THE ULVERSCROFT F⊂ _____
(registered UK charity number 264873)

was established in 1972 to provide funds for research, diagnosis and treatment of eye diseases. Examples of major projects funded by the Ulverscroft Foundation are:-

- The Children's Eye Unit at Moorfelds ⌐e
  Hospital, London
- The Ulverscroft Children's Eye Unit at Great Ormond Street Hospital for Sick Children
- Funding research into eye diseases and treatment at the Department of Ophthalmology, University of Leicester
- The Ulverscroft Vision Research Group, Institute of Child Health
- Twin operating theatres at the Western Ophthalmic Hospital, London
- The Chair of Ophthalmology at the Royal Australian College of Ophthalmologists

You can help further the work of the Foundation by making a donation or leaving a legacy. Every contribution is gratefully received. If you would like to help support the Foundation or require further information, please contact:

THE ULVERSCROFT FOUNDATION
The Green, Bradgate Road, Anstey
Leicester LE7 7FU, England
Tel: (0116) 236 4325

website: www.ulverscroft-foundation.org.uk

THE COLLIER'S WIFE

Leeds, 1918. When Amy visits her husband Hugh at Beckett's Park Hospital, he doesn't recognise her. Broken after serving four devastating years in the First World War, Hugh is a shadow of the man he once was. Can he ever again be the man Amy knew and loved?

Barnsborough, 1912. The first time Hugh and Amy meet, the connection between them is instant and electric. While a librarian's assistant and a collier might not be the most conventional pair, the two come together over a love of books that quickly turns into more. Neither suspects their families have secrets that threaten to tear them apart . . .

CHRISSIE WALSH

THE COLLIER'S WIFE

Complete and Unabridged

MAGNA
Leicester

First published in Great Britain in 2020 by
Aria
an imprint of Head of Zeus Ltd
London

First Ulverscroft Edition
published 2021
by arrangement with
Head of Zeus Ltd
London

This is a work of fiction. All characters,
organisations, and events portrayed in this novel
are either products of the author's imagination or
are used fictitiously.

A catalogue record for this book is available
from the British Library.

ISBN 978–0–7505–4871–7

Published by
Ulverscroft Limited
Anstey, Leicestershire

Printed and bound in Great Britain by
TJ Books Ltd., Padstow, Cornwall

This book is printed on acid-free paper

In memory of my brother John E Manion,
(1945–2020).

'A brother shares childhood memories and grown-up dreams.'

1

Beckett's Park Hospital, Leeds

2nd September, 1918

The crowded train came to a juddering halt, metal wheezing against metal and steam billowing up to the station's glazed roof. Amy Leas lifted her bag down from the luggage rack above her head. The passenger nearest the door opened it, the acrid stink of overheated axle grease and smoky fumes wafting into the carriage. Amy's nose curled at the unfamiliar smell. This was the first time she had travelled by train, the first time she had ever been to Leeds, and the first time she had ever been so far from home. The hand gripping the bag feeling unpleasantly clammy and her stomach as if it were inhabited by a swarm of butterflies, Amy stepped onto the platform.

Bewildered, she stayed where she was, buffeted by the constant flow of people passing in both directions, several of the men wearing British Army uniforms. Eight grey-faced soldiers marched by, and Amy wondered if they were returning to battle or they had just returned from some awful hellhole in France. Whichever, her heart ached with pity for them as she watched them disappear into the swirl of bodies.

Then, a hefty shove galvanising her feet, she pushed her way through the throng to what, she hoped, was the station's exit.

Out on the street, Amy studied the map that she had received with the letter, the maze of streets blurring as she struggled to find her bearings. Having no idea of the distance between Leeds station and Beckett's Park Hospital, she threw caution to the wind and hired one of the many hackney carriages waiting at the station's entrance. Damn the expense, she thought, giving instructions to the driver then climbing into the rear seat. The sooner she saw Jude, the quicker she would have answers to the questions that crowded her mind with every breath. Shell shock, that's what the letter had said. She didn't like the sound of it.

Bolt upright in her seat, and oblivious to the view from the cab's window, Amy saw none of the city's fine civic buildings or its grand shops as she sat wringing her hands and interlocking her fingers so tightly that they ached. Her thoughts clattered in her brain, thoughts and half-thoughts colliding with fears and notions that buzzed inside her head as each turn of the cab's wheels brought her closer to Jude. Taking her to what . . . she had no idea.

The cab rumbled to a halt outside a formidable grey building. Amy paid the driver then, down on the pavement, she took a deep breath and throwing back her shoulders she marched up to the imposing front entrance. Once a stately home, Beckett's Hall was now a hospital that treated soldiers suffering from nervous disorders. Inside the foyer, at a small office marked 'Reception' she showed her letter to the Voluntary Aid Detachment clerk. The young, pretty VAD clerk gave a sympathetic

2

smile and asked her to take a seat; someone would come and take her to meet the doctor in charge of Jude. She pointed to a row of chairs near to a pair of double doors.

Amy perched on the edge of a hard seat and gazed up at the high ceiling and then at the tiled floor, wondering how long it would be before someone came for her, hopeful it would be soon; time was of the essence if she was to spend it with Jude and catch the last train back to Barnborough. She listened to the buzzing of an intercom in the office and the VAD clerk's soft voice. Perhaps she should have made arrangements to stay somewhere overnight. That way she could have visited Jude again the next day. As she muddled over the idea, four young women bustled through the double doors in a flurry of bright red capes: Queen Alexandra's nurses. Laughing and chattering, they headed for the front door. Amy glanced down at her own navy coat that had seen better days and thought how attractive and confident the nurses looked. A spike of envy had her thinking: *If I had their skills, I'd speed Jude's recovery.*

'Mrs Leas?'

Amy tore her eyes from the backs of the departing nurses and turned her head sharply. A bespectacled young man wearing a white coat smiled down at her. 'Mrs Leas,' he reiterated, 'I'm Dr Mackay, if you'd like to come with me, I'll take you to your husband.' He pushed open the double doors.

A long corridor loomed before them, and as they walked Dr Mackay talked, his soft Scottish burr calming Amy's nerves. Even so, the palms of her hands were moist and her bag's handle sticky as she swapped it from one hand to the other. By the time they arrived outside a green door, Amy had learned that Jude no longer suffered from severe bouts of diarrhoea and was beginning to eat again, and managing a few hours of unbroken sleep each night. Poor, dear Jude, thought Amy, her heart aching at what he must be going through. The doctor opened the green door.

Much to Amy's surprise, he led her into a small office; she had been steeling herself to find Jude lying in bed in a ward filled with injured men. Her legs feeling decidedly insubstantial, she was relieved when Dr Mackay said, 'Take a seat, Mrs Leas; we need to talk.'

Seated rigidly upright at one side of a large desk with Dr Mackay at the other, Amy gazed intently into his face, her hands clasped in her lap to still their trembling. He was sitting at ease, his hands folded his against his chest as he looked into her wide, blue eyes thinking how sad it was that this young, pretty woman would, most likely, live the rest of her life with a man who, at best, was bitter and morose or, at worst, violent and abusive. A thousand questions burning her tongue, Amy was about to ask them, but the doctor stole her opportunity.

'Mrs Leas,' he said softly, 'it might help you better understand your husband's state of mind if you consider that he has been forced to indulge in a behaviour of a kind that is thoroughly repulsive to his natural instincts. Not only has he had to commit cruel and sadistic acts, he has witnessed horrors beyond our imagination and his senses

4

are burdened down with the memory of these.' He paused, allowing Amy time to consider his words.

A gamut of expressions flitting across her face, Amy gasped. 'Cruel and sadistic. Jude was never that. He's kind and thoughtful; he's the most sensitive, caring man I've ever known.'

'And that is probably why the rigours of war have had such an effect on him. Exposure to lengthy periods of heavy bombardment and witnessing unspeakable acts of violence have changed him, made him lose his sense of reason. The problem is psychological, and the way we treat it is to get into his mind to help him eradicate that which is making him react in the way he does.' He looked deeply into Amy's eyes, his expression conveying sympathy and the need to be understood.

'And can you do that?' she whispered, her eyes begging a positive response.

Dr Mackay's answering smile was pensive. 'Given time, and with plenty of rest and useful exercise, Jude may be able to put it all behind him.'

'How long might that take?'

'It's impossible to say,' he replied, steepling his fingertips and resting his chin on them. Amy noted how clean his nails were. Jude's had always been rimmed with coal dust. She wondered what they were like now. Dr Mackay coughed discreetly and Amy, aware that he had noticed her attention wandering, flushed and smiled apologetically. 'Jude is dealing with his problem by obliterating his memory — when he can,' he continued. 'It may be that he will not recognise you, and if that's the case I advise you to refrain from making any overt gestures on this visit.'

5

'Overt gestures,' Amy echoed.

'Hugs and kisses — that sort of thing. It could distress him.'

'But I'm his wife. I haven't seen him for ages. Isn't that how I should greet him?' She was almost begging for Dr Mackay's approval.

'As I've already said, he might not remember you.' He paused, smiling hopefully as he added, 'If he's having a good day, maybe he will.'

Wanly, Amy returned the smile, but she was saddened by the lack of conviction in his voice. He stood, and in a heartier tone he said, 'Come, we'll go and see him now.'

Amy followed him, sure that he must hear the thudding of her heart.

They entered a large, airy room with windows looking out onto lawns and trees, their leaves a riot of gold and russet. It was not a ward filled with beds as Amy had anticipated, but an elegant drawing room teeming with men. Bewildered, she cast anxious glances at men clustered round tables playing cards or board games and then at those sitting in chairs by the windows. Amongst them were nurses wearing grey uniforms. Every now and then the hum of voices was penetrated by unintelligible shouts and low groans.

'Let's see how the good man is today,' said Dr Mackay, striding out, Amy walking behind him on feet that felt as though they didn't belong to her. Several pairs of eyes followed their progress as they made their way to a high-backed wing chair facing a window, its occupant hidden from view. Dr Mackay stepped round it, saying, 'Someone to see you, Sergeant Leas.' He beckoned Amy to come forward.

Amy hesitated. She felt tears building behind her eyes. Biting on her lip to stop them from flowing, she stepped in front of the chair. And there he was: her Jude — but not her Jude. Gaunt and pale, his lips clamped in a bitter line, he stared straight ahead with no sign of recognition that she was within arm's reach. She longed to embrace him, but recalling the doctor's advice all she could manage was a wobbly, 'Hello, Jude, how are you?'

Jude blinked as though wakening from a long sleep, and his lips twitched as if he was searching for a smile he couldn't find. Then he fixed his dark eyes on hers, and as Amy gazed into their depths, she saw a soul in torment, a man stripped naked and crying out for help. 'I'll leave you alone with him,' said Dr Mackay. He hurried to attend to a man who was gibbering and swaying wildly.

Amy let her bag fall to the floor. Then, down on her knees, she took Jude's hands in her own. He seemed to have forgotten she was there, his gaze on a point above her head. Amy kneaded his flaccid hands, hands that had once felt so strong and capable, but Jude did not respond. 'What is it, love, tell me what's wrong?' she urged gently. He pulled his hands free, and still he did not look at her. Amy sat back on her heels. 'Talk to me, love,' she pleaded.

Jude leaned forward, his forearms resting on his knees in that same old familiar way but whereas before he had merely clasped his hands, he now twisted them savagely. A strange gurgling from somewhere deep in his throat bubbled to the surface, mangled sounds escaping his lips, and as his

7

wild eyes searched the distance, she thought he said 'Kezia.'

Her heart leapt. 'Yes, love. Kezia. She sends her love. She's settled in at school. Doing very well. Fancy, it doesn't seem two minutes since she was born, and now our little girl's learning to read and write and do all kind of things. We love you and want you to come home.' Amy knew she was babbling but, in her desperation to gain his attention, she was afraid to stop.

Jude's limbs began to twitch. He placed his hands on the arms of the chair, and as he struggled to come upright a stream of foul epithets spewed from his lips. They erupted from deep in his throat, the monstrous threats so vile that Amy jumped to her feet but did not move away from him. Jude towered over her, his eyes unseeing but his face close enough for her to feel his hot breath blasting her cheeks.

Time seemed to stand still.

Rooted to the spot, she flicked her eyes from Jude's ugly, contorted features to elsewhere in the room, seeking assistance. Amy almost cried with relief as Dr Mackay and a nurse hurried to her side. With gentling hands and calming words, they silenced his shouts and snarls. Eventually, his body sagged and like a burst balloon he slumped into the chair, his head lolling on his chest and his mouth hanging loose. A thick string of frothy saliva swung pendulously from his lips.

'Don't get upset. It's to be expected,' said the nurse, seeing Amy's panic-stricken face. Amy goggled, but neither Dr Mackay nor the nurse seemed unduly perturbed. Amy was itching to wipe Jude's

8

chin, thinking how mortified he would feel to be seen in such a state. As though she had read Amy's mind, the nurse dabbed it away.

Dr Mackay stood, hands behind his back, quietly observing Jude. His eyes were closed, and the only sign of life was the rhythmic rise and fall of his chest. The doctor nodded to the nurse and then to Amy. 'Good day, Mrs Leas. I'll leave you with Nurse Brennan,' he said. He walked over to a young soldier who was rhythmically tapping his forehead against a windowpane. Amy watched him go, feeling somewhat cheated that his attention was on another man, and not on Jude. But when she looked at Jude, he was oblivious to everything, including her.

Nurse Brennan took hold of Amy's elbow. 'You should leave him now; you'll not get any response.'

Amy shrugged her off. 'But I've hardly had chance to talk to . . . '

The nurse lightly tugged at her arm. 'I know you're upset, but you'll not get anything out of him now. Maybe next time, eh?'

Reluctantly, Amy picked up her bag. 'I brought him some socks and underwear,' she said forlornly, filching them from her bag.

'I'll see he gets them.' The nurse tucked the parcel under her arm. Amy's gaze lingered on Jude. He seemed to be asleep, his eyes tight shut and his mouth twisted in a bitter line. With a sinking heart Amy realised there was nothing more she could do.

'Did you come far?' asked the nurse, as they walked back along the corridor. Amy told her she had and then added, 'I'll come again tomorrow.'

9

'We're trying to limit visitations, what with this dreadful flu epidemic; we can't risk infection. I'd leave it for a day or two if I were you. You'll not see much change in him. Sometimes it's more disturbing for them if you come too often.'

Amy dearly wanted to protest, but knowing it would be useless she thanked Nurse Brennan and walked out of the front door on leaden feet. What the nurse had said about the flu that was ravaging the country was true; Barnborough already had its share of victims. Yet, thought Amy, she should be with Jude all the time or she'd never get through to him. He couldn't have forgotten she was his wife.

She felt like running back inside and making one unholy fuss, but a hackney cab was just dropping off a passenger so she spurted towards it. On the way back to station she recalled the moment Jude had said 'Kezia', and the way he had searched her face as she talked. She felt sure he had recognised her then, and had wanted to talk to her if only he could have found the words. For a moment her spirits rose, only to sink again when she recalled the foul and filthy words he had found.

Well, she told herself, sitting up straight and pushing back her shoulders, *next time I'll make damned sure he knows me. Even if there are doctors and nurses all round him, I'll hug and kiss him and show him how much I love him. I'll do anything it takes to bring him back.* She felt inside her bag for her purse to pay the cabby, her fingers brushing against the book she had put there that morning. Jude had asked for it in his last letter. How could she have forgotten to give it to him?

Amy's face broke into the first proper smile of the day as she pulled the copy of Kipling's *The Man Who Would Be King* from her bag. She had the answer to Jude's problems in her hand.

★ ★ ★

On the station platform, she concentrated on how best she could help Jude. Next time, she'd give him the book, talk about it and other books, sure that his face would light up when he held a book his hands. In the past she'd often joked that he loved books more than he loved her. It wasn't right for him to be sitting staring out of a window all day. He should be reading, getting back to normality. She thought about the comfort he took, had always taken, from literature. It was a major part of his life. Reading wonderful stories would surely drive away the horrors that were filling his mind.

Confident that she had found the answer, and already planning her next visit, when the train for Barnborough chugged to a halt she boarded with a ready step. Come hell or high water, she would bring Jude back from his living nightmare.

But when she was settled on the train, lulled by its persistent clickety-clack, her thoughts refused to dwell on Jude's predicament, terrible though it was. Before long, she was recalling another family tragedy, one that had its beginnings long before she was born and had ended cruelly and needlessly — and all because of the war.

11

2

Intake Farm, Barnborough

Spring, 1906

Amy Elliot was curled up on the window seat in her bedroom at Intake Farm, a copy of *Pride and Prejudice* in her lap. Like many thirteen-year-old girls, she loved romantic stories, but today Elizabeth and Mr Darcy held no fascination. Something was going on below in the kitchen, and with her ear close to the open window Amy was doing her best to hear what it was her parents and her older sister, Beatrice, were arguing about: something serious, that was for sure.

Amy was the youngest of Bessie and Hadley's children, and Hadley's favourite child. Blonde and bonny, she was the image of the young Bessie he had ardently courted and won, but she had none of her mother's guile or bossiness. Amy was a sweet-natured, thoughtful girl, unlike Beatrice whose dark complexion and surly demeanour was, and had been for many years, the cause of Hadley's present aggravation. Now, as he attempted to silence his wife's bitter words, he was saddened to think how different the female members of his family were. Amy heard his pleading tones, and thought how like her mild-mannered dad it was to attempt to pour oil on troubled waters.

She craned her neck closer to the open window. They were talking about Beatrice; that much she understood. Her father sounded sad. Her mother sounded furious. What had Beatrice done now, she wondered? Not that it was unusual for Bessie to be angry with Beatrice, for no matter what she did she rarely escaped her mother's waspish tongue and flailing hand. Poor Beatrice, thought Amy, a sudden rush of guilt at her own privileged rearing making her kind heart ache.

For as long as Amy could remember, Beatrice had always been the wrong shape and the wrong colour as far as her mother was concerned. She didn't understand why; all she knew was that no matter how hard her older sister tried — and she did try — she never managed to please their mother. Then, she was sullen and cheeky, refusing to respond when spoken to, or answering back in an insolent manner that usually earned her a clout. Bessie's wooden spoon beat Beatrice's knuckles and the back of her head or her legs as frequently as it beat pudding batter, and Amy often wondered why she persisted in provoking their mother; after all, she knew what the outcome would be.

Of late, now that she was older, she had begun to question her mother's cruelty towards Beatrice. Neither she, nor her older brothers, Samuel and Thomas ever felt the weight of Bessie's hand, or the razor edge of her tongue. Recently, she had taken to defending her sister, but whenever she did Beatrice had turned on her snarling that she needed nobody's pity, least of all hers. Yet seeing how lost and lonely

13

Beatrice seemed, Amy wanted to befriend her and was tempted to run downstairs. However, cold reasoning telling her it would make matters worse — it always had done in the past — she stayed where she was, her ears alert to the angry voices.

★ ★ ★

Down below, Beatrice sat at the kitchen table with her shoulders hunched and her head down, her long, black greasy hair hiding her face. Her mother towered over her. At the opposite end of the table, her father's bulbous blue eyes, troubled and slightly moist, looked into his wife's. Hers flashed spitefully. He ran a fleshy hand over his florid face and said, 'She's not the first, and she won't be the last. Don't be so hard on her, Bessie.' He sounded weary.

Hearing her father's sympathetic tones Beatrice raised her head and, tucking her hair behind her ears, she stared defiantly at her mother.

Bessie glared back. 'I always knew she'd come to no good,' she shrilled, 'bringing shame on this house, and at her age.'

'What do you mean, my age? I'm twenty-three, well old enough to be married,' Beatrice said sullenly.

'Aye, but not old enough to know better,' snarled Bessie. 'Oh no, not you. You had to go and get yourself pregnant. Was that the only way you thought you'd get him?'

'Now, now, Bessie, that's a cruel thing to say,' Hadley chided, 'she says the lad's willing to marry

14

her. And like I said, she's not the first to make her vows with a baby in her belly.' He added weight to his last remark.

Bessie shot him an agitated glance. The bland expression that met hers stilled the fluttering in her stomach.

'We don't even know who he is, Hadley. Her ladyship didn't have the courtesy to introduce him to us before getting herself in the family way.'

'Well, I'm sure we'll meet him soon enough things being what they are.'

Hadley headed for the outer door, eager to put an end to the wrangling. He was saddened by Beatrice's predicament but he detested confrontation, particularly when it involved Bessie. 'I'm sure he'll turn out to be a grand sort of chap,' he said, hurrying out to the yard.

Left alone with her mother, Beatrice gazed at her sullenly, her long, sallow face the picture of misery. 'I've never done anything that pleased you,' she whined. 'All you care about is your blue-eyed boys and your precious little darling.' She scowled at Bessie, daring her to deny it. Bessie strode over to the sink, Beatrice's grievances competing with the rattle of crockery. 'It's always been our Sammy, our Thomas and our Amy before me, and once I was old enough you made me skivvy after them like I was a servant. Don't think I don't know you've never loved me like you love them.'

'Don't be ridiculous!' Bessie half-turned, spitting out the denial although she knew it was a lie. She hadn't wanted Beatrice like she had wanted her other children, their blond hair and blue eyes making them the image of herself and Hadley. But

15

then, Beatrice wasn't Hadley's daughter.

Bessie turned her back to Beatrice, her thoughts burning with memories of Raffy Lovell. She could still feel his hands about her waist and his thighs pressed to hers, his hot breath on her neck. It had been the night of the Easter Fair, and she had been riding on the Cocks and Hens when he'd jumped up behind her. She'd turned, looking into a pair of mischievous eyes as black as currants. By the time Bessie had known for certain that she was pregnant, Raffy and the fair were long gone.

Drying her hands, Bessie lifted a little dustpan and a bird's wing from the shelf above the range. At the table she brushed crumbs from the tablecloth, her eyes on Beatrice. She sighed heavily. Whereas Raffy's dark complexion and finely sculpted features were rakishly handsome, his daughter's swarthy skin and sharply angular cheekbones and chin made her downright plain, and like him she left a nasty taste in Bessie's mouth.

'I thought you'd be glad to see me wed. You're never done reminding me I'm still on the shelf,' Beatrice moaned, twisting her lank hair round her work-worn fingers.

Bessie brushed crumbs, her mind on her own marriage and the haste in which it had been arranged. Hadley had courted her for some time, bringing little gifts of a clutch of duck's eggs or a posy of flowers to woo her. But he wasn't the sort of man she'd wanted for a husband. More than twice her age, he carried too much weight, and his florid complexion, sparse fair hair and bulbous, blue eyes were in sharp contrast to the dark and dashing good looks of Raffy Lovell.

16

The bird's wing idle in her hand, she broke out in a sweat as she recalled the panic and the anxious nights she had spent when first she realised she was pregnant. To this day she still marvelled at how quickly a solution had come to her, amazed that she'd not thought of it sooner. She'd married Hadley Elliot.

Poor dear Hadley, she thought guiltily, as she crossed to the door, tossing the crumbs into the yard for the birds. When he had first proposed, Bessie had prettily refused him, her father berating her roundly and calling her a fool.

Fool or not, she had faced up to the truth. Raffy Lovell was gone, Hadley Elliot her only hope. And now she was the respectable wife of a prosperous farmer, and mother to his children. When she had given birth to a daughter some six months later Hadley had shown no surprise at the premature arrival of his firstborn, and if anyone else thought it suspicious they were careful not to voice their opinions in his company. As for his daughter's dark complexion, he merely commented that she must take after his grandmother and that they should name the child for her: Beatrice.

From the kitchen door, Bessie watched a flurry of wagtails descend on the crumbs and felt the sourness of her duplicity oozing through her pores. Shaking her head to dispel the feeling and then turning about briskly, she set the dustpan and feather on the shelf. *Pull yourself together*, she silently intoned, going over to the sink and dabbling her hands in the washing-up water, rinsing the clamminess from her palms. Memories had made her fearful. She had much to lose should

Hadley ever find out.

An unexpected wave of sympathy washed over her. She wiped her hands on her apron and turned to face Beatrice. 'Aye, well, if you are to be married, and you can't not be in your condition, you'd better bring him to meet us,' she said flatly.

Upstairs, from her perch in the window seat, Amy had caught snatches of the angry words enough to make sense of Beatrice's predicament. Poor Beatrice, but at least the man wanted to marry her; with a home of her own she'd escape Bessie's cruel tongue. And, Amy acknowledged, what Beatrice had said about their mother favouring the boys and her was nothing but the truth — although she hadn't liked being referred to as the 'precious little darling'.

Amy set the unread book aside and got to her feet. She'd go downstairs, pretend she knew nothing of what she'd heard, and be nice to Beatrice. Her sister needed a friend right now.

* * *

On Sunday afternoon, Amy helped Bessie lay on a spread; Beatrice's young man was coming for tea. Hadley was already seated at the head of the table ready to make their visitor welcome, and hopeful that Bessie would swallow her bitterness and be pleasant. Thomas, his youngest son, always hungry, sat eyeing the large sponge cake. As Amy set out cups and saucers, she wondered if Beatrice's young man would be as bad as her mother made him out to be (even though she'd never met him) and how she, Amy, should behave towards

18

him. You could never be sure with Mother who you had to be nice to and whom you didn't. Amy decided she'd be nice; reasoning that it wasn't his fault Beatrice was having a baby. Then she took a fit of giggles at her foolishness. Of course it was. That's what men did. She didn't know quite how they did it, but she knew that babies didn't happen without them.

'What's tickling you?' Hadley asked fondly.

Amy wasn't supposed to know about the baby. 'The idea of me getting married,' she lied, as she sat down at the table.

The door opened, Beatrice almost pushing Bert Stitt into the kitchen. Eyes barely focused, he stared at the group round the table: a pretty, young girl with blonde curls; a gormless looking, fair-haired fellow of about twenty and a corpulent older man with blue eyes like marbles whom Bert presumed was Hadley Elliot.

Averting his gaze, he looked into the face of the stout, yellow-haired woman standing guard by the range, arms folded across her bosom, her blue eyes cold and unwelcoming. Beside her stood a fat, fair young man with a slack mouth, his blue eyes equally unwelcoming. Bert quaked, at the same time wondering fleetingly why Beatrice resembled none of them.

Beatrice let go of his arm. 'This is Bert Stitt,' she said. Bert mumbled a greeting.

'Come an' sit you down, lad.' Hadley, half-standing, beckoned Bert to the table. Seeing an empty chair at the foot of the table, Bert shuffled into it.

'Not there, that's our Sammy's chair.' Bert shot upright. 'Sit there,' said Bessie, pointing to the

19

chair next to the young girl and then snapping, 'and if you please, Hadley, I'll do the bidding in my own house.'

Hadley sank back into his chair, an embarrassed smile creasing his face.

'You can sit next to me, and welcome,' Amy chirped, and when Bert sat down she nudged him with her elbow and whispered, 'Nobody's allowed to sit in our Sammy's chair but him. He's the boss in this house.' Although she had lowered her voice, her words were still audible enough for all to hear.

'Now Amy, mind your manners. None of your cheek,' Bessie reprimanded as she brought the teapot to the table.

'Aye, watch your lip, girl.' Samuel threw Amy a threatening look, his expression equally unpleasant when it came to rest on Bert. He sat down pompously at the end of the table, Bessie at his right hand.

Tea poured and sandwiches handed round, Bessie began her interrogation. 'So, Bert, where do you and our Beatrice intend to live once you're wed?'

Bert noisily swallowed a mouthful of ham and pickle. 'A pit house by t'colliery. Grattan Row, there's one come empty, so I wa' lucky.' Words garbled, face bright red, he looked beseechingly at Beatrice. Head down, shoulders hunched, she stared stolidly at her plate.

'You're a collier then? It's not a job I'd choose,' Samuel said, his tone indicating he had little respect for those who did. 'Crawling about in t'pitch black wouldn't suit me, an' you've never done but what you're on strike half the time.' He helped himself to another sandwich, and then carefully considering which was the largest slice of cake, he lifted that also.

'Sammy's scared of the dark,' Amy whispered.

Bert choked back a giggle before responding to Samuel. 'Sumdy's got to do it, an' we only strike 'cos we want better wages an' conditions,' he said.

Samuel's sneer was ugly.

Hadley intervened. 'It takes a brave man to go underground and dig for coal that we might be warmed at the fireside.' He gave Bert a nod of acknowledgement.

Buoyed by her father's praise for Bert and annoyed at Samuel's antagonism, Amy said, 'You couldn't work down the pit if you wanted to, Sammy. You'd get stuck in the seams.'

Beatrice sniggered. Sponge cake exploded from Samuel's lips.

'Amy! I won't tell you again. Any more of that and you'll leave the table. Apologise to your brother.' Bessie patted Samuel's arm comfortingly. Amy mumbled an apology and Bessie turned her attention back to Bert. 'What I want to know is, can you keep our Beatrice in the manner to which she's accustomed?' she asked imperiously.

Beatrice sniggered again.

'I think so.' Bert didn't sound too sure so Beatrice answered for him.

'Me and Bert'll manage just fine. After all, I'm not accustomed to much, am I?' Her challenging gaze met Bessie's. Bessie was the first to look away.

For the most part of the next hour Bert silently observed the members of the family he was about to marry into. Although he was not markedly astute, he couldn't help but notice his future mother-in-law's discrimination. She fussed over Thomas as though he was half his age and was almost deferential to Samuel, paying particular attention to his every word.

However, it was Bessie's attitude towards Beatrice that struck him most, indeed hurt him, for whenever she addressed her daughter there was a hard edge to her voice.

Beatrice pretended not to notice, sullenly obeying Bessie's orders to replenish the teapot or mend the fire. Had Bert been an impetuous man he would have jumped to her defence, but wisely he held his tongue concluding that his heroics could only cause Beatrice more suffering in the long run; her mother was a termagant, her eldest brother a lout, the younger lad a simpleton and her father henpecked. Only Amy had made a good impression.

Bert left Intake Farm with the distinct impression he was rescuing Beatrice.

3

Barnborough

Spring 1912

'Another whodunit, Mrs Winterbottom? You love a good mystery, don't you?' Amy took one of Sexton Blake's books from the elderly widow's hand.

Nellie Winterbottom chuckled. 'Since you put me on to him I've read nowt else. Your advice has filled many a lonely hour since I lost my Freddy.'

'I'm pleased to hear it; there's nothing like a good book to keep you company,' Amy said, placing the date stamp firmly on the flysheet. Nellie smiled her thanks and trotted out of the library.

'I'll put these back on the shelves,' Amy said, addressing the other assistant librarian, Freda Haigh, and indicating the cart full of returned books. 'You can take over here for a while then go for your tea-break.'

Freda was Amy's friend from schooldays, and it was Amy who had recommended her for a job in the library — something she now regretted. From the outset, Freda had made it quite plain that she envied Amy's position of superiority, and she frequently attempted to undermine her. Now, she jumped at the chance to work behind the desk checking books in and out. It was an improvement on dusting shelves and rearranging books.

However, she was fully aware that the borrowers preferred Amy. They even said so, asking to be attended by the pretty young lady. Yet another thing that rankled, for Freda was a plump, pasty girl with a protruding jaw. She lifted the date stamp to attend to her first client.

Mr Porter, the chemist, shoved the books he was returning across the counter, gruffly enquiring, 'Where's the girl who knows what I like to read? She knows every book in this library.' Freda clenched her jaw and then, imitating Amy, she plastered on a smile and attempted to placate the chemist, at the same time sourly and silently admitting that what he had said was mainly true.

By the time Amy Elliot was nineteen she had read most of Dickens, laughing with the Pickwickians, detesting Uriah Heap and crying with Little Dorrit and Tiny Tim. Hardy, Gaskell and Twain helped shape her view of the world and Louisa May Alcott and the Brontë sisters had opened her eyes and mind to the complexities of family life and the turbulence that falling in love can bring.

Amy was a lovely, outgoing young woman with a lively mind capable of forming opinions and justifying them, but she was never arrogant where other people's ideas and feelings were concerned. Her love for reading had served her well, and on leaving school she was rewarded with the post of assistant librarian in Barnborough's newly opened library. The job not only immersed her in a wonderful supply of literature, it provided independence outside of Bessie's domineering reach and Samuel's bullying.

Amy considered herself blessed.

24

Today being a Monday, the library was busy. Amy wheeled the cart filled with books between the stacks, depositing books in their rightful places and every now and then stopping to chat to a customer about a book they had just read or offer some friendly advice. The last book in place, Amy returned to the desk. Reluctant to surrender the date stamp and her position behind the counter — one which she was sure raised her position in the eyes of the community — Freda went for her tea-break.

Amy served the doctor's wife, and then bent down to take a replacement inkpad from the cupboard. When she came upright, she found herself looking into the ready smile of a tall, darkly handsome boy with deep-set, warm brown eyes. As he placed his books on the counter, she could tell straight away how he earned his living; the scrubbed but not quite clean fingernails and the fine traces of coal dust blackening his eyelashes let her know he was a collier.

He handed over the books he had chosen, the flash of white teeth against his swarthy skin making Amy's heart flutter and her fingers clumsy as she removed the index cards and stamped the date. But it wasn't just the smile that intrigued her; it was his choice of books. Not for him the usual thrillers or Wild West cowboy tales that miners usually selected but Erskine Childers' *The Riddle of the Sands* and Forster's *Howard's End*.

'A good bit of reading there, Mr . . . ' Amy paused to glance at his library card, but she already knew his name, had stamped it on her heart as she had stamped the books.

'Leas,' they said in unison, and chuckling after they had said it.

'I've not read this one,' Amy said, handing him *The Riddle of the Sands* and thinking how she might keep him there a little bit longer, 'but I thoroughly enjoyed *Howard's End*.'

'Then so will I, seeing as how you've recommended it. After all, you're the librarian.' His smile roguish, Jude was also searching for a way to prolong his stay. 'Have you read *A Room with a View*?' he asked, and when Amy said she had, he said, 'I'd like to go to Italy.'

'Oh, yes, me too,' Amy said. For several minutes, the magnificence of what they thought Florence had to offer kept them talking, both of them thinking they could talk to one another forever.

'Miss Elliot!' Phoebe Littlewood's grating voice brought Amy and Jude back to reality, Jude flashing the head librarian a charming smile and then pointedly saying in a loud voice, 'Thanks for your advice, Miss Elliot, you've been most helpful.' He picked up his books, and giving Amy a rueful grin, he left.

Amy apologised to the queue of borrowers that, until now, she hadn't noticed was steadily lengthening. She dutifully stamped a book, her eyes on Jude's departing back and her mind on how lovely he was. Later, when Miss Littlewood chastised her for keeping them waiting, Amy recalled Jude's gallant attempt to deflect her annoyance. For the rest of the afternoon she had the feeling that something special had happened. She couldn't wait to see him again.

Later that day, after work, Amy made her way across the town to the home of Beatrice and Bert Stitt and their children, a bulging shopping bag over her arm. She made this journey twice a week, and had done so for the past six years because Beattie, as she now called herself, never visited Intake Farm. Although Amy made these visits to keep in touch with her sister, her chief interest was the welfare of her nieces and nephews. Five children, ranged like steps and stairs, their mother's neglect and raucous chastising worried Amy. Sadly, Bessie and Hadley were almost strangers to their grandchildren, their visits rare and brief.

After walking for ten minutes, Amy arrived at an ugly little row of pit houses crouched in the shadow of a giant slagheap. Here the air tasted acrid, and cinders blown by the wind from the mountain of waste crunched under her feet as she walked up to the shabbiest house in Grattan Row. She opened the door, her nostrils assaulted by the stench of boiled cabbage and unwashed bodies. She shuddered involuntarily as she stepped inside.

'Beattie,' Amy called from the untidy parlour to the tiny kitchen beyond. When there was no response, she addressed Maggie, the oldest of her sister's five children. 'Where's your mam?'

'Dunno,' said Maggie, hefting baby Henry from one hip to the other and then kicking one of the two small boys squabbling over a broken toy wagon. Albert, nearly six, bit four-year-old Fred. Fred screeched. 'Shurrup! Auntie Amy's here,' yelled Maggie, her tangled copper curls bouncing angrily around her flushed, freckled face.

'Did you miss school again?' Amy's voice was heavy with disappointment.

The copper curls bounced again. 'I had to stay home and mind the young 'uns.'

Maggie jiggled a whinging Henry. Not yet seven, she looked and sounded as though she carried the worries of the world on her shoulders, her unwashed face and grubby cotton smock reminding Amy of a pauper child from a Dickens novel.

Amy glanced at the clock on the mantelpiece: quarter past six. 'Have you had your tea?' she asked, tossing her coat over the back of a chair. Maggie didn't reply.

Amy carried her bag into the kitchen. The unlit stove, clogged with dead ashes, answered her question. She rolled back her cardigan sleeves and filled the kettle, setting it on the single gas ring on the cluttered draining board. Unwashed crockery and pans malingered in a sink full of greasy water. As she rinsed mugs and plates Amy wondered, not for the first time, if Beattie deliberately negated Bessie's domestic skills in sheer defiance of her mother's strict rearing.

Emptying her shopping bag, Amy filled four plates with sausage rolls and one with ginger biscuits. Intended to be a suppertime treat they'd now suffice as the older children's first proper meal of the day. She set the plates and a pot of tea and mugs on the table. The bottle of warmed milk was for Henry.

'Here, give him to me.' Amy took Henry from Maggie's arms, at the same time wondering how a child of less than six months old managed to attract so much dirt; his tiny face smeared with snot and sticky muck lurking between his fingers and toes. 'Sit down and eat your tea nicely,' she said, her warning aimed at Albert and Fred who were grabbing biscuits. Only then did she realise one child was missing. 'Where's Mary?' Maggie pointed to the corner under the stairs.

Dumping a protesting Henry into a chair, Amy went and found the toddler asleep on a pile of coats. Gently wakening her, Amy carried Mary to the table and then filled five mugs with milky tea. Like ravening dogs, the children chewed and slurped. With Henry fed and in his pram, Amy moved from parlour to kitchen bringing order to the chaos. Finally, she heated two large pans of water.

'Strip off, you're all in need of a good wash,' Amy ordered Maggie and the boys. She undressed Henry and Mary. From the clotheshorse she took dingy underwear and nightclothes, and with the children clean and ready for bed, she glanced at the clock. She really should be getting home, but the children shouldn't be left alone at this time of night. She began to tell them a story but her mind was on Beattie. Her sister's slatternly housekeeping annoyed Amy but her sympathy for the young Stitts who, she felt, had a raw deal in life always provoked her into doing something to make their home life pleasanter. She glanced at the clock again.

The front door scraped open and Beattie tottered in. Spying Amy, she pulled up, sharp. 'Oh, are you here?' She didn't sound best pleased.

'It's as well I am,' Amy retorted, 'you shouldn't

leave them alone for so long. Maggie's too young to be in charge — and it's way past teatime — they were starving.'

'Oh, don't start on at me,' whined Beattie. 'I were only two doors down wetting the head of Carrie Heppenstall's new baby.' She threw her coat on the couch and walked into the kitchen. Amy caught the sweet tang of gin on Beattie's breath as she passed by saying, 'I'll make a pot of tea. Do you want some?' The remorseful look in her eyes told Amy she wanted to be friends.

'Go on then,' Amy said, in a show of sisterly solidarity. A fresh pot brewed, they sat by the living room fire.

'Well, anything exciting happen in the library today?' Beattie's attempt to make pleasant conversation was spoiled by the distinct lack of interest in her tone.

Amy gave a half-smile. 'No, just business as usual.' She loved her job, but there was no point in elaborating; books meant nothing to Beattie. And she wasn't going to mention the devastatingly handsome man she had met, even though he had never really left her thoughts. Instead she asked, 'Is Bert working?'

Beattie's lip curled at the mention of her husband. 'Aye, he's on afters this week,' she replied, referring to the shift at Barnborough Colliery that started at two in the afternoon and finished at ten at night.

Amy glanced at the clock. It showed twenty minutes to eight. 'You'll not be going out again then, Beattie?' She worried that once her sister had the taste of drink in her she might go looking for more.

'Is that all you come here for? Checking up on me to see if I'm looking after this lot?' Beattie waved a hand in the direction of the four older children now huddled quietly in the corner under the stairs. They knew better than to play or make noise in their mother's presence, and not once since she came in had Beattie looked at Henry in his pram. Amy's hackles rose.

'I come because I care about you, Beattie,' she said tartly. Then softening her tone she added, 'I want to help you. You always seem so unhappy, and you never seem to get on top of things.' Amy gestured hopelessly.

Beattie stood, belligerent. 'Aye, well, I don't need your pity. I've told you that before, and if I seem unhappy it's because I bloody am, so you can bugger off. And you lot,' she yelled at the children, 'get up them bloody stairs and get to bed.'

The children jumped and after calling 'Goodnight, Auntie Amy', they scampered upstairs. Amy put on her coat. There was no dealing with Beattie when she was in one of her moods.

Amy walked briskly to Intake Farm, puzzling over what more she could do to help Beattie; all her efforts seemed to make little difference, and things were going from bad to worse. Maggie shouldn't be missing school to let Beattie go out drinking. Amy had tried talking to Bert but he'd shrugged in that lackadaisical way of his saying, 'talk to Beattie not me.' Amy didn't doubt he loved his children, playing silly games with them and taking them on country walks, but he failed to protect them from Beattie's cruel hands and tongue. *Perhaps*, thought Amy, as she approached the kitchen door at Intake Farm, *if I'd done more to protect Beattie from our mother's hands and tongue when we were younger, she might have turned out differently. But I was just a child*, she reasoned, *a spoiled little girl too full of my own importance.*

'You're late,' said Bessie, emphasising the words and glowering as Amy stepped inside. 'What kept you?'

'I called with Beattie to see the children.'

Bessie's expression darkened even further. 'I don't know why you bother. I wouldn't set foot in the place. She's nothing but a slattern for all my good rearing.'

Amy raised her eyes to the ceiling.

4

Beckett's Park Hospital

4th September, 1918

Amy's second train journey was far less daunting than the one she had made two days ago. Confident that this time she knew where she was going, she sat back watching the ever-changing scenery as it flashed by: here a little village, there a grimy town, and next a sprawl of open countryside. All had gone unnoticed on her first visit to Leeds and Beckett's Park Hospital. Today, the bag on her knee contained her purse, four new men's handkerchiefs, a bag of mint humbugs — Jude's favourites — and a copy of Kipling's *The Man Who Would Be King*.

Outside Leeds City Station, she glanced up at the large clock above the entrance. Plenty of time to walk to the hospital; no need for a cab now she knew the way. She set off briskly, twice stopping to ask directions, making sure her memory wasn't playing her false. The city streets were busy, the bright September sun encouraging people to be out and about: women shopping, nannies pushing their charges in high, glossy perambulators, and businessmen in smart suits hurrying in and out of office buildings. Amy almost envied them, for the nearer she came to Beckett's Park the lower her spirits sank.

She felt the weight of the book in her bag bumping against her thigh as she walked. She'd set out full of optimism, thinking she had the answer to his problem in a few hundred pages bound in cheap leather-cloth, but as she walked up to the hospital's imposing doors, she knew that she had been clutching at straws.

The VAD clerk behind the reception desk recognised her from her previous visit.

'Hello, it's Mrs Leas, isn't it?' she said, smiling. 'If you just sign here, Mrs Leas, you can go through. You know the way.' She slid a book with lined pages across the desk. Amy added her signature to the list already there.

She walked down the long corridor, past the green door of Dr Mackay's office and on to the double doors that would take her into the large, airy room, and Jude. She paused before entering, thinking how she should approach him, and wondering if she would find any change in him. She pushed open the door.

The room was just as it had been two days ago: soldiers, nurses and, like her, those who had come to visit their loved ones, sitting at tables playing board games or by the windows, talking. A nurse came to greet her, and after ascertaining who Amy was, she pointed to where Jude was sitting — exactly where he had been two day ago. Amy approached him on legs that trembled and feet that felt as though she were moving through treacle. Afraid to breathe, she rounded the chair and stood in front of him.

Jude gave no indication that he saw her. He sat rigidly, his hands clamped to the arms of the chair.

He was staring straight ahead, the same blank, bitter expression twisting his mouth and narrowing his eyes. Amy pulled an empty chair closer to his and sat down. Still, he showed no sign of knowing she was there. Tentatively, she placed her hand on his arm, and squeezing it gently she said, 'Hello, Jude. It's me, Amy. How are you, love?'

He turned his head, glancing briefly at her before turning away, but he let her hand rest on his arm. She had half-expected him to shake it off as he had done before. He looked at her again, his eyes dark and brooding as they scanned her face. She smiled.

He blinked, and blinked again, his face contorting and lips beginning to move. Amy held her breath, only releasing it when he turned his gaze back to the window. *Does he know it's me*, she wondered? She thought she had seen a flash of recognition, and encouraged by this she reached into her bag and took out the book.

She placed it on his knee. He made no attempt to lift it.

'I brought it because you asked for it in your last letter,' she said. 'It's *The Man Who Would Be King*.'

Jude lowered his gaze. Amy's nerves jangled and she felt slightly nauseous. She was sure she and the book were having some effect on him. She waited. Out of her eye corner she saw Nurse Brennan looking over at them. She turned her head and smiled. Nurse Brennan nodded, as if to say is everything all right. Amy nodded back.

They sat for twenty minutes or so, the book lying on Jude's knee exactly where she had placed it. Then, cautiously he removed his hands from the chair arm and lifted the book. He rubbed his right thumb over the cover, backwards and forwards. Gradually, the dark blue leatherette began to peel, the flakes clogging under his thumbnail and tiny fragments of grey card curling like maggots into his lap. Amy placed a restraining hand on Jude's. He looked at her, his eyes rolling wildly and saliva sputtering from his lips.

'Jude! Jude!' she cried.

The book sailed over her head, landing with a thud at the foot of the window.

Nurse Brennan came rushing over. Jude was rocking back and forth, guttural noises escaping his throat. She held him firmly until he stopped rocking. 'You're safe, Jude, you're safe,' she said over and again. She wiped his face. He closed his eyes, his breathing slowing.

Amy stood impotently by, silently cursing herself for her presumption. Why had she ever thought that a book could be the answer?

Nurse Brennan picked it up. She handed it to Amy, her expression a reprimand. 'Dr Mackay doesn't allow books,' she said, 'you should have asked first.' She took Amy by the elbow and moved her out of Jude's hearing.

Amy looked at her, askance. 'But why?' she gasped. 'Jude loves reading. I thought it might liven his mind, give him something to think about. All he does is sit and stare out of the window.' She glanced at him and saw that he was doing just that. 'Look at him,' she said, exasperated. 'He needs something to bring him back to normality.'

'And he's doing just that in his own way,' Nurse

36

Brennan said dryly. 'He's tackling his demons, and had you seen him when he first arrived here, you'd know that. No diarrhoea, no projectile vomiting, no screaming and shouting all night long.' She softened her tone. 'He still has a long way to go but he is improving, believe me. Now you go and say goodbye and — ' she tapped the book in Amy's hand '—take that home with you and leave it there. Dr Mackay believes reading only disturbs them further, and he's the expert. Leave it up to him to get Jude in a fit state to go home.'

★ ★ ★

After Amy had gone, Jude sat quietly picking at his thumbnail and letting that lovely smile and the gentle voice play inside his head. There was a scent in his nose, a clean fresh smell that reminded him of meadow flowers. His eyes were closed, but behind his lids he saw a large room filled with stacks of shelves and row upon row of books. A pretty girl with a mass of blonde curls came walking towards him. She was wearing a pin-tucked blouse and a smart skirt, and she was smiling. The scent sweetened.

5

Barnborough

Spring, 1912

In a rented room in a house in Barnborough, a darkly handsome young man was lying on his bed thinking about the girl in the library. She was something special. It wasn't just her bouncing, blonde curls and bright blue eyes that attracted him, it was her lively mind and the way she talked that fascinated him. He was glad he'd come to Barnborough, even though he didn't care for the job he had taken to earn a living.

He had left the sparsely furnished cottage in Bird's Well six weeks ago, bringing with him nothing but a pack containing all his worldly goods, a pack that had sagged under the weight of Hardy, Stevenson, London and Conan Doyle. *You're heavy fellows*, he had silently told them, but to leave them behind was unthinkable. He had yet to come to terms with how quickly his life had changed. Less than two weeks before, he had been working the smallholding with his father and mother, now both dead within days of each other, and despite offering Jude his condolences the landlord had repossessed the tenancy.

Jude had been sad to leave Bird's Well, the only home he had ever known, and sadder still at losing the kindly couple that, having taken him in as a baby, had reared him with fondest love. He was twelve when Henry and Jenny Leas told him he was not their natural son, his birth mother dead and his father unknown. Rather than deterring him it had made him all the more grateful for his nurturing. Henry had been a quiet, thoughtful man with a wealthy knowledge of plants, birds and country matters. Jenny had been a reader of good literature, fond of poetry and storytelling. Education that had not been provided at home had been given at the nearest school, a tiny establishment with a dedicated teacher, and so, at twenty years of age, Jude had arrived in Barnborough looking for a place to stay and a job that involved using his brain rather than brawn.

He had no difficulty finding lodgings, but after a week of fruitless enquiry — no experience, no paper qualifications — he had walked across the pithead at Barnborough Colliery, his boots kicking up spurts of the black dust that coated everything in sight. He'd gazed up at the towering winding gear and the mighty slag heaps beyond it, ranged like mountains. It all looked black and ominous but it was the most likely place to find work and earn some much-needed money. As he had pushed open the door into the pit office, he had recalled the words his teacher had said on his last day in school. 'You're clever enough to work in business, start out as a clerk and work your way up.' Jude had put her prediction to the test. Afterwards, he cringed whenever he thought of it.

'I'd like to apply for a position in clerking,' Jude had said to the two men behind the counter who, having curtailed their conversation were eyeing him expectantly. Then, thinking his capabilities needed embellishing he had told them, 'I'm an able writer and good with numbers.'

The men had exchanged sardonic smiles, the taller of the two pushing his spectacles further up the bridge of his nose before asking his colleague, 'Do we require a clerk, Mr Heslop?'

'Not that I recall, Mr Clifford, not even one who can write and add up.'

Jude had flushed. They were making game of him. He'd turned on his heel.

'Hold on, hold on,' spectacles called out. 'Do you want a job or don't you?'

And so — as Jude contemplated future visits to the library, he was grateful for a job at the pit because with money in his pocket he could afford to ask the delightful Miss Elliot if she would accompany him to the theatre or any-where else she might choose. He would have been even more pleased had he known that up at Intake Farm, Amy also was contemplating his next visit and wondering if she should wear her new white shirtwaist with the pin-tucked bod-ice later in the week on the off-chance that he read quickly and would return his books before the week was out.

★ ★ ★

On Thursday afternoon of that same week, Jude dashed from the pithead back to his lodgings. He bathed hastily and put on a clean shirt and trou-sers. 'I'll leave that brown stew for later,' he told his landlady, Lily Tinker.

40

In the library, a stout, rather plain girl with a superior attitude checked his returned books. Disappointed, he went in search of replacements, and Amy. She was slotting a handful of returned books into their rightful places when she saw him at the far end of the aisle. Heedless of where the books really belonged, she shoved them onto the shelf and watched him approach.

How strong he looks, she thought, admiring his tall, muscular frame, pleased that she was wearing her new blouse and skirt.

She's even lovelier than I remember, thought Jude, admiring her pert figure as he closed the distance between them. Their eyes met, the blue of hers sparkling and his darkly glittering. They smiled at one another, but before either of them had chance to say a word, Phoebe Littlewood came barging down the alley.

Amy saw her first. Her eyes widening, she gulped, 'You'll find it in the arts section, sir,' and stepping around him, she hurried towards the head librarian. Surprised at being so suddenly and curtly abandoned Jude swung on his heel to follow her, but quick to assess the situation he stayed where he was. When he heard Phoebe ordering Amy to go and work in the storeroom until closing time, Jude trudged down the alley in search of a good book to salve his disappointment.

★ ★ ★

'That's the second time he's been in this week. Is he pestering you or are you encouraging him, Amy? Miss Littlewood won't like it, you know,'

41

Freda said, as they were putting their coats on at the end of the day.

Amy hid her reddening cheeks and her annoyance by picking up her bag and heading for the door. Freda hurried after her. She and Amy were old friends, but just lately Amy was beginning to find her irritating. Working in the library had turned Freda's head. She had joined the staff less than a year ago, Amy having put in a good word for her, but the longer she worked there the more superior she considered herself. Demeaning and bossy, her know-all attitude had provoked Amy into telling her, 'Just because you work in a place full of knowledge and culture doesn't mean that you know the answer to everything.' But what annoyed Amy most of all was Freda constantly telling her what she should think and do — that and the way she was all too keen to curry favour with the head librarian. And right now, she just wanted to get away from her.

'Who is he, anyway?' Freda continued, catching up with Amy on the library steps.

'He's a very pleasant young man, and I don't need either your permission or Miss Littlewood's to talk to him,' Amy said tartly.

'I'm just looking out for you, that's all. You don't know anything about him. He's not from round here, and you need to be careful.'

'Careful of what, Freda? Of making a friend without your approval? You don't own me, but just lately you're never done telling me what I should and shouldn't do. And don't think I don't know it was you told Miss Littlewood I was talking to him.'

Freda shrugged. 'Like I said, I thought he might be pestering you.' She wouldn't admit that she would have preferred it had Jude been pestering her. It was always the same. Amy always attracted the best-looking fellows.

★ ★ ★

Early the next morning, Jude was still thinking about Amy as the cage carrying a motley bunch of colliers began to rattle its way down the shaft. Up until now he had worked on the pit top; this was his first day underground. His stomach lurched painfully, and his nose clogged with the stink of human sweat and the acrid stench rising from below. He heaved a gusty sigh.

'What makes a lad like you come to work in t'pit?' asked Bert, the hewer Jude had been assigned to that morning. It was his job to shovel the coal that Bert hewed into huge tubs, ready to be lifted to the surface.

'It's not by choice. It's all I could get.'

'None of us are 'ere by choice, lad, it's cos we 'ave no bloody choice,' said Bert caustically, 'but never mind, you'll get used to it.' Jude wondered if that was true.

The cage clunked to a sickening halt, the doors scraping open. The miners stepped out into cold, damp, eerie gloom. Jude tagged along behind, dreadfully aware that above his head were tons of rock and soil. He shivered. Before him stretched a long, underground road hemmed in on both sides with slimy walls. Underfoot was rough and uneven and above his head the roof dipped then rose and

43

dipped again.

'What do you do when you're not workin'?' asked Bert. 'I've not seen you in t'pub.'

'I'm not much of a drinker. I spend most of my time reading.'

'By, bloody hell, that's not much fun; tha' wants to get out an' about,' Bert exclaimed. They trudged onwards, the lights from their helmets casting elongated, menacing shadows against rugged walls.

About to disagree, and conscious of Bert's advice to get out and about, Jude suddenly thought of the notice he had seen on a board outside the library. Instead he said, 'I don't know anybody in Barnborough to go out with, but I did see a notice advertising a dance in the Church Hall on Saturday night. Is it just for older folks or will there be young 'uns as well?'

'Oh, aye, there'll be a good crowd there. They don't allow drink, mind, so you'll not see me there, but you should go. You might be lucky an' meet a nice lass.'

Jude knew exactly which nice lass he'd like to meet there. Lost in his imagination, he failed to react quickly enough to Bert's 'mind your head,' and his helmet clanked resoundingly against low-hanging rock.

Jude plodded on, a sharp pain above both ears advising him to look where he was going. Gradually the procession of colliers grew fewer as, in twos and threes, they filed into stalls along the coal seam. Bert stopped at the next entrance and Jude followed him in. A short while later another coal hewer joined them. 'How do, Seth?' Bert said.

'Has tha come to gi' us a hand?' Then stashing their tins that, like Jude's, contained their dinners into a cleft in the stall's wall they stripped off their jackets and shirts. Jude followed suit, his vest embarrassingly white and novice-like compared to Bert's dingy grey. Laughing, Bert pointed a finger. 'Tha'll get that mucky afore t'shift's over.'

He lifted a short-handled, double-edged pick that was leaning against the wall. 'This is a nadger,' he told Jude, swiping at the seam of coal running along one wall of the stall. 'It's a bloody good seam is this, it's like hackin' shite,' he gasped, as glistening lumps of coal fell at his feet. Seth joined him. Jude shovelled coal into the nearest of the two huge metal tubs, Bert laughing raucously and shouting, 'Keep up, lad! Put your back in it. We can't do wi' standin' knee-deep in bloody coal.' Jude laughed back, knowing that the good-natured Bert was only joking; he had been keeping up.

Midway through the shift they stopped to eat, squatting with their backs against the stall's wall, Bert and Seth with their snap tins on their knees. Jude set his on the ground, opened it and took out a corned beef sandwich. Still munching, he reached for another. 'Bloody hell,' he roared, tossing the sandwich across the stall along with a writhing mass of shiny black beetles. Bert and Seth had laughed. 'That's summat else you'll have to learn. Never leave your snap uncovered. Them buggers 'ud eat you given t'chance,' said Seth. Hungry and embarrassed, Jude thought he would never get used to working down the pit.

By the end of that week every muscle and sinew in his body ached, but he'd kept pace with Bert

45

and Seth and enjoyed their company. Bert droll and Seth placid, their ready humour and friendly advice made every day less onerous, and Jude had reached the conclusion that if he must work down the pit then he'd become a hewer; the men who cut coal earned three times that of a man shovelling it into tubs.

★ ★ ★

At Intake Farm a flurry of activity spilled from bedroom to kitchen as Amy and Freda prepared for the Easter dance in the Church Hall. Bessie smiled fondly, recalling the days when she had done much the same, anticipation of what the evening might hold always making her blood sing.

'There,' she said, fiddling with Amy's lace collar, as Amy twitched impatiently.

'Will you fasten my necklace?' Freda dangled a string of gaudy beads under Amy's nose. As Amy secured the clasp, she couldn't help thinking that her pale blue tunic with its lace collar, worn over a long, straight skirt of deeper blue looked rather insignificant against Freda's velvet dress. In a violent shade of emerald-green, it swathed Freda's plump body in drapes and rolls. The necklace fastened, Freda performed a twirl, exclaiming, 'I feel like a willow in this dress.'

Bessie held her tongue. Had she let it wag it would have said, 'Aye, an' look more like a Savoy cabbage.'

Silently and proudly, she noted that her daughter was by far the prettier of the two. Amy had pinned back her long, blonde tresses with tortoiseshell combs then let them fall into the nape of her slender neck, the whole effect enhancing her china-blue eyes and finely shaped brows. Far more attractive than Freda's severely rolled, drab brown hair and eyes of a nondescript colour, thought Bessie, vainly attributing her daughter's beauty to her own.

She watched Amy pirouette, and suddenly, from nowhere, she recalled the joy on Hadley's face when she had presented him with a bonny, blue-eyed, blonde-haired daughter. It had been some seven months after she had left a mother-less boy with her barren friend, Jenny Leas; a boy who was the image of Raffy Lovell. *Had I known I was pregnant then I'd have most likely used it as a persuasive ploy*, she thought, *make Jenny jealous of my fertility had she refused to take the child.* But Bessie didn't want to remember that unsavoury incident so she shook her head vigorously to dispel the memory and cried, 'You look a picture, our Amy; you remind me of when I was your age.' Amy responded with a smile.

'Are you ready for the off? The trap's ready and waiting,' barked Samuel, coming in from the yard, his best waistcoat and jacket straining at the seams. Used to seeing him dressed for work in a loose smock and corduroy britches, Amy thought he looked decidedly uncomfortable and even fatter. She had scant sympathy for the brother she considered to be a self-indulgent bully who, with his bulbous, blue eyes and fleshy bottom lip, was ugly inside and out. That he had no girlfriend didn't surprise her in the least, although she suspected that Freda fancied him, goodness knew why.

Samuel glowered at Amy, and almost as if he had read her thoughts on his love life or the lack of it, he said, 'And think on, our Amy, if Albert Sissons asks you to dance, don't refuse him. He's a good catch, is Albert. Don't be dancing wi' any colliers.'

'We won't,' chirped Freda, 'we don't associate with mucky pit lads.'

Amy bristled. Who did Sammy and Freda think they were, telling her whom she could or could not dance with? She threw Samuel a disdainful glance. 'Is that because you think Albert's dad'll sell you one of those new tractors cheaper?' she asked sarcastically. Ernest Sissons owned a farm machinery business in Barnborough.

'Just do as you're told,' growled Samuel, barging to the foot of the stairs. 'Come on, Thomas. Get a move on. I'll not wait all night.'

Thuds on the stairs heralded Thomas's arrival. He blundered into the kitchen, a hint of fear on his gormless features at having kept his older brother waiting. 'I can't get this right,' he moaned, indicating his clumsily knotted tie. Not dissimilar in appearance to Samuel, Thomas also carried too much weight but whereas his brother's features were tightly supercilious his were flaccid, and his pale blue eyes held none of the malevolence that gleamed in Samuel's. Indeed, for much of the time Thomas appeared utterly vacuous.

'Come here, little lamb, let me do it for you.' Thomas hurried to his mother, glancing nervously at Samuel as Bessie fixed his tie. Another roar from Samuel had them all hastily making their way out of the house and piling into the trap. 'Think on now, girls. Mind who you keep company with and don't keep our Sammy waiting when he's ready to come home,' Bessie called out as she waved them off.

★ ★ ★

At the same time as the young folk at Intake Farm were preparing for the dance, a similar scene was being played out in a small terrace house in Barnborough.

'There you are; that'll do you.' Lily Tinker handed Jude a freshly ironed, crisp white shirt. It was his one good shirt, worn only on special occasions, the last time being when he had applied for a clerk's job at Barnborough Colliery. It hadn't brought him much luck that day but tonight he hoped it might do the trick.

'Thanks, Mrs Tinker,' he said, thinking yet again that Lily was a smashing landlady and how fortunate he was to have made his home with her. A gregarious widow with a witty tongue and a warm heart, Lily mothered Jude just as she did her own son, Tommy.

'Think on now, don't be getting any lipstick on that collar — it's a bugger to wash off,' she said, her eyes twinkling.

Jude grinned. 'Just on me lips then,' he quipped, at the same time wondering if the girl whose lips he'd like to kiss would be at the dance. With her in mind he climbed the stairs to the bedroom he shared with Tommy. He hung the shirt on the same hanger that held his one good suit. Tailor-made

49

from fine quality black worsted the suit was Jude's pride and joy. He'd bought it from a secondhand stall in the market, its previous owner, no doubt deceased, having had good taste and a much larger income than his own. He didn't object to wearing a dead man's suit, not when it fitted him to perfection.

Tommy Tinker looked up from the shoe he was polishing. 'I'm going to try for Mary Stockdale tonight, Jude. Do you think I'm in with a chance?'

Jude smiled into the homely face of the seventeen-year-old lad who was three years his junior. Tommy had flattened his unruly, brown hair; and now he had a frill of greasy curls above each ear. 'I don't see why not but . . .' Jude reached for a towel hanging over the end of the bed. 'You've been a bit heavy handed with the Brilliantine. Rub it off and wear it like you always do.'

Tommy grinned sheepishly. 'I were trying to look like a man about town,' he said innocently.

'You look more like Coco the clown.'

There was no malice in Jude's remark but just in case it was misconstrued he added, 'You're good-looking enough without it.' The white lie sprang easily from his lips. He liked Tommy and didn't want him to be seen as a figure of fun. As Tommy towelled his hair, Jude peered into the mirror on the dressing table and brushed his own thick black hair. It flopped over his forehead and curled round his ears and in the nape of his neck, softening his aquiline features. Finely shaped eyebrows topped his dark, penetrating eyes, eyes made all the blacker by the permanent lines of coal dust embedded in his lashes. A tiny blue scar in the shape of an arrowhead marked one swarthy cheek, the sharp flint that had caused it lending a rakish enhancement to his good looks.

'My, I could fall for you meself,' Lily remarked when Jude clattered downstairs, Tommy at his heels. For all Lily wouldn't see forty again, she flirted outrageously with her young lodger.

'I'm hoping somebody else thinks the same,' Jude replied, at the same time fretting that the object of his desire might not be at the dance. *But if she is*, he thought, *I'll make sure to strengthen our brief acquaintance.*

'You look a treat an' all, our Tommy.' Lily tweaked his greasy mop. 'Off you go now and behave yourselves,' she said, wiping her fingers on her apron. 'Watch out for them lasses, don't be doin' owt I wouldn't.' She gave a lewd, throaty chuckle.

Jude thought he wouldn't mind being led astray.

'Don't wait up, we might be late,' the lads chorused, chortling at the coincidence and throwing friendly punches as they scuffled out the door.

★ ★ ★

The five-piece band struck up a foxtrot. Several young women took to the floor, partnering each other in the absence of offers from the men lounged nonchalantly against the hall's walls, hands in pockets and chins jutted upwards. Older couples dipped and swayed, as did a few young men who had plucked up enough courage to find a girl to partner.

'We'll dance with each other and just stay with the girls when we're not dancing,' Freda told Amy,

51

conscious that her prettier companion would attract far more offers than she herself. Freda didn't fancy being a wallflower.

They made their way onto the dance floor.

Leaned against the wall, a Woodbine clamped between his lips, Jude felt his spirits lift as he watched the slender, blonde-haired girl in the blue dress glide by in the arms of her plump friend dressed in green. His eyes followed them as they circumnavigated the floor. His scrutiny did not go unnoticed.

'That fellow from the library's here and he's watching us,' Freda hissed, peevishly aware that she was not the focus of his attention.

'Who? Where?' Freda pointed. Amy's heart fluttered when she saw it was Jude.

'He's awfully handsome, isn't he?' she said.

Freda scowled, piqued that Jude had eyes only for Amy. 'Let's get a drink,' she said, dragging Amy away from Jude's close proximity. Amy glanced his way again.

Freda tugged her arm, saying, 'Ignore him. We don't want him pestering us.'

Lemonade glasses aloft, Amy and Freda manoeuvred their way through the throng to stand with the girls. Amy turned in the direction she had last seen Jude, surprised to find him standing close behind her.

'Can I have the pleasure of the next dance?' he asked.

'No, you can't. We're sitting it out,' snapped Freda.

'I wasn't asking you,' Jude retorted. 'I think the lady can answer for herself.'

Amy's heart drummed and her throat went dry. She gulped at the lemonade. Then, shoving the glass into an affronted Freda's hand, she smiled sweetly at Jude.

'I'd love to dance,' she said, taking hold of his outstretched hand.

The band played a slow waltz, Jude pleased that the slow pace and tender music allowed conversation. In the space of the dance they merely acknowledged their meetings in the library and how fond they were of reading. Several dances later, they agreed that a breath of fresh air would be most welcome. Hand in hand they slipped outside, Freda looking distinctly peeved as she watched them go.

They wandered into the graveyard, a mellow moon lighting the way and cherry blossom scenting the air. Seated on a large, flat tombstone they swapped potted histories: Amy telling him about her family and Intake Farm and Jude recalling his earlier days in Bird's Well.

When she asked about his job, he said, 'It's not what I would choose, but I aim to work my way up from shovelling coal to hewing it, so it will suffice until I've saved enough money to explore my options.'

'And what might they be?'

'I'm not exactly sure. I'd like to go to college and qualify for something that uses my brain rather than my muscles. Literature's my thing.' He chuckled wryly. 'When I was growing up Jim Hawkins and The Three Musketeers were my best friends. My mother gave me the love of reading and . . . ' He paused dreamily. 'Maybe I'll be a writer or a publisher of other writers' great works. Anything to do with books.'

Amy warmed to him all the more. 'I loved Jim Hawkins as well, but I loved Heathcliff even more,' she confided. 'I'm a romantic at heart. I adore Jane Austen and the Brontës. I can't read enough, and would you believe it, just as I left the girls' grammar, they opened the public library and I got the job of assistant librarian. I couldn't have hoped for better. It was pure luck.'

'Luck plays a large part in our lives,' Jude said, thinking how disappointed he would have been if Amy had not come to the dance.

'Luck's only part of it.' Amy was going to add that hard work played its part but Jude interrupted her, his thoughts turning for no reason to the disaster that had occurred a week or so earlier. 'What if you'd bought a ticket to sail on the *Titanic* then missed the boat? That's pure luck.'

Amy clutched at her throat. 'Oh yes,' she gasped. 'I read about that in the papers. Wasn't it terrible? They said the ship was unsinkable, yet all those people drowned in freezing cold water. Surely the boat's owners must have known there weren't enough lifeboats for all those on board.' Amy shuddered.

'They did, and the worst of it was they let the rich passengers get into the lifeboats first. Them that travelled steerage on the cheap tickets were locked down below until it was too late to save them.' Jude's voice shook with anger. 'It's one law for the rich and another for the poor. I hate man's inhumanity to his fellow man.'

Amy couldn't believe she was having such an

interesting conversation with a man, even if the topic was sad. All the other lads she knew showed little interest in anything other than farming or football. Jude continued talking about the division that existed between the social classes, Amy contributing her own opinions and at the same time thinking what a caring, thoughtful young man he was; his beliefs were in tune with her own and she liked him all the more for it.

The night air was balmy and the quiet of the graveyard a welcome respite from the bustle and noise in the Church Hall. Neither of them wanted the evening to end. The church clock struck ten. Jude turned his head at the sound, Amy remarking, 'You've the sweetest heart-shaped mark just below your left ear. Is it a birthmark?'

Jude fingered the mark and chuckled. 'Aye, my mother said I'd been kissed by an angel. She told me it would bring me luck, and I'm beginning to think she was right now that I've met you.'

Amy flushed with pleasure.

★ ★ ★

Inside the Church Hall Thomas sought out Freda and Amy, a panic-stricken expression on his pasty face. Finding Freda alone he blurted out, 'Our Sammy's ready to go and he'll not like being kept waiting. Where's our Amy?'

'Off outside with a mucky collier,' Freda said spitefully. 'I don't know what she's playing at.'

Thomas turned and ran. He had to find Amy.

Over at the trap, Samuel Elliot savagely stubbed his boot toe into a clump of daffodils, cursing under his breath as he waited for his passengers. The evening had turned sour. For the first hour he had stood outside the Hall drinking with the men who had brought crates of bottled beer from the pub and then, venturing inside, he had found himself a girl who was easy, or so he'd been told. After plying her with drink he'd tried his hand, furious when she'd laughed in his face. 'I don't do it wi' great lumps o' lard like you,' she'd jeered. He'd given her a clout then stomped off to find Thomas, telling him to find the girls. They were going home.

Now, as Thomas and Freda approached, Samuel roared, 'Come on, get a move on. I've had enough of this bloody place.'

'I can't find our Amy,' Thomas stuttered. 'She's not in the Hall. Freda says she's gone off with a fellow.'

'He's a collier,' Freda sneered adding fuel to the fire.

Just then, Jude and Amy walked out of the graveyard. Seeing them, Samuel set off at a run, throwing himself at Jude and yelling, 'Get your dirty hands off my sister.'

Amy screamed. Jude staggered sideways but, quick on his feet, he soon righted himself and raised his fists. Only then did Samuel take stock of his opponent. A full head taller, his muscles honed from long hours shovelling coal, Jude braced himself ready for the onslaught. Samuel stepped back.

'Amy, get in the trap,' he bellowed, spittle flying from his blubbery lips. He glared at Jude. 'Keep away from her if you know what's good for you.'

Amy climbed into the trap, thoroughly dis-comfited. Jude, outwardly unperturbed, stood his ground waiting for Samuel's next move. Samuel scuttled round the trap and from the safety of the driver's seat he threatened, 'Don't go near her again.'

Jude, thinking it wise not to aggravate the fellow further and cause Amy more distress saluted cockily and then said, 'I'll be seeing you, Amy.'

Feeling utterly humiliated, she responded with a pathetic little wave.

6

When, on the night of the dance in the Church Hall Jude had said, 'I'll be seeing you, Amy,' he had meant it, and so, on Monday morning he walked into the library. When he looked at Amy, he felt his heart float. Hers fluttered and she looked back with a smile that told him all he wanted to know. He was wearing the same black suit that he'd worn the night of the dance and under it a crisp, white shirt. Slender and sinewy, with eyes darker than the night and shining black curls caressing his forehead and swarthy cheeks, Amy wondered if he would be Mr Darcy to her Elizabeth.

'Wait for me in Religion and Theology,' Amy whispered, sending Jude to a secluded corner of the library that didn't attract many borrowers. When she joined him there, they both quickly agreed that the altercation with Samuel made no difference to their friendship, and when Jude asked to see her after work, maybe go to the theatre or do anything to spend time together, Amy readily accepted. However, Jude was on 'afters' that week, working two till ten, so nights out would have to wait. Jude left the library feeling as though the world was a different place, and for the rest of that week during the long hours underground he willed time to fly, and was barely able to conceal his impatience to see her again. Amy found herself counting the days, each morning appearing brighter than the one before and every passing hour filled with pleasurable anticipation.

On the next Monday afternoon, Jude deliberately lingered between the shelves until hatchet-faced Phoebe Littlewood curtly told him it was closing time. When Amy stepped outside a short while later, she found him perched on the wall by the steps, waiting for her. It was a warm evening, and when Jude suggested they walk along the river-bank behind the library and past the church, Amy saw no reason to refuse.

Immediately, just as on the night of the dance, they felt a connection, and they only had to look at or listen to each other to see it and feel it. As they walked by the river, the melancholy sound of a violin drifted through the open window of a garret in one of the houses on its banks. The ten-der strains of 'Love is the Sweetest Thing' floated on the air. How apt, Amy thought. She glanced at Jude to see if he heard it too.

His head was cocked and his eyes on the garret's window. When he stopped walking and lowered his gaze, Amy could tell his thoughts matched her own, and as their eyes met Jude leaned in to share their first kiss. Then he wrapped his arms around her and kissed her again, more ardently this time. Beneath his shirt she felt the steady beat of heart, but her own felt as though it was melting. When the kiss ended, they drew apart, breathless, and simultaneously gasped, 'I love you.'

★　★　★

After that first evening by the river they met when-ever time allowed, every minute precious for they

59

knew they were meant to be together. Meetings flew by in a whirl of shared interests: books, politics of the day, natural history, and each other. They swapped stories from their respective childhoods, Jude neglecting to mention the truth about his parentage. These walks, too brief and infrequent for their liking, brought with them an understanding that neither of them had ever before experienced.

Jude had always loved poetry and, encouraged by his mother Jenny, he had read many poems. Now, for the first time he understood what it was the romantic poets were trying to say: it was love, pure and beautiful love. For her part, Amy was lost in the wonder of his company, the pleasure of seeing him never diminishing and her heart beating that little bit faster whenever they met.

However, Amy chose not to mention any of this to her family or to Freda although the latter was curious as to why she made excuses for not spending time together after work. Afraid of Samuel's reaction, she took care to hide it from him. On the evenings she stayed out late for a trip to the theatre or simply sitting in the comfort of Lily Tinker's parlour, she told Hadley and Bessie she was with Freda or Beattie. She felt guilty at the pretence but she dared not chance their interference spoiling her romance, not when it was so beautiful. But some secrets are hard to keep.

★   ★   ★

'What's this about me and you going to the theatre to see *Hindle Wakes* last Saturday?'

Amy froze midway between taking off her coat

60

in the library's storeroom, ready to start work. Her back was towards Freda so she was able to hide the guilty flush that sprang to her cheeks, but Freda's accusatory tone had her desperately searching for an excuse. Finding none, she turned to face her.

'Who said that?' Amy tried to sound uncaring.

'Your Samuel. He asked me had I enjoyed it.'

'And what did you say?' Amy heard the wobble in her voice and knew that Freda heard it too.

Freda smiled smugly. 'Oh, I didn't let on, if that's what you're thinking. I knew who you were with so I pretended I'd seen it.' Relief flooded Amy's face but before she could offer her thanks, Freda said, 'But don't think I'll lie for you the next time.'

'I didn't ask you to lie this time,' Amy said tartly, having recovered her composure.

Freda smirked. 'No, you didn't, but you've been lying to me. Your Sammy seems to think we're never done gallivanting but we haven't been out together for ages. All you've done this while back is make excuses, saying you had to go straight home.'

'I'm sorry, Freda. I shouldn't have used you like that but I'm not yet ready to tell Mam and Dad about Jude, and you know what Sammy will say.' Amy gave Freda an appeasing smile. 'He really took a dislike to Jude on that night at the dance.'

'I wonder why?' Freda said sarcastically. 'Still,' she shrugged carelessly, 'if you're that ashamed of him being a collier, I can see why you're keeping it a secret.'

'I'm not ashamed,' Amy retorted hotly. 'I'd never be ashamed of Jude. He's the most decent man I ever met.'

'In that case you won't mind me telling your Samuel who you're out with the next time he asks, 'cos it's certainly not me.' Freda spun on her heel and flounced out.

Amy stayed where she was. It now seemed despicable to have cut off her friendship with Freda after all the times they had shared. She should have been honest about Jude and how much he meant to her. But, Amy reasoned, Freda would have tried to talk her out of being with him. *Poor Freda*, thought Amy, *I understand why she feels annoyed at having no one to go out with, and that she's jealous of Jude, but I can't let her, or our Sammy, rule my life.*

★ ★ ★

And so Amy's secret love was secret no more. She was almost glad Freda had found her out, but common sense ruling that her romance would not meet with Samuel or her mother's approval, she couldn't help but worry.

Since that night at the Easter dance, Samuel had raised the incident with Jude more than once. Amy felt hurt when he accused her of having loose morals, and furious to be told she was a poor judge of men. Of course, Bessie had taken his side, warning Amy of the dangers of dallying with low-class colliers who were only out for one thing. Samuel had told her she should set her sights on Albert Sissons and Bessie had agreed. Amy had laughed scornfully, declaring that Albert was an insipid, inarticulate bore with droopy eyes and big ears,

62

and as for his money . . . 'It's you that finds his assets attractive, not me,' she had told them forcefully, 'and as for marrying him, I'd sooner be a nun.'

But, like any other young girl in love for the first time Amy yearned to shout it from the treetops and share this new and wondrous feeling with someone who understood what it felt like to wake each morning and see the future in a completely different light. Freda should have been the obvious person to confide in but Amy hadn't done that, so whom could she tell?

Against her better judgement, Amy decided to tell Beattie. Growing up, they had never been close enough to share hopes and dreams or secrets, the age gap too great and Beattie's surly manner discouraging. But the new, grown-up Amy needed to talk to someone about Jude, and who better than her older sister? After all, Amy pondered, Beattie must know something about love. She'd married Bert and given him five children. With this thought in mind, she left work and walked to Grattan Row.

Beattie was in the kitchen cooking Bert's tea. Amy dumped a large paper bag on the cluttered table. 'Apples and ginger snaps for the kids,' she said.

For once, Beattie was pleasantly welcoming. She smiled her thanks and offered Amy a cup of tea. 'Let's have a natter before Bert comes in,' she said, this friendly gesture sneaking its way into Amy's heart. Cups of tea in hand they lolled against the sink, gossiping.

When Amy reflected on what next took place,

she was undecided as to whether it was finding Beattie in such a good mood or her own pensive feelings that made her say what she did — without thinking.

'I'm in love, Beattie.'

Beattie raised her thick, black eyebrows, her face lighting up in surprise. 'Who with?' Before Amy could answer she said, 'Don't tell me it's Albert Bloody Sissons. He's awful.'

Amy grimaced. 'No, it's not him,' she squealed. The grimace became a dreamy smile as she said, 'His name's Jude Leas and he's absolutely wonderful. He works at the pit and lodges with Lily Tinker.'

The house door scraped open and Bert Stitt walked in. 'How do, young'uns,' he cried, fondling heads and patting bottoms as he made his way across the living room and into the kitchen. He beamed at his wife and sister-in-law. Bert was unfailingly cheerful despite having a cantankerous wife, too many mouths to feed, and empty pockets for most of the time.

'Our Amy's got a chap, Bert,' Beattie blurted out, her delight apparent.

'By bloody hell! It's taken you long enough to find one.'

'I think you know him,' Beattie said. 'Didn't you tell me you work with a fellow called Jude?'

Bert grinned. 'Aye, Jude Leas. He's a grand lad is Jude. Right educated but not pushy wi' it, if you know what I mean.'

Amy flushed with pleasure at his words. Then, her surprise showing, she said, 'He mentioned working with a Bert and Seth, but I didn't think

64

of you.' She didn't add that the industrious, efficient and highly skilled Bert that Jude talked about bore no resemblance to the Bert she knew. Jude credited Bert with having taught him all he had learned about mining coal. He'd said it was thanks to Bert's excellent tuition that he had been promoted to hewing coal rather than loading tubs. Amy looked at her feckless brother-in-law through new eyes.

Bert continued to sing Jude's praises then sat down to his tea. Amy joined Beattie at the fireside. 'What do that lot up there think about it?' Beattie's sour remark let Amy know she referred to just their parents and Samuel. Thomas didn't think.

'They don't know I'm seeing him,' she said miserably. 'I've had to keep it a secret because of our Sammy.' She told Beattie about the night of the dance and Samuel's ongoing animosity.

'And no doubt our dear mother agrees with our Sammy,' Beattie said scornfully.

Amy clamped her lips together and nodded her head. 'Dad's being supportive but he doesn't say much, and when he does, they shout him down,' she said despairingly.

'Take no notice of 'em. It's always been the same in that house; Mam and our Sammy calling the tune and Dad letting them away with it.'

'Aye, that's right,' Bert called from the table. 'When your Beattie married me, it got her away from that bloody lot up there. She couldn't believe her luck. Now she's got me an' a nice little home an' five bonny bairns to make her happy.'

Beattie gave him a look of utter disbelief. Then

she burst out laughing, a bitter-sounding cackle that brought tears to her eyes. Amy went home wondering if Beattie's enthusiasm for her romance with Jude was partly motivated by the notion that now she and Amy were more equal; they'd both earned Bessie's disapproval.

★ ★ ★

'Late again,' Bessie said, as Amy hurried into the farmhouse kitchen. 'I've kept this warming for over an hour.' She slammed a plate of steak pie, potatoes and vegetables down on the table. 'I don't know why you can't come straight home to eat with the rest of us.'

'I do,' snarled Samuel. 'She's been wi' that collier I told you about; the one I gave a bloody good hiding that night of the dance.'

Amy widened her eyes at Samuel's lie. 'You did no such thing. You just made a fool of yourself. Jude's too much of a gentleman to brawl with the likes of you.'

Samuel looked abashed then blustered, 'Jude, is it? I should have wiped the bloody floor with him, what with him traipsing you outside to do God knows what once he got you on your own in the graveyard.'

'Keep your dirty insinuations to yourself, Sammy. Not all men are like you.'

'Now, now,' Bessie reprimanded, 'don't speak to our Samuel in that tone. He was only looking out for you.'

'No he wasn't, he was doing what he always does; ruling the roost.' Amy pushed the plate of

66

dried-up food aside. 'I don't want any dinner,' she said, storming to the foot of the stairs, 'nor do I want him telling me who I can or cannot be friends with.'

Just then, Hadley came in from the yard. Hearing Amy's angry words, he asked, 'What's to do?'

'Ask him!' cried Amy. 'Our Sammy seems to think he has the right to tell us all what to do, and I've had enough of it.' She looked beseechingly at Hadley. 'Dad, I've met the most wonderful young man and I'd like bring him home to meet you, but our Sammy's decided he isn't good enough for me — even though he doesn't know him.' She stood tall, her clasped hands pressed against her chest as she spoke, her heart thudding and her expression begging understanding and approval.

Hadley's eyes found hers, his half-smile conveying love and sympathy. 'If you think he's the one, I'd be happy to meet him.' His smile broadened, and he had a twinkle in his eye as he asked, 'Go on then, let's be knowing. What's he called and where does he hail from?'

Amy blushed, and directing her words purely for her father's hearing, she said, 'He's called Jude Leas. He comes from Bird's Well. His parents had a smallholding but they're both dead so he came to work in Barnborough. He's working down the pit at the moment to earn enough money to put himself through college.' Her voice was tinged with pride.

Hadley nodded, pleased, but Bessie's insides froze. Leas! Bird's Well! Surely not! It couldn't be — it mustn't be. Cold sweat trickled down her spine and her hands shook so violently that the tealeaves she was spooning into the teapot scattered onto the countertop. She thought she might be sick.

'He sounds like a grand chap,' said Hadley. 'Bring him, and welcome.'

'Bring him here an' I'll give him another bloody good hiding,' Samuel growled.

In another mood Amy might have fought back, but she had got her dad's approval, and that was what mattered.

'Our Samuel knows what he's talking about,' Bessie piped defensively, 'so you think on, Amy . . .'

But Amy, sickened by the argument didn't stay to listen. She ran upstairs to her bedroom, raging at her mother for always taking Samuel's part.

7

Bessie didn't sleep well after her confrontation with Amy and Hadley. Try as she might, she couldn't stop the thoughts that whirled round inside her head although, as yet, she had no proof of their validity. Her fears could be totally unfounded, she told herself, as she lay staring at the ceiling. There could be any number of young lads called Leas from Bird's Well — a nephew of Henry's perhaps, or maybe Leas was a surname common to that area; she just didn't know.

She dozed, but when she wakened her thoughts returned to the same problem, and a day some twenty years before. She'd been out collecting eggs from the chicken coops when a man carrying a bundle close to his chest came into the farm-yard. Now, as she tried to find a cool place on her pillow to rest her aching head, she recalled how she'd stopped dead, her heart thudding wildly, and a flush of blood springing to her cheeks; she had thought it was Raffy Lovell. What the devil was he doing here after all this time, she'd asked herself. What did he want?

Then, a sudden gust of wind catching the man's long cloak and swinging it wide, she'd puffed out her cheeks, her breath whistling through her teeth. Relief mixed with disappointment as she'd realised it wasn't him; this man wasn't as lean as Raffy.

The man had raised his free arm and waved,

white teeth flashing a broad smile. 'Bessie, my love, my beautiful Bessie,' he'd called across the distance. The lilting tones achingly familiar, she'd dropped the egg basket, her hands flying to her face as she'd struggled to control pleasure and panic.

Then he was by her side, his boots trammelling the shells and splattered yolks at her feet. She'd felt his closeness, the heat from his body and the musky scent she remembered so well. Craving for him to hold her, she'd felt her pulse quickening and her stomach clenching. He'd reached out to touch her. Like a frightened hare she'd leapt away, springing back even further as the bundle against his shoulder writhed and bawled. The burlap had fallen away to reveal an angry, red face, eyes tight shut and the mouth an ugly shouting 'O' — it was a baby.

Bessie inched her way to the edge of the bed, Hadley rolling into the space warmed by her body and then noisily breaking wind. She swung her legs from under the covers and planted her feet on the floor, urged on by the noxious smell wafting from under the covers as much as the need to drink a strong cup of tea, and think. Could that baby now be the young man her daughter had fallen for? The baby boy she had given away to her friend Jenny? If so, she had to put a stop to Amy's romance before it went any further.

Downstairs in the kitchen she sat at the table, tea scalding her trembling lips. A poor, motherless boyo, Raffy had called him, his son by a poor dead Welsh girl. She'd been jealous then, thinking of him giving himself to someone else. On cue, the baby had squalled, as though he understood the parlous state of his short life. She had begged Raffy to leave immediately, before the children arrived home from school but, too late, they had caught her in the yard, Bessie arguing for him to go, he prevaricating and begging for a place to rest for the night.

The children had stared, goggle-eyed, and she had pretended he was selling pegs. Raffy had greeted the children cheerily, laughing when they enquired as to why he had an earring in his ear. 'Cos I's a king,' he had said, his black eyes twinkling wickedly. Then he'd looked closely at the little girl with swarthy skin and black hair, so unlike her pink-skinned, fair-haired brothers.

He'd crossed the yard, Bessie at his heels telling him to be gone, and when they were out of the children's earshot he'd said, 'The little missy — she's mine, isn't she? 'Twas like looking in a mirror, looking at her.'

'Keep your mouth shut,' Bessie had warned. 'Say nothing. I've too much to lose.'

'And what if I don't?' he'd replied mischievously.

She'd hidden Raffy and the baby in a disused pig crib, telling him he could stay there for the night. Later, she'd taken milk for the child and food for Raffy, giving him strict orders to leave before Hadley wakened and learned of his presence. She had intended to walk away smartly but Raffy had smiled endearingly, his eyes crinkling at the corners, just how she remembered. Blood singing in her ears, she had stayed until daybreak.

When she had wakened, Raffy was sleeping, his long, greasy locks snaking the straw under his head, and his long black lashes, pretty as any girl's, fanning the hollows beneath his almond-shaped eyes. He looked like an Asian prince from some exotic land far across the sea. His face was more lined than she remembered it, his hair not so lustrous, yet he was still the handsomest man she'd ever known. Oh, but she had loved the boy he had been when first they met, still did if she were honest. Hadn't he filled her dreams often enough, and how many nights in the bed she shared with Hadley had she pretended that it were Raffy making love to her. But that was the past, and rising quickly to her feet, Bessie did as she had always done and dealt with the present.

Then she'd glanced down at the sleeping child, her blue eyes glinting spitefully. Raffy had left his mark. Below the child's left ear was the same bluish heart-shaped patch as was on Raffy's neck. Her daughter also bore it, but Bessie hadn't told him that. As far as she was concerned Beatrice was Hadley's, and Raffy must never be allowed to think he had any claim on her. Not now, not ever.

She had wakened him with a kick. 'Take yourself off,' she'd flared, running as fast as she could back to the farmhouse.

By now, her tea grown cold, Bessie glanced at the clock on the dresser. Hadley would wake anytime soon. She stood, and stirring the embers in the range she tried to clear her head, but the secrets she had buried in the deeper regions of her mind refused to shift, the memories still rising to the surface, sharp and clear.

She sliced strips of bacon, whisked eggs and plopped a blob of lard into the frying pan. As it melted and began to spit, she stiffened, recalling Hadley's stern expression of the night before. Was he, after all this time, letting her know he wasn't the fool she'd played him for? She shuddered.

At the breakfast table Hadley was still wearing that same authoritative face he had worn the night before, and as Bessie served him with bacon, eggs and fried bread he neither thanked nor engaged her in his usual early morning banter. Her heart fluttered uncomfortably as, every now and then, she caught him looking at her in a strange, thoughtful way.

Samuel shuffled into the kitchen, bleary-eyed and surly. He slumped into his chair at the table, and as Bessie set a plate of bacon and eggs in front of him, Hadley said, 'Don't take all morning over it. That barn roof needs fixing. I want it done. *Today.*'

Samuel's eyes boggled, not so much at the order but at Hadley's curt delivery. His eyes slid to meet Bessie's, as if to say: what's eating him? Bessie shook her head. She needed to get away, sort out her problems and clear her head.

'I'm going into town. We're out of dried fruit and flour. I'll bake your favourite fruit loaf when I come back, Hadley,' she said, trying to sound cheery. She threw her husband an endearing smile.

Hadley responded with a brief nod, and pushing back his chair he bent and began to lace his boots. Thomas blundered into the kitchen, smiling stupidly as though surprised to see his family there. 'Is me breakfast ready?' he asked.

'It is,' said Hadley, 'and when you've had it,

73

get out there and help Samuel fix that barn roof.' He stamped towards the outside door and then paused, his hand on the latch. 'And if you're thinking of baking, Bessie, make something nice for when our Amy brings her young man for his tea on Sunday.' He slammed the door behind him.

Samuel's eyes boggled for the second time that morning. 'Is our Amy bringing that collier here?'

'Not if I have anything to do with it,' snapped Bessie.

★   ★   ★

It was a bright, crisp morning and the fields and trees were bathed in autumn's final glow, but Bessie saw none of this as she drove the trap into Barnborough. Amy's romance had opened up a can of worms and if she, Bessie, was to prevent them snaking into Hadley's mind she had to put a lid on it, and soon.

Now, as the pony clip-clopped along the road at a steady pace with Bessie at the reins, she recalled another day and another journey she had made twenty years before, not to Barnborough, but to Bird's Well.

That day, she had risen at first light and rushed out to the pig crib to make sure Raffy had done as she had ordered. When she saw that he and his pack were gone, she'd sagged with relief. Then she'd screamed. The baby screamed too.

Panicked as to how she would explain the baby's presence, she'd hared back to the farmhouse, and as she warmed a pan of milk and sought out some clean rags, she did what she had done before: she hatched a plan to save her reputation.

Within the hour she was on the road to Bird's Well, with the baby — now fed and his soiled nappy hidden in the straw in the pig crib — sleeping in a clothesbasket in the bottom of the trap. It was ten years since she had last visited her old friend, Jenny Leas, but local gossip had kept her privy to the fact that Jenny was still childless.

'I thought of you straight off,' she'd said, as soon as she had arrived at the remote smallholding that Jenny now lived in with her husband Henry. As Bessie explained the reason for her visit, she had gazed at the woman some two years her senior, thinking that time had not been kind. Whereas her own hair was still bright as summer corn and her plump cheeks smooth as a peach, Jenny's hair was streaked with grey, her face lined and drawn. These thoughts in mind, Bessie said, 'He'll put new life in you; make you feel young again. He's a blessing from heaven, Jenny, someone to care of you in your old age.'

To Bessie's distress, Jenny had prevaricated. 'But what about his own kinfolk? Surely he . . .' Jenny got no further.

'It's like I've already said; the poor girl fell for the child with a travelling man. An orphan she was, with not a soul to care for her. I did what I could but she died on me when this mite was but two months old.' The lies had tripped off Bessie's tongue.

Jenny had stroked the baby's swarthy cheek, her forefinger sliding into the folds of his neck, gently pushing aside a straggle of black, greasy curls. 'Oh, look, he's been kissed by an angel,' she'd gasped, tracing the purple, heart-shaped mark below the child's left ear. 'Motherless he might be but that's a sign of good luck if ever I saw one,' she'd said, the words coming out on her breath.

Bessie had inwardly rejoiced. 'So you'll keep him then?'

'Henry will have the final word.'

Bessie's heart sank. She was itching to be on the road home.

Jenny had then lifted the child from the basket, and bidding Bessie to take a seat, she sat also, dandling the child on her knee. 'Your Beatrice has a similar mark,' she said, innocently enough, 'and she come early as I remember, very early.' Bessie had bristled but Jenny had not taken notice. Her brow had wrinkled thoughtfully and she'd gazed hard at the child. 'He's a proper little prince. Do you know, he not only puts me in mind of your Beatrice, he has a look of . . . ' Her eyes had brightened and she'd given Bessie a sly wink before whispering, 'That lad at the fair, the one who . . . what was his name? The one who stole your virg — '

Bessie's blood had run cold. 'Can't say as I remember,' she'd said, through gritted teeth. 'And as for names, you can call this one whatever you choose, for he has no name as yet.' Jenny had smiled at that, the smile fading when Bessie had rounded on her, telling her in no uncertain terms that Beatrice was Hadley's, and that she took after his grandmother for her dark looks. Jenny hadn't looked convinced. She'd shrugged apologetically, saying, 'Must be my memory playing tricks again.'

But Bessie hadn't been appeased. 'I got a good

man when I married Hadley, one who's given *me* four fine children,' she'd said, the spiteful remark sharp as an arrow.

It had taken some artful persuasion on her part, but in the end she had convinced her childless friend to keep the child. 'It's best you say nothing to anyone about how you came by the child. You don't want to encourage gossip,' she'd advised, 'and I'll not expect you to keep in touch.' This last remark sounding rather like a threat, Bessie had left the Leas' little cottage, and thankful for its remoteness, she had rattled merrily along the roads back to Barnborough and Intake farm.

Now, as she drove into the centre of Barnborough and parked the trap in the inn yard, she wondered how much Jenny and Henry Leas had told their son about the true nature of his birth and how they had come by him.

Still, I have no proof the lad's the one I gave to Jenny, she thought, as she impatiently watched the grocer weigh out raisins and currants. *But what if he is?* said an insidious little voice inside her head. By now, she was sweating so profusely that the coins she had taken from her purse slipped from her fingers and scattered. Making no attempt to gather them up, Bessie grabbed her provisions and dashed out of the shop, leaving the grocer staring after her.

Out on the street, Bessie paused to ease the thudding in her chest. Panicking like this wasn't good for her, it could give her a heart attack, she told herself crossly, and to lessen the palpitations she took several deep breaths, trying to convince herself that her fears were unfounded. It was a

77

chance in a million that Amy's young man was Raffy Lovell's son. That sort of coincidence only happened in the penny dreadfuls she sometimes read. Feeling foolish at allowing her imagination to get the better of her — it wasn't one bit like her — Bessie stepped smartly along the pavement.

Then she saw them.

Amy and Jude were walking hand in hand towards her, laughing at something one or the other had said.

Bessie came to a standstill.

So did they, Jude swinging Amy into a loose embrace and pecking her cheek. They lingered for a moment and then resumed walking, not a care in the world or so it appeared.

Bessie drew breath so sharply it pierced her throat, all the optimism she had fostered in the past few minutes snuffed out like a candle in the wind. Her brow and palms turned clammy again, fear mixed with burning anger bubbling in her chest.

Now there was no escaping the fact. That same tall, rangy stature and the aquiline features were the mirror of Raffy Lovell's, even the way the lad had caught Amy up in his arms made him his father's son. Without a doubt he was the boy child she had handed over to her friend Jenny Leas, some twenty years before. Bessie thought to take flight, cross the street, avoid Amy and Jude's path, but her feet refused to budge and before she knew it, they were face to face with her.

'Mother!' Amy's cry was high with surprise. 'I didn't expect to see you in town.'

'Apparently not,' Bessie replied acerbically.

'Otherwise you wouldn't have been canoodling in the street for all the world to see.' Her steely tones caused Jude to raise his brows, his comical expression making Amy giggle and then give an exasperated sigh before saying, 'Oh, Mam, we were hardly doing that.'

Amy tugged at Jude's hand, drawing him forward. 'Allow me to introduce you,' she said, mockingly formal. 'Mrs Bessie Elliot, meet Mr Jude Leas.' Bessie heard the pride in her voice.

'Good afternoon, Mrs Elliot, pleased to make your acquaintance at last.' Jude proffered his hand. Bessie ignored it. Was there implication in the way he had said 'at last' or was it just her imagination, she wondered? Had Jenny told him about her? Had he remembered the name and made a connection? Jude met her gaze, a half-smile playing at the corners of his mouth.

'Mother!' Amy cried, annoyed by Bessie's rudeness. Then, attempting to dispel the unpleasantness she said, 'I've told Jude that you've invited him for tea on Sunday.'

'And I'm more than pleased to accept,' said Jude, giving Bessie a warm smile.

Unappeased, Bessie looked sour.

'Mother!' Amy's cry bit the air. 'Why are you being so unpleasant?'

Bessie had neither the desire nor the integrity to divulge the reason for her unseemly behaviour. 'I'm late. I have to get home,' she said, and looking pointedly at Amy she added, 'and you'd better come with me.'

'I'm going back to work. This is my dinner break.' Amy linked her arm through Jude's. 'Come on, I don't want to be late.'

Bessie swung on her heel and strutted down the street.

'Good day, Mrs Elliot,' Jude called cheerily at Bessie's rigid back. He gave Amy a rueful smile. 'That didn't go too well, did it?'

'Our Sammy's to blame for that,' Amy said, her cheeks flaming. 'He's turned her against you even before she met you.'

Jude pulled her close. 'Don't fret. I'll win her round. Nothing and nobody will come between us.' He dropped a kiss on Amy's drooping head. Amy leaned her head on his chest, felt the thud of his heart and told herself that she loved Jude Leas with every breath in her body. He let her go. 'Now, let's get you back to the library and me to bed so I can catch some sleep before I go on the night shift.'

★ ★ ★

Deep in thought, Bessie walked to where she had left the trap. In the yard behind the Red Lion public house, she saw a dishevelled young thug leaning against the wall. She didn't know him personally but she knew all about him, and the very sight of him set her thoughts and her pulses racing. Deliberately fiddling with her shopping as she set it in the trap, and giving herself time to think things through, she decided he might be the solution to her problem. Hopeful that he was sober, she walked over to him.

'Is your brother out of prison?' she asked. 'Because if he is, I've a bit of business to put his way. Yours too, if you want the job.'

After a few brief, whispered words, Bessie drove out of Barnborough assured that the thug and his brother knew exactly what to do, and to whom they should do it. Her purse was several shillings lighter but she felt rather pleased with herself. She had always made it her business to know everybody else's, and even though she would have denied it, she knew who did what in Barnborough. Now it was paying off.

Unfortunately, her euphoria was short lived. What if her plan failed? What if she was found out? Bessie drove on in a state of morbid confusion, oblivious to the road and the speed at which she travelled, panic rising with every covered mile. *It's well this pony knows its way home*, she thought, as the little horse clattered into the yard at Intake Farm.

★   ★   ★

Late that same day, Jude picked up his snap tin and headed for the door; he was going on the nightshift.

'Don't work too hard,' Lily quipped, 'you'll need all your strength for dealing with Amy's mother now that you've been invited to tea on Sunday.'

Jude paused, his hand on the latch. 'I'll give her some of me old charm. It works on you so why not her?'

'Because Bessie Elliot's a stuck-up piece of work. Ever since she married Hadley, she's given herself airs and graces — and why I don't know. She was three months gone when she got wed — he had to

81

marry her.'

Jude raised his eyebrows, surprised by this piece of information about his prospective mother-in-law, but having no time to linger and learn more he stepped outside. A chill wind had brought a touch of frost to the pavement, the slabs glistening in the light from the streetlamp outside the pub on the corner. Under it he spotted two lads. Although he had only lived in Barnborough a short while he knew them from the pub, and knew also of their reputations. Bob and Jed Benson were petty criminals: a couple of brawlers. Paying them no heed he took the short cut up a back lane to the colliery, his warm breath pluming into clouds of vapour in front of his face.

Jude hadn't walked far when he sensed someone behind him. He glanced over his shoulder, expecting to see a fellow miner also making his way to the pit. The figure that ran at him wielded a short, stout length of wood. It connected with Jude's shoulder. He leapt back, and then righting himself he charged forwards, fists raised. As he lashed out, his assailant swung the piece of wood again. It clouted Jude's cheekbone at the same time as he felt soft flesh under his knuckles and heard the satisfying crunch of bones. Bob dropped his weapon, his hands clutching at his broken nose as he slumped to his knees. Then Jed barrelled forward, Jude instinctively raising his right foot and kicking out, his heavy pit boot catching the lad between his legs. Howling, Jed staggered backwards, frantic hands groping his injured manhood as he turned and tottered into the darkness.

By now, Bob was back on his feet but there was no fight left in him. As he turned to follow his brother, he gasped, 'You're to keep away from Amy Elliot if you know what's good for you.' This so incensed Jude that he considered going after them but, common sense telling him there was little to be gained by prolonging the fight, and that he was already late for his shift, he hurried to the pit.

'Eeh! Somebody's not happy wi' you.' Bert pointed to Jude's swollen cheek and blackened eye. 'I hope you gave 'em as good as you got.'

'I think I did better than that,' growled Jude. He told Bert what had happened, and then said, 'If you ask me why, I'd say it smells like some of Samuel's dirty work.'

★　★　★

Bessie woke next morning with a headache. Beside her, in the huge double bed with its iron and brass ends, Hadley's rumbling snores reverberated in the darkened room. Outside, a moaning wind shivered against the windowpanes. Its sound made Bessie tremble. She had slept intermittently, the face of the young man she had met in town the previous day haunting every waking moment. Jude Leas — Raffy's son.

Now, sweat moistening her brow and armpits, she watched the first lights of dawn peek through the gap in the curtains as she mulled over what she had done. Whatever had she been thinking of? She must have been crazy to pay those thugs to give him a beating. That was all she had wanted them to do, to frighten him off, but supposing they had killed him?

Her head thumped mercilessly at the dreadful thought, tears seeping from her eye corners and trickling into her ears. She'd been a fool, and it was all Raffy Lovell's fault. He'd brought her to this, him and his wily ways. She wished she'd never met him. But then, she sadly told herself, she would never have known what it was to really be in love — and it had been wonderful whilst it lasted. She could never love Hadley like she loved Raffy.

Almost as though he knew he was in her thoughts Hadley heaved his bulk towards her and broke wind. Bessie rolled to the edge of the bed, the foul smell wafting from beneath the loosened bedclothes breaking her last reserve. She leapt out of bed and went downstairs.

In the cold light of morning, pottering about the kitchen, Bessie looked back on her madness as though she had been some other woman when she had planned the attack. And what for, she asked herself? If Jude knew anything about his birth, he'd have told Amy, and surely she would have mentioned it. Consoled by this thought, Bessie sliced rashers of bacon and put them in a pan.

Bessie's head still ached, and as the bacon began to sizzle so did her brain. But what if, when Jenny had told Jude she wasn't his natural mother she had then told him the detail of how her old friend, Bessie Elliot from Barnborough, had brought him to Bird's Well? Furthermore — Bessie shuddered at the thought — had Jenny gossiped about Raffy Lovell and Beatrice's birth? Bessie's heart missed a beat. God forbid Jude told Hadley.

The smell of burning fat brought her back to the present, and flinging the burned rashers into the slop bucket she replenished the pan whilst firmly telling herself to gain control of her emotions before she gave the game away. After all, tomorrow afternoon Jude Leas would be here in her kitchen. What then?

★ ★ ★

'Oh, my dear God, what happened to you?' cried Lily Tinker, as Jude entered his lodgings the next morning. 'Did you get in t'way of a flying lump o' coal?'

'Aye, summat like that,' replied Jude, shedding his jacket and then dumping it outside the open kitchen door for Lily to beat against the wall. Knocking the dust out of a collier's pit clothes was usually a wife's job but, Jude being single, Lily insisted on performing the task in the same way she did for her own son, Tommy.

When Lily went outside, Jude stripped and stepped into the tin bath in front of the fire. He'd let Lily believe the lie. Accidents happened down the pit all the time, and he didn't want her gossiping to her neighbours about his altercation with the thugs. Lily came back inside, and fishing his trousers from the floor, she went out again to beat them also. As Jude washed away layers of coal dust and towelled himself dry, he decided to tell the same lie to Amy; he didn't want her worrying over what Samuel might do next.

'Are you decent?' Lily popped her head round

the door and found Jude sitting at the table dressed in the clean underwear and shirt she had left out for him. Two minutes later, she set a plate of meat and potato pie, cabbage and gravy in front of him. 'Tuck into that, and when you've finished, I'll put some salve on them,' she said, pointing to Jude's grazed cheek and his blackened eye. 'You've got a right shiner, lad. You need to be more careful.'

'I will be, next time,' Jude grunted, wondering if and when the next time might be.

★　★　★

On Saturday afternoon, Jude waited for Amy outside the library. She was shocked when she saw his battered face and, like Lily, believed he had sustained the injuries at work. Jude didn't disabuse her. 'You poor darling,' she said, tenderly stroking his bruised eye and then lightly kissing his grazed jaw.

They walked to Jude's lodgings, Jude keeping a sharp eye out for the Benson brothers should they strike again. He didn't think they would, but it did no harm to be vigilant. Seated by the fire in Lily's cosy parlour, he asked Amy if Samuel was friendly with them, dropping it casually into a made-up story about something that had happened in the pub.

'Good Lord, no! Our Sammy wouldn't go within a mile of them.' She giggled before adding, 'that's because when they were at school together, they bullied him. Besides, our Sammy thinks he's far too good to bother with the likes of the Bensons.'

Deeply puzzled, Jude dropped the subject but,

for the rest of the evening, his thoughts kept toying with the fact that the Bensons had been hired to attack him — and that the reason was this lovely girl nestled in his arms. If it wasn't Samuel Elliot, then who the hell was it?

8

Beckett's Park Hospital

September, 1918

Throughout the month of September, Amy made her twice-weekly visits to Jude. By now, she no longer found the train journeys daunting but whenever she entered the hospital she felt as though her heart was in her mouth. Never knowing quite what to expect she had, for two interminable hours every Wednesday and Sunday, sat beside him praying for him to acknowledge her presence, say her name, or give her a smile. More often than not he sat quietly gazing out of the window, his eyes like two pits of empty blackness and his mouth twisted in a sardonic sneer.

Not one to give in without a fight, Amy talked and talked, her voice gentle as she told him about Kezia's progress and what she herself had done since she last saw him. Jude sat with his hands clamped to the arms of his chair, and as she talked Amy stroked the back of the nearest one. He gave no indication that he felt her fingers caressing his skin. One day, when his hands were rested in his lap she had reached out and held them. Then, he had looked directly at her. His mouth had twitched and she thought he was about to speak, but just as her spirits soared, he had tugged his hands free. She'd held his hands again on the next visit and he hadn't resisted, but since then she had had to be content with stroking. Nurse Brennan had told her it was a good sign; he was improving. But then, from somewhere deep inside, the growls and yells and blaspheming would pour in torrents, outbursts of such extreme anger that had Amy fearing for her own sanity, let alone Jude's. On those days, she had gone home feeling as though there was no hope.

Now, on the last Sunday in September, she sat with her chair angled towards him, almost forcing him to look at her as she talked. The afternoon was drawing to a close, almost time for her to leave to catch her train. She had been talking and stroking the back of his hand for almost two hours without any response from Jude. Her mouth was dry and her fingers ached but she still battled on. 'Kezia says to tell you that she's been helping Granny Bessie feed the chickens and milk the goats. She loves spending time on the farm whilst I'm here with you,' she said, keeping up a steady patter of the one-way conversation. 'Oh, and by the way, Mrs Hargreaves gave me some more books to add to your collection. Our bedroom's coming down with books, books, and more books, everywhere you look.'

Jude blinked. He leaned forward, his face close enough for her to smell his breath; it was sour. He blinked again, and it was as if someone had drawn back the curtain from a window in a darkened room. His eyes gleamed as they searched her face. Amy let the silence swell and grow. Then, tentatively loosening his grip on the chair's arm, she lifted the hand that she had been stroking and wrapped both her own round it. It felt like a dead fish between her warm palms. She gave it a gentle squeeze. Jude continued to stare at her, his eyes troubled, as though they were fixed on a puzzle he could not solve.

Amy smiled warmly, loving him with a pain that almost cleaved her heart in two. His eyes widened, and then she felt it: a faint responding pressure, steadily increasing as the squeeze was returned. Amy's heart lurched. She held her breath.

She lost track of time as they sat, eyes for no one but each other and her fingers starting to numb as he held on, but she didn't care — he was telling her something, she was sure of it. Tears seeped from the corners of her eyes, but Jude did not see them. He had closed his eyes, and the bitter sneer that had been on his lips each and every visit had been replaced by something resembling a smile.

They had turned a corner.

9

Intake Farm

Autumn, 1912

On the Sunday morning of the day that Jude was coming to tea, Amy overslept. When she finally wakened, a rush of nervous anticipation overwhelmed her. In a few hours from now, Jude would arrive to meet her family, albeit he had already met two of its members in less than pleasant circumstances. Pushing that unfortunate factor aside, Amy determined to make sure nothing marred the occasion. After all, she told herself as she stepped out of bed, it was her father that Jude was coming to meet, and Hadley held none of Bessie and Samuel's petty preconceptions. Her dad judged a man at face value. Surely he would see Jude's true worth.

Bolstered by this premise Amy ran downstairs, only to meet a barrage of abuse from Samuel. 'If you think that bloody collier's welcome to come for his tea, you're mistaken,' he said, his tone of voice and face ugly.

'He is coming, and it's nothing to do with you, Samuel,' Amy snapped back.

Samuel's eyes narrowed. 'He's scum, only out for what he can get. He's been wi' umpteen lasses in Barnborough whose fathers have a bit o' brass,' he taunted, smirking as he judged the effect of this accusation.

Undaunted, Amy fought back.

'You can spin your filthy lies till the cows come home but you won't convince me. I know all there is to know about Jude, Sammy; I know the truth.'

Truth! Bessie cringed. What did Amy know? She clutched the sharp stab of pain under her left breast. These unanswered questions were killing her. She glanced uneasily at Hadley. He surveyed the unpleasant scene with utter repugnance.

'An' I know he's a playboy out for an easy catch and you, you daft bitch, can't see it,' bawled Samuel.

'That's enough!' Hadley thrust back his chair and marched across the kitchen to face Samuel. Samuel blinked his surprise as Hadley, his jowls quivering with rage, prodded him sharply in his chest. 'You're getting above yourself, lad, and you,' Hadley swung round to address Bessie, 'stop egging him on. I'm sick of it, and so is our Amy. Now — ' He got no further.

'She doesn't know what she's getting into,' Bessie screeched, fear staining her cheeks a dull red and darkening her eyes. 'Our Sammy says — '

'Our Sammy says!' Hadley's roar bounced off the walls and ceiling. 'I'm master in this house and I say the lad's welcome.' He gave Bessie and Samuel a warning glare, and his tone softening, he addressed Amy. 'Bring him to meet us, lass.'

Shocked by Hadley's intervention and feeling thoroughly peeved, Bessie wittered, 'We're only doing it for her own good.'

'No you're not,' said Hadley, his expression

cynical and his voice menacing. 'The pair of you were doing it for your own ends, whatever they might be.'

Bessie shuddered.

★ ★ ★

At a quarter to three Amy was waiting for Jude at the end of the lane, her heart skipping a beat as he strode towards her. *How smart and handsome he looks in his good black suit and white shirt,* she thought. *He even manages to wear his black eye like a badge, a mark of his bravery.* She ran to meet him, his confident bearing quelling the anxiety that Samuel had caused.

Although Jude appeared perfectly at ease, he was a sack of nerves. He had barely slept knowing that the impression he was about to make would decide his future one way or another. Up until now he had been reasonably content to let life take its course but meeting Amy Elliot had changed the way he saw himself and the world. He wanted nothing more than to spend his life with her; share her hopes and dreams as they explored the years ahead. Bessie and Samuel's animosity didn't particularly trouble him. It was Hadley he had to impress. He'd pondered on how he should respond were he to quiz him about his rearing; he might be averse to his daughter marrying a bastard foundling. Yet, he had had the finest upbringing and he would make sure Hadley knew it. With this in mind he ran the last few steps into Amy's open arms.

In the kitchen at Intake Farm, the table was set

for afternoon tea. At Hadley's insistence Bessie had reluctantly prepared a spread of boiled ham and roast beef sandwiches, cake and biscuits. 'Let's show the lad we know how to entertain,' he had joshed, 'let him know that our Amy's used to nothing but the best.'

Bessie had curled her lip.

Now, seated in his place at the head of the table and dressed in his Sunday best, Hadley looked from one son to the other, Samuel lounging in a chair by the hearth and Thomas at the table. 'Think on now. Behave like gentlemen,' he said, the faintest warning colouring his tone.

Samuel jerked upright. 'We're not stopping. I'll not sit at the same table as that fellow,' he said haughtily. 'Come on, Thomas, we're leaving.'

'But ... but ... ' Thomas gazed longingly at the cake and biscuits.

'Up! Now!' Samuel bawled.

Thomas jumped to attention.

When Jude and Amy entered the kitchen, Amy was relieved to find neither of her brothers present. Hadley welcomed them warmly but Bessie fussed over the teapot, avoiding Jude's courteous greetings.

'My, my,' said Hadley, noting Jude's black eye, 'you look as though you've been in the wars, lad.' Yet again, Jude trotted out the same lie. 'Accidents happen all the time down the pit.' Bessie stole a glance at his bruised face and murmured something about taking more care.

Amy ushered Jude to a chair at the table and sat beside him. Bessie brought the teapot and sat down. Hadley began talking about the dangers

94

of working in the pit, chuckling before saying, 'I thought our Amy had brought home a brawler — you know — one of them chaps that likes to fight after a few pints in the pub.'

'Oh, Dad! You couldn't be more wrong,' said Amy.

'She's right, Mr Elliot. I'm no fighter.' Jude paused. 'But I can handle myself when needs be.' He grinned at Hadley and then looked across at Bessie, surprised to find her gazing at him watchfully. Did she doubt his story, he wondered? Had he been able to read Bessie's mind, he would have learned that she was regretting having wasted her money; if a black eye and a grazed cheek were all that the Bensons had managed to give him then he was a fighter, and they weren't worth paying. And why was he telling the tale about getting hurt down the pit?

They began to eat. Shedding their nervousness, Amy and Jude soon settled into easy conversation with Hadley, the subjects flitting from one to another: Jude's occupation and his plans for the future, the politics of the day (Amy quite animated when the talk turned to the suffragettes and Mrs Pankhurst's recent imprisonment), and Hadley equally animated as he told Jude the history of the Elliot family and Intake Farm.

Bessie spoke little, her sullen demeanour not escaping Jude's notice. Rather than distress him, it made him all the more determined to win her over. He started by praising the splendid tea, adding that he hoped Amy was as wonderful a hostess as her mother. Bessie blushed at his flattery and Jude, quick to spot this, told her it wasn't difficult to see where Amy had inherited her beauty. Bessie found herself warming to his charms, her vanity almost her undoing. Then she remembered; he was Raffy Lovell's son.

★ ★ ★

On Monday evening Amy called with Beattie. Bert's whippet, Towser, lay in the doorway. Amy stepped over him and then picked her way round Albert and Fred sprawled on the linoleum. Emptying a chair piled high with cast-off garments she sat opposite Beattie, feeling as though she had successfully completed an obstacle course.

'Jude came to tea yesterday,' Amy said, leaning forward so that her sister could hear over the children and Bert's chatter.

'And . . . ' Beattie's dark eyes flashed with curiosity.

Amy grinned. 'It wasn't half as bad as I thought it might be. In fact, Jude was so charming I think he won Mother over.'

'My, he must be a charmer if he managed that,' Beattie hooted. 'I can't wait to meet him.' Then, she too leaned forward, almost conspiratorially, and said, 'But watch out for her. Mother can rip the heart out of things quicker than you can bat your eyelids.' She didn't add, 'and I should know,' but Amy knew Beattie thought just that.

★ ★ ★

The mellow autumn weather of late September and early October lent a vivid background of scents

96

and colour to every meeting Amy and Jude now shared. Snatched meetings no longer necessary, they freely walked the streets of Barnborough or, time allowing, wandered further afield to Wentworth Park or Stainborough Castle delighting in the mystery of these historic places and each other's company. As the last leaves withered on the trees and the nights chilled, they stayed in the comfort of Lily Tinker's happy little home, or at Intake Farm.

Hadley welcomed evenings spent with his lively, sweet-natured daughter and the knowledgeable young man he had grown to respect and was much better company than his bickering wife and sullen sons. They always found plenty to talk about, Amy loving the way Jude leaned forward with his forearms resting on his knees as he listened earnestly to Hadley reminiscing about days gone by, and Hadley impressed by Jude's knowledge of country matters, or laughing heartily at Amy's amusing accounts regarding the peculiarities of some of the library's clientele.

Bessie hovered on the edge of these gatherings, ever watchful should Jude reveal what he knew about his upbringing but, as winter approached, her fear of being incriminated lessened. He talked fondly of Jenny and Henry Leas, giving no indication they were anything other than his natural parents. There were, however, one or two sticky moments that made Bessie's blood run cold.

One evening, Jude remarked on the insularity of his home in Bird's Well. 'It was my father's home place, not my mother's. She came from Barnborough. She was Jenny Parkinson to her own name.' He glanced at Bessie. 'You might have known her,' he said.

Bessie denied it with an impatient shake of her head. Hadley frowned, and gave her an enquiring look. 'Wasn't that the name of your friend? The one you ran about with afore you married me.'

'She was *Patterson*, Jenny *Patterson*.' The lie flew from Bessie's tongue far more fervently than she intended.

Amy blinked at the vehemence of Bessie response. 'There's no need to get cross,' she said, thinking not for the first time how oddly her mother behaved in Jude's company, her watchful nervousness quite at odds with her usual bossiness.

Another occasion was when Hadley asked Jude how he came by his name. 'It's not common in these parts,' he said. 'Is it a Leas family name?'

Jude chuckled. 'I didn't have a name when my mother got me and seeing as how she believed St Jude was the saint of lost causes, and that her cause was lost until I arrived, she named me after him.' He smiled at the explanation.

Samuel, who had come into the kitchen a short while before, sniggered. 'That's a funny way of putting it. Nobody has a name when they're born. You sound as though she found you under a gooseberry bush.' He smirked at his own wit.

Bessie clasped the handle of her teacup so tightly it snapped off with a sharp click. Tea spilled into her lap, the colour seeping from her plump cheeks as she waited for Jude to confirm that he'd been delivered in a basket. By a woman called Bessie Elliot.

98

Jude, realising he had said too much, and still of the opinion that being a bastard foundling was his business and no one else's, rushed to her rescue. 'Here, mop it up with this.' He handed her a teacloth and then asked, 'It didn't scald you, did it?' He smiled sympathetically into Bessie's stricken face. She essayed a smile, touched by his concern. What a pity it was that he couldn't have been someone else's son. He was kind and gentle, intelligent and hardworking, and no doubt he'd make Amy a good husband, thought Bessie. *But although Jenny Leas is dead and Raffy Lovell long gone, I can't be sure my secret's safe as long as he's around.*

Towards the end of the evening, Samuel announced he was going to check on the animals. 'I'll give you a hand,' said Jude, and when they were out in the yard he bluntly asked, 'Was it you set the Bensons on me the other night?'

Samuel looked blank, and then spluttered, 'What are you on about?' Jude told him, and after a brief interrogation, Samuel robustly denying having any involvement, Jude was left believing him. Amy had been right, but if Samuel wasn't the Bensons' accomplice then who was?

Back in the kitchen, helping Amy into her coat, Jude was aware that Bessie was observing him in that strange manner he had seen many times before. He frequently sensed she was waiting to catch him out — but in what, he didn't know.

★ ★ ★

Amy wanted to share her happiness. She also wanted to make Beattie happy. So, on some Saturday nights she and Jude went to the house in Grattan Row and babysat whilst Bert and Beattie went to the Miners' Welfare Club. At other times they all stayed in, Bert fetching bottles of beer from the pub for himself and Jude and bottles of milk stout for Amy and Beattie.

'Be quick an' shut that bloody door. It's bringing t'smoke down t'chimney,' Bert Stitt yelled, one blustery November evening as Amy stepped inside, Jude at her heels. A gust of black pother clouded the fireplace, Beattie flapping at it with a newspaper and calling out, 'Come in, come in.' She was wearing a neat brown dress and her hair was smoothly coiled; she looked almost pretty. Amy could tell she had cleaned the house in honour of their visit. It pleased her.

'Auntie Amy! Uncle Jude!' chorused the young Stitts, happy to greet the aunt who brought treats and the uncle who showed them magic tricks. Jude had bought a game of Ludo and whilst he showed Maggie, Albert and Fred how to play it, Amy helped Beattie put Henry and Mary to bed.

'Your Jude's gorgeous. I bet he's smashing in bed,' Beattie gushed, as she stripped Mary down to her knickers. 'If I wasn't wed to Bert, I'd make a play for him meself.'

'You'll do no such thing,' Amy expostulated, at the same time wondering when it was that her sister had acquired a lust for men other than her husband. Beattie was a strange creature, and Amy never really understood what was going on inside her head.

Later, all the children in bed, the two sisters and their husbands sat gossiping and playing cards, Beattie flirting with Jude and Amy thinking how different her sister's temperament might have been had the younger Beattie been exposed to the fun and friendship she now enjoyed. Amy had never understood Bessie's apparent dislike for her firstborn child. It was at complete odds to the affection she showed for Amy herself and her brothers, and somehow Amy felt responsible for this. Therefore, making Beattie happy had its rewards — as long as she kept her hands off Jude.

When the card game ended, Beattie and Amy went into the kitchen to make suppertime tea and sandwiches. 'And how are the good folk up at Intake Farm?' Beattie asked archly.

'Dad's being lovely as usual. He's really taken to Jude, but he's mad as hell at Sammy for not fixing the barn roof. Mam's never done refereeing the rows between them.'

'How's she taking to him?' Beattie flicked her thumb in the direction of the parlour and Jude.

Amy responded with a puzzled frown. 'Strangely,' she said slowly. 'She's not openly unpleasant like she was when they first met, but neither does she waste any of that old Bessie Elliot charm on him. In fact, she seems almost afraid of him — you know, dithery and distracted, as though she's expecting something awful to happen.'

'What! Bessie Elliot, queen of the kitchen, mistress of all she surveys, nervous of your Jude. I don't believe it.' Beattie looked smugly pleased.

'It is hard to fathom,' said Amy, grinning at

101

Beattie's show of delighted revenge before sarcastically adding, 'Maybe she fancies him for herself, like you do.'

They both burst into laughter.

At times like this, Amy and Beattie felt more like sisters than they ever had before.

And whilst Bessie's initial coldness towards Jude had been replaced by jittery acceptance, Amy was still wary of her mother's moods. As Beattie said, she could turn in the wink of an eye.

★   ★   ★

When Amy announced that she and Jude would marry early in the New Year, Bessie bitterly objected. 'You haven't known one another long enough,' she argued on one occasion. 'It's an unseasonal time for a wedding, wait till spring,' was another of her excuses. One day she said, 'Why don't you get married after Jude's completed his college course?' Secretly she hoped the romance would run its course, for although her fear of Jude revealing her secrets had lessened, she still didn't want Raffy Lovell's son for a son-in-law.

10

Raffy Lovell hobbled down the deserted street, the pack on his back weighing heavier with every step. His feet were paining him badly, the sole of his boot flapping on the pavement where it had parted from the upper. Head down, he plodded on, his steps faltering as a sudden sharp wind threatened to unbalance him. It was close on midnight, shops and houses in darkness, the town's inhabitants safe in their warm beds, and Raffy was looking for a place to sleep on this cold November night. He had been travelling the roads for three days to come this far, hitching rides from the borders of Wales to Barnborough, and walking for much of the way.

In the shelter of a deep-set shop doorway he offloaded his pack, and pulling the edges of his cape together, he lowered his long, lean body to the ground. Raffy Lovell was weary of wandering. He had come to stay.

It was too late to seek lodgings so he rested his back against the shop door and pulled his broad-brimmed hat low over his face. He itched to remove his boots and rub his feet with the salve a gypsy woman in Mumbles had given him but, afraid of being disturbed by a constable on night patrol, he made do with packing a piece of rag inside the loose sole. As he prodded it into place he pondered on the past and what the future might hold. He didn't regret his wandering days.

He'd seen marvellous sights, met interesting men and bedded many beautiful women. But now he was weary. He wondered what sort of a man his son had grown to be. Had Bessie taken good care of him? He felt not a jot of guilt at having left the baby boy with her. He was certain she would have given him a better rearing than he himself could have provided. Maybe she'd made a farmer of the lad, glad to have an extra strong pair of hands about the place. Bessie had always put the farm above all else.

And what about the girl child? She'd be a woman now. Had Bessie come clean? Had she whispered in the girl's ear that the gypsy man she'd briefly met one day when she was no more than ten years old was her father? He doubted it. Hadley Elliot wouldn't take kindly to that. And Bessie had too much to lose by telling the truth.

Raffy shuffled into a more comfortable position and closed his eyes, picturing a buxom Bessie with her head of blonde curls and sharp blue eyes. She often came to him in dreams. She was his woman, no matter they had travelled such different paths. And the lad and the girl were his also, a son and a daughter who were strangers to him. But not for much longer, he thought, as sleep claimed him.

★ ★ ★

Hadley woke at first light, the wind rattling the windowpanes and a rhythmic clanging of metal against metal disturbing his sleep. He listened for a while, his temper rising by the minute. Damn

Samuel! If he'd fixed the barn roof it wouldn't be flapping and banging fit to wake the dead.

Over breakfast Hadley glowered at his two sons. 'That barn roof needs fixing — *today*,' he growled. 'Leave it any longer and the whole lot will come tumbling down.'

Samuel shoved a loaded forkful of bread dripping with egg yolk into his mouth as though he hadn't heard. Thomas glanced nervously at his father and then at his brother. He helped himself to another slice of bread.

Hadley's cutlery clattered to his plate. 'Did you hear what I said?' he barked.

Samuel swallowed noisily then belched. 'We'll do it after we've been to see that new tractor I'm thinking of buying,' he said lazily.

'Tractor? And where's the money for that coming from?' Hadley asked scathingly.

Samuel's eyes slid to meet Bessie's. She smiled indulgently. 'Our Sammy says . . . '

Harumphing noisily, Hadley got up and walked to the outer door, and pulling on his topcoat he said, 'I'll bring the cows down for milking. Be up on that roof by the time I get back.' He opened the door, a savage gust lifting the edges of the tablecloth and ruffling Bessie's curls. Samuel shrugged and carried on eating. Staring vacantly, Thomas chewed on a crust.

Amy glanced disparagingly from one brother to the other. 'You boys don't pull your weight on the farm. You can't expect Dad to do all the work,' she said, buttoning her thick, navy blue winter coat then wrapping a woollen scarf round her neck, ready to go to work.

Thomas shuffled to his feet. 'I'll get the trap,' he said.

'Don't bother; I'll walk,' Amy retorted, 'you just make a start on that roof.'

★ ★ ★

Raffy Lovell had risen at first light, leaving the shop doorway long before the proprietor arrived to open up the shop, and before a passing constable could apprehend him. He lingered in the streets until the Red Lion hostelry opened its rear gates, and sneaking into the yard, he visited the closet then washed at the pump, running damp hands over his dusty trousers and waistcoat. Spotting some twine dangling from the end of a clothesline, he sliced it off with his knife then bound it tightly round his broken boot. It wouldn't do to arrive at Intake Farm looking less than presentable.

Back on the street, the wind tugging at his cloak and threatening to whisk his hat from his head, he looked for a place to shelter. Spotting the high curved wall to one side of the steps outside the public library, he went and sat in its lee. He'd bide his time till a more respectable hour. He dozed, waking with a start some time later.

Out of the corner of his eye he saw a pretty, young woman wearing a navy-blue coat hurrying towards him, the tails of her scarf flapping and long tendrils of blonde hair escaping her neat little cloche where the wind had caught them. Raffy jerked his head in surprise and stared. For one fleeting moment he had thought it was Bessie but, common sense to the rescue, he acknowledged the passing of time. Smiling ruefully, he rubbed his grizzled jaw.

The girl drew level with him, and giving a dazzling smile and a friendly 'good morning' she bounced up the steps and into the library. Raffy watched the trim figure retreat, his thoughts on Bessie and days gone by.

★ ★ ★

In the library's storeroom Amy slipped off her coat, and as she smoothed the collar of her white, pin-tucked blouse and the pleats of her grey skirt she thought about the man on the steps. He wasn't a customer, of that she was sure. She would have remembered a gypsy with a golden earring. Yet, there was something about his dark, brooding eyes and the way he smiled that seemed achingly familiar. Shaking her head, she put him out of her mind.

★ ★ ★

By the time the cows had been milked and the churns left at the end of the lane for collection, neither Samuel nor Thomas had returned from Sisson's Farm Supplies. Hadley lumbered about the yard, his head tilted and his eyes scanning the barn roof. Gusting wind lifted the loosened corrugated sheets. When it released them, they crashed down on the creaking roof trusses. The walls swayed and Hadley, looking as though his heart was about to break, stamped into the barn. Reappearing, he propped the ladder against the side of the barn, its top rested beneath two flapping corrugated sheets. Back inside, he stuffed a handful of nails into his smock pocket and then lifted a hammer from the bench.

Harry Sykes, the farm labourer, came in behind him. 'I've finished in t'dairy, Mester Hadley,' he said, and giving Hadley a quizzical look asked, 'What's to do wi' t'ladder outside?'

'I'm fixing this blasted roof before it comes down on top of us,' Hadley growled, blundering past Harry and out to the foot of the ladder.

'Nay, tha nivver is,' bleated Harry, hurrying after him. 'Leave it to t'lads, Mester.'

'I already did, and look where it got me.'

'It's too windy, mester. Them sheets are liftin' rightly.'

Hadley gave him a withering glare and mounted the ladder.

'It'll not hold your weight, Mester Hadley,' yelled Harry, looking doubtfully at Hadley's bulk on the insubstantial ladder.

Hadley began to climb. Harry glanced sharply round the yard, willing Samuel or Thomas to appear. When he raised his gaze, Hadley's head was almost level with the razor-sharp edge of the roof.

A rushing noise like a thousand angry birds gusted between the house and the barn, and as Harry heard it coming, he shouted at the top of his lungs. The corrugated sheets lifted, flapping crazily before crashing down with a sickening thud.

Like a slaughtered bullock Hadley toppled into the yard.

★ ★ ★

108

Outside the library, Raffy mulled over what he was about to do. Seeing the girl and thinking she was Bessie had left him feeling somewhat unsteady. Maybe it would be wiser to put the past behind him and forget about the seed he had scattered; he had left it too late. Bessie didn't need him, and his son and daughter didn't know him. Yet, he thought, he would like to know them, and they had a right to know he was their father. Reaching the decision to at least seek them out, Raffy left his perch and shuffled down the street. He'd go and see Bessie; she could tell him where to find them. Nearing his destination, Raffy left the road, making his way over the fields to Intake Farm. This way he could spy on the yard, hopeful of catching Bessie alone.

He heard the commotion before he saw the cause of it. A woman's shrill screams and a man's angry shouts pierced the air, Raffy quickening his pace up the slope to the wall surrounding the yard. He peered over, his sharp eyes quickly taking in the scene. This was no time to come calling. He turned back the way he had come.

★　★　★

Bessie was distraught, but as she grieved she couldn't help feeling relieved. Hadley would go to his grave never knowing the truth about Beatrice's birth, or the part Bessie had played in Jude's fostering. Now, there was no chance of her husband disowning her. Her position at Intake Farm was assured. Furthermore, she could use Hadley's death as an excuse to delay Amy's wedding plans and buy time to devise her own plan for getting rid of Jude Leas.

After the funeral, attended by a hundred or more members of the local community, the family and a few close friends returned to Intake Farm to mourn the loss of a highly respected gentleman, husband and father. Later, when only the immediate family remained, Bessie firmly addressed Amy and Jude.

'You'll not be able to marry for at least a year,' she said. 'It would be disrespectful to your father's memory.' In her stiff, black widow's weeds she looked every inch the domineering matriarch.

Amy gasped. Jude frowned and opened his mouth to object. Before he could speak, Samuel intervened. 'She's right,' he said, looking pointedly at Amy. 'There'll be no wedding from this house until we've mourned him for a year.'

'You hypocrite!' Amy hissed, rising from her seat to give vent to her feelings. 'You've disrespected him for years. Now you're pretending to grieve him. It was your idleness that killed him. If you'd mended the barn roof when he asked, he'd still be alive.' Tears coursed her cheeks, her voice cracking as she spoke. Jude placed a comforting arm around her shoulders, but she shook him off.

Two short strides took her to where Samuel lounged in Hadley's chair by the hearth. She leaned in, her face close to his, and his head shrinking into his neck as he felt her hot breath on his cheeks. Contempt etched her features. 'You might be master of Intake, Sammy, but you're not my master. I'll marry when I please,' she said, her words as sharp as broken glass.

110

She swivelled on her heel, and giving Jude a warning glare when she saw he was about to intervene, she caught hold of his arm as she swept to the door.

'Take me away from here,' she said.

★ ★ ★

Amy married Jude on a chill day in February 1913. She wore a white linen dress trimmed with Broderie Anglaise and a white fur cape to fend off the cold. She rode to the church in a hired car, tears threatening as she thought how proud Hadley would have been to be with her on this special day. But, with no father to give her away and Amy unwilling to let her brothers or Bessie take his place, she travelled alone.

At the church, Amy handed the cape to Beattie who was waiting in the doorway with an excited Maggie and Mary. Pretty in spotted blue organdie, Amy's bridesmaids were inspecting their frilly knickers, dazzled by their beautiful attire and the important role they were about to play. Bringing them into line with sharp clouts, Beattie left them to take her seat inside, leaving Amy to calm the girls and compose herself.

From the arched doorway, Amy saw the empty pews to the right of the aisle. Lily and Tommy Tinker and three of Jude's workmates and their wives filled just one. To her left she saw the sea of slicked male heads and ladies' hats that were her family and friends, this imbalance in the congregation causing her to feel sad for Jude.

The organ pealed out the bridal march. 'Right,

you two, let's go,' Amy said, her voice wobbling as she addressed her nieces. How she wished she had her father's arm to lean on. At the altar rail, wearing his good black suit and a new white shirt, Jude waited with Bert, his best man. Hearing the music Jude half-turned, his eyes alight with love and admiration as he watched Amy's approach.

Bessie sat alone in the front pew, stiff in her lavender suit and cartwheel hat, her displeasure hanging like a dank fog above her head. Beattie and her sons sat behind, the boys wearing new white shirts (bought by Amy) and Beattie resplendent in pink crepe (Amy's choosing), the soft, rosy colour enhancing her swarthy complexion. Beattie stared at Bessie's lavender back, a rebellious delight running through her veins at having eschewed the drab browns Bessie had made her wear. Across the aisle Lily Tinker's orange hat blazed like a beacon, Lily and Tommy beaming their delight as Amy and Jude exchanged vows.

When the vicar asked, 'Who gives this woman in marriage?' Amy said, 'I do.'

A flurry of gasps, frowns and curious glances followed her bell-like response but the vicar, primed by Amy for this irregularity, smiled beatifically and carried on.

To save face, Bessie had prepared a splendid tea at the farm, her social standing in the community demanding it and Amy and Jude grateful for the effort she had made. It lent another dimension to the wonderful occasion. Now, happily accepting gifts and felicitations, they stood arm in arm in the parlour congratulating each other on this being the perfect day.

The afternoon was progressing nicely, neighbouring farmers and their wives chatting pleasantly with Phoebe Littlewood from the library, Bessie's sister and her husband with the colliers, and Lily Tinker flirting with a bachelor friend of Hadley's. Tommy Tinker came and stood with Amy and Jude, and was just about to replenish his glass from the barrel of beer Jude had ordered for the occasion when Raffy Lovell appeared in the open doorway. Clean and tidy in a dark suit of indiscriminate age and a bright red scarf at his throat, he leaned against the doorjamb and surveyed the pleasant scene. He might have gone unnoticed had it not been for the gasp escaping Bessie's lips and the way she surged forward to meet him.

'I just called by to congratulate the happy couple.' Raffy smiled into Bessie's beetroot-red face. Her blue eyes flashed dangerously, the twist of her mouth letting him know he wasn't welcome. Unfazed, Raffy looked past her into the assembled crowd. 'So where be the happy couple then?'

Raffy's eyes lighted on Amy. He knew she was the bride, his devious enquiries in the town having furnished him with knowledge that the pretty girl he had seen outside the library was Bessie Elliot's daughter and that today was her wedding day. He had been told that the groom was a young lad from Bird's Well, by the name of Jude Leas.

Bert Stitt grabbed Jude with one hand and Amy with the other, ushering them forward and crying, 'Here they are. Come in and drink their health.'

Raffy needed no second bidding. Sidestepping Bessie, who was standing rigidly in front of him and looking as though she had sucked on a dozen lemons, he stepped jauntily into the kitchen and up to Jude and Amy. Then he faltered, visibly, his outstretched hand falling loosely to his side. He stared long and hard, utterly overwhelmed by the memory of his twenty-year-old self.

Amy and Jude stared back, she because she recognised him as the man on the library steps, and Jude because an icy hand clutched at his insides; it was like looking into the future and seeing what he would look like in thirty years' time. Recovering his composure, Raffy thrust out his hand, Jude and Amy automatically extending their own as Raffy enthusiastically proffered his good wishes. They thanked him, and as he moved away, Amy whispered, 'I saw him outside the library a while back. Who is he?'

'I've no idea,' Jude said, the strange feeling that he should know him persisting.

Bert pushed a drink into Raffy's hand, Raffy gulping it to settle his nerves. He had fully expected the bride to resemble the young Bessie he so fondly remembered, but he hadn't given a thought to the groom. Now, covertly watching Jude as he mingled with the guests, Raffy was almost certain that Amy Elliot had married his son. He made his way across the room to Bessie.

Bessie watched Raffy approach, her heart thudding painfully. She had excused his presence with a lie, telling Bert and anyone else who asked that he had worked for Hadley many years ago. Now, as he stood close enough for her to feel the heat from his body and breathe-in that musky smell that was his and his alone, she was mired in deceit.

'Why did you have to come on today of all

days?' she hissed.

Raffy's eyes gleamed, and he gave her his old, familiar smile — the smile that always filled her with regret and yearning. 'I came to wish you well, Bessie. What better than a wedding be there but to renew old acquaintances?' He leaned into her, his breath warm on her cheek. 'And to meet new ones; who be the groom, Bessie?' Bessie's heart fluttered, her thoughts in turmoil. She might have confessed had the kitchen door not crashed back on its hinges.

Samuel swaggered in with Thomas close behind. Having refused to attend the wedding, they had taken the day off and gone to the pub. They swayed in the doorway, their faces red and engorged with drink. Samuel stared sneeringly at the assembled guests and then pointed to the door. 'You can all bugger off home,' he yelled. 'This is my house and I want you out. Now!'

In the ensuing melee, Bert punched Samuel and Thomas and the colliers joined in the fray. 'You're to blame for this. It's you made our Sammy the ignorant pig he is,' Beattie shrieked at her mother. Bessie retaliated with a stinging clout and, 'You ungrateful slut,' before barging into the throng to pull on Bert's shirttail lest he do Samuel any further damage.

Amy's cry rose above the rumpus. 'Stop! Please stop! Don't spoil today.'

But by then it was too late. Although Jude's fists itched to beat the living daylights out of Samuel he waded in and broke up the fracas, intent on saving the day for Amy's sake. Raffy joined him, and between them they separated the combatants.

In the uncertain calm that followed, Jude chivvied Samuel to the foot of the stairs. 'Go to bed and sleep it off,' he growled. Samuel slumped down on the bottom step.

Bessie, ashamed and embarrassed that her sons should humiliate her in front of her guests, smoothed her dress and patted her hair and then, with Raffy's help, urged the guests to fill their cups and carry on with the party as though nothing had happened. Thomas fell into a chair and slept.

Suddenly, having got second wind Samuel lurched up from the step. Hurling abuse at Jude, he lashed out. Jude's determination to be the peacemaker sank into oblivion.

He silenced Samuel with one swift punch, knocking him unconscious.

The wedding party ruined, the guests drifted off in twos and threes leaving only the immediate family and Raffy in the kitchen. As Bessie fussed over Samuel, Bert and Beattie stormed out threatening to never come back, and a short while later Amy and Jude made their way to the little house they were renting in the town. They walked along the road hand in hand, a fine drizzle shimmering in the light from a pale moon and the ghostly shapes of trees casting ugly shadows on the way ahead.

Jude breathed deeply, struggling to curb his anger and attempting to comfort Amy, telling her that drink was to blame and that all families fell out at one time or other; but it didn't make her feel any better. In an attempt to dismiss the awfulness, she said, 'He was a strange fellow, the one that looks like a gypsy.'

116

'But good enough to help calm the situation,' said Jude, sensing the same uneasy feeling he had had when he first saw Raffy. 'I know this might sound ridiculous,' he continued, 'but when I looked at him, I had oddest feeling; a bit like Jonathan Harker in Bram Stoker's *Dracula* or maybe *Dorian Grey*. It was like looking at myself.'

Amy gasped. 'That's why he looked so familiar the day I saw him outside the library. He reminds me of you.' She giggled. 'They say everyone has a double somewhere and now you've found yours; but don't go getting any ideas about growing your hair or wearing an earring,' she added.

Chuckling at the strange coincidence they quickened their steps, the amusing interlude lifting Amy's spirits. However, by the time they reached Wentworth Street the unpleasantness at the farm came back to haunt her. The day that had started out so beautifully had been ruined, and the beautiful memories she had hoped to hold on to would forever be marred by bitterness and violence. She wondered if it was an omen of worse to come.

11

Still wearing her wedding dress, Amy Leas stood by the bed in the larger of the two upper rooms in number 2 Wentworth Street, breathing in the fresh, clean smells of soap, bleach and new paint. Three weeks before the wedding Jude had acquired a pit house and now, having spent days and nights scrubbing, painting and papering, they would sleep here, together, for the first time.

Letting her gaze drift around the room, Amy told herself she should be deliriously happy but she was struggling to come to terms with the violence that had spoiled her special day. And now she was faced with another problem.

Anxiously, she gazed at the bed she had made up the day before with brand-new, white sheets and a blue patterned bedspread. Would she know what to do once she lay under them with Jude at her side? Would he? Did men automatically know? She didn't think she would. Shivering, she crossed the room to the small fireplace with its chipped green tiles, and taking comfort from the glowing embers in the grate she spread her trembling fingers.

Jude watched her, his dark eyes bright with love and anticipation. He would have given anything to prevent Samuel from spoiling the day, and on the journey home he had mulled over how he should have handled things, but in the heat of the moment all he had wanted to do was bash the living daylights out of the lout. Still, he thought, it would all blow over, and he wasn't going to let his brother-in-law spoil his wedding night as well.

He began to undress, and sensing that Amy's disappointment and nervousness was no less than his own, he removed only his jacket and shirt before going to stand behind her. He leaned with both hands on the mantelpiece, his lips brushing the nape of her neck. He felt the tension leave her body, her shoulders relaxing under his kiss. Bringing his hands round to her back he undid the buttons of her dress, his calloused fingers fumbling over the tiny loops. Amy stepped out of the pool of linen at her feet, and turning, she fixed her eyes on his with a thoughtful, considering stare. Jude gazed back, his dark eyes gleaming with love and desire. Amy felt a sudden loosening, as though he had pulled a string deep inside her.

★   ★   ★

Afterwards, Amy had no idea how they had progressed from the fireplace to the bed, only that time had been filled with the most wondrous sensations. Jude lay contentedly by her side, his hand cupping her breast, his smile euphoric. Amy turned to gaze into his face, her smile telling him that this marriage was destined to be a marvellous journey

★   ★   ★

In those first heady weeks of married life Amy and Jude lived a charmed life. Each weekday Amy

119

worked in the library and Jude his appointed shifts down the pit, time spent apart filled with anticipation for the time they spent together in their own little home. Nestled on the shabby couch in the parlour, the room's only piece of furniture, they read from their ever-increasing collection of books kept in two stout cardboard boxes at either end of the couch, Jude's to the right and Amy's to the left. They read favourite passages out loud, sharing the joys of literature, new ideas and old histories. They talked at length, weaving dreams of the future and they made love, often.

On a blustery day at the end of March, Amy stepped backwards out of the dry-dropper closet into the yard behind the house. She hated the closet with a passion. Shared with her neighbours, she took her turn to clean it every other week. But today wasn't cleaning day. She was there this morning because, like every other morning in the past week, she had vomited her breakfast.

At first, she had blamed it on the fish they had eaten in a cafe in town. Now, she was certain she was pregnant. Clammy perspiration moistened her hands and forehead. This wasn't what they had planned. They had only been married seven weeks and Jude was going to college in September. Fear clutched at Amy's heart.

Jude was sitting at the table when she returned to the kitchen.

'Oh, are you up already?' she said. He didn't start work until two that afternoon and she had hoped to slip away to the library without having to face him. She turned her back, pinching her cheeks in case she looked as pale as she felt.

120

'I couldn't sleep,' he replied, riffling the pages of the book in front of him. 'I thought I'd do a bit of studying. That syllabus says this chap's an absolute necessity.' He held up a battered copy of *The Complete Works of William Shakespeare*.

Amy's heart plummeted.

'In that case I'll leave you and Mr Shakespeare in peace,' she said, trying to sound cheerful enough to hide the feeling that she was sinking into a bottomless pit. She pulled on her coat, and instead of sharing their usual warm, parting kiss on the lips she pecked Jude's cheek and then hurried to the door, saying, 'I'll see you at ten.'

''Shall I compare thee to a summer's day; thou art more lovely . . . '' Jude called after her, disappointed by the fleeting sign of affection.

Amy left him to his reading and walked to the library thinking that reading hadn't done either of them much good if she was pregnant. After that first night of unbridled passion they had reluctantly agreed to practise birth control until Jude had completed his course and obtained work. To that end they had read Charles Knowlton's book quoting Annie Besant's words on family planning. But Annie, a woman Amy admired for her socialist views, seemed to have let her down.

* * *

Jude came home from work, and Amy let him take his bath and eat his supper before telling him what, she was sure, he would not want to hear. Now, as he sat on the couch in the parlour she watched as *The Complete Works* slipped from his grasp.

'I don't understand how it happened,' Amy concluded, her voice barely above a whisper. She was standing in front of the hearth facing him, and although the heat from the fire warmed her legs her insides felt cold as ice. She stooped slightly, her blue eyes begging understanding as they sought his.

Jude raised his gaze, his eyes widening as his brain slowly registered her words.

'It changes everything doesn't it?' Amy's voice wobbled, her throat thick with unshed tears.

'You could be mistaken. We've been so careful.' Jude sounded desperate.

Amy shook her head. 'I called with the doctor after work. I *am* having a baby.'

This time her voice refuted any misunderstanding. She went and sat beside him, wanting him to take her in his arms.

Jude sat stock-still, couldn't move, because once he moved time would start rolling again, and when it did, he knew that nothing would ever be the same. Amy watched him struggle with his thoughts, her own a mixture of sorrow tinged with disappointment; sorry for quashing his hopes but disappointed that he found not one ounce of joy in what they had created.

'I'll have to forfeit my job in the library,' she said, flinching at the thought of it, and at the same time inwardly willing him to show some signs of pleasure.

'And I'll have to carry on hewing coal,' Jude said, the feeling of loss so deep that his words sounded completely hollow. He prodded the copy of Shakespeare out of reach with his toe, lit a cigarette and then stood up. 'I'm off for a breath of fresh air,' he said, walking out to the yard. He closed the door quietly behind him.

Amy watched him go, the disappointment she had felt earlier now swelling into full-blown anger. It wasn't her fault alone. It had taken both of them to make a baby and the least Jude could do was accept it with some grace. When she heard him come back inside, she hurried upstairs and began to undress. She didn't want to talk to him. A few minutes later Jude entered the bedroom.

Amy slipped off her chemise, naked for a moment before her nightdress enveloped her. Jude eyed her willowy figure. They might yet be saved; miscarriages were common enough. Disgusted by the wickedness of the thought, he joined Amy in bed. She was lying flat on her back gazing at the ceiling.

He made no mention of his dashed hopes to further his education. Instead, he leaned over her, brushing her lips with his before saying, 'I'm sorry.' He laid his hand on Amy's stomach. 'This baby's blessed to have a mother as wonderful as you.' He crushed her to his chest. 'I love you, and I love our baby. We're a proper family now.'

Amy felt reassured, yet secretly she grieved for his lost opportunity.

12

Beckett's Park Hospital

October, 1918

Amy walked the length of the large airy room, pausing now and then to greet the nurses and family members of other Jude's fellow patients. He was sitting in his usual chair gazing out of the window at the burnished sycamores and beech that vied with fatheaded chrysanthemums of various hues. Whether or not he appreciated the glorious riot of colour was difficult to tell, but Amy admired them fulsomely, saying that she would like a garden like that, one day.

Jude nodded his head. On her last two visits he had focused his attention on her for much of the time, meeting her gaze with a benign expression on his face. He had let her hold his hand without pulling it away, and at the end of her most recent visit he hadn't flinched when she pecked his cheek.

The gardens duly commented on, she pulled up a chair so that she was facing him. Then, throwing caution and the doctor's advice out of the window, she took the battered copy of *The Man Who Would Be King* from her bag and began to read aloud: 'The Man Who Would Be King.'

She glanced at Jude. He stared back, his eyes glittering.

Amy continued, 'Brother to a prince and fellow to a beggar if he be found worthy. The law, as quoted, lays down a fair conduct of life, and one not easy to follow. I have been fellow to a beggar again and again under circumstances which prevented either of us finding whether the other was worthy.'

Amy paused, and raising her head she saw that Jude's eyes were riveted on her face. She carried on reading and had just read 'and was promised the reversion of a Kingdom, army' when gurgling noises in Jude's throat had her glancing up, alarmed. Perhaps Dr Mackay was right. Was Jude about to start shouting and blaspheming? Was reading a disturbing influence? She bit down on her lip, watching and waiting. His lips twitched, and then he muttered, 'Go on.'

Amy's blood sang, and a hot, excited feeling invaded her entire body as she began to read again. He had spoken to her.

Barely able to decipher the words, her eyes blurred with unshed tears and her voice shaking, she read, 'But today, I greatly fear that my King is dead, and if I want a crown I must go and hunt for it myself.' Then the words stuck in her throat and she croaked to a stop.

'Kipling,' said Jude.

'Yes, love, it's Kipling,' she stammered, beside herself with joy.

He closed his eyes. The taut, bitter lines round his mouth relaxed into what Amy could only describe afterwards to Samuel and Bessie, as the way he used to look when he'd heard, seen or read something wonderful, the one with his lips pressed together as he stretched them slowly and nodded his head.

13

Barnborough

Summer, 1913

The night of Amy and Jude's wedding, Raffy Lovell had stayed at the farm long after everyone else had left, and Samuel and Thomas were in bed. Bessie had made a pot of tea, and as they sat by the hearth Raffy softly asked, 'Whatever happened to my boy that I left ye to care for?'

Bessie swallowed, almost choking on a mouthful of tea. It brought tears to her eyes, and thinking fast, she forced more tears to join them. 'He died,' she whispered, her wet cheeks and stricken features giving credence to the lie. 'Measles,' she added, keen to convince Raffy.

Raffy shook his head sadly and rubbed his jaw. 'Measles,' he repeated slowly. His brow wrinkled and his eyes darkened as he looked searchingly into Bessie's face. Then he gave a little shrug and said, 'So he never grew to be a man?'

'I did my best for him but it wasn't enough,' she mumbled, squeezing out a few more tears, and looking suitably penitent. Then, eager to change the subject, she began to talk about how the farm had suffered since Hadley's death, Raffy listening patiently and making sympathetic noises. He made no mention of Jude or Beatrice, or of his intentions to stay in Barnborough. Bessie had seemed glad of his company, content to unburden herself to one who understood farming, and before he left, he had kissed her gently on the cheek and promised to call again when he was passing. Bessie, sad to see him go, had told herself it was for the best; it was dangerous to have him near and Samuel wouldn't want Raffy about the place.

Raffy was well aware of that and was biding his time, waiting for the opportune moment to return to Intake Farm. To his good fortune, Kitty Rose, a gypsy woman he had met on his travels had pitched her caravan on the edge of the town and Raffy was sheltering there. Sly and smooth-tongued, he had a way of persuading the townsfolk he met in the inns to gossip about the Elliot family. How were they managing now that Hadley was dead, he asked, his voice thick with concern? Rumours that Samuel and Thomas were drinking heavily and the farm going to pot were just what he wanted to hear. When he had heard enough, he made his move.

★   ★   ★

It was a bright May morning, Bessie in the dairy feverishly cleaning churns and worrying over the cows in the milking parlour. Harry Sykes, the farm labourer, had refused to work with Samuel, and Samuel's reputation being what it was, no replacement could be found. Wearily, Bessie rolled a churn into the milking parlour then came to an abrupt stop, the churn clanging on the flags.

Raffy lolled in the doorway, smiling ruefully.

'What the . . . ?' Bessie stuttered, her hands

flying to her hot, pink cheeks then up to her dishevelled hair. She patted it ineffectually, embarrassed to be caught performing a labouring man's task.

'How be ye, Bessie?' Raffy asked softly. 'It looks to me like you be needing a hand.' The gentle words brought tears to Bessie's eyes. Raffy moved closer, placing his arm about her heaving shoulders. 'Now, now girl, don't take on. I'm here to comfort ye and put things right. Where be those sons of yours?'

'Still in their beds,' Bessie said, moving out of Raffy's reach to upright the churn. She moved with none of her usual sprightliness.

Raffy shook his head disbelievingly. 'Still abed, and Top Clough only half ploughed and Low Fold run to weeds.' He sighed at the sorry state of the farm, but secretly he was pleased.

Before Samuel and Thomas appeared downstairs, the milk churns had been filled and delivered to the gate for collection, the cows released from the milking parlour to the meadow and the horses hitched to the plough, waiting to be taken to Top Clough.

'If you're to stay there's to be no mention of your kinship to Beatrice,' said Bessie, and believing that everyone had a guilty secret and that Raffy truly loved her, she made him swear to keep hers.

Raffy had just cleared his plate of eggs, bacon and sausage when Samuel and Thomas lumbered into the kitchen. They made a sorry-looking pair, their blubbery features still wearing signs of the drink they had consumed the night before.

'What the bloody hell is he doing here?' bawled Samuel, squaring up to Bessie. Thomas stood a pace behind trying to copy him.

Bessie glared first at Thomas and then at Samuel. 'He's here because this farm needs him,' she said, mentally adding 'and so do I.' She lifted two heaped plates. 'Sit down and get your breakfasts.'

Lured by the sight of eggs, bacon and sausage, Samuel and Thomas sat down. Bessie slammed a plate in front of each of her sons and then placed her hands palms down firmly on the table. 'This farm's gone to rack and ruin since your father died, and I'll not stand by and let that happen when there's a good man offering to save it.'

'A good man! He's a bloody gypsy, I'll not let . . .' Samuel struggled to rise. None too gently, Bessie prodded him back into his chair. When he opened his mouth to object, she shouted him down.

'You'll do as you're told,' she snapped, fetching him a smart clip across his ear. Samuel's bulbous blue eyes moistened and his bottom lip wobbled, but it didn't soften Bessie's heart. She marched over to the dresser, and returning to the table with a ledger, she slammed it down in front of Samuel and flicked it open. In a voice thick with scorn, she read out the list of debts. 'And who's going to settle them? Tell me that, Samuel.'

For a moment there was a deathly silence, Samuel too shocked and Thomas understanding none of it. Bessie raised her hand and Samuel flinched but Bessie simply ruffled his hair. 'Let's not fall out, love, you know I'm right, and now's the time to make some changes.' Lies tripping from her tongue she said, 'Raffy worked for your father before you were born. He's an old friend and your dad trusted him; so do I and whether or not you

130

like it, he's here to stay.'

Samuel and Thomas looked at one another and then at Raffy, their expressions a mixture of suspicion and dislike tinged with relief. Raffy eyed them back sombrely. 'You'm a bit late for planting, lads,' he said, 'but get the seed in today and ye'll have a crop of sorts. An' I be thinking that if ye sells the bull it'll cover much of what ye owe. He'm knackered, but only ye know that so don't be letting on.'

Sullenly, Samuel nodded his head. He had fallen for Bessie's story that Raffy was an old friend of his father's — he vaguely remembered seeing a gypsy about the place when he was a small boy — and if the old fool wanted to do the work then he'd let him. Lazy as Samuel's brain was, it told him the farm might not survive otherwise. Thomas gave Raffy a sloppy smile, all teeth; if this man was a friend of his dad's then he must be a good man.

Raffy now hired, he chivvied Samuel and Thomas out to Top Clough, Sammy carrying the sacks of seed and Thomas the drill. Bessie watched them go with a complacent smile; Intake Farm was in safe hands, and she had got her man.

★ ★ ★

On Sunday afternoon, Amy and Jude walked to Intake Farm to tell Bessie she was about to become a grandmother yet again. They walked in silence for much of the way, each turning over their thoughts on the matter, Amy conscious that her mother would make some objection, and Jude reflecting on his lost opportunity. When

131

they entered the kitchen, they found Raffy Leas sprawled in a chair at the hearth. Amy blinked her surprise. She looked to her mother for answers. Bessie looked flustered as the same lies she had told Samuel and Thomas sprang from her lips; she'd fooled her sons into believing her story and had been certain Raffy would keep her secret, but now, faced with father and son together in her kitchen she panicked.

Afraid her lies would find her out, Bessie fluttered and fumbled as she made tea and Amy, puzzled by her mother's highly nervous state, almost forgot the reason for her visit. Bessie received the news with a distracted frown and a curt, 'Isn't it a bit soon?'

Raffy congratulated them heartily, adding, 'You'm going to be a grandmother, Bessie.' She curled her lip, and what should have been a reason for celebration wasn't mentioned again. Amy wanted to cry.

Bessie clumsily poured tea, her nerves jangling like a hurdy-gurdy as Raffy engaged Amy and Jude in conversation. 'Have you no work to attend to?' she asked pointedly, nodding her head at the door. Raffy's eyes narrowed wickedly. 'None that can't wait,' he said nonchalantly. Bessie pursed her lips.

Within the next hour, Raffy successfully gleaned Amy and Jude's histories, Bessie quaking when Jude recalled his younger days in Bird's Well. Twice she slopped tea from her cup into her lap, Amy anxiously asking if she was feeling unwell.

'Just a headache,' Bessie retorted, 'I'll lie down when you've taken yourselves off.' The hint unmistakeable, Amy and Jude took their leave. After waving them off, Bessie flopped into a chair fanning her blazing cheeks and waiting for her heart to resume a steady rhythm.

Raffy watched, his eyes steely, his mouth twisted in a cynical smile. 'You'm a liar, Bessie Elliot,' he said. 'My boy didn't die, you gave him away when he was a babe, an' now he's back and wed to your daughter.'

'Don't be a fool,' Bessie snapped, 'Jude's not your son. He told you he belonged to a couple in Bird's Well.'

'Aye, he did, but I suspects it was you gave him to them. I trusted him into your care.' Raffy's voice was heavy with disappointment.

'You didn't care what happened to him,' screeched Bessie. 'You couldn't wait to offload your responsibilities. And I'm telling you, Jude's not your son.'

'You be right I abandoned him,' Raffy said solemnly, 'but if he's not my son, why do he carry my mark?'

★   ★   ★

'That was uncanny,' Jude said to Amy, the minute they left the farmhouse. 'They say everyone has a double, and give or take twenty years, I'm Raffy's.'

'It's like I said, I thought I knew him from the moment I first saw him, but now I realise it's his similarity to you that had me thinking that way.' Amy pictured Raffy's lazy smile, so achingly familiar before adding, 'He must have been awfully handsome in his younger days.'

'He's a real charmer, no doubt about that. A mystical gypsy with a tale to tell.'

133

Amy giggled. 'I couldn't help thinking of Jane Eyre's Mr Rochester — that bit where he disguises himself as a gypsy — or then again, he's a bit like a pirate.'

'Aagh, shiver me timbers an' pieces of eight,' cried Jude, walking down the lane with a rolling gait, his hands a pretend telescope to his eye. They reached the road, and reverting to his normal stride, he said, 'Gypsy or not, the fellow's pulling the farm back into shape. Your mother must be pleased about that.'

'She didn't seem overly thrilled about the baby,' Amy said dismally. Although she had expected it, she was surprised by how hurt she felt at Bessie's reaction.

Jude flinched. *She isn't the only one*, he thought miserably. Then, cursing inwardly at his disloyalty, he pulled Amy into a warm embrace saying, 'It's the most wonderful thing in the world and as long as it makes us happy, why care about anyone else?' He saw the delight in Amy's face as she heard the words but, even so, he couldn't resist adding, 'I suppose your mother's just as shocked as I am.'

After that they barely spoke as they walked back home to Wentworth Street.

★ ★ ★

Beattie was delighted to learn of Amy's pregnancy; yet another reason for her to consider them equal. Considering herself an expert, she gave Amy countless lectures on childbirth, her lurid descriptions of what to expect both fascinating

134

and terrifying. When Amy could no longer hide her condition from Phoebe Littlewood, the head librarian pursed her lips distastefully and issued her with a month's notice.

Out of work, and watching every penny she spent, Amy endured long, lonely hours in the little house in Wentworth Street. Now, for the first time, she became startlingly aware of its inferiority, the initial excitement of married life having masked the poverty of her surroundings. She stood by the window watching the snow fall relentlessly into the yard, making igloos of the closets and ash pits, and whilst everything was pristine white out there, her thoughts were black. Dismally, she walked out of the kitchen.

The parlour with its lone couch looked ridiculously bare, its only saving grace the green velvet curtains and the fire grate she had polished till her fingers were raw. The kitchen, lit by one tiny window was a small, depressing room. Even the newly limewashed walls and cupboards that Jude had painted a bright sky-blue could do little to detract from the ill-fitting doors and the worn flagged floor. Inside the cupboards were pots, plates, mugs and cutlery, two of everything, and against the wall two shabby kitchen chairs and a table. Beneath the window there was an ugly stone sink and a worn slop board. However, the range gleamed blackly and the brass knobs twinkled brightly in the gloom, further evidence of Amy's polishing.

Upstairs, their bedroom held nothing more than the bed and an old chest of drawers, more of Bessie's cast-offs. The second bedroom was bare, as were the floorboards throughout the house. Miserably, Amy came to the conclusion that compared to the spacious, well-appointed rooms at Intake Farm, her own home was no fit place to raise a child. Before, it hadn't seemed to matter. They had happily denied themselves comforts to save money for Jude's college fees. Now, without Amy's wages to support them whilst he studied, he would have to be the breadwinner. The money they had so far saved was needed for an equally important shift in their domestic arrangements.

'I won't be extravagant. I'll buy secondhand,' she told him, after listing the furnishings she thought they needed.

Jude listened to her proposal. Sombrely, he agreed, but Amy could tell by the way he clamped his lips and the darkening of his eyes that it pained him to see his hopes and dreams turning to ashes. It pained her also.

★ ★ ★

Deep underground, in the gloom and stink of the pit bottom, Jude crawled under the low coal seam in which he was working with the ease of a contortionist. Rhythmically swinging his nadger, the short-handled pick bit out shining black lumps of coal, his movements so fluid that the pick appeared to be an extension of his muscular arm.

And as Jude hacked at the seam he thought about Amy and the baby.

He loved Amy; of that he was sure. She was his soul mate and he wanted to spend the rest of his life with her, make a happy home and a family.

So why was he blaming the baby for condemning him to hacking coal for the foreseeable future? He hadn't so much minded being a collier when he'd known every penny he earned was going towards furthering his education in order to obtain a fulfilling job and make Amy proud of him. He hated feeling this way, but he couldn't help it. He wondered if he would fall in love with the baby as easily as he had fallen for Amy.

Jude rolled out from under the overhang and stood upright, flexing his aching shoulders. Pallid streams of perspiration coursed through the black dust coating his skin, his torso streaked like a roadmap. He took a swig of cold tea from a bottle in his snap box. 'Is there any more word of us striking?' he asked the collier working alongside him.

Bill, a Union man, grinned. 'Aye, we'll be putting it to t'members at next meeting. We've asked for ten bob more an' so far t'owners have offered nowt. We've given 'em till t'end o' t'week, an' if they don't meet our demands we'll call a strike. If we get enough votes to carry it, we'll be out afore t'month's end.'

Jude smiled cynically. If he had to be a collier, he'd be one who fought to improve working conditions and wages. 'You can count on my vote,' he said.

★ ★ ★

Amy had sensed a change in Jude from the moment she had told him she was pregnant. Outwardly, for much of the time, he was the same loving, caring Jude, content to sit and talk about matters of interest or share views on whatever it was they were reading. They still made love (passion somewhat diminished) and they still laughed at the same silly things, but Amy couldn't deny there was an undercurrent of altered feelings and unspoken words. They no longer speculated as to what they might do and where they would go once Jude had gained his qualifications, nor did they weave dreams for the future, a favourite topic before the pregnancy. Now their future was planned for them and, at times, Amy felt as though Jude was simmering inside; that, if she were to open him up, red-hot lava would gush out.

He had taken Bill Gascoigne's words to heart and was now a prominent member of the Mineworkers Union. He attended every meeting, often stopping off in the pub afterwards to continue airing his, and his workmates, grievances. He borrowed books from the library on social inequality and read Union documents in detail. According to Bert he was looked on as a leader, his knowledge and articulate delivery valuable tools for fighting the cause. Whilst Amy wholeheartedly agreed that Jude's stance against the mine owners was justified, she did not like the tough, argumentative attitude he adopted to deal with it. When she tried to talk about it, he pulled down the shutters refusing to meet her eyes or made jest that she was a woman and couldn't possibly understand. That he should doubt her intelligence angered Amy.

When they paid their usual Sunday afternoon visit to Intake Farm, Samuel immediately aired his views. 'I see you're threatening to strike again, Jude,' he said sarcastically. 'You should try being a farmer; you'd soon know what hard work was.'

Jude clenched his fists and bit his tongue. For Amy's sake he held himself in check whenever he was in his brother-in-law's company.

'I'd never accuse you of working hard, Sammy,' Amy retorted, equally sarcastic.

Samuel eyed her malevolently. 'Don't get cocky wi' me,' he said, 'because afore long when there's no wages coming in to your house, whose will you be running to?' He smiled pompously. 'And I'll tell you summat else. As long as you stick with him, you'll never have owt. He's not good enough for you.'

The spit in Jude's mouth suddenly tasted sour and a frisson of anger burned his throat and chest. What gave Samuel Elliot the right to think that he, Jude Leas, wasn't worthy of his sister? Jude leapt from his seat, clenched fists raised. Samuel cowered in his chair. Before the blow landed, Amy pushed between them, the bump straining at the front of her dress and the horrified expression on her pale face making Jude drop his fists. Breathing heavily, he clumped to the door. Amy ran after him and they walked down the lane in a silence so deep they felt bathed in it.

14

Amy bent over the crib, scrubbing brush in hand. She had bought it secondhand, just as she had promised, and was eradicating every trace of its previous occupant. Made from light oak, it would be perfect once she'd waxed and polished it. Upstairs, the smallest bedroom awaited its arrival. It would join the cupboard that Amy had painted white to match the prettily patterned yellow and white curtains and the cream rug.

The parlour also had a new rug, one that Amy had pegged out of an old blue coat of Bessie's and a brown one of her own. The old couch kept company with a small table and an old bookcase Amy had refurbished, Jude grudgingly admitting that these new acquirements took the bare look off the place. Amy said that the shelves filled with books gave them their own little library and the table made it look more like a home fit for a new baby. With the purchase of every item, Jude saw his hopes and dreams slipping away.

★ ★ ★

Up at Intake Farm, Raffy was now more or less accepted as a permanent member of the family. In the months since Hadley's death, the farm had teetered on the brink of bankruptcy so, for Bessie's sake and his own security, Raffy toiled night and day. Chivvied by their mother, Hadley's sons reluctantly worked alongside him.

Big, blond and blue-eyed, Samuel and Thomas were Hadley Elliot's sons to the core in all but his work ethic, yet they knew the value of their inheritance and were covetous of the land. To this end they tolerated Raffy, grudgingly acknowledging his worth, and Raffy, to suit his own ends, turned his hand to any task without presuming any kind of authority or ownership. He left that to Bessie; she still held the purse strings.

It hadn't taken long for Raffy to worm his way into Bessie's bed, although neither of her sons was aware of this. Had they been, they most likely would have killed him. Bearing this in mind, every now and then and long after they were asleep, Raffy cautiously left his room behind the scullery and mounted the stairs to Bessie's bedroom, leaving long before Samuel and Thomas woke. Bessie was a happy woman.

Each morning she counted her good fortune, her mirror telling her she looked younger than her years, no matter that she was somewhat plumper than the girl in the fairground almost thirty years before. She was the mistress of a fine farm and, to all intents and purposes, a respectable widow. Sure in the knowledge that she still captivated Raffy and confident he would never reveal the truth about Beatrice and Jude, Bessie buried her fears.

★   ★   ★

Raffy was in Barnborough to buy flour and dried fruit so that Bessie could bake her Christmas loaves. It being a chill November day threatening snow, she had declined to accompany him. Deep in thought, Raffy strolled along the street to the grocery. He had no objections to being an errand boy but, of late, Bessie's domineering manner had begun to irk. He could pack his bags and leave, but winter was a bad time to go travelling and, furthermore, roaming the roads no longer held any fascination. Besides, he had a son and a daughter in this town, and by rights they should know he was their father. He saw no reason to persist with the secret now that Hadley Elliot was dead. It would be grand to have kin of his own, mused Raffy, and Jude was a son to be proud of. As for Beatrice, he couldn't say. He didn't know her.

The flour and fruit stowed in the trap, Raffy was about to head back to Intake Farm when who should he see but Jude, walking past the yard behind the Red Lion. He called out to him. Jude came into the yard, and at Raffy's suggestion he joined him for a pint before returning home.

Inside the pub, Raffy deliberately chose seats in a secluded corner of the bar. He perched on a low stool, his eyes and face mysteriously alight. Jude took the stool opposite and sipped at his pint. Raffy made small talk and Jude, intrigued, responded by asking him about his past life. Raffy reeled off the names of numerous places he had been. Jude was fascinated to be in the company of a man who, amongst many other journeys, had seen dawn rise at Stonehenge, dug for coal in the

Rhondda Valley and crossed the Clifton suspension bridge.

Raffy called a second pint, and over it he turned the conversation to Jude's earlier days in Bird's Well. Jude was shocked to the core when Raffy, gazing enigmatically at him said, 'Henry and Jenny? Not your natural parents, be they?'

Jude listened, aghast, as Raffy told his story, doubting what he heard then utterly convinced when Raffy swept back the long, greasy curls dangling below his left ear to reveal his mark. Jude leapt up so quickly his glass smashed on the floor. Then he ran.

Amy was washing cabbage for the dinner when Jude burst into the kitchen, his face ashen. As he struggled to catch his breath, Amy dried her hands and hurried to his side. 'What's the matter?' she cried, thinking something dreadful had occurred at the pit.

'Him! Raffy!' Jude cried. 'I met him on my way home — stopped for a pint — good God — my father — Beattie's . . . ' Incoherent, he rattled on, Amy trying to make sense of it until a loud knock at the door diverted her attention.

Before she could answer it, the door opened and Raffy stepped inside. 'I be sorry for upsetting ye,' he cried, reaching out to Jude.

Jude shook him off, shouting, 'Go on, tell her what you told me.'

Then it was Amy's turn to listen to Raffy's story. Wide-eyed and trembling, she struggled with the detail, and when it came to Raffy admitting that he was Jude and Beatrice's father she let out a howling wail. If Beatrice and Jude were Bessie and Raffy's children, she had married her brother.

Then it was her turn to run, out of the house and up the street, the baby in her womb heavier with every step. Unable to run further, she flopped down on a low wall outside the Methodist church, and nauseated by the hideousness of what she had heard, she vomited onto the pavement. Jude found her there.

Amy stared up at him, the look in her eyes and the lines etched round her mouth bearing all the horrors of the world. 'You're my brother,' she croaked. 'I married my brother.' Her shoulders sagged and she would have slipped from the wall had Jude not grabbed her in time.

He held her closely, afraid she had lost her sense of reason. 'I'm not your brother, I'm your husband,' he said gently.

Amy began to gabble, and as Jude listened, he began to chuckle. 'Oh, my poor love, you've got it all wrong. Beatrice is Raffy and your mother's daughter. I belong to Raffy and some other woman, not Bessie.'

★　★　★

Back in the house, sitting round the kitchen table over a strong cup of tea Raffy reiterated his tale, Amy feeling slightly foolish for the misunderstanding and hugely relieved to learn the truth. Even so, she found it hard to believe her mother's duplicity. And now she understood why Bessie behaved so strangely towards Beattie and Jude. It felt like swallowing stones to take in so many truths all at one go.

144

'Will you tell Beattie?' she asked, the question no more than a whisper.

'The girl have a right to know who her father be,' Raffy said solemnly.

Apart from clarifying some of Raffy's story, for Amy's benefit, Jude had said very little. Now, Amy looked searchingly at him to see what effect the revelation had on him. Calmly, he returned her gaze, and almost as though he had read her mind he said, 'Raffy might have provided the seed that gave me life, and if that's the truth so be it, but it was Henry and Jenny Leas made me who I am and nobody can replace that.'

Shadows lengthened and still they talked, Jude asking a hundred questions and Raffy, in that practised way of his, supplying him with vague answers. Amy stood to light the lamps. As she stretched to reach the lamp on the mantelshelf water whooshed down her thighs, spattering the flagstones. She grabbed the edge of the mantelshelf, her heart lurching and her cheeks reddening that this should happen in front of Raffy. In all the recent confusion she had blamed her flight up the street for the nagging pains in her back and abdomen. Through clenched teeth she managed to say, 'Jude, fetch May Jackson.'

Jude tore his attention from Raffy, and seeing Amy's agonised expression and the puddle at her feet he ran for the midwife.

★ ★ ★

Dawn's early light streaked the sky, probing fingers of watery winter sunlight slanting between

145

the gaps in the bedroom curtains. May Jackson laid the baby in Amy's outstretched arms, saying, 'Well done, lass. You've got a bonny daughter.'

Amy sank back into the pillows, the baby against her breast, a rapturous feeling of release suffusing her body. She gazed into the puckered face of this perfect little stranger, her heart swelling with a love so powerful it made her catch her breath. She lay, almost in a trance as May completed her duties then, everything tidy, she smiled and nodded at the midwife. May marched out to the landing and at the head of the stairs shouted, 'You can come up now. Your daughter's waiting to meet you.'

Thudding feet sounded in the stairwell, Jude the first to arrive in the bedroom. He stood, gazing in awe at his wife and child. Up until now, he'd thought of the birth as far off. It seemed unthinkable that now his daughter was here in this room. Amy met his gaze, love and pride gleaming in her eyes, and Jude felt as though his heart would burst. He knelt beside the bed, one hand gently stroking Amy's flushed cheek and the forefinger of the other carefully tracing his daughter's face.

Raffy stepped closer, peering at the snuffling baby. 'She's yours all right, boyo,' he said, glancing at Jude for confirmation that the tiny girl's swarthy skin, limpid brown eyes and straggling black locks were similar to those of her father.

'I never doubted she was, you old fool,' Jude replied tersely, feeling annoyed that this man who had suddenly claimed to be his own father was there to share this momentous occasion. Jude had had time to do some deep thinking whilst they waited for his daughter to be born, and in that time he had wondered what kind of man could so easily hand over his child to a woman he barely knew then disappear for twenty years. Now, looking at his daughter asleep in her mother's arms, he knew he would fight tooth and nail to keep her by his side. He also wondered how he could ever have regretted her conception. His eyes settled on the baby's rosebud mouth. How could a college course compare with treasure such as this?

'I'll be off,' May Jackson said, picking up her bag. 'I'll call back in a couple of hours. You've two lovely lasses there, Jude. Make sure you look after 'em.' Jude assured her he would, and he meant it.

'What be you calling her?' asked Raffy.

'I'd like Catherine, but Jude prefers Jennifer,' Amy said.

'You should call her Kezia,' Raffy said, leaning forward to take closer look at the sleeping child.

'What sort of a name is that?' Amy asked.

'Jude's mother's name, that's what sort of name it be,' Raffy replied tartly. 'Child is the image of her.'

Jude scanned the tiny heart-shaped face the colour of cinnamon and cream. He saw, a short, straight nose and brown eyes the shape of almonds and above them a high forehead banded with ribbons of oily black hair. Had his mother looked like this?

Raffy nudged Jude. 'The image of your mother, isn't she so?'

Jude spun round to face him, his eyes glittering angrily. 'How the devil would I know?'

'I suppose not, boyo,' Raffy said softly, 'an' I'm

sorry for that.'

The last thing Amy wanted to do right now was referee a row between her husband and father-in-law, so she said, 'It's a pretty name. Different. I like it, Raffy. Thanks for telling us.'

'Do you mean that, Amy?' Jude's expression had changed from belligerent to sad and thoughtful. 'Would you really call her after my mother?'

Amy didn't answer immediately. She had seen how disturbed he was to learn that Raffy was his father, and knew that his present anger stemmed from the shocking realisation of his true identity. She also knew that with Raffy now part of their lives it was up to her to build bridges and keep the peace, because the last thing she wanted was a dark Raffy-shaped cloud hanging over Jude's head.

'I think it's a perfectly beautiful name,' she said, genuinely liking the name and knowing she had done the right thing when she saw Jude's smile. 'How do you spell it, Raffy?'

'K-E-Z-I-A,' Raffy explicated.

★   ★   ★

Much to Amy and Jude's surprise, Beattie accepted Raffy as her father in much the same way as she had accepted the callous treatment doled out by Bessie and Samuel when she was younger.

'I always knew I wasn't an Elliot,' she said, shrugging carelessly and grimacing when Jude told her he was her half-brother. 'An' I don't just mean because I don't look like them — it was the way that bitch looked at me. I knew from no age

148

that the miserable cow had something against me.'

Amy cringed when Beattie referred to their mother in such ugly terms but she didn't condemn them — as far as Beattie was concerned, they were true. What she couldn't understand was Bessie's acceptance of Raffy. There he was, living and working alongside her mother, Bessie forever praising his loyalty to her whenever Amy and Jude paid their weekly visits. Later, when she mentioned this to Jude he replied, 'She needs Raffy more than he needs her. Without him Intake Farm would go to the dogs and she knows that. She's as cunning as a fox is your mother, not that I hold it against her. When she gave me to Henry and Jenny, she did me a favour.'

'Will you tell her that you know Raffy's your father?' Amy asked Jude and Beattie.

Beattie snorted. 'I'll not be telling her. I haven't spoken to her since that carry-on at your wedding, and I don't care if I never speak to her again.' She tossed her head dismissively.

'Aye, what difference does it make to Beattie who her father is?' said Bert. 'She's a grown woman wi' a family of her own. She doesn't need anybody but us.' Bert lifted Kezia from her pram as he spoke, cradling her with such consummate ease that Jude, still nervous of the precious little bundle that was his daughter, felt a twinge of jealousy coupled with guilt. He hadn't wanted Kezia but now she was more precious than anything he could imagine.

'I never did need Bessie bloody Elliot an' I've managed this far without Raffy,' Beattie sneered. She glanced at Jude. 'You can tell her if you want.'

149

Jude shrugged. 'I think we'll let Raffy tell her,' he said, grinning as he added, 'although I don't think she'll be pleased to hear it.'

Amy was inclined to agree.

Visits to Intake Farm became something of a trial, Amy seeing her mother in a new light, and often finding it difficult to keep the secret. Whilst she had always been aware of her mother's cruelty towards Beattie, she still didn't understand why. Bessie plainly adored Raffy, anyone could see that, so why had she treated his daughter so abysmally? Guilt, she supposed for having deceived Hadley. And as for giving Jude away then pretending she didn't know who he was, Amy didn't know what to think. Fortunately, with Kezia the centre of attention on these occasions, Amy was sufficiently distracted and Bessie none the wiser that her secrets were secret no more.

15

Kezia was ill. Dr Hargreaves told Amy it was a touch of bronchitis, and to give her plenty of fluids and keep her warm. To that end, Amy had slept with her, listening to her laboured breathing and wishing that Jude wasn't on the nightshift. Now, as the six-o'-clock hooter blew, she climbed out of bed and went downstairs to put the kettle on. A few minutes later, Jude stepped into the kitchen.

'How is she?' he said, his first concern for his precious daughter.

'No better,' Amy replied, as she followed him upstairs.

Kezia tossed restlessly, half-asleep. Her cheeks were flushed and they could hear her rasping breaths. 'She hardly slept a wink, her little chest's so tight,' Amy said despondently. 'I'll go up to Mam's later and borrow her tin of Kaolin. I'll make a poultice to help her breathe.'

'I'll go now,' said Jude, fear clutching at his insides as Kezia gave a hacking cough. 'Raffy'll be up by the time I get there.'

Amy showed her gratitude by pecking his cheek. 'I'll have your breakfast ready by the time you get back,' she said, as they went back downstairs.

⋆   ⋆   ⋆

Raffy had slept too late in Bessie's bed. Now, seeing it was already daylight, he hastily got up and gathered his clothes in a bundle. On the landing, his eyes boggling, Samuel saw Raffy sneaking out of his mother's room wearing only his underwear.

'You dirty, rotten swine,' he bawled, flinging himself at Raffy's back. Caught unawares, Raffy reeled forward, tumbling down the stairs into the kitchen. The noise wakened Thomas and Bessie.

Raffy got to his feet ready to defend himself as Samuel lunged after him. They grappled, Samuel holding Raffy in a bear hug. Thomas blundered into the room, Bessie at his heels. 'Stop it! Stop it!' she screamed.

Raffy struggled to free himself, Samuel shouting to Thomas for assistance. He waded forward, kicking Raffy in the middle of his spine. He was still kicking him when Jude burst in.

Shocked to see Jude at that hour of the morning, Samuel loosened his grip. Raffy broke free. Jude dived at Thomas. He landed on his backside, puffing and panting. Raffy found his second wind and laid into Samuel, Jude dragging them apart and tossing Samuel to the floor. Bessie was still screeching.

'My God,' Jude gasped, 'what's going on here?'

'Him, the filthy swine,' Samuel yelled, pointing a finger at Raffy. 'He's been sleeping with my mother.' He got to his feet, but before he could attack Raffy again, Jude's fist landed on his chin, knocking him back to the floor.

Bessie rushed to Samuel's aid screaming, 'Don't you dare hit him again.'

'Aye, Jude, you keep out of it; it's nowt to do with you,' Samuel growled. 'Why are you defending that stinking, old reprobate?'

Jude's eyes glittered blackly as he hissed, 'Because he's my father.'

Bessie paled. Sagging visibly, she fixed her eyes on Samuel, a ghastly expression twisting her features.

'Your father?'

'Aye, Samuel, my father — and Beattie's.' Jude measured his words carefully, taking an unseemly pleasure in Bessie and Samuel's reactions: one terrified, the other horrified. 'Your mother'll tell you all about it, Sammy.'

He turned to Raffy. 'You'd best come along with me for the time being,' he said, and remembering his errand he asked Bessie for the tin of Kaolin, telling her why he needed it.

She tottered to the cupboard, her hands shaking as she took out the tin and handed it to Jude. 'What have you done?' she hissed.

★ ★ ★

Amy's expression mirrored disbelief when Jude told her what had happened. 'So Mam knows you know the truth of it. She must be beside herself.'

'Something like that,' said Jude, running his fingers through his hair, 'but I wasn't going to stand by and let them beat the shit out of him.' He glanced at Raffy who had flopped into the nearest chair and was rubbing his back to ease the pain. 'Come on, old lad, let's get you onto the couch. When Amy's warmed the Kaolin and made a poultice for Kezia's chest, she can make one for your back.'

Ignoring the aroma of sizzling bacon and the

153

rumbling in his belly, Jude made Raffy comfortable and then washed and changed his clothes before going upstairs to assist Amy in applying the poultice to Kezia's chest.

Raffy's face lit up when Jude applied a poultice to his bruised back, but it was plain to see that the ordeal had taken its toll. Later, after Jude had slept for a few hours and Raffy had rested on the couch, he limped into the kitchen, his face haggard and his devil-may-care rakishness withered. It was then that Jude realised his father was growing old.

'Do you fancy a pint before I go back on nights?' Jude asked. 'I could do with one myself.' A touch of the old Raffy flared. 'Why not, boyo?' he said, his voice shaking.

Amy nodded her approval, and the two men walked to the Miners Arms on the corner of the street. Raffy took a long pull on his pint. 'I thank ye for coming to my rescue,' he said, clinking his glass against Jude's.

Jude gave a wry smile. 'You might not be much of a father, but I wasn't going to let those two louts beat the hell out of you.'

Tears beaded Raffy's lashes. He brushed his eyes with the back of his hand. 'I don't deserve it. I didn't stand by you when you needed me, I gave you away but . . . ' He shook his head. 'I didn't know what else to do. Your mother dying left me in a sorry state. I thought Bessie was the next best thing. She be a good woman.' He looked to Jude for confirmation.

Jude grunted. He wouldn't go so far as to agree but he did say, 'She did me no harm.' He paused

154

thoughtfully. 'Will you go back there?'

'I don't know as I'd be welcome — not now Bessie's secret is out,' growled Raffy, a hopelessness colouring his words.

'You'd better stay with us then,' said Jude, draining his glass.

'Do you mean that, boyo?' said Raffy, choking on the words and rising so quickly his stool toppled over.

Before Jude left for work, he and Raffy talked as fathers and sons should do, and in that short space of time they formed a lasting bond. 'He's staying the night,' Jude told Amy. She smiled. She knew it was what Jude wanted and, surprisingly, she discovered she wanted it for him.

On the night Jude had learned about his true parentage, he had told Amy that it had filled a gap in his life, and that whilst he would always be grateful for Henry and Jenny Leas' loving care, to go through life without knowing your true origin leaves a void full of unanswered questions. 'Whether or not Raffy's the sort of man I would have chosen for a father, he is mine,' he'd concluded, smiling wryly.

★ ★ ★

Bessie muddled through her chores with an aching head and a broken heart. She couldn't look Samuel in the eye, and when he looked at her, the disgust masking his face ripped her insides to tripe. Time and again she wished that he had never learned the truth but, if Jude and Amy and Beattie now knew it, she had nothing to hide. Although

155

Jude's revelation had shocked her to the core it brought with it a strange sense of relief. She was sick of living with unbearable guilt whenever she was in Jude's company, or when Amy hinted at the unforgivable way she had treated Beattie. Now, as Samuel stamped into the kitchen, she steeled herself to face him.

'I need money to buy a new hoe,' he growled, holding out his hand belligerently.

Bessie knew it was a lie and that he would spend the money on drink. Both he and Thomas had rarely been sober since the morning of the fight. Taking consolation in the fact that she still controlled Intake's finances she fished the key to the safe-box from between her breasts, leaving it dangling from the gold chain round her neck as she walked over to the dresser. Her fingers trembling, she opened the box and extracted a handful of coins.

'We can't go on like this, Sammy love,' Bessie said, handing him the money.

Samuel's baleful glare told her he intended to do just that. 'I don't need a trollop like you telling me what to do,' he snarled.

'Think of the farm,' Bessie pleaded.

'Aye, that's what you thought of when you fooled my dad into marrying you, and once he were dead you had the bloody cheek to bring that filth in to take his place.'

'The farm needed him. You were letting it go to ruin just like you are now, but it needs you, Sammy, and so do I,' Bessie cried, clutching at his arms in an attempt to embrace him.

'Aye, well bugger the farm and bugger you. I

156

don't need either,' Samuel yelled, and calling to Thomas who lolled in the doorway, he barged out.

Bessie leaned against the sink and did what she had been doing for the past eleven days; she cried piteously.

★ ★ ★

'I'm worried about Mam,' Amy said, when she returned from a visit to Intake. 'Our Sammy's still not speaking to her, or if he does it's to call her vile names, and him and our Thomas are drinking their heads off.'

Jude looked up from the book he was reading. 'I'm not sure there's anything we can do to change that. Samuel put your mother on a pedestal, and now she's fallen off it his head's all over the place. One thing for sure is that they'll come to terms with it.' He chuckled. 'Your brothers need her to feed 'em and she still holds the purse strings so they'll have to learn to live with one another whether they like it or not; the farm's their livelihood. And anyway,' he went back to his book, 'we've enough to contend with now Raffy's living here.'

Amy nodded sombrely. She had readily agreed with Jude that Raffy should stay, and couldn't deny he had made himself useful fixing the leaking tap, fettling the stove and mending a broken chair, but his presence had altered their way of life. He talked too much, repeating the same stories time and again, the peaceful quiet of the little house disturbed by his restlessness.

'I suppose I shouldn't begrudge letting him

stay but he does get on my nerves,' Amy said, lifting Kezia from her pram and handing her to Jude, 'and I'm glad he's taken to Beattie and she to him. They get on like a house on fire.'

'Two of a kind,' said Jude, 'I think I must take after my mother, thank God.'

★ ★ ★

Less than a week after this conversation, Raffy surprised both Amy and Jude by announcing that he was moving in with Beattie. 'It's not that I'm not grateful to ye for your kindness, it's just that Beattie wants it.'

He wasn't going to tell them that he did too. That he found Amy and Jude's neat, quiet house restrictive, and though he was fond of Amy he considered she was far too particular about the way things should be done.

'It just be a case of me takin' the truckle bed off your landing and puttin' it on Beattie's,' Raffy continued. 'Ye'll no doubt be happy to see it go.'

Amy certainly was, and neither she nor Jude pressed him to stay.

'Birds of a feather,' said Jude, after he returned from carrying the truckle bed up to Beattie's. 'It's our good fortune they get on so well.'

★ ★ ★

A couple of days later Amy dropped by the house in Grattan Row, her spirits sinking when she heard the howls and roars emanating from behind the

158

door. Leaving Kezia outside in her pram, she cautiously stepped inside.

Raffy was down on his knees roaring and growling. The children sat, mouths agape and shivers running down their spines as they watched Granda Raffy battle with sharks and swordfish before killing the whale with the golden tooth.

'Twas the gold I used to make this,' he boasted, flicking his earring.

'It was an elephant had the golden tooth, the last time I heard that story,' Amy said, her laughter high with relief that the awful noises she had heard from outside were nothing but good fun. She glanced into the kitchen. 'Where's Beattie?'

'Out. Took off an hour ago.'

'Go on, Granda, tell the next bit,' Maggie cried, directing an annoyed glare at Amy. Albert and Fred added their pleas as Amy stepped back outside to bring Kezia in. Raffy finished his story, and roaring and growling, the boys ran outside to play their own version.

'Can I take Kezia for a walk, Auntie Amy?'

'Yes, Maggie, and take Mary with you. Don't go too far, I'm not staying long.'

In the silence that ensued, Amy said, 'Beattie's taking advantage of you.'

'I don't be complaining.'

'Did she say when she'd be back?'

Raffy pretended not to hear. He didn't object to Beattie taking a few gins with Lizzie Heppenstall, but he knew Amy did.

'I hope she comes home sober,' Amy said tartly. She opened the door, and with a curt 'tell her I called' she walked out. Catching up with Maggie,

159

she relieved her of Kezia and headed for home feeling rather disgruntled.

After Amy had left, and as Raffy made tea for himself and the children, he mulled over his situation. Moving in with Bert and Beattie had been the right thing to do but his heart was still aching from Bessie's refusal to have him back at Intake Farm. That bastard Samuel had seen to that. He wondered how long it would take for the farm to go to rack and ruin. Slurping his tea to the dregs, he told himself it was none of business. Living with his daughter, and his son close by suited him fine.

Walking home, Amy too did some thinking. She supposed she should be grateful that Raffy was living at Beattie's but she worried that, given leeway, it left her unhappy sister free to neglect her children and seek pleasures in all the wrong places.

16

Careful not to waken Amy, Jude slipped out of bed and padded over to the crib to soothe Kezia's wails. Gently, he lifted her to his shoulder, her breath dampening his ear and the heat from her tiny armpits warming his fingers. Sniffing and snuffling, she shuffled up his shoulder, her sharp little toes using his ribs as a ladder. As he walked the floorboards between window and door and back again, he pondered on what the future might hold for his little girl. Germany had invaded Belgium and Britain was at war.

Colliers were exempted from the call to arms, the country needing coal to fuel the vast furnaces that produced the metal for weapons and Amy delighted at knowing Jude wouldn't be expected to volunteer but Jude didn't share her opinion. As he gently lowered Kezia back into her crib he struggled with the concept of loyalty. Where did it lie: with family or king and country?

Later that day, it being a Sunday and the August weather exceedingly warm and sunny, Amy, Jude and Kezia went to Miller's Dam for a picnic along with the Stitts. Whilst Maggie, Albert and Fred ran wild by the water and Kezia and Henry dozed in their prams, the adults lolled on the grass, Bert and Beattie with bottles of beer and Jude with his Sunday newspapers. Amy sat with little Mary on her lap and read Joseph Conrad's *Heart of Darkness*.

Bert looked over Jude's shoulder and har-rumphed. 'Bloody war, newspapers are full of it. Sarry Jevo's wa' nowt to do wi' us and neither is bloody Belgium.' He paused thoughtfully. 'Where is Sarry Jevo anyway?'

Jude grinned. 'It's Sarajevo,' he said, giving its correct pronunciation, 'and it's in the Balkans.'

'Ball cans? I never heard of them either.'

'I suppose we'll hear of lots of places we've never thought about before,' said Amy, her brow creasing as she rhymed off a list of countries. 'We're all involved and it's going to get worse.' She gave a little shudder and thought how apt the title of the book she was reading was.

Beattie gave Amy a withering look. 'You're a right wet blanket, you are. Like Bert says, them places are a million bloody miles from here. And anyway, we've nowt to worry about, it's not as though Bert and Jude will have to go and fight.'

Amy smiled, secure in that knowledge.

★　★　★

The next night, as the lurching cage gravitated to the pit bottom in Barnborough Main, Jude sensed a feeling of loss and aggravation. Hal Sykes, Tommy Tinker and Jimmy Snell, none of them had turned up for this stint. Familiar faces, he'd grown used to the closeness of their bodies, the rank stink of Sykes' breath, Snell's irritating cough and Tommy Tinker's wisecracks.

'Where's Tommy and the others?' he asked Wally Hamby, although he already knew the answer.

Wally, a muscular man in his fifties and head and shoulders shorter than Jude half-turned, speaking into Jude's ribcage.

'Joined up this morning, the silly buggers.'

'Aye, answered Kitchener's call,' cackled an older man with a humped back.

The cage juddered to a stop. The colliers walked along the in-bye leading to the coalface, elbows knocking elbows where the tunnel narrowed and heads lowering or bodies bent double where the roof swooped down. Sharp flints crunched under their clogs. The shot-firers had opened new seams earlier that day, the air thick with dust. Brattices that directed the airflow hung like filthy curtains hiding the entrance to hell.

Jude stooped for the umpteenth time, his eyes on the cartwheel backs of two elderly miners in front of him. Would he end up like that, he wondered, or would he meet his end in a different country far away from the pit? Lost in thought, he raised his head too soon, his helmet clanking on the roof. He pushed it off his forehead, irritated not so much by his carelessness as the confusion that plagued his conscience.

At the coalface, Jude hacked at the seam. Coal shards flew in all directions, his manic vigour causing Willy Hamby to yell, 'Oy, Jude! Are you tryin' to give Lloyd George all t'coal he wants in one day?'

Jude hacked all the harder. His mind made up, he knew what he was going to do.

★ ★ ★

163

'But you don't have to go. Colliers are exempt.'

Amy's crossed arms hugged her shoulders as she rocked back and forth in anguish, her forlorn plea ringing in Jude's ears. He gazed at her stricken face, her eyes wide with disbelief and reddened from crying. Jude's heart went out to her.

'I'll be back before you know it. They're saying it won't last long.'

To Amy he sounded as though he was popping out for a jaunt. Her tears turned to anger. 'Isn't it enough that the poor Belgians are being massacred by the Germans without you losing your life? It's not your war. You're not a soldier,' she cried.

'No, but I am a man who knows what's right. If we don't stop the Germans we'll end up like the Belgians.'

'But you could be killed!' Amy waved her clenched hands to add impact to her words, Jude catching hold of the little fists dancing before his eyes. Amy tore them free. 'I never took you for a fool,' she spat contemptuously.

'I'm not being a fool, I'm doing my duty,' Jude contradicted her, his words ringing with authority. Amy's back visibly stiffened.

Jude placed his hands on her shoulders, and this time she did not pull away. He held her to his chest, shaken by the intensity of her outburst. 'I want to go. I need to go. I wouldn't think I was much of a man if I didn't.'

'But what if you don't come back?' Amy sagged against him.

A grimace twisted Jude's lips. He looked as though he was about to laugh out loud.

'When I go down the pit, do you spend the

whole time worrying about me?' he asked gently, his hot breath fanning Amy's cheek.

Amy shook her head and whispered, 'No.'

'Then maybe you should,' Jude said, stepping back to look at her. 'You can't have forgotten the accident at Barrow Pit — the cage released too soon, seven men dead at the bottom of the shaft. They weren't even hewing coal where the real danger is. And what about the explosion at Wharnecliffe when nobody knew the gas was building up until a spark blew them all to kingdom come?' He smiled cynically. 'And you worry that I might get killed if I enlist. I could just as easily end up dead if I didn't.' He paused to let his words sink in. 'And as for fighting the Germans — if we don't, we might lose our freedom and all that we hold dear.' He pointed to the ceiling above which Kezia slept. 'I'm doing it for her.'

Amy quailed as the truth of his words hit home.

$$\star \quad \star \quad \star$$

The kitchen door almost flew off its hinges as Beattie Stitt flounced in, her hair on end and a malevolent gleam in her eye. Amy groaned inwardly. She had slept badly, afraid to rest on the darkness of the night, and now she felt in no fit state to deal with one of her sister's tantrums. Affecting calm, she carried on stirring the porridge. 'Good morning, Beattie,' she said.

'Don't good morning me.' Beattie wagged a threatening finger. 'Just who does that bloody husband of yours think he is?'

At a loss, Amy left off stirring and gave Beattie a

quizzical glare. Beattie glared back. 'That bloody husband of yours has persuaded my Bert to join up,' she shrieked.

Amy felt a spurt of anger in her chest. Jude had obviously told Bert before he told her. She should have been the first he talked to so that they could make a rational decision as to whether or not he should join the army. Last night had ended in tears, Amy feeling as though her words were knocking against a brick wall, and Jude refusing to discuss it further.

'I don't like it any more than you do, Beattie, and when Jude comes home from work, we're going to thrash it out reasonably.' Amy spoke firmly but deep inside she felt no conviction.

'How am I going to manage all them kids on me own?' Beattie wailed. She burst into tears, her raucous crying that of a wounded animal as she tore at her greasy hair.

Amy took control of the situation. Clasping her sister in a tight embrace she forced her into a chair, the unpleasant odours emanating from Beattie's armpits and hair quickly curtailing the sisterly hug. Then she grabbed the kettle. A strong cup of tea was in order. Still muttering at Jude's betrayal, Beattie slumped at the table, her head on her forearms. Amy offered no words of comfort for she also felt betrayed. Yet, when she set down the cups of tea and sat at the table, she found herself repeating Jude's reasons for going to war. There was little point in railing against the inevitable, she decided. What both women needed now was to be strong.

The tea worked its magic, Beattie's sobs mere

sniffles she peered over the rim of her cup. 'I don't suppose you've a drop of summat strong to go in this tea.'

Reluctantly, Amy produced the brandy kept purely for medicinal purposes. The bottle was almost full. Beattie slopped a generous measure into her cup then drank deeply. 'I'll not manage on army pay,' she moaned. 'Lily Tinker says its nowt compared to what t'miners are earning now, what with all t'coal they need for t'war.'

Again, Amy found the voice of reason. She talked of duty to king and country, the need to support comrades, defend the nation against the Hun. She didn't know if she truly believed it but she managed to calm Beattie who, having helped herself to several tipples of brandy, was feeling quite cheerful.

'We'll get by, Beattie, you'll see,' Amy said positively. 'In wartime everyone suffers but we'll manage. We'll manage together. I'll give you a hand with children.'

Amy didn't know then how much she would come to regret this remark.

'Aye, you're right,' said Beattie, pouring brandy into her empty cup. 'And think on. No more mucky pit clothes to wash, nobody farting and breathing beer in your face when you're in bed unless,' she giggled girlishly, 'unless of course you look for a bit of company now and then.'

'Beattie Stitt! You are incorrigible,' exclaimed Amy. Although she laughed out loud, she couldn't help thinking that in Bert's absence Beattie's unseemly behaviour would further deteriorate.

Beattie stood, wobbling against the table. 'I

don't suppose I can take this to steady me nerves,'
she asked, lifting the depleted brandy bottle. She
tottered to the door.

Amy shook her head despairingly. She really
must talk to Jude tonight.

17

Beckett's Park Hospital

Late October, 1918

Amy plodded through the hospital gateway, thick fog like damp, grey blankets hanging in front of her face. It had dampened her coat and her hair, but it hadn't dampened her spirit. She had walked but a few paces when Eileen Brennan, the lovely Irish nurse whom Amy now considered to be her friend, caught up with her.

'Ye managed to get here, then?' she said cheerily, linking her arm into Amy's. 'I had one heck of a journey, what with the buses crawlin' along and a car blocking the road after it had run into a lamppost. I walked most of the way.'

'Poor you,' said Amy, giving her a friendly grin, her heart warming at the thought of this dedicated nurse's determination to get to work. 'I was in two minds whether to come or not when I saw how bad it was this morning, but I didn't want to let Jude down, and fog doesn't seem to bother the trains. It was only a few minutes late, but then I couldn't get a cab for love nor money so I had to walk as well.'

Eileen chuckled. 'The things we do to put these fellas right, eh. They'll be makin' saints of us before we're done. Mind you, it takes a lot more than a bit o' fog for me to miss me work. My Liam says there's a tinge of the burning martyr about me. He says I give Our Lady a run for her money.'

Amy laughed. 'You're the Blessed Virgin Mary in disguise as far as I'm concerned. You're doing a marvellous job with Jude. I can't thank you and Dr Mackay enough,' she said, as they climbed the steps to the hospital doors.

Eileen flushed at the compliment. 'Thanks, it's nice to be appreciated — an' I know Dr Mackay didn't agree with the book reading,' she continued, as they entered the foyer, 'but no two men are the same, and the doctor's not always right.' She waited for Amy to sign in, and then as they entered the long corridor she said, 'You're not doing such a bad job yourself.' Now it was Amy's turn to blush.

'It's just that I know Jude loves books, and I thought that if anything might help him, it'd be reading. He even ran a library for the troops in his section, you know, carried the books from place to place giving the chaps something to read when they weren't fighting.'

'Wow!' Eileen looked surprised. 'That's admirable. Good old Jude. He's made of strong stuff, an' isn't it just great that he's talking again?'

'It's absolutely wonderful,' Amy gushed. 'There was a time when I thought the only words he'd ever say again were those awful swear words. It scared me.'

They were outside the door of the room where they would find Jude. Eileen paused. 'He still has a fair way to go, so don't rush him. He'll get there in his own good time.'

'I know that now, thanks to you. I'll just keep

on with the reading and the talking. Last week he asked about Kezia — just said her name — and more than once he's repeated a few words of what I've just read. We've yet to have a proper conversation, but it's better than nothing.'

Eileen pushed open the door. 'Well, off you go an' do your bit an I'll do mine,' she said with a grin. 'Look, he's seen you coming.'

Amy hurried across the room to Jude. He was half in and half out of a chair that was nearer to the door than the one he used to sit in, his eyes riveted on her as she approached. 'Hello, love,' she said, reaching for his hands. He didn't reply, but to her surprise and joy he pulled her close, holding her against his chest for a moment before almost pushing her into the chair next to his. In that moment, Amy breathed in his old familiar smell, the smell that she associated with Jude alone. The sour smell that had seeped from his pores during the past weeks had gone, as though it had been washed away along with the horrors that haunted his troubled mind. She held the scent in her nose, butterflies dancing in her heart.

She reached into her bag for a book. Jude's eyes lit up. During the past weeks they'd finished the Kipling and *The Diary of a Nobody*, and were now partway through *Three Men in a Boat*, Jude smiling wryly at the adventurers' misfortunes. Amy opened the book where she had left off on her last visit and began to read. She had read no more than two pages when Jude stretched out his hand, taking the book from her hands then closing it.

Amy stiffened. She looked anxiously up into his face, expecting to see it twist and the foul words to spurt out, but to her relief he was smiling a proper smile that reached his eyes and spoke of recognition, and love.

'Amy, my lovely Amy,' he said, his voice thick with emotion. He repeated the words as though he was tunnelling through dense clouds of long forgotten memory. When he said the words for the third time, he sounded almost surprised, and this time he added, 'It's you. Amy.'

'Yes, it's me, love. Your Amy,' she replied, her voice no more than a whisper. Then, almost delirious with joy she leapt from her chair, its legs rattling against the floorboards as she threw her arms round him. He rose to meet her, his chair almost toppling as he hugged her in a fond embrace. They held onto each other, afraid to let go.

Eileen, hearing the scrape of the chairs and seeing them desperately clinging to one another hurried over, wanting to ascertain that all was well. When she saw the joy on their faces she grinned, saying with a tinge of sarcasm, 'Ah, I see you two have made up at last; an' not before time.' Amy giggled.

'I knew you'd come,' Jude said in a shaky voice. He released his hold, stepping back and shaking his head in wonderment as he gazed at Amy. 'I just knew you'd come to find me.'

'And now I have, my love, and this time I'll not lose you again,' Amy said, feeling like a child whose birthdays had all come at once.

18
Barnborough

October, 1914

On a bright, blustery Friday morning in October 1914, Jude Leas and Bert Stitt joined a long, straggling line of men outside the Territorial Drill Hall in Barnborough. Men of all ages, shapes and sizes, creeds and classes gradually shuffled nearer the open door. Some chatted convivially, others waited silently, no doubt contemplating the wisdom of their actions. Every so often men exited the dark blue doors, some triumphantly waving a Bible and clutching the King's shilling whilst others slunk off hands deep in trouser pockets, disconsolate or relieved at having failed to be recruited.

The long wait unnerved Bert. Taking no part in the banter Jude was enjoying, he darted his eyes up and down the street as though looking for a means of escape.

'Cheer up, Bert!' Jude clapped him on the shoulder. 'You look as though you're at a funeral.'

'I might be afore too long. Me own. I'm beginning to think that I'm not cut out for soldiering.'

'You'll be right enough. Stick by me and we'll soon show Jerry what Barnborough colliers can do. They'll not know what's hit 'em once we get over there.'

The queue shuffled forward and Bert and Jude entered the Drill Hall. Inside, they were each guided to a different table behind which sat a recruiting officer. Jude's was an elderly chap who had seen service in the Boer War. One look at Jude and he told himself this man was just what the British Army needed; a finer, fitter-looking chap you couldn't hope to meet. However, he was a collier. Coal was vital to the war effort. About to return Jude to his labours underground, he looked up into the dark eyes and recognised desire when he saw it, the need to be in the fray. Writing with a flourish and stamping with alacrity, he handed Jude his papers.

Over at another table Bert drooped miserably in front of the officer who, tired of vetting a continuous stream of men, barely raised his eyes as he signed and stamped Bert's papers.

'Well, we've been and gone and done it,' Jude remarked cheerfully, as they waited to be sworn in. Bibles in hand, they listened to and repeated the Padre's words that sealed their allegiance to king and country.

They left the Drill Hall, one marching proudly, the other dazed and stumbling. As they paused outside for Bert to get his bearings, a poster on the wall caught Jude's eye. Lord Kitchener's defiant eyes stared back at him. 'Join Your Country's Army' he commanded.

Jude was convinced he'd done the right thing.

* * *

In the days leading up to Jude's call to arms the atmosphere in the little house in Wentworth Street fluctuated between cold resentment and passionate nurturing. Resigned to the fact that her husband would soon be gone, Amy cooked his favourite meals and calmly discussed how she would manage in his absence. They made love, often. At times it sparked with the passion that had filled those heady first months of marriage, and at others it gently burned with a new maturity that made the bond between them ever stronger. However, there were days when Amy's heart hardened towards what she still thought of as an unnecessary need for his departure and she could neither bring herself to speak nor look at him. Jude weathered her moods patiently, knowing that their love would stand the test.

'I'm sorry for being so prickly this morning,' Amy told Jude, as they walked through the woods one afternoon in late October, three days before Jude reported for training. Jude brought Kezia's pram to a halt, and taking Amy in his arms, he buried his face in her hair. It smelled of the woody scents of autumn.

'Don't be sorry. I understand how you feel. It's a big step for both of us.'

Amy took a deep breath. 'I've been unfair,' she said, 'I was letting my own needs obscure the bigger picture. You're right to go, and I was wrong to try and deter you.' She pulled away to gaze up into his face. 'I fell in love with you because you had ideals, because you want this world to be a better place. I also want that, and if letting you go is the price I have to pay then I'll do it proudly. You're a good, brave man, Jude, and every day we're apart I want you to know I love you and admire your courage. However,' her voice lightened, 'you'd better come back safe and sound 'cos if you don't, you'll have me and Kezia to answer to. We girls won't let you off that easy.' Amy slapped his chest playfully, Jude catching her round the waist and swinging her high into the air. Kezia chuckled, her gummy smiles wrenching at the hearts of her adoring parents.

★ ★ ★

In the Stitt house, chaos reigned. To show how much he loved them, Bert played rumbustious games with his children from dawn till dusk, Maggie, Albert and Fred revelling in the fun yet dreading his departure, and little Mary and Henry unaware they were about to lose their father. The high jinks frayed Beattie's nerves and she ranted and raved, and Raffy took himself off to stay with Kitty Rose.

The night before Bert was due to leave for training Beattie watched as Bert, down on all fours buried beneath his children, yelled at the top of his lungs for mercy. Mary and Fred slid off his back, Maggie roughly tickling his ribs before he rolled over, laughing up at them.

Beattie's mouth was turned down at the corners, petulant and spiteful-looking. 'I'll be glad to see the back of you,' she said.

Bert curled up like a foetus. There were times when crouching in the trenches in France seemed preferable to living with Beattie.

Jude had been gone no more than a week when Amy received his first letter. Having missed him more than she had thought possible, her fingers quivered as she opened the envelope. It seemed strange to receive a letter from the man with whom she'd traded thoughts and feelings simply by speaking whenever they were together.

Amy blinked back tears, her vision blurring as she read that Jude was stationed in the Arcade Hall in Barnsley. Less than twelve miles away, it seemed like a million.

Amy chuckled at the part where Jude had written *'we sleep on the draughty floor, one blanket each, and if anyone had told me I'd be cuddling up to Bert like I cuddle up to you in bed, I wouldn't have believed them. (By the way, they let us smoke in bed, something you don't allow.)'* He went on to tell her how interesting it was to meet men from all walks of life, shopkeepers, solicitors, Boer War veterans and landed gentry, but that the training was repetitive and tedious. It warmed her heart when she read *'the food's not bad but I miss your brown stew and meat and potato pie. Some of the lads say they've never been better fed. All I can say is they mustn't be used to much.'*

He described his uniform as navy blue stuff with brass buttons like Post Office workers wear. Amy formed a mental image of him; he looked particularly handsome. In conclusion he wrote tenderly and poetically of how much he loved and missed her and Kezia, Amy's tears smudging the ink and sobs turning to giggles at the postscript:

'*P.S. Don't let Beattie borrow any money — keep her sober.*'

Amy sat for some time with the letter in her lap, thinking how much she missed Jude. Now, there was nobody with whom to share the plot of the latest book or exchange opinions on the latest news. Neither was there any urgency to keep to a task. Jude wouldn't come clattering down the street looking for a hot bath and a tasty meal shortly after the pit hooter signalled the end of a shift. Waking hours seemed somewhat empty, and at night she yearned to feel his hard, warm body next to hers. Kezia's cries reminding her there were still tasks to attend to, Amy put the letter behind the clock on the mantelshelf. She'd share some of it later with Raffy.

★ ★ ★

Raffy called every day to lend a hand or sit and gossip. He'd dance to and fro in the kitchen with Kezia in his arms, the tap of his boots on the flags accompanying the strange ditties he sang to keep her amused. Amy was glad of his company, and grateful for the tasks he undertook that would normally have been Jude's.

'That tap's leaking again, Raffy,' said Amy, setting a steaming mug of tea at his elbow shortly after he'd arrived one chilly Wednesday morning in December. Raffy dandled Kezia on his knee for a minute or two longer before handing her to Amy.

'She be bonnier by the day,' he said, his warm, brown eyes glowing with admiration.

178

Amy sat Kezia in her highchair and gave her a ball of dough to play with. 'She stood on her own two feet this morning. She'll be walking in no time,' Amy said proudly, her smile clouding as she added, 'It's such a pity Jude wasn't here for her first birthday.' She crossed to the hearth, sweeping it unnecessarily to hide her sadness. As she swept, she heard the flap of the letterbox in the parlour. Dropping the brush, she hurried to lift the letter. It had to be from Jude. She stayed in the parlour to read it.

Raffy was sprawled on the flags, his head underneath the sink when Amy went back into the kitchen. 'Jude's got leave. He'll be home this Friday and stay till Sunday evening. Bert's coming too,' she cried, sounding girlish and giddy. Lifting Kezia she performed an impromptu jig across the floor, Raffy cheering and waving a spanner triumphantly from under the sink.

'I'd better let Beattie know.' Amy's purposeful tone changed to one of reproach as she said, 'Jude says she never answered Bert's letter so he said he wasn't going to write again.' Amy sounded rather self-righteous.

'She'm not be much at letter writing, do our Beattie,' came the reply from under the sink. 'She don't have the time.'

'Time!' Amy snorted. 'She doesn't spend it cleaning — the house is a tip. And you do all the cooking and minding the children.'

Raffy scuttled from under the sink, squirming his way upright with the help of the draining board. 'She be an unhappy woman do Beattie. I blames Bessie for that,' he said sombrely. 'Beattie don't know how to be happy. Nobody ever showed her.' The penetrating look in his dark eyes made Amy feel guilty.

'I'll go and tell her Bert's coming on Friday,' she said, reaching for her coat behind the door. 'I'll stay a while and help her tidy round,' she added contritely, thinking how different things might have been had her mother not been so cruel and she herself so uncaring when they were young. She took a warm romper suit off the clotheshorse. 'I'll take Kezia with me. You finish off here.'

Dejectedly, Amy walked to Grattan Row wondering what she could do to boost Beattie's morale; for that's what was needed, she told herself. Any self-esteem her sister might have had when she was young had been eroded by Bessie's constant criticism and Samuel's sneering disregard. But how could she undo a lifetime of misery? Amy asked herself, lifting Kezia from the pram then opening Beattie's door.

'Bert's coming home for the weekend, Beattie,' she called cheerily, though she felt anything but as she eyed the filth and clutter. 'Your daddy's coming home,' Amy told Mary who then toddled over to Henry in his pram. 'Daddy coming home,' she lisped.

Beattie was sitting by the hearth puffing on a cigarette. Smoke billowed from her curled lips as she acknowledged Amy's presence.

'Did you not hear me, Beattie? Bert's coming on leave.'

Beattie shrugged. 'Aye, I heard you all right. What do you want me to do about it?' She flicked the butt of her cigarette into the fire. 'I'll not be doing owt special to welcome him back, I'm skint.'

Amy's hackles rose. 'You could at least try to look pleased,' she snapped, 'and as for having no money, you always seem to find it for cigarettes and gin.' She could have bitten off the end of her tongue. Where was the compassion she'd felt on her way to the house? She tried again. 'Sorry Beattie, that was unkind. Let's not fight.'

Beattie was about to make a stinging reply when Raffy walked in.

Quick to sense the tension between the two women, he said, 'Put the two young 'uns in Kezia's pram an' me an' Mary will take 'em for a walk.'

Amy shot him a grateful smile and then did as he suggested.

'Me come, Granda Raffy.' Mary hurried to the door.

'You can go an' all,' Beattie said, ungraciously thumbing Amy. But Amy wasn't giving in without a fight. She set the kettle to boil, lifted cast-off clothing and swept the floors, and as she cleaned, she had an idea.

'I know what we'll do, Beattie,' Amy cried enthusiastically, 'we'll have an early Christmas, give Bert and Jude something to remember before they go too far away to come home.' Amy warmed to the theme. 'I'll bake and get a chicken or a duck from Intake. We'll invite a few friends, make a night of it.' Amy's cheeks were pink with excitement.

'Have you finished?' Beattie lit another cigarette, sneering at Amy through the cloud of smoke escaping her lips. Feeling deflated yet unwilling to admit defeat, Amy began mopping the floor. Beattie watched, petulantly dismissive and then cloaked in shame. 'Why are you being nice to me when I'm such a bitch?' she asked, her voice wobbling.

'I do it because I care,' Amy replied, the uncertainty in Beattie's question tugging at her heart. *How vulnerable she is*, thought Amy. *Beneath that rough exterior there's a woman crying out for help.* Amy knitted her brow, gathering words that didn't sound patronising or condemning. 'When we were young, I was the one that got all the favours and you got the brickbats. You fought back in the only way you knew how by being sullen and cheeky, and I don't blame you for that, but it didn't help matters.' Beattie's eyes flashed and she opened her mouth to intervene but Amy pressed on. 'I can't undo or excuse our mother's nastiness but you mustn't let it poison your life. Mother couldn't love you because she felt guilty at betraying my dad, but there are others who do. There's Bert, the kids, me and Jude;even Raffy in his funny old way. Let us make it up to you, Beattie. Just accept that you're not the worst in the world.'

By now, Beattie's cheeks were wet with silent tears. 'I bloody nearly am when I get going,' she croaked, essaying a quivering grin.

Amy grinned back. 'Oh, Beattie, what would I do without you? I'd have nobody to clean up after or give off to when I feel like it,' she chuckled.

'In that case I'll carry on being a useless sod,' Beattie responded, doing her utmost to sound perky. They both laughed at that. They were still laughing when Raffy came back with children. He smiled when he saw that amity had been restored. Amy was clever when it came to making people

182

see reason, he thought, giving her a conspiratorial wink. Amy gave an imperceptible nod as she smiled back.

'I'll do your hair for you tomorrow if you come down to mine,' Amy offered, thinking that if Beattie smartened herself up it would help lighten her spirits.

'Aye, go on then,' said Beattie. 'I'll want to look me best for Bert.'

Amy returned home feeling far happier than when she had set out for Beattie's.

★　★　★

That afternoon, as Amy walked up the lane to Intake Farm, the happy mood she had set out with dissipated. Low Fold was overrun with thistles and dock, and a fence blown down in recent high winds lay exactly as it had on her last visit. Peeling paint mottled the barn door and weeds sprouted in between the flags in the yard. *Dad would be heartbroken to see it like this*, she thought, bringing the pram to a halt outside the kitchen door. Visits to her mother were awkward these days, Bessie still hurt by Raffy's betrayal and angry with Amy and Jude for offering him a home.

'Hello, Mum.' Amy stepped inside, Kezia in her arms.

Bessie was plucking a duck. She stuffed a handful of feathers into a sack at her feet and then swished her hands under the tap. 'Hello, love,' she said wearily, coming forward to take Kezia from Amy's arms and then quickly following it with 'you're getting too big to lift, young lady,' as she set her granddaughter down. Kezia crawled over to the cat on the hearthrug.

'I'll put the kettle on,' Amy said, pained to see how tired her mother looked. The skin beneath her eyes was loose and drooping, her movements slow. 'We'll have a cup of tea then I'll finish plucking that duck.'

Bessie plodded to a chair by the hearth. 'How's Jude?' she asked, Amy fully aware she asked not out of concern but only because it was expected.

'He's coming home for the weekend this Friday. That's partly why I'm here. I want to make an early Christmas party so I wondered if I might have a chicken or a duck.' She handed Bessie a cup then sat down in the opposite chair.

'You might as well take that one,' said Bessie, gesturing to the carcass by the sink. She leaned her head back on the chair cushion and closed her eyes, showing little interest in her tea, Kezia or the party. Amy felt a stab of deep concern. Where was the bossy, bouncing woman who once seemed to rule the world?

'Are things still as bad between you and Sammy, Mum?'

'How's Raffy?'

The response to her question caught Amy by surprise. Since his ignominious ejection from Intake Farm, Amy had not heard Bessie once mention Raffy's name. Now, she saw the yearning in her mother's eyes.

'He's well enough,' she replied, pausing before saying, 'he misses you.'

A tremor ran through Bessie's ample frame. Tears welled in her eyes. 'I miss him,' she said

184

softly, 'and so does the farm.'

'So I noticed,' Amy said, thinking of the neglected fields and broken fences. 'Is Samuel still taking too much drink?'

Bessie nodded. 'They both are. Thomas has always followed our Sammy's example.' It was Amy's turn to nod, dispiritedly. She reached for her mother's hands, squeezing them between her own.

'Why don't you ask Raffy to come back?'

Bessie paled. 'Samuel would never allow it.'

'You're still mistress of Intake Farm, mother,' said Amy, her repugnance for her arrogant, bullying brother sharpening her words.

'I can't cross Samuel. He runs the farm.'

Amy snorted. 'You could have fooled me. The place is a disaster.'

Bessie's face crumpled further. 'It is. We've had to sell Top Fold to keep going. It'll be the cattle next. We only get by on what I make on the butter and the fowl.'

'Then get Raffy back before it's too late. Ask him when you're at the party.'

* * *

Amy whipped off her apron, did a little twirl and clapped her hands as she danced across the kitchen to lift Kezia. 'Daddy's coming home, Daddy's coming home,' she chanted, swinging the toddler in a merry little jig. Kezia giggled, her rosebud lips forming the word 'Dada' over and again. Amy glanced at the clock. 'Oops! Better get a move on,' she said, giving Kezia one last twirl. 'You play with your dolly whilst I get ready.'

185

Leaving her daughter on the hearthrug, Amy dashed over to the mirror above the sink. Peering into it, she saw a flushed, pretty face with sparkling blue eyes staring back at her. She giggled. *I look like a girl fresh from her first romantic meeting*, she thought, tucking stray blonde curls back into her chignon. Satisfied with her appearance, she went and stood in the centre of the room breathing in the savoury aroma of roast fowl that wafted from the fireside oven. Smoothing the skirts of her best blue crepe dress she mentally took stock: duck in the oven, apple tarts, sponge cake and buns in the cupboard and potted meat in the cold press. She had spent most of her separation allowance and used up her entire butter and sugar ration but it all seemed worthwhile if the party was to be a success. Amy glanced at the clock again, butterflies fluttering in her tummy and her heart beating that little bit faster. It was almost midday. Where was Jude?

The thud of footsteps out in the yard had her rushing to the door. 'How do, Amy.' Ernest Dixon clattered by in his pit clogs. Amy's spirits drooped. She went indoors, and down on her knees she played with Kezia and her dolls in the parlour. Maybe Jude wasn't coming after all.

'I think it's time for your nap, lady.' Amy settled her daughter on the couch. Two lullabies and Kezia slept. Amy watched the steady rise and fall of her little chest and listened to her whispering breaths, and then sensing that someone else was in the room she turned. And there he was, tall and proud in his navy blue uniform, brass buttons gleaming and his dark eyes alive with anticipation.

Amy's breath caught in her throat. She leapt up, throwing herself at his chest, clinging on, laughing and crying at the same time. Jude kissed her tenderly and then again slowly and sensuously until she was melting with desire.

Tearing his lips from hers Jude gasped, 'Kezia?' and went and stood by the couch gazing down at her. 'She's beautiful, and look how she's grown,' he said, his voice cracking and his rugged features softening, only to brighten mischievously as he added, 'but we'll let her sleep for now.' Lifting Amy into his arms, he carried her upstairs to bed.

★ ★ ★

Bouncing impatiently on the balls of her feet at the end of Grattan Row, Maggie Stitt let out a yell, and with Albert, Fred and Mary on her heels she ran to meet Bert. He saw them coming and dropped to his knees, his arms and his grin wide, the force of their hugs almost bowling him over. At last he struggled to his feet, children hanging from his limbs as he went into the house. Beattie came out of the kitchen smiling, the teapot in her hand.

'I thought you'd fancy a brew,' she said by way of welcome. Bert's heart soared. He'd been expecting a tongue-lashing.

'You look grand, lass,' he said softly, his pale grey eyes admiring Beattie's clean pink dress and freshly washed hair. That she'd smartened herself for his homecoming brought tears to his eyes. Accepting the tea, Bert gulped it then set the cup on the table. Grabbing Beattie about the waist, he plonked a wet kiss on her mouth.

'Gerroff, you daft beggar.' Beattie shoved him away but the push and the words were not unkind.

'Kiss her again, Dad,' shouted Albert.

'Kiss us all again,' Maggie cried, throwing her arms about her parents, hardly daring to believe that they weren't fighting like they usually did. She thought her mam looked very pretty and happy today. She wanted her to stay that way.

Bert and Beattie caught Maggie, then Albert, Fred and Mary in one big embrace. 'We've forgotten Henry,' yelled Maggie, yanking the toddler into the laughing huddle of bodies. Bert laughed loudest of all. His welcome home was like nothing he'd imagined.

★ ★ ★

'You overcooked that duck.' Bessie cast a critical eye over the spread on Amy's kitchen table. Resplendent in navy blue serge and a string of pearls, she was the first to arrive at the party.

Amy blushed. 'I got carried away doing something else,' she said, her body warm and languid from Jude's caresses and her lips still tingling from his kisses. Jude stepped forward. Like Amy he was wearing the clothes he'd had on before hastily scattering them on the bedroom floor.

'My, you look smart,' Bessie said, appraising him with none of her old dislike. Her secret out, she no longer feared him. In fact, she was glad the truth had been told.

Amy's spirits soared. It was going to be a good night.

188

The Stitts tumbled in, Bessie greeting Beattie and Bert with a tight smile. They responded likewise. Amy shooed the children into the parlour, telling them to play nicely. 'You're in charge, Maggie, and you boys, don't get too rough. All of you watch the little ones.'

Maggie drew herself up to full height, her copper curls bouncing as she said, 'I'll mind us, Auntie Amy,' and none of them ever having been to a party before, they promised to be on their best behaviour.

When Amy returned to the kitchen, she saw that Lily and Tommy Tinker had arrived along with Jude's colliery mates Seth and Harry, and their wives. There was no sign of Raffy, and Amy wondered if his absence was due to Bessie's presence.

The men opened bottles of beer. The women made do with tea, except Beattie, Bert having nipped to the pub for a half bottle of gin in honour of the occasion. Amy took lemonade and buns, slices of cake and jam sandwiches into the parlour for the children, leaving the adults to help themselves. Someone produced a pack of cards.

'Come on, Amy,' Beattie called out, 'let us women beat this lot at gin rummy.' She waved a handful of cards, her swarthy face flushed with excitement and gin.

Amy sat down at the table, pleased that the party was having the desired effect on her sister. The card game began, noise levels rising as the participants shouted the odds.

Bessie had declined to play, and when Amy looked over a short while later, she saw her deep in

189

conversation with Raffy. She hadn't even noticed his arrival. His mouth was set in a grim line. A knot of anxiety made her lose a trick, Beattie squawking at her to pay attention. Feeling flustered, Amy excused herself from the next hand and went out into the yard for air. A handful of stars glinted in a purple-black sky, a watery moon silvering the frost rimed walls and flagstones. It looked so peaceful it was hard to believe there was a war on, and Jude was going to fight it. Amy shivered, about to go back inside when Bessie and Raffy joined her.

'Thank you for a lovely evening.' Bessie placed a hand on Amy's arm. 'Me and Raffy are going back to Intake. We've an early start in the morning.'

Amy threw an arm about each of them, hugging them close. Before she let go, she whispered in Raffy's ear. 'Don't let our Sammy drive you away.' Raffy stepped back, giving her a sly wink and a grateful smile.

As Amy watched Raffy hand Bessie into the trap, she promised herself that the next time she was alone with her mother and Raffy she'd get to the bottom of their strange relationship.

After everyone had departed, Amy put a weary, over-excited Kezia to bed whilst Jude tidied the parlour and kitchen. 'Did I see your mother and Raffy leaving together?' he asked when Amy came downstairs.

Amy grinned. 'You did. He's going back to the farm.'

Jude caught her in an embrace. 'You're a miracle worker,' he exclaimed. 'You have the knack of making people happy. Raffy's back where he belongs, Beattie and Bert and the kids went off home looking like they belonged in *David Copperfield* and everyone here tonight had fun.' He paused to kiss the top of Amy's head. 'That's what I love about you. You see other people's miseries and their needs and you do something about it, not ostentatiously but subtly and with love.'

Amy blushed at his praise and was about to modestly protest, but he gave her no chance. Sweeping her off her feet, he headed for the stairs saying, 'And now I'm going to show you just how much I love you.'

★   ★   ★

Amy accepted Jude's return to camp stoically, the glorious weekend all too short for her liking. He was soon to be transferred to another camp, this one a much greater distance from Barnborough so rumour had it. With each move taking him further away, she would have to resign herself to communicating by letter and parcel.

'I'll write every week,' she said, clinging to him on the station, clouds of steam and slamming doors indicating the train was about to depart.

'Don't forget to send a book or two whenever you can afford it. It helps while away the hours off duty.' Jude lifted Kezia for one last kiss, and embracing Amy with his free arm the little family held onto one another for what might be the last time for a very long time.

★   ★   ★

Early the next day, Amy walked to Intake Farm, eager to find out if Raffy had met with a favourable reception from Samuel. She doubted it. A thick frost rimed the hedges and the rutted lane, Amy shivering as much from anxiety as the cold air. She heard the raised voices even before she opened the farmhouse door. Dismayed at having her doubts compounded, Amy lifted Kezia out of her pushchair and stepped inside.

Samuel was glaring at his mother, his drink-sodden face purple with rage. 'I told you to get rid of him,' he yelled, thumping the tabletop with such force that Kezia jumped and the cutlery on Raffy's plate rattled. Kezia hid behind Amy's legs. Raffy calmly continued severing fat from a slice of bacon as carefully as a surgeon removing damaged tissue.

'And I told you he's here to stay.' Unfazed, Bessie stood with her arms folded across her ample bosom, her implacable expression grim. 'This farm is mine, and I hold the purse strings,' she sniffed contemptuously, 'not that there's much in the purse these days, what with your idleness and all that carousing you do in the Bull and Ram.' She held out her hands, palms upward, her expression and tone softening. 'See sense, Sammy,' she pleaded.

'Mam's right, Sammy. You need help. Thomas isn't much use but Raffy is. You know that,' Amy insisted. 'By the way, where is Thomas?'

Bessie sighed. 'In bed, he's not well.' Raffy's snort was derisible.

'See,' said Amy, 'you need help, Sammy.'

Samuel barged to the door. 'Help from a bloody

gypsy,' he bawled. 'I'll see him dead before I take orders from him.' The windows shook as he slammed outside.

'What will you do?' Amy asked, looking anxiously from Bessie to Raffy.

'I'll do what needs to be done. He don't frighten me,' said Raffy.

Bessie's smile was watery and her voice wobbly as she said, 'I ruined that lad by giving into him at every turn but I'm not going to let him ruin Intake.'

'Neither you will, my love,' Raffy said softly.

'Tell me what's between you two,' Amy asked curiously. 'It's plain you love one another so how come you didn't stay together?'

With a warm and meaningful smile, Bessie gave Raffy the stage. He told his story honestly, shouldering all the blame for keeping them apart. 'I didn't know she was pregnant with Beattie. We were young an' I was trying to earn a living at the fair but I allus meant to come back for Bessie. When I did, she was married to Hadley so I went on me travels with a broken heart. I never stopped wanting her.'

Amy listened avidly, a lump in her throat.

When Bessie took up the story, Amy's heart ached for the panic-stricken, young girl her mother had been when she duped Hadley into marriage. She forgave Bessie's lies, for after all, her mother had been a good wife to Hadley. Amy wondered how she would cope if she had to carry a burdensome secret throughout her life with Jude. As for Bessie, she was glad to tell her daughter the truth.

'Guilt makes you do terrible things,' she said,

Amy understanding that she referred to the cruelty Beattie had suffered.

Amy left Intake Farm feeling much older and wiser.

19

Amy smiled as she handed the neatly wrapped parcel bearing Jude's regimental address to the clerk behind the Post Office counter. Still smiling, she stepped outside thinking of the pleasure Jude would derive from the long, newsy letter, Kezia's homemade Christmas card and her own Christmas gift to him: Saki's short stories and H.G. Well's *Around the World in Eighty Days*.

In Jude's last letter he'd written, '*Most of the lads read only magazines or nothing at all, so when 2nd/ Lieut. Milford saw the books I'd taken with me he suggested we keep one another supplied; it's a good deal. Him being an upper-class toff, he receives some smashing books.*' When Amy read this, she hoped 2nd/Lieut. Milford had not read the ones she had just posted — to where, she didn't know, Jude not allowed to divulge his whereabouts for security reasons. He'd also told her he now had a rifle and was a good shot, unlike Bert. She had laughed when she read, '*Bert fired five rounds at the target; only one hit it. When the instructor bawled "where are the others, you useless bugger?" Bert told him they had all gone through the same hole. Bert's a crafty bugger but he's not cut out for soldiering.*'

Pleased that her package was winging its way to Jude, Amy stopped off at Beattie's. 'Mam's invited me and you and the children to have Christmas dinner at the farm,' she said cautiously, unsure of Beattie's reaction.

Beattie's jaw dropped, surprise then contempt masking her features. 'Bit bloody late in the day,' she said. 'Our Maggie's nine an' she hardly knows her. She's seen our Henry just once.'

Although Amy understood Beattie's annoyance, she desperately wanted to heal the rift between Beattie and Bessie so she said, 'Mam regrets the way she treated you but she had her reasons.'

Beattie sniggered. 'Reasons be buggered. She's a lying, vindictive cow who couldn't admit she'd had it off wi' a gypsy. An' look at her now, all cosied up to him an' pretending it never mattered.'

'That's because it did matter, Beattie; it mattered very much. She loved Raffy — still does — but he left her pregnant and she panicked. Think what you'd have done if Bert hadn't married you.' Beattie's lips wobbled and Amy, seeing she had struck a nerve, said 'sit down and let me tell you how it was.'

Amy made a pot of tea then told Beattie all that Raffy and Bessie had told her.

When she had finished, Beattie said, 'Poor bugger, living wi' all that guilt. She never looked as though she were suffering.' Her lip curled and she growled, 'But by bloody hell, she made up for it by making me suffer.'

'She was wrong; she knows that now. If you can find it in your heart to forgive her, I think you'll feel better about yourself, Beattie. You were never to blame, you've nothing to be sorry for, so don't let it ruin your life.'

Beattie shrugged. 'I suppose I can try.' She grinned wryly. 'An' if it all comes to nowt, at least she might give me a few bob an' the kids'll get a

196

decent Christmas dinner.'

Amy gave a lopsided grin. Trust Beattie to think of it that way, but at least it was a start. On the way home, she dwelt on the tangled web that was her family. Was it destiny that had led Bessie to the fair, and for Raffy to father both Beatrice and Jude, and she herself to fall in love with the motherless boy her own mother had hidden away in Bird's Well? Amy didn't know, and she decided she didn't care. She had a loving husband whom she adored and a daughter who was the love of her life. Bessie and Raffy were reunited. Her dad, Hadley, had gone to his rest never knowing he'd been cuckolded, and Beattie might yet be saved.

★　★　★

Kezia Leas and the Stitt brood sat round the Christmas tree playing with the gifts Bessie had bought them: dolls for Maggie, Mary and Kezia, trucks for Albert and Fred, and a spinning top for Henry. The tree had been Raffy's idea, and Amy had decorated it the day before. In this festive atmosphere the adults sat convivially, everyone replete after a splendid Christmas dinner and Samuel and Thomas mollified with strong drink.

'Have you seen how fat our Thomas has got?' Beattie whispered. Amy nodded, Beattie adding, 'He looks fit to burst.'

Amy glanced at her youngest brother and frowned. He glugged on a tankard of ale, his huge, flabby face resembling a blood moon and the rolls of fat beneath his chin a plough horse's collar. When he set the tankard down, he had to stretch his arm to reach the table, his enormous belly denying him closer access. Amy hoped the children wouldn't remark on it.

After a while, Samuel and Thomas lurched off to find more drink. The minute they were out of earshot, Maggie piped, 'You know that one you said we'd to call Uncle Thomas, well, I think he must be the fattest man in the whole wide world.'

'Shush, don't be rude.' Beattie glanced nervously in Bessie's direction. To her surprise, Bessie laughed. So did everyone else.

⋆ ⋆ ⋆

'That wasn't too bad, was it?' Amy said, as they made their way home, Raffy driving the trap and the sleepy children lolling on their mother's knees.

'It were grand,' Beattie replied, 'but I'm still not sure how to take her. She can be sweetness and light one minute and the next she's a bloody harridan.'

Amy didn't argue. Hopeful that the bridges built that day would not collapse, she contented herself by mentally composing her next letter to Jude and puzzling over how she might acquire more books to send without having to buy them from a bookshop. Perhaps she should approach Dr Hargreaves or Mr Lionel Grey, the retired schoolmaster, gentlemen like them were sure to have books they had read and no longer wanted. Back in her own house, with Maggie who was staying overnight and Kezia in bed, Amy sat down to write to Jude. Close to midnight, she doused the lamps and climbed the stairs to bed. She fell into a deeply satisfying sleep.

A furious knocking on the street door wakened her. Who could it be at this time? It was barely daylight. Pulling on a robe she dashed downstairs. When she opened the door Raffy almost fell inside.

'You'm better come quick,' he gasped. 'It's Thomas! The doctor be going ahead o' me but I be thinkin' there's little he can do for him.'

Oh my God, thought Amy, *what now? After we had such a lovely day.* Out loud she cried, 'What happened to him?' She grabbed her coat from where she had left it on the chair the night before and dashed to the foot of the stairs. 'Maggie, are you awake?'

No reply, Amy hared upstairs to the small bedroom. Awake now, Maggie sat up in the bed, her copper curls tossed and her eyes fearful. 'What is it, Auntie Amy?'

'It's Uncle Thomas. He's been taken bad.'

'Did he burst?'

Amy's stern expression let her know this was no time for jokes. Maggie listened carefully to her aunt's instructions.

'You mind Kezia, and when you get up, go home and take her with you. I'm going back to Intake with Granda Raffy. Tell your mam the doctor's been called. Tell her Thomas is very sick.' Or worse, she thought, recalling Raffy's words.

Her voice wobbling fearfully, Maggie said, 'I'll do that, Auntie Amy.' She bit her lip. 'Sorry for what I said about Uncle Thomas.'

'It's all right,' said Amy, fondling Maggie's tatty head and hoping it was. 'You're a good girl, Maggie, and so is Kezia.' Curled up against her cousin's back Kezia slept soundly, her dreams undisturbed.

Outside, a light covering of snow fallen during the night muffled the swishing of the trap's wheels and the thud of hooves as Raffy urged the little pony into a canter. Huddled beside Raffy, Amy tracked the lingering stars in the murky dawn light as he recounted what had happened.

'They two boyos were still carousing when me an' Bessie went to our beds. The next thing I hears is a mighty crash, and Samuel roaring like a bull. I goes down to find the big fellow lying on the floor, a chair in bits against the stove. I be thinking they'd been fighting but Samuel said no, and when I took a look at Thomas, I'd say he were dead afore he hit the ground.'

Stunned into silence, Amy pictured a young Thomas. His sweet, vacuous smile and innocent blue eyes that always seemed to be trying to make sense of what went on round him. When she spoke it was merely a whisper. 'Dead? Are you sure?'

'Sure as sure, but Bessie wouldn't have it. Screamed for me to get the doctor, so I did.'

They heard Bessie wails before they stepped inside. Thomas lay where he had fallen. Dr Hargreaves was assuring Bessie he hadn't suffered any pain, and when he saw Amy and Raffy he turned to include them. 'A massive heart attack. He wouldn't have felt a thing. He was dead before he hit the floor.'

Raffy gave Amy a 'I told you so' look. Amy went and knelt beside Thomas gazing sorrowfully at his monstrous bulk; Maggie's jest had proved true. Gently, she stroked pale strands of hair from his

200

forehead. Purple patches mottled his flabby face. Other than that, he looked quite peaceful, the corners of his mouth quirked as if he had been caught by surprise. His eyelids were closed but Amy imagined his bulbous, blue eyes struggling to make sense of wherever it was he had gone, and his lips curving in a slow, simple smile when he thought he understood. Her tears wetting his cheeks she bent to kiss him and then, her legs wobbling, she went to embrace her mother.

Samuel sat at the table, his head in his hands. His shoulders heaved as guttural sobs escaped his chest. Amy had never seen him so desolate. Long after the undertaker had been and Bessie gone to her bed, Samuel sat on. Not a word passed his lips, and when Raffy announced he was going to bring the cows down for milking, Samuel followed him.

Later, after calling at Beattie's to collect Kezia and tell her sister the news, Amy sat in her own home hugging the fire, the chill in her bones too deep to ignore. Was Thomas's death the culmination of the bad omen she had foreseen on her wedding day? Had fate played its hand in the all-too-soon pregnancy that prevented Jude from taking his college course, and this terrible war that had stolen him from her? Her friend, Freda, often said that trouble strikes in threes. Was the awful, unnecessary loss of her youngest brother the last part of the trilogy, or was there worse to come? Amy just didn't know. On that sad note she turned out the lights and went up to bed.

★ ★ ★

Thomas's funeral was all the more poignant for being in the festive season, the rest of the world still celebrating Christmas and waiting for the New Year that would, so they were led to believe, see an end to the war. Bessie was distraught, her skin grey and her blue eyes like Thomas's as she struggled to make sense of his death. Supported between Samuel and Amy, she seemed incapable of putting one foot in front of the other.

Afterwards, back at the farm, Amy couldn't help noticing how close Samuel and Freda appeared to be. Yet again, she was puzzled as to why her friend was attracted to Samuel. Freda's pale face oozed compassion as she held Samuel's meaty paws in a comforting way. He leaned in, his head almost resting on her bosom as he quietly poured his heart out. As Amy watched them, it occurred to her that Samuel must have loved Thomas deeply. The thought took her by surprise, and she felt guilty at not realising it before now. Silently, she acknowledged that Thomas's death had changed Samuel, and that she found the now shrunken, morose Sammy far more tolerable than the bombastic bullyboy she had so disliked.

20

Barnborough: autumn 1915

Maggie Stitt put down the book she was reading and attended to Kezia's demands. 'Lid, Maggie, find lid,' she chanted, holding up a miniature tea-pot.

Maggie scanned the toys scattered on the rug. Spying the tiny porcelain lid in amongst a clutter of doll's clothes she handed it to her cousin then eagerly returned to *Anne of Green Gables*. The opportunity to read wonderful books in the haven that was Auntie Amy's house was one she never had in her own chaotic home. Therefore, Maggie sought sanctuary whenever possible.

Amy joined the girls in the parlour. Perched on the couch next to Maggie, she divided her attention between the two girls.

'Can I have a cup of tea, please?'

Kezia solemnly poured non-existent tea into a tiny porcelain cup. 'Maggie find lid for me,' she lisped.

Amy smiled at Maggie. 'How's Anne getting on?'

'She's just fallen out with Gilbert because he called her 'carrots',' Maggie replied, her freckled nose just visible over the top of the book. She flicked at her copper mane. 'I hate it when the boys at school call me that.'

'Take no notice, your hair's beautiful,' said Amy,

patting Maggie's head and thinking that lovely as Maggie's hair was, it could do with washing. She sighed inwardly. Beattie was letting things slide again — her own appearance unkempt, the children neglected and the house filthy.

No wonder Maggie prefers to be here, Amy thought, half-wishing Maggie lived with her. She was a bright, big-hearted girl, wise for her ten years. Amy enjoyed introducing her to good literature then answering the intelligent questions she posed. As for Kezia, she was like a bottomless bucket ready to be filled with stories, rhymes and pretend games. Spending time with both girls gave Amy immense pleasure and helped ease the loneliness in Jude's absence.

'Is there any cake to go with this tea, Kezia?' Her daughter proudly handed Amy a brightly coloured Plasticine confection. Amy pretended to munch.

'When you've finished with Anne, I think we'll try Oliver Twist; you'll love him Maggie,' said Amy, lifting Kezia into her lap. 'As for you, young lady, it's bedtime, so choose a story and then it's up the wooden hill you go.'

When Kezia was sleeping, Amy went downstairs and said, 'It's time you went home, Maggie.' She hated having to say it, but Beattie objected to Maggie spending time at Amy's, and she didn't want to burden her niece with yet more unpleasantness; Maggie suffered enough of that already. To Amy's sorrow, Beattie's attitude to Maggie was a replication of Bessie's to Beattie, poor Maggie left too often to care for her siblings and do household chores instead of enjoying the freedom

204

a child should expect.

Reluctantly, Maggie put the book back on the shelf — she wouldn't take it home for fear her brothers might tear it to shreds. 'Thanks, Auntie Amy,' she said, pulling on her coat and then hugging Amy and adding, 'I love you. Night-night.' She slouched out, a sorry figure in a coat far too small for her and shoes broken down at the heel. From the doorway Amy watched her go, an immense sadness coupled with anger at Beattie's fecklessness burning in her chest.

Dusk had fallen, the autumnal evening air fragrant with the sweet, musty smell of fallen leaves. It was warm for October, the sort of evening Amy and Jude would have put Kezia in her pram and walked along the riverbank beside the church.

Yearningly, Amy recalled the walks she had taken with Jude when first they met. How long would it be before they walked together again, she wondered?

It seemed a lifetime since she'd last seen him, and whilst his letters brought him close, it wasn't close enough. Pieces of paper covered in loving words were a poor replacement for warm lips, gentle hands and lively conversation. That he was still in England was some consolation, but for how much longer? She tried to put France out of mind but it kept sidling back, unbidden. Already the local newspaper's obituary column carried the names of husbands and sons of families she knew. Only last week her neighbour, Betty Briggs, had lost her husband, Amy paying her condolences and wondering how long it might be before Betty reciprocated. The thought had made her blood run cold.

The balmy air making her feel restless, and her annoyance at Beattie niggling, Amy couldn't settle. Beattie was out of control. Amy had heard the rumours that a young collier called Larry Hamby had been seen making late-night visits to Beattie's. Maggie had denied it, her eyes unable to meet Amy's and her words no more than a whisper. Amy suspecting that she had been threatened into not mentioning it now wondered if, later, she should slip up to Beattie's and find out for herself but, with Kezia in bed, she dismissed the idea and went inside to write to Jude. It always made her feel better.

★　★　★

The next night, as Amy sat by the fire knitting a pair of thick woollen socks for Jude, Beattie dropped in. 'I just thought I'd pop down and keep you company for a bit,' she said, her fawning tone making Amy suspicious of her real reason for calling. She never called unless it was to borrow something.

'That's kind of you.' Amy put aside her knitting and then set the kettle to boil.

'Don't bother making tea for me,' Beattie said, 'I'm not stopping that long.'

Amy sat back down and picked up her knitting. Beattie fidgeted restlessly and attempted to make small talk. When Amy could bear it no longer, she said, 'What did you really come for, Beattie?'

'Can you lend us half-a-crown?'

'That's the second time this week.'

'I'll pay you back when I get me separation money.'

'No you won't because I'm not lending it. You want it to buy drink, don't you?' Amy sounded disappointed rather than accusing.

'It's none of your bloody business what I want it for,' bawled Beattie, jumping up ready to leave. Amy also stood, her face creased with concern. She put out a staying hand but Beattie shook it off, crying, 'And don't go giving me that holier than thou look. I'll do as I please.' She made for the door.

'And does doing as you please involve Larry Hamby?' Amy spoke calmly but deep inside she burned with frustration and disgust.

Beattie's step faltered. She swung round and glared at Amy. 'And what if it does?' she sneered. 'Aren't I entitled to a bit of pleasure?'

'Pleasure! You should be ashamed of yourself,' cried Amy. And before she could contain herself, her hurt and annoyance spilled over like boiling porridge. 'You have the morals of an alley cat, you neglect your children, and your house is muckier than the pit bottom. If you had one ounce of decency, you'd stop feeling sorry for yourself and think about your children and Bert.'

For an instant Beattie looked shocked. Then giving a careless shrug she said, 'So you're not going to lend me owt then? I suppose you don't care if my kids go without bread and milk for their breakfast.'

Amy reached for her purse on the mantelpiece. She tossed a florin into the air.

Beattie lunged and caught it. 'Thanks,' she said,

and without a backward glance she left. Feeling utterly defeated, Amy stared at the closed door.

★   ★   ★

The next morning Amy called with Lionel Grey, as much to take her mind off Beattie and the previous evening's unpleasantness as to beg for books to send to Jude. Burnished copper and golden leaves rustled underfoot and twirled upwards as she and Kezia walked along the country lane leading to the retired headmaster's house.

Lionel was in the garden, deadheading late roses and dahlias. He greeted her request with interest. After a pleasant walk round the beautiful garden, Amy admiring his herb parterre and Kezia fascinated by the fishpond, he took them into his study. The delightful interlude restored Amy's spirits, and she came away with her faith in human nature and the beauty of God's world renewed. Later that day she posted two volumes of the popular Sexton Blake detective stories along with the letter she had finished writing after Beattie's visit. She'd keep the other three books to send later.

Back in the house, she debated whether or not to visit Beattie, try to reason with her and heal the rift. The more she thought about it, the less inclined she felt. She'd leave time for Beattie to cool down, and to get her own opinions under control. Flying off the handle like she had done last night served no purpose.

Her mind made up to stay indoors, Amy lit the parlour fire, a little luxury during the week. She sat with Kezia on the couch, a large bright picture book between them, Amy linking the characters to the illustrations as she told the story. The kitchen door scraped open. Amy waited for one of Beattie's children to call out, for that's whom she expected. When she heard nothing but a dull thud she got to her feet, her curiosity aroused.

'I thought I'd surprise you,' Jude said, a warm smile on his face and a huge kitbag at his feet. Amy flew into his arms, words tumbling from her lips and Jude doing his best to still them with kisses as, in between, he told her he had seven days' leave.

Seven days! Amy was overjoyed. However, when he told her his battalion's next move would take him to France, she was gripped by an ugly sinking feeling that turned her insides to water. Valiantly, she hid her fears from him. She wasn't going to let anything spoil the pleasure of having him home again.

'We've finished training,' Jude said, as he sat down to eat, Amy glad that she had made a meat and potato pie that morning. 'I've learned how to fire a Lewis gun and what to do with a Mills bomb, but I spend most of my time digging.' He grinned ruefully. 'I can't get away from it. They're using us colliers to show the other lads how to work below ground. That's what I'll be doing in France: digging trenches.'

'What's a Mills bomb?' Amy asked anxiously. To her mind any kind of bomb was highly dangerous.

'Do you remember the picture of a pineapple in one of Kezia's books? These things look like them only they're smaller and made of metal. You pull out a pin, count to seven then throw it as far as you can before it explodes. Hold it too long and it'll blow you to bits. That happened to a chap in our battalion last month.'

Amy shuddered, and decided to ask no more questions about weapons and warfare.

★　★　★

Those next few autumn days were spent roaming the woods on fine days, collecting conkers for Jude to polish then thread on long strings for Kezia to play with. Amy gathered leaves to press and mount, making a collage to hang on the parlour wall as a reminder of what, she secretly and painfully thought, might be the last autumn they spent together. When it rained, they hugged the parlour fire, playing with Kezia or reading and exchanging ideas, a thing they both missed dreadfully in their time apart.

On the day they visited Intake Farm, Freda was helping Bessie pluck hens for market. Although Amy had known Freda was keeping company with Samuel, she was surprised to see her performing such a menial task.

'I usually help Mother Elliot on my day off from the library,' Freda said smugly.

Amy gave Bessie an enquiring look, wondering why her mother had chosen not to mention it. Bessie gave Amy a sly wink then told Freda to call Samuel in for tea.

'She's only helped me once before,' Bessie said, as soon as Freda was out of earshot. She sounded exasperated and her face clouded as she added, 'She has her heart set on our Samuel and he doesn't seem to mind, but it's her that does all the running.'

'She always had a fancy for him, and it 'ud do our Sammy good to get married.'

Bessie pursed her lips and folded her arms across her bosom. 'Just as long as she remembers whose kitchen this is. I'm still mistress of Intake.' Her matriarchal stance and no-nonsense tone made Amy smile.

Samuel and Freda came in and they all sat down at the table. As they ate, Amy took stock of her family, Jude and Raffy talking about the rabbits that had overrun Jude's last camp in Rugely, and Bessie and Freda vying for Samuel's attention. Amy gazed at her elder brother thoughtfully. It was hard to believe that this rather morose, but almost pleasant, man was the same arrogant bully who had once made her life a misery. *Thomas's death hit him hard*, she thought, *but Freda seems good for him*. She watched Bessie plying him with another piece of cake. *Mother's afraid of losing him to another woman, and Freda will have her work cut out if she hopes to untie the apron strings.*

On their way home, Amy and Jude called with Bert and Beattie. Bert was sitting by the fire staring disconsolately into the flames, a bottle of beer in his hand and Henry on his knee. He glanced up when Jude said, 'I see you're enjoying your last night of freedom?'

Bert's expression conveyed anything but. He gestured with his thumb towards the kitchen. 'Call this freedom. She's making my life a misery.'

'Don't be sad, Dad.' Maggie stroked Bert's sparse hair. She was hanging over the back of his chair and Mary, Albert and Fred were lolling against his legs, all of them conscious their dad was about to leave them again.

Amy walked into the kitchen, Beattie catching her by the elbow and pulling her into a corner away from the door. 'Don't you be saying owt about Larry Hamby to him,' she hissed.

'I wouldn't dream of it,' Amy hissed back, 'although he's most likely heard about it in the pub.' She sighed heavily. 'Poor Bert, he's going to France and goodness knows when he'll be back. Try being kind to him for once.'

Amy marched back into the living room to sit with Jude and Bert. Beattie stayed in the kitchen. Chatting about nothing in particular, both Amy and Jude attempted to lighten the mood, without success.

'I'll call for you tomorrow, mate,' Jude said to Bert as they were leaving.

Bert nodded wearily.

Jude put Kezia into her pushchair. On the way back to Wentworth Street, he said, 'You do realise that with me in France it could be ages before I get the chance to come home again.'

Amy nodded sadly and squeezed the arm through which her own was linked that little bit tighter. Blinking back tears, she gazed up to where a few stars had begun to speckle the violet sky, and afraid to speak she wished on every one of them: let him come back safe.

Almost as though he had read her thoughts, Jude said, 'If by chance I don't survive, promise

212

me you'll not stay lonely. Look after Kezia and find yourself a decent chap to be a dad to her and a husband to you.' His tone matter-of-fact, he tried to lighten the mood, chuckling wryly as he added, 'You're a beautiful young woman, Amy, and you'll not have any bother finding someone, so don't spend the rest of your life grieving.'

Knowing how much it must have pained him to say these words, Amy stopped walking. The arm linked through his holding him back, Jude brought the pushchair to a halt. They turned to face one another, sad blue eyes meeting eyes darker than the night as Amy said, 'I could never make such a promise, Jude.'

★   ★   ★

That night, Jude made love to Amy with all the passion and tenderness he could muster, and Amy responded as eagerly as when they were first wed. Afterwards, their bodies still entwined and Jude sleeping, she thought how strange it was that parting should bring out the best in each of them. She gazed at the handsome face on the pillow next to hers, long, dark lashes hiding eyes as black as coal and firm lips inviting a kiss. She brushed them with her own as Jude woke to make love to Amy for what, he thought, might be the last time ever.

In the morning, after breakfast, Amy bundled Kezia into her pushchair whilst Jude packed his bag: clothing, soap and razor, the Bible he'd been given when he was sworn in and a photograph taken in a studio on the day they'd christened Kezia. Packing done, Jude lifted Kezia, hugging her to his chest. It beggared belief to think that there had been a time when he had resented this little girl, he thought, fondling the tiny skull so fragile beneath Kezia's silky hair it almost made no impression on his fingertips. An unfamiliar sweetness clogged his throat. He'd make sure he came back in one piece, for her sake, he vowed as he set her down.

Amy watched with tears in her eyes then flung herself against Jude's chest, feeling his heart beat in tandem with her own. Jude's lips met Amy's, and joined as one they fondled as if to stamp the memory of taste and touch on their minds. When they drew apart, Amy smiled brightly, her face set for the street. There would be no outward display of emotions that might embarrass him, she told herself. She would see him off proudly as he would want her to do.

A few neighbours came out to bid Jude farewell. No doubt they had been watching behind curtains until the door to number 2 opened. Jude accepted their good wishes with courtesy, Amy grateful for the respect they showed. As they approached the Stitts' house Bert stumbled out through the door, closely followed by his kitbag. Beattie stood in the doorway yelling, 'Go on, bugger off and don't bother to come back.' She folded her arms, sneering as Bert stooped to retrieve his kitbag.

Maggie pushed past her mother's hip, trailing Mary by the hand. Albert and Fred tumbled out behind, all of them aware that their last defence against Beattie's flailing hands was going off again and leaving them to their fate. 'Don't go, Dad, don't go,' they howled in chorus. Maggie let go of Mary and flung her arms round Bert's neck. The boys yanked at his trouser legs almost pulling him to the ground. Mary stuck her thumb in her mouth and wet her knickers.

Bert hunkered down, arms stretched to embrace his children. Amy blinked back tears. Lackadaisical he might be, she thought, but there was no denying Bert loved his children and they loved him. He would miss them, she knew, but they would miss him all the more. Snotty kisses accepted and delivered, Bert struggled upright, children hanging off him like windblown rags on a bush.

Jude and Amy stepped forward in tandem to stand either side of Bert. 'I'm not sure I can go through wi' this,' he said, his voice ragged. 'What's going to become of these bairns whilst she's playing away?' Bert's head drooped.

Amy felt his pain. 'I'll be here, Bert. I promise you they'll come to no harm.' She laid a comforting hand on the back of his neck, stroking gently. Jude patted Bert's back, assuring him that Amy would be true to her word. Beattie slouched in the doorway, a sullen expression coarsening her features.

'It's too late to back out now,' Jude said softly. Bert shuddered, guttural sobs leaping from his throat.

'Dry your eyes, Bert.' Amy handed him a handkerchief. 'Don't let the kids remember you like this. Give them a smile before you go.'

Bert rubbed his face, shoved the hanky into his pocket and squared his shoulders. Stretching his lips in a travesty of a smile then widening his eyes, he danced a little jig. The children laughed. So did Bert.

'Hey up,' he cried, 'we can't have this. Me cryin' like a bairn an' you upset. I'll be back afore you know it an' when I am, you'll think I'm Father Christmas. I'll bring French dolls wi' velvet dresses an' lace knickers for you lasses an' two big guns for you lads.' He bent down. 'Now, t'sooner I get off, sooner I'll be back so give us a kiss an' I'll be on me way.'

The children hurled themselves into his arms. More snotty kisses exchanged, and Bert stood tall and straight. 'I'll be off then, Beattie,' he said, stepping towards her, but before he reached the doorway Beattie went inside, slamming the door in his face. Bert covered his embarrassment with a foolish grin, but Amy saw the hurt in his eyes. She ran and linked Bert's arm, squeezing it encouragingly.

'Come on, kids,' she cried cheerily, 'let's give your dad and Uncle Jude a rousing send-off.'

At the station they met Raffy. 'You've come to see us off then,' said Jude, his tone indicating surprise.

Raffy tossed his head. 'You didn't think I'd be letting you go without saying goodbye did you, boyo,' his tone suggesting he was hurt by Jude's lack of faith.

Jude slapped him on the shoulder, and leaving his hand there, he walked along the platform with his father. Although Amy felt as though her heart was breaking, she smiled fondly as she followed behind with Kezia.

The station was crowded with mums and dads,

sweethearts and wives and jostling children waiting to say goodbye to a loved one. When the train arrived, it was already filled with enlisted men from further down the line. They gazed forlornly out of the windows. They had made their goodbyes.

Jude took Raffy's hand. 'Watch over Amy and Kezia, old man. I'm leaving them in your care.' He paused and grinned. 'And keep a close eye on our Beattie. I'll hold you responsible if anything goes wrong.'

Raffy's eyes flashed at the challenge. 'You can rely on me, boyo, never you fear.'

Bert was down on his knees kissing dirty little faces and patting heads.

Jude lifted Kezia then pulled Amy close. First he kissed Kezia then Amy. 'Look after each other. I love you,' he said.

'Be safe,' Amy whispered back against his cheek, the words sticking in her throat. She gulped unshed tears and said, 'We'll think about you every minute of the day. We love you.'

The train belched steam. The whistle blew. Jude and Bert boarded, hanging out of a window and waving wildly as the train snaked out of sight.

21

Jude stood in line on the quay at Devonport docks warily eyeing the ship that would take him to France. Like his companions, many of whom had never seen a ship of this size let alone boarded one, he had never even sailed a rowing boat across the pond in Barnborough Park. At a signal the line shuffled forward, the men grumbling and cursing and not a few of them afraid for their lives as they boarded the vessel for the first time.

For the next three days, Jude found himself tramping up and down gangplanks, descending ladders into the hold or scurrying for and aft as crates and cartons were loaded and military equipment was dragged aboard. On the morning of the fourth day they set sail and as the coastline slipped away, even the toughest of men had tears in their eyes. Waving their helmets aloft to a small crowd assembled on the harbour they gazed on — what for some would be the last time — the shores of England. Exhilarated by the newness of his surroundings, yet fearful of what lay ahead, Jude scanned the coastline with misted eyes and when a voice started to sing 'Homeland' he joined in lustily. As the voices rang out across the water the feeling of companionship that swelled his heart was to stay with him and spur him on in the darkest hours.

From the moment the *Megantic* steamed out into the English Channel Jude realised he was a landlubber. As the vessel rolled and pitched in heavy seas the pit of his stomach came up into his throat and he was violently seasick. However, he discovered that if he lay prone on the deck the nausea eased and as they approached the coast of France, Jude lay gazing up at the racing clouds.

'Come on, mate, gerrup on thi feet,' Bert urged, 'we're bahn to land.' Surprisingly, he had endured the journey without a qualm and had passed the time below decks playing cards, and losing. Groggily, Jude got to his feet and made his way to the side of the ship. So this was France. Beyond the harbour a domed building dominated the view and beyond that a high hill, on top of which stood a church with a tall spire.

The port of Marseilles bustled with confusion as the accumulated possessions of the entire 13th Battalion, Yorkshire and Lancashire Regiment, along with those of companies from the 14th Battalion, were discharged onto the quayside by a horde of French dockhands. Crowds of French men, women and children thronged in and out of the mountains of crates, boxes and military equipment, cheering every now and then in their excitement.

About an hour later, the troops disembarked, Jude glad to feel solid ground beneath his feet. They formed marching lines, Bert and Jude waiting patiently for the order to move on. Lost in thought, Jude was taken by surprise when an elderly woman rushed up to him and clasped his hand. She delivered a toothless smile and a torrent of words before hurrying further down the line to repeat her actions. 'Well, Bert, somebody seems pleased to see us,' Jude chuckled.

Bert laughed. 'Pity she's ninety if she's a day,' he said. 'I think I'd rather be welcomed by the likes of that one over there.' He pointed to a young woman with long, red hair and voluptuous figure. She turned and swayed away in the opposite direction, hips jiggling under a tight, blue satin skirt.

'Aye, right enough, I see what you mean but it looks as though you're out of luck.'

'I could murder a pint,' Bert said.

Jude's stomach flipped. 'I don't think I could keep one down.'

As they bemoaned their lot, the call to move out rang down the line and the troops reluctantly shuffled to attention. Whilst they were glad to feel dry land beneath their feet after the constant pitching and tossing at sea, they were less enthusiastic about the march that lay ahead.

A short while later they arrived at the railway station and were bundled into a row of covered wagons built of wooden slats. As Jude waited his turn to board, he wondered what the words and numbers painted on the side of each wagon meant, and regretted not knowing one word of French. He read out loud: 'Hommes, 32/40, Chevaux, (en long) 8'.'

'What does it mean?'

'I haven't a bloody clue, Bert, but they look like cattle trucks to me — there's no seats in 'em.' Jude surmised correctly, the mixture of straw and horse droppings on the floor of the wagon leaving them in no doubt.

The wagons got underway, the soldiers settling

down on the straw with their backs against the wagon sides or against one another. Some played cards whilst others intermittently dozed. Jude gazed out over the patchwork fields, and wishing he was walking them. 'Stop wriggling about,' he said to Bert, who was propped against his right shoulder.

'I can't stop scratching.' Bert simultaneously delved one hand under his armpit and the other down the back of his neck.

'Me neither, it's this bloody straw; it's crawling wi' insects.' Billy Cooper turned over a handful. Small, black lice scurried in all directions.

'I'm being eaten alive,' moaned a big, fat sweaty lad, scratching furiously. 'The buggers have gotten inside me trousers.'

Before long Jude, along with every man on board was itching, scratching and cursing as, for the next fifty hours, the wagons lurched and swayed along the track. Stopping and starting, speeding up and then slowing down, the train trundled its way through Provence and from there it clanked and rattled its way up the Rhone Valley. At Orange it came to a halt, the thirsty men cheering as Red Cross nurses filled their tin mugs with tea before they continued their journey through the French countryside to Lyon, Dijon and Paris. Finally, it pulled into the station at Pont Remy, a few miles southeast of Abbeville.

Utterly weary, bones cramped, skin bitten and scratched raw, the battalion climbed down from the wagons and once again began the tedious task of unloading their equipment. Then under the weight of large field packs, shouldered high

221

up on their backs they marched the six miles to Doudelainville. The pretty, rustic countryside and the warm welcome they received in the billets in Doudelainville did much to brighten their spirits, as did the return to soldierly duties: rifle drill, route marching and the cleaning of kit. But each passing day was taking them a little nearer to the ultimate goal: the front line.

Jude set aside the rifle he was cleaning and lit a cigarette, pensively drawing the smoke into his lungs and then letting it out slowly. Bert lolled at his feet. Jude gazed down at the sloppiest soldier in the Battalion according to the RSM, his feelings a mixture of overwhelming fondness and fear. 'We're getting close to the real thing now, Bert. It'll not be like training so you make sure to do as you're ordered. Don't go playing silly buggers. I want us both to get back home in one piece,' he said.

Bert, recognising the sincerity of the sentiment didn't, for once, crack a joke. Instead, he replied, 'I know what you mean, Juddy, I'll be careful. I don't want to get killed so — ' he brightened visibly '— I'll stick wi' thee. Me an' you make a good team.'

★　★　★

Rumours that the war was almost won filtered down to Doudelainville and Jude jokingly suggested that they might all be home in time for 'Barnborough Feast,' an annual holiday traditionally held the last week in August. His suggestion was met with ribald comments and serious doubts from the more pessimistic.

'They told us it'd all be over by Christmas,' Bert reminded Jude, 'an' that were in 1914. I'll not believe it's over until I'm standing in t'Miners Arms wi' a pint in me fist.'

Heavy rain and freezing temperatures made the troops even more discontented for by now they were weary of waiting to see some action. A gruelling march to Mailly Maillet helped satisfy the urge to be in the thick of battle. For the first time since leaving Barnborough the Battalion were within firing distance. Along the way they had billeted in abandoned houses and barns, in villages that were battered and broken, but each step of the way reinforced Jude's reason for having enlisted in the first place. This was why he'd left the coalface, Amy, Kezia, and all he knew.

* * *

Amy watched the rain lashing against the kitchen window. It was mid-June and the summer of 1916 was turning out to be particularly wet, cold and miserable, though not as miserable for them as it was for Jude, she thought, recalling his last letter. In it he had complained about the tiring route marches and being soaked to the skin in torrential rain. He had also described the pretty villages and towns they had marched through, one with a bridge about which a song had been written. One of the officers sang it for them, Jude wrote, but she had no idea what the town was called because all the place names had been obliterated with thick, black ink so she still had no idea where he was although she studied the map in the atlas trying to picture him in unpronounceable places.

'It looks like we'll have to stay indoors again,' Amy said to Kezia. Kezia glanced up from the picture she was crayoning, her smile saying she didn't object; she enjoyed quiet pursuits. She scribbled a large splodge, pressing down on the bright pink crayon. 'Is it a flower?' Amy asked, and began peeling potatoes for the dinner.

'No, a piggy,' said Kezia, and carried on colouring, the tip of her tongue poking from the corner of her mouth. Amy's heart flipped; Jude did that when he was concentrating. The scuffling of feet and loud voices outside the door had them looking at one another, their faces falling.

The door burst open and Beattie's children tumbled in. 'There's nobody in our house so we've come here,' Maggie announced loudly. She shot a warning glance at her siblings. Albert failed to interpret it.

'There is,' he said. 'Me mam's in wi' that chap what goes round the doors selling stuff.' Maggie kicked him sharply on the ankle.

'Ouch!' cried Albert before adding, 'She's up in t'bedroom wi' him.'

'She is,' Fred corroborated. 'He didn't have his trousers on.'

'Shurrup!' yelled Maggie, then turning sheepishly to Amy she said, 'Me mam told us we hadn't to let you know she was in.'

Amy's heart sank. When she'd promised Bert Stitt that she would keep an eye on his children whilst he was away, she had truly meant it. What she hadn't bargained for was the reality of the situation, and as she towelled their wet heads and

224

hung their coats to dry, she couldn't help thinking: *keeping an eye on them, they're hardly ever out of my sight.*

Albert and Fred began to squabble over a marble and Mary and Henry wailed.

'They're hungry, Auntie Amy,' Maggie said.

'Go into the parlour and play quietly, dinner won't be long,' said Amy, hastily adding, 'and see they don't break anything.'

'I'll watch 'em, Auntie Amy,' Maggie replied fervently, for she above all of them knew they would go hungry if it wasn't for Auntie Amy.

'I know you will, love,' Amy said, saddened by the weight of responsibility Maggie carried on her young shoulders.

Maggie shooed her siblings into the parlour, calling out, 'Are you coming, Kezia?'

Kezia stayed where she was.

Kezia was not yet three, but Amy's gentle nurturing and tutelage had made her a thoughtful, caring child with a lively mind that showed an understanding far beyond her years. She preferred books and crayons and 'let's pretend' to the rough and tumble games Albert and Fred played, and she was no match for five-year-old Mary who fought selfishly over dolls and tea sets. Maggie and little Henry were Kezia's favourites.

Amy peeled more potatoes.

★ ★ ★

The dinner ready, Amy marched into the parlour. Her cheeks were alight with bright red blotches, not so much from the heat of the stove as from

225

exasperation. 'Stop that noise, right this minute or you'll get no dinner,' she bawled.

This unexpected threat from one who was usually placid and gentle had the desired effect. Like chastened sheep they filed into the kitchen.

Amy wiped the snot that ran from Mary's and Henry's permanently dirty noses and then, holding the pan aloft and fighting the urge to bang it off Fred and Albert's heads, she spooned dollops of mash onto plates then drowned each pile with gravy. At her instruction to 'sit properly and eat nicely' they tucked in, gravy dribbling from the ends of their chins and mashed potato riding high up the handles of the spoons to form sticky blobs between their grubby fingers. Throughout the rumpus Kezia had been sitting quietly at the table. Now, her eyes meeting her mother's, she gave her a complicit smile. Amy smiled back, giving a little nod to show she understood that her daughter was on her side.

It was stuffy in the overcrowded, little kitchen so Amy opened the door and leaned against the doorframe gazing at the children. Nine months had passed since their fathers had gone to fight in France. *What a difference a year makes*, she thought. Jude would be amazed by how much Kezia had grown, and how clever she was. *That's if he ever gets to see her again*, she reflected sadly. And Bert would be pleased to know she was feeding his children, but what would he think if he knew Beattie was neglecting them in such a shameful manner? She mulled over what Albert and Fred had said earlier about the man with no trousers. It left a distinctly unpleasant feeling in the pit of her stomach.

Plates cleared and the rain off, the boys went out to play and Maggie took Kezia, Mary and Henry for a walk. As Amy washed up, she decided to go in search of the elusive Beattie, and when she found her she'd give her a piece of her mind. She'd tell her in no uncertain terms that she'd had enough: that Beattie was abusing her good nature and demoralising her children. However, the opportunity to do this arrived sooner than she expected.

The kitchen door scraped open and Beattie tottered into the kitchen, the clatter of high heels on the flagged floor jarring Amy's jangled nerves. Taken aback by the unexpected sight of her sister Amy dropped the dishcloth and stared. Beattie was dressed to the nines in what Amy took to be a new outfit, yet she still managed to look every inch a trollop. Her greasy hair was held in place with cheap, gaudy combs and her swarthy cheeks smeared with rouge.

Amy eyed the new rig-out: a green dress with a wide, white collar and drop shoulders, the hem of the bell-shaped skirt cut well above the ankles. Where had Beattie got the money from to buy it, she wondered? She was always asking for handouts to pay the rent or buy food. Amy's heart thumped uncomfortably against her ribs.

Beattie fumbled in her handbag for a packet of Woodbine and a box of matches. She had painted her lips in a bright, red cupid's bow and as she placed the cigarette between them and then lit it, she reminded Amy of the gypsy fortune-teller she had once seen at Barnborough Fair. Beattie puffed nervously. 'Can you do us a favour?' she wheedled.

Amy ignored the request, every muscle in her neck and shoulders aching with frustration. 'Not before you've heard what I've got to say.'

'Never mind that,' Beattie interrupted, 'I was wondering if you'd keep the bairns for a few days till I get back.'

Amy's jaw dropped. Then gathering her wits, she asked tartly, 'And where might you be going?'

Beattie tried to look apologetic. 'Scarborough,' she simpered. 'Me friend's going to visit his brother what's just come home from France and he's taking me with him for a bit of a holiday.'

'Taking you with him on a holiday.' Amy's incredibility was patent. The cheek of the woman: had she no decency? 'You're a married woman, Beattie Stitt! And in case you forgot, you've five children who need you.'

'I know that,' whined Beattie, 'that's why I'm asking you to mind 'em till I get back. Our Maggie can't manage 'em on her own.'

'She shouldn't have to. You've no right to even consider leaving them whilst you go gallivanting off with . . . '

Amy had no idea as to the identity of Beattie's holiday partner. It could be any one of a number of colliers who regularly visited Grattan Row. Gossip amongst the neighbours was rife and Amy had heard Beattie's name linked to three or four since Bert's departure. Distastefully, she looked Beattie up and down, realisation dawning.

'Is it the travelling salesman? Did he give you the fancy clothes?'

Oblivious to Amy's disgust, Beattie said, 'Aye, he wants me to look nice for the visit.'

'Nice! There's nothing nice about you, Beattie.' Amy's voice was harsh with condemnation. 'Poor Bert doesn't deserve this. He's far away from home, fighting for his life and you're behaving like a trollop in front of your children.'

'Aw, don't be so bloody stuck up,' retorted Beattie. 'It wa' Bert's choice to go off and leave me on me own. I didn't make him go. I'm just having a bit o' fun, and for all I know he'll be having his own bit o' fun wi' some French women over there.' She smirked at her own wit.

'Don't be so stupid. There are no women where they are, just men up to their knees in muck and mud, dodging bullets and choking on gas. You're a hateful bugger and I want nothing more to do with you. As for your children, you can stay at home and mind them your bloody self.'

Shocked by the use of words that rarely passed Amy's lips, Beattie blinked then raised her eyebrows, and lighting another cigarette, she drew deeply on it before drawling, 'Eeh, you've got your bloody hackles up today, lady.' She walked out, her back rigid with disdain. Shrouded in failure, Amy watched her go.

* * *

Beattie went to Scarborough and Amy dutifully looked after the children. What else could she do? Five days later, a disillusioned and dishevelled Beattie returned. She slunk into Amy's kitchen and flopped down on a chair at the table, her woebegone expression pleading for sympathy. She received none from Amy who listened to her sorry tale with grim satisfaction.

'He buggered off an' left me to pay the bill,' Beattie moaned. 'When I told the woman that kept the boarding house that I had nowt, the bitch said she'd call the police if I didn't settle up wi' her. I've spent the last two days washing and ironing, me hands are fair rubbed off me, an' if ever I set eyes on that bugger of a tally man again, I'll make him pay, see if I don't.'

Amy told her she had got what she deserved. 'And in future, Beattie, I won't be free to mind your children. I've joined Mrs Hargreaves' comfort group. I'll be there every afternoon knitting socks or packing parcels to send to men like my Jude or your Bert.' She looked pointedly at Beattie. 'They need all the comfort they can get and I'll be more use there than doing your job which, in case you've forgotten, is caring for your children. Now, take them with you and go.'

Although Amy spoke firmly, she knew in her heart that she would continue to look out for Beattie's children. She wouldn't break her promise to Bert.

22

Bright sunlight shone through the trees dappling the vegetable patch in Dr Hargreaves' garden. Down on her knees, Amy prised out clumps of chickweed and newly sprouted dandelions from in between rows of cabbages. The vegetable plot had been her idea, as well as the plan to distribute the fresh produce to needy families in Barnborough. Mrs Hargreaves was delighted to add yet another strand to the good works she oversaw at the comfort meetings, leaving Amy and the gardener to tend the plot.

At Amy's side, wielding a small trowel, Kezia turned over the rich soil looking for worms. Unearthing a particularly lengthy specimen, she picked it up with her thumb and forefinger, dangling it teasingly close to her mother's right ear. Amy sat back on her heels and laughed. 'You cheeky little madam,' she chuckled, 'are you trying to frighten me?'

Kezia swung the worm closer to Amy's face. Magnified by a shaft of sunlight, its reddish-brown segments glistened moistly. The worm wriggled, attempting to escape. Amy watched it, a mental image of the worm's natural habitat conjuring a different image of Jude underground sweating and straining beneath the fields of France. His letter, received that morning, had told her he was tunnelling under a hill near the German lines. 'No matter where I am, I spend my life underground.

Please God send me a bit of sunshine, or a handful of stars,' he had written.

Amy shuddered and shook her head to expel the comparison. 'Put it back on the soil. You don't want to hurt it, do you? Worms are good for the garden,' she said, lightly catching hold of Kezia's wrist.

Kezia puckered her face, but when Amy insisted a second time, she set the worm down. Hastily, it slithered into its earthy lair. Amy continued weeding, but the image of Jude scrabbling like a subterranean creature amidst the muck and mud of endless narrow passageways troubled her and the pleasure was gone from the task.

Setting aside the fork she shifted her weight, her hands flat on the grass behind her hips and her legs stretched out. Tilting her face upwards she peered through the leafy shade of a beech tree that deflected the sun's glare and then closed her eyes. 'Please God, send him home safe,' she prayed.

A warm, soft yet solid weight plopped across Amy's thighs. She opened her eyes. Kezia wrapped her arms about Amy's neck and Amy hugged the wiry, little body tight. 'Stop moping,' she silently advised herself, 'don't let silly imaginings spoil the day.' Playfully, Amy pushed the little girl off her knee so that she rolled onto the grass squawking with glee when Amy reached out and tickled her. As Kezia wriggled and rolled away out of reach, Amy stood and dusted bits of grass from the knees and hem of her old navy-blue skirt.

'Ah, I thought I'd find you here.' Mrs Hargreaves walked across the lawn to Amy, a brown paper carrier bag in her hand. She cast an inspecting eye over the vegetable plot. 'Splendid, quite splendid,' she boomed, handing Amy the bag. 'Just a few books for you to send to Mr Leas. How is he, by the way? Bearing up, one would hope.'

Amy assured her that Jude was doing just that. On the way home, the string handles of the carrier bag biting her fingers, Amy wondered about the books. Ever since she had asked Dr Hargreaves if he had any books she could send to Jude, his wife had taken it upon herself to ask her friends and acquaintances for their unwanted books. Amy sent only those that weighed the least and that she thought Jude and his fellow soldiers might find interesting. Heavy religious, historical or political volumes she kept on the shelves in her bedroom, awaiting his return; the room was coming down with books.

'We'll have to ask Uncle Sammy to build more shelves,' she said to Kezia, as they walked down Wentworth Street. 'We'll ask him tomorrow.'

★　★　★

Early next morning, Amy and Kezia walked to Intake Farm. These days Amy looked forward to visiting her family. There had been a time when she dreaded Samuel's company but, since Thomas's untimely death, her brother had changed beyond recognition. He no longer drank heavily and much to Bessie's delight he worked willingly with Raffy, the farm thriving.

'Who have we here then?' Samuel said, as Kezia trotted into the kitchen. His niece ran to him, eager to be picked up and swung in his beefy arms. To

233

Amy he said, 'You must be able to smell the kettle boiling. Mam's just about to make a pot o' tea.'

Amy grinned. She had deliberately timed her arrival to coincide with Samuel and Raffy's tea break. 'I hoped I'd find you in from the fields,' she said, 'I need more shelves. I've more books than I know what to do with.'

'You should sell 'em,' said Raffy, 'take a stall on the market.'

'I couldn't do that. They're for Jude when he comes home. Besides, I had them given. It wouldn't seem right.'

'No daughter of mine is working on a market stall,' said Bessie, bustling to the table with the teapot. 'Amy has enough to do with her war work and minding Kezia.' The mention of her granddaughter reminded her of her other grandchildren and their mother. 'What's Beattie up to thesedays? Still playing the trollop, is she?'

'Unfortunately, yes,' Amy replied. 'I still spend half my time looking after her children even though I told her I wouldn't, but I can't see them go hungry or shut out when it's raining.' She heaved a sigh. 'They're not to blame for whatever it is that eats away at Beattie.'

'Innocent victims, all of 'em,' muttered Raffy.

Bessie's face crumpled. She knew that he included Beattie in that remark. To hide her distress, she hurried into the pantry. Blinking unwanted tears away and forcing a smile, she brought out the cake tin.

'I could always lend a hand,' she said brightly. 'After all, I am their grandmother.'

As Amy struggled to hide her surprise, Raffy

chipped in with 'Them two boyos could help out rightly on the farm when they're not at school.'

'Aye, so they could,' said Samuel. 'They can pick stones in Low Fold and give a hand wi' making silage.'

'That's a brilliant idea,' Amy said, pleased to think that in a roundabout way she was keeping Bert's sons from harm. 'Maggie's no bother, and she's very good with the young ones. I enjoy having her about the place, but those lads are so lively I never know what to do with them, Sammy.'

'We'll keep 'em occupied, an' I'll give 'em a few coppers. I wouldn't want 'em working for nowt.'

'And you could send Maggie up here now and then to help with the hens,' Bessie said, her satisfied smile suggesting that she had masterminded the solution to Amy's problem.

★ ★ ★

And so, in the month of June 1916, whilst Amy tended the vegetable plot in Dr Hargreaves' garden or knitted socks and packed comfort parcels, and sorted out Bert's children, Jude was toiling underground.

Although he believed he had left mining behind him, probably forever, it made perfect sense that his regiment — most of them coalminers in peace time — should be called upon to tunnel under the German lines. Beaumont Hamel was the objective and Jude once again found himself deep in the bowels of the earth, this time beneath the Picardy Hills, toiling alongside the Royal Engineers in charge of hacking away the thick chalk deposits

235

that lay beneath the surface. It was heavy work, and the close proximity to the front line meant that he could hear the rattle of heavy gunfire and the whistling explosion of shells. The dangers of war were now reality.

Whilst Jude and his compatriots in the 13th Battalion breathed chalk dust and heaved dirt, the 14th were deployed to the front line. At first, Jude felt cheated of a chance to demonstrate his skills as a fighting soldier but when news filtered down the lines of the horrors of trench warfare and the heavy casualties the 14th had sustained, he consoled himself with the thought that maybe mining was the better option.

The most hazardous part of any shift was the journey to and from the tunnels and several of Jude's pals were killed or wounded as they made their way to and from the mines. Shells and shrapnel became an expected hazard on the journey and they knew to run for cover at the first explosion but there was no escape from the lethal gas canisters if the wind was blowing in the wrong direction. Jude feared being gassed more than death itself. The sight of men, dazed and confused, their wits befuddled by the poisonous fumes tortured him. Better to die than return home with your brain addled, an object of pity to all who knew you.

Jude's world centred around Mailly Maillet, Auchonvillers (or Ocean Villas as the troops called it), Beaumont Hamel and the road to Serre. His life was repetitive and tedious but Bert's, on the other hand, was anything but; he was here, there and everywhere. From the moment he received his first driving lesson at Hurdcott Camp, Bert had found his true vocation. Behind the wheel of a truck, Bert felt like a god in command of a powerful beast. Not only was he a skilful driver, he knew every part of the vehicle like the back of his hand. He could nurture the most cantankerous rattletrap into action. As the officer in charge of transport commented, 'That man's a bloody marvel. Put him behind the wheel or under an axle and he'll keep that vehicle driving to hell and back.'

And on a warm, overcast evening in the middle of June that's exactly what Bert was doing. They might not have made a marksman out of him, but where transport was concerned, they had uncovered a genius.

As he swung the lorry over the ruts and hollows of the New Beaumont Road, returning from an ammunition delivery up towards Serre, a flurry of shellfire cascaded down from a German redoubt above Beaumont Hamel. Regardless of his own safety Bert swerved in and out of the bombardment, oblivious to the fact that a stray shell could blow him and the remains of his precious cargo to kingdom come. He'd seen a troop of fellows making their way back to the billets in Mailly Maillet and was intent on picking them up from the roadside and speeding their journey.

Putting his foot to the floor, he put enough distance between the lorry and the range of the shellfire and slewed to a halt at the side of the road. The miners, white-faced from a mixture of chalk dust and fear piled aboard and Bert gunned the engine.

'You took your bloody time,' a voice called

above the roar of the engine. Bert glanced over his shoulder and saw the grinning face of Jude Leas. 'What kept you? If you'd come earlier you could have saved us having to walk half a mile.'

'I were takin' tea wi' General Haig,' Bert yelled back. 'He come over specially to ask me what I thought about all t'carry on here. I told him it wa' about time we finished Jerry off an' got back home.'

Wry laughter rose above the rattle of the engine, some of the lads adding their own ribaldry to Bert's, but this quickly petered out at Bert's next remark.

'I'll tell you now, there's summat big bein' planned. I wa' up doin' a bit o' listenin' in as you might say when I wa' up at the front. There's talk of a big push an' we'll all be in it. So you lot what's never been further than a bloody hole in t'ground 'ud better watch out. You could be up there afore you know it.'

23

Samuel fixed a final screw into the new bookshelves in Amy's bedroom. Amy stood back to admire his handiwork. 'They're grand, Sammy. Jude always said he wanted a library of his own and now he's got one. I can't wait to see the look on his face when he comes home.'

Her heart flipped at the presumption, and swallowing the thought that he might never come home, she gabbled, 'Jude's set himself up as the librarian for his unit. What with all the books I send and those that the other chaps get, he's persuaded the drivers of the supply trucks to carry them in used ammunition crates from place to place. He makes a note of whoever borrows them so that he can get them back.'

Samuel looked slightly bemused. 'I wouldn't o' thought they had time to read,' he said, shoving his screwdriver into his overall pocket and then brushing the palms of his hands together. 'Mind you, I'm not one for books meself.' He shook his head as though he couldn't understand why anyone would be and then pointed to the shelves. 'You must have nigh on a hundred here.'

'Seventy-seven to be precise,' replied Amy, walking out to the landing and calling down the stairwell. 'Put the kettle on, Maggie. Uncle Sammy's earned a cup of tea.'

Maggie served the tea and then joined Kezia, Mary and Henry in the parlour, leaving Amy and

Samuel in the kitchen, Samuel remarking, 'She's growing into a right grand lass, isn't she?'

'She's a treasure, Sammy; and clever too. What about the lads? How are they getting on?'

Samuel smiled into his cup. 'Grand. They're two right good little workers and they're as happy as Larry when me mam lets 'em stay over at weekends. She says they can stay all t'time when school breaks up for t'holidays.'

'I can't imagine Beattie objecting to that, she'll be glad to see the back of 'em, but she raises Cain if I keep Maggie too often.' Amy pulled a face. 'And that's only because she wants her for the housework.'

Samuel sniggered. 'From what I've heard, our Beattie doesn't have time to do it, she's too busy doing her own bit o' war work for them that never joined up.'

Amy gave a sad smile. 'Maggie's awfully loyal to her mother, you know. She'd do anything for her, and she turns a blind eye to what Beattie gets up to. I think she feels sorry for her.'

'She shouldn't have to,' growled Samuel. He thumped his cup down on the table. 'When t'time comes I'll make sure I earn my children's loyalty.'

Amy blinked her surprise. 'Your children?'

Samuel flushed. 'Aye, Freda's talking of us getting wed.'

'And what are you saying, Sammy?'

'I'm saying yes,' he chortled, his bulbous blue eyes shining.

Amy laid her hand on his and squeezed it. 'I'm happy for you, Sammy. You'll make a grand husband and father.' She smiled warmly at the brother she had once despised. Sad though it was, something good had come out of Thomas's death after all.

Sammy smiled back, his eyes watering. 'Do you think so, Amy?'

'I know so,' she said, giving his arm a friendly punch.

'I'd best be off.' They both stood, Samuel giving Amy a brief hug and saying, 'You're a lovely woman, Amy.'

'You're not so bad yourself,' she said, following him to the door, 'and as long as we keep Bert's kids out of harm's way, I'll be keeping my promise and you can practise being a good father.'

Samuel walked away laughing.

After he'd gone, Amy stood at the sink peeling potatoes and reflecting on how life was full of little blessings: Sammy, about to get married, and Bessie mothering Albert and Fred like she had her own sons. *I just hope she doesn't spoil them rotten*, Amy thought, plopping potatoes into a pan. Still, it was good to know that the boys were in safe hands for much of the time, just as Maggie and Mary and Henry were when they stayed with her. She was pleased to see that in her care the children were thriving. Maggie read her books and learned from Amy and, following Kezia's example, Henry and Mary were learning to play properly. What a blessing Kezia is, thought Amy, hearing her daughter's merry laughter through the open parlour door. Jude would be so proud of her — *and he's still alive and doing the best he can so life's not so bad*, she concluded. The only fly in the ointment was Beattie.

'I'm doing the best I can, Bert,' Amy said silently to the pan on the stove, and at the same time wishing she could do something to change her sister's heartless ways.

★ ★ ★

Lizzie Wainwright groaned and pulled the eiderdown up over her ear. Living next door to Beattie Stitt was no joke, she told herself, as thuds and yells penetrated the thin party wall. She buried her head deeper into her pillow only to bolt upright as an almighty crash shook the wall and a bloodcurdling scream split the night air. Tossing aside the eiderdown and blankets, Lizzie was on her feet as quickly as her aged bones would allow. A second scream sent her tottering down the stairs, her bare feet flapping against the worn linoleum.

When she opened her front door, she came face to face with Sam and Gert Barrett, Beattie's neighbours on the other side. As they exchanged looks of alarm, the door to the Stitt house flew open and Maggie, clad only in her shift, catapulted out on to the flags, wild-eyed and shaking.

'Come quick!' she screeched. 'He's killin' me mam an' I can't gerrim off her.'

Sam Barrett hesitated. At eighty years of age and fearing for his own safety he wasn't about to commit any foolish acts of bravado for the likes of Beattie Stitt, but Lizzie Wainwright, some five years younger, had no such fears.

'Run and fetch Billy Warton,' she shouted, before lumbering into Beattie's house. Lizzie reckoned that what with Billy being a brawler he'd soon sort out who it was up Beattie's stairs.

Maggie ran, heedless of the sharp flints piercing the soles of her bare feet.

Bawling and shouting on every step, Lizzie heaved her bulky body up the narrow stairs, the noise above abating as though whoever was up there paused in their frenzy, listening for the intruder's approach. Just as Lizzie reached the landing a clatter of footsteps below signalled Billy's arrival. Lizzie stood to one side as he bounded up to the landing and into the front bedroom, fists raised.

Larry Hamby, his flies undone and his shirt flaps askew, folded like a pack of cards. Billy grinned and lowered his fists. Larry's eyes begging for mercy, he gabbled his excuses. 'She asked for it, Billy. I'd already given the bitch half a bottle o' gin an' two bob. I caught her emptying me pockets when she thought I wa' asleep.'

Billy laughed out loud. 'More fool you,' he said, swivelling on his heels to look at Beattie. 'Are you all right?' he asked, his tone suggesting he didn't particularly care.

'Do I look as though I am?' Beattie, half-naked, was sprawled on the bed midst the shards of a broken chamber pot, a dent in the wall above her head indicating where Larry had thrown it. Her left eye was swollen and her bottom lip split. Livid bruises were fast blooming on her arms. Apart from that she appeared to be unharmed.

'I'll get back to bed then.' Billy glanced at Larry. 'An' you gerroff home, yer daft bugger.' The young collier shouldered past Billy and ran. Billy jauntily saluted Lizzie, Gert and Maggie before following him.

Eyes wide, Maggie stared at her mother. Beattie grimaced, her injured lip curling to reveal blood-stained teeth. 'You lot can bugger off an' all,' she grunted.

Nobody moved.

'Cover thi sen up,' Lizzie briskly ordered, as Sam Barrett slunk into the room.

Shamefaced, Beattie dragged at the bed-spread. 'I think that bugger's broken me arm,' she moaned. From wrist to elbow, her right arm was a livid shade of purple.

Lizzie sent Gert for a bowl of warm water and a cloth. 'Once we've got you cleaned up, we can see how bad you are,' she commented pragmatically. 'See if you need t' doctor.'

'I don't want a doctor,' snapped Beattie. 'Our Maggie'll see to me.'

★　★　★

'We'll keep the lads up here full time.' Bessie showed not an ounce of sympathy when she heard about Beattie's misfortune. She was more interested in keeping Albert and Fred close by. 'Raffy'll run 'em to school in the morning and they can walk back in the afternoon. That way she'll not have to bother about them.'

Amy agreed that it made sense. 'Maggie's looking after her and I'm minding Mary and Henry,' she said, nodding over at Beattie's youngest children and Kezia who were playing with a new litter of kittens by the hearth. 'I'll help Maggie out where I can but there's not much more I can do.' She shrugged disconsolately. 'I suppose we should be glad that Beattie's in no fit state to entertain her gentlemen callers,' she added sarcastically. 'She just sits there moaning and grumbling.'

'She doesn't have a grateful bone in her body,' Bessie retorted.

Amy gathered the children, and as she walked back to Wentworth Street she contemplated on the state of affairs. How many times had she wished something would happen to make Beattie change her ways? Well, she hadn't reckoned on her getting a beating, but if it had knocked some sense into her sister she wouldn't complain. She decided she wouldn't mention it in her letter to Jude; he had enough to worry about. And she would advise Maggie to do the same in her next letter to Bert.

When they arrived back at the house there was a letter on the mat behind the door. Amy settled the children in the parlour with milk and biscuits. Alone in the kitchen, she sat holding the letter against her breast, praying as she always did that its contents would tell her Jude was safe and well and then tearing it open with trembling fingers.

She read that he was in good health but tired much of the time, and glad to be no longer working underground. He was on the move, marching. *'I've so much to carry I'm loaded like a packhorse and clank with every step,'* he wrote, *'and whilst I can't tell you too much, we are heading for one almighty dust up. They are saying this will be a battle to end all battles and I can only hope I survive it to come home to you and Kezia. If luck is against me, know that you have given me the greatest joy in my life and that I love you both dearly and will still love you should we be parted.'*

245

Amy wept.

The following day, the *Barnborough Chronicle* reported that something the generals were calling the 'Big Push' was about to take place, an intensive that would finish the Germans once and for all. The article mentioned places called 'The Somme' and 'Serre' and although Amy had no idea where they were or where Jude was, as she read she prayed for his safety. Fortunately, for her balance of mind, she was totally unaware that Jude's first taste of action in the front line would shortly be in Serre.

24

'Warnimont Wood . . . '

'Matthew, Mark, Luke and John: four small copses.'

'The first objective . . . '

'Point of entry . . . '

The officer's words buzzed in Jude's ears commingling with his thoughts. Wood and copses; it was as though they were about to embark on a countryside ramble. If he'd been at home it would have been Stainborough Park, Wentworth Forest and Miller's Wood.

'Our job is to capture Serre and to do so we . . . '

Jude shook his head and blinked his eyes rapidly. *Pay attention,* he sharply told himself; *lack of it could cost you your life.* Weary from days and nights spent tunnelling under Beaumont Hamel and Hawthorn Ridge and then the long march, this unaccustomed lack of activity was having a soporific effect. He forced himself into a more upright position to take better notice. The young officer's voice droned on.

Jude listened.

He'd realised days ago that something big was coming up. On his way to and from the tunnels he had observed huge quantities of trench mortars, small arms ammunition and Mills bombs, crate after crate of them, being taken from the dump and loaded onto trucks. Bert had confirmed that the stuff was being taken up to the trenches. It looked as though the 'Big Push' was beginning to take shape. Jude had wondered what part he might play in the 'Big Push.' As like as not he'd be left digging tunnels, he'd thought, as it seemed that was all that life had in store for him. Now, as he listened to the officer outline the plan, he knew otherwise.

To play their part in the 'Big Push' the 94th Brigade, of which he was a very small part, would cross No-Man's-Land and capture Serre, a heavily fortified village and an intimidating German stronghold. Prior to their walk into No-Man's-Land there would be several days of heavy bombardment by the Artillery, to cut through the German wire and weaken the frontline trenches. The first wave of British troops would then walk some one hundred and fifty yards across No-Man's-Land, capture the first four lines of the German trenches in front of Serre, stay there and strengthen their position. The following waves would pass over them and drive the Germans out of Serre. This would then make way for the mighty Fourth Army to crush any German resistance.

'It all sounds so simple and straightforward,' Jude said sarcastically to the man sitting next to him when the officer stepped down from the platform.

'I wouldn't know, I've never been in a battle afore,' his companion replied lugubriously.

'Me neither,' said Jude, sounding equally doleful. 'Our lot had four days' training up at Gezaincourt, that place where the Royal Engineers have made a model of Serre for us to practise on. Four days' training for the first real fight I've ever been in.'

'We got ten. You were unlucky.'

'Aye, fighting in t'pub or on t'pithead doesn't prepare you for this sort o' thing.' Had Jude known this was the biggest battle the British Army had ever faced he might have felt even less prepared.

'I only joined because o' Kitchener,' said a young lad of no more than seventeen.

'And now he's dead and gone to the bottom of the ocean, torpedoed off the Orkneys aboard HM Hampshire,' a knowledgeable-looking lad remarked.

'I blame it on those flashing blue eyes and that pointing finger,' said Jude. 'That's what brought me here.'

'What day is it?' asked a forlorn little voice to Jude's rear.

Over his shoulder, Jude replied, 'Thursday, the 29th of June.'

A short while later, several lusty speeches were delivered by those in command, but to be told that they were about to fight in the greatest battle in the world, and in the more just cause, did not ring with confidence in Jude's ears. The words, 'Keep your head, do your duty and you will utterly defeat the enemy' made more sense, for these words he understood. Working down the pit, he was used to counteracting the long hours of toil with camaraderie to keep up his spirits but in between laughing off the hardships was the ever-present sense of duty; one man's life depended on another's vigilance. He knew how to keep his head in a crisis.

Darkness fell, the distant boom and crash of gunfire mingling with the wood's night noises.

For a while, Jude lay listening to the scrabbling of a small creature close to his head. Most likely a rat, he thought, sitting quickly upright. Then, to ease the tension of endless waiting, he oiled and then re-oiled his rifle bolt. The 'Crown and Anchor' lads had unfurled their little squares of linen and were out to make a few bob but Jude was not tempted. He wandered to the edge of the clearing and leaned against the gnarled trunk of a tree whose name he did not know. He thought about the trees in the woods at home, beech, oak and chestnut and remembered the day he had collected conkers with Amy and Kezia. In his mind's eye he saw their happy faces and he thought he heard their laughter as they'd kicked up the carpet of gold and russet leaves in search of the spiky, green balls. They'd do it again when he got home — if he got home.

Saddened by the thought, he slumped down on his hunkers and withdrew a tattered copy of '*The Riddle*' from his knapsack. Losing himself in the thrill of espionage, he eventually fell asleep.

The following evening, the 30th of June, the 94th Brigade moved up to the front. They trekked along muddy paths that led from Warnimont Wood to the assembly points in the trenches, and Serre. The long, straggling lines of men weighed down with a conglomeration of equipment reminded Jude of the tinkers who travelled the roads at home, the rhythmic clanking and clunking of mess tins against haversacks like jangling harness and pots and pans. Their bodies were like hat stands in busy hotel foyers, hung with entrenching tools, gas masks and shovels and their pockets bulging with Mills bombs; everything but the kitchen sink.

Jude slipped and slithered along the water-logged tracks, attempting wherever possible to avoid the murky pools of water that were deep enough to cover his puttees. He wore the yellow armband that denoted him as a wire cutter. The bright yellow band was not a mark of superiority, merely a marker; a marker that would make the wearer more visible if and when he fell. In such an event his comrades could spot him more easily and retrieve the wire cutters for future use.

'It's a bugger to think that these wire cutters are considered more valuable than the man himself,' Jude had said angrily when the NCO explained the purpose of the band. Even so, he understood the logic.

The man marching ahead of him shouldered a Bangalore Torpedo as well as his standard equipment. An hour into the journey and he swore his right arm and shoulder had lost all feeling. The men carrying Vermoel sprays huffed and puffed behind him. 'Hey up, do you think you can do summat about black spot? It played havoc wi' my roses last year,' the Bangalore carrier asked them, amused by the idea that a spray used to kill green-fly had now been adapted to neutralise the effects of chlorine gas.

Jude trudged doggedly in line, his body and brain an automaton, and as the hours slipped by and his feet kept moving, his brain repeated again and again the strategies he would soon turn into actions. Nine hours later he filed into Rolland trench along with the rest of the lads in 'B' Company; nine hours to cover a journey of no more than six miles. It was just after 5 a.m. Jude sat down on the fire step, and oblivious to the rumble of big guns and the incessant screech of shot and shell, he slept.

Weary though he was, he might not have slept so easily had he been aware that the Artillery had failed to pulverise the German batteries, and had he known that the Germans were expecting him and his companions he would not have slept at all.

Several hours before the troops had trudged into the slimy morass of the assembly trenches a party of Hull 'Commercial' had cut lanes through the British wire to allow access to No-Man's-Land. Shortly after that a party from the Sheffield City Battalion had crept out to lay lengths of white tape, intended to guide the lines of British troops to the German trenches once they had crawled through the wire. At first light, although the scrubland was veiled in a light mist, the swathes of cut wire and the bright white lines of tape were frighteningly visible to the enemy. As the Artillery continued their onslaught on the German batteries, the Germans, now fully aware that the British were coming, replied with a fusillade of shot and shell, pounding John Copse and the entire length of the front line behind which 'B' Company now waited.

Shortly before seven o'clock Jude was roughly shaken and brought back to his senses. Thinking he had slept for only a matter of minutes he was amazed to learn he had slept for almost two hours. Peering cautiously over the parapet of mud and sandbags he saw dense smoke drifting over Gommecourt Wood. This he knew was part of the distraction planned to draw German fire before the whistle blew at 7.30 a.m. and the first wave of infantry entered No-Man's-Land.

He sat down again and rubbed his hands over his grizzled cheeks and shaven head, willing the blood to rush to his brain and keep him alert. He arched his neck as far back as he could until the top of his head rested on the mud wall of the trench, gazing up into a perfect summer blue sky. In a sudden lull between salvos he thought he heard a bird singing. Did it know that it was in the middle of a battlefield? Was it not afraid of being blown to kingdom come by a bloody German sniper? He was.

A massive explosion, rending the air asunder, abruptly broke his reverie. He leapt to his feet. Far to his right, he saw a mountain of soil flying heavenwards and felt the ground beneath him tremble and, as the mighty rumbling faded, he heard the increased rattle of German guns. He knew what had happened. The mine beneath Hawthorn Ridge had gone off: too early. He'd helped dig the tunnels for that mine. It shouldn't have gone off until they were over the top, and here they were, still lying in the trenches waiting for the whistle to blow.

In the minutes that followed the thunderous fulmination, the Artillery ceased its rigorous bombardment of the German batteries and withdrew to allow the British troops to take the crater. With the cessation of heavy guns, a strange, uneasy quietness hung in the foul air. Jude thought he heard the same bird chirp its song. The calm was shattered as a Stokes mortar spluttered into action, immediately followed by the rattle of German machine guns. Jude lit what he thought might be his last cigarette and pulled deeply on it, enjoying the simple action of something so familiar and comforting.

A frisson of expectancy flurried along the trench, and a voice cried out, 'Uphold the honour of the regiment as you go over the top.'

This is it, thought Jude. *I've waited for this for two years and now it's come I'm not sure what it was I waited for.*

He hoisted his pack and the wire cutters, shuffling forward in the footsteps of men loaded down beneath the weight of their equipment. The whistle blew and a blur of bodies scrambled up the ladders. Jude followed suit, rolling himself over the top of the trench and making for the holes cut in the wire and out into the unknown territory that was No-Man's-Land. Wave upon wave, men climbed, rolled and crawled out into the unforgiving landscape. Wave after wave, one hundred yards apart, they walked with rifles held at port arms, following orders not to charge, but to walk. Britain's finest and Barnborough's best, the very best, walked into the jaws of hell.

Following orders to keep the lines straight, Jude looked anxiously ahead then to right and left and behind. The chaos of zigzagging men all around him made him realise that there was no order, no tapes to outline the way, no one to call the tune: it was every man for himself. Head down, he kept going towards the German wire. That was the only order to follow. Get to the wire; get through it. Take the position.

Machine gun bullets hissed in the grass and the air was foul with the acrid stench of explosives. Ribby Atkins, a wiry little bloke struggling under the weight of a bag of Mills bombs, hurried alongside Jude. Jude reached out a hand to help him over a hazardous ridge raked up out of the scrub, but before he could make contact the piercing whine of a shell snatched Ribby away.

'That one was too bloody close by half,' grunted Jude to the man on his left, but he received no reply. Although the man was still on his feet the life had gone out of him several seconds before. *What's that they say?* Jude contemplated as he ducked and dodged. *If your name's not on it, it's not meant for you.*

He struggled on, some of the time running low to the ground, at other times crawling over the scrub and several times half burying himself in earth gouged up by shell and mortar. He stumbled over the lower torso of some poor chap whose head and shoulders were gone. He thought he recognised the boots. Sammy Dawson could only ever get a shine on the left one, no matter how hard he spat and polished. He passed the inert bodies of fallen men, some he knew and some whom their own mothers wouldn't recognise.

As he neared the German wire the ground exploded around him and searing fragments of hot metal rained down on him. He threw himself face down in a deep shell hole, rolling over onto his back as excruciating heat penetrated his lower leg. Swiping the burning area with the palm of his hand, a singed scrap of his trouser leg fluttered loose. Crossing his wounded right leg over the left he inspected the damage. A tiny fragment of shrapnel had burned its way through his trousers and was now stuck to the skin on the fat of his calf. He groped for his water bottle. The shard of metal sizzled and he flicked at it with his thumbnail, freeing it from his flesh. A livid indentation the size of his thumbnail glared angrily through the hole in his trousers. He fumbled in the top pocket of his tunic for a field dressing and clumsily attached it to the wound.

A movement to his right whisked away any thought of his injured leg. His rifle cocked, Jude turned to see Charlie Sykes crawling towards him wearing a half-crazed expression, his naturally prominent eyeballs bulging even more than usual. 'You nearly had your chips, creeping up on me like that.'

Charlie's teeth chattered as his lips tried to form words. Jude pulled him roughly down into the shell hole and they huddled together as the carnage continued. At last Charlie's shuddering limbs and teeth stilled and he managed a sickly grin.

'They never told us it 'ud be like this. They said Jerry 'ud be gone by t'time we got here.' Charlie sounded as though he might cry at any moment.

'Aye, and now we know they were lying because they're still there, and what the bloody hell we're supposed to do about, I don't know. And the buggers have burned a hole in me trousers, never mind me bloody leg.' He grinned at this last remark and Charlie grinned back.

'I was coming to get the wire cutters. I saw t'yeller band on your sleeve before you went down,' said

Charlie, covering his shame with reason.

'Right,' said Jude, not wanting to doubt him. 'In that case I suppose we'd better make a move before Mr Hitler spots us. We've been lucky so far but we can't stay here all day. They're expecting us for tea. Jerry'll have boiled the kettle by the time we get there.'

Jude's light-hearted banter boosting Charlie's spirits, he laughed and raised two derogatory fingers. 'They can keep their bloody tea,' he said. 'I'd piss in it.'

Jude grinned back at him, but his heart was full of pity for the boy. *Sykesy's only a young lad,* he thought, as he adjusted the dressing on his leg. *He can't be more than eighteen, if that. He's seen nothing of life yet, 'cos you can't call this living.*

'Hey up,' said Jude as they prepared to move out. 'Look over there. It's Ernie Snell an' that big lad from Heaton.' The sight of familiar faces added to their determination to carry on and together they crawled over to where their mates were crouched. Shortly afterwards they were joined by four other 'pals' from 'C' Company. Above them the fortress that was Serre stood proud and impenetrable. Covertly they neared the German wire.

Ernie Snell snorted. 'It's not been cut anywhere as far as I can see; there's not a bloody break in it. What the hell wa' all that about artillery cutting through t'wire afore we got here? They've hardly bloody touched it at this end.'

Jude appraised the wire in both directions. Thick tangles of impenetrable razor-sharp barbs stretched as far as the eye could see. Here and there the remains of khaki clad figures hung like last week's washing, suspended from the tangles.

'They didn't have much luck getting through,' croaked Charlie, tears choking his throat.

A maelstrom of bullets from a machine gun nest above their heads had them diving for cover. When the fusillade slackened, they bellied forward, Jude attacking the wire with the cutters. His arms and hands growing weary the others took their turn and soon a hole large enough for a man to crawl through appeared in the mesh. They looked at the hole and then looked at each other. Who would be the first to enter?

Before such a decision could be taken a volley of shots from a sniper's rifle dispatched three of the lads from 'C' Company and seriously wounded the fourth. Seconds later the lad from Heaton took a direct hit in the head. With all the strength he could muster Jude rolled to his left, and scrambling to his feet darted for the cover of a shell hole some yards away, screaming for Snell and Sykes to follow him. Plunging into the shell hole, Jude landed on something warm and soft. It was the body of a young officer. He lay there as though he were sleeping, not a mark on him. Just as Jude was attempting to feel for a pulse in the handsome chap's neck the breath was knocked out of him as Charlie landed on top of him, closely followed by Ernie Snell.

'Bloody hell! Are you trying to kill me?' gasped Jude. They wriggled apart, making space for each other. Jude was still partially lying on top of the officer.

'Is he dead?' asked Charlie. 'He doesn't look as though he is.'

Jude put his cheek against the lips of the fair young man. Not even the faintest of breaths fanned his skin. The finely shaped mouth was cold to his cheek. 'Aye, he's dead,' muttered Jude. Charlie began to cry, thick guttural sobs that wracked his body and made pink rivulets in his dust-stained face. Jude ignored his sobbing, and easing his own body sideways, he unceremoniously folded the long, slender legs up and across the top half of the officer's body and pushed it further into the shell hole, away from his own.

The sun, now high in the heavens on what had turned into a glorious summer's day, beat down on them unmercifully. A putrefied stench seeped through the trench. The officer had soiled his trousers. Jude threw handfuls of soil over the officer's rear in an attempt to mask the sickening smell. They lay silent, not daring to raise their heads, not knowing what to do next. Out on the battlefield lay the dead and dying: husbands, fathers, brothers, nephews, cousins, sweethearts — loved ones all.

Through a haze of smoke, Jude watched as daylight faded into rosy pinks and yellows then fiery red. Under the dark canopy of a velvet sky streaked with purple and a handful of stars the screeching shells and frenzied clatter of guns seemed at odds with the tranquillity of the heavens. The guns fell silent, the screams and cries of wounded and dying men echoing eerily over No-Man's-Land. Jude flinched at each desperate call and cursed his impotence. What could he do?

He calculated that dawn was some three hours away: three more hours before the light of a new day would peel away the blackness to reveal the horror of what lay out there; three more hours to hide under the cloak of darkness. Sitting upright, he fiddled with his puttees and tightened the strap on his helmet. Shifting his bulk in the confined space so that he was on his knees he brusquely announced, 'I'm going back the same way as I came and if you two want to join me, I'd appreciate your company.'

25

And so, as Jude crawled out of a shell hole in No-Man's-Land, his sister, Beattie, wallowed in a pit of her own making in Barnborough. She was pregnant.

At first, she had lived in hope that copious tipples of gin might bring on a miscarriage but all they had done was make her drunk and depressed. Amy was furious — not because she knew about the pregnancy; she didn't. She was angry and disappointed because after Larry Hamby's vicious attack Amy had hoped that Beattie would mend her ways.

Maggie, faithful as ever, ran the house and nursed her mother lovingly, even though Beattie showed scant appreciation for the girl's efforts. Amy dropped by every day, more to support Maggie than to listen to Beattie's grumbling and moaning. Her arm had healed but the black dog of depression hung over her like a shroud and she would sit for hours by the hearth smoking one cigarette after the other. Initially, Amy had suggested distractions that might please Beattie such as a shopping trip or a walk in the countryside, or the offer to cut and style her hair or freshen up the paint in the house. Nothing worked, and now her drunkenness wore Amy's patience to a frazzle.

Besides, she had other things to worry about. Jude had yet to reply to her last letter, and the newspapers were now full of the most horrific stories. In the first few days after what the papers referred to as the 'Big Push' Amy had smiled when she read 'The Big Advance: All goes well for Britain and France' and 'only a few casualties'. This must be 'the big dust up' Jude had mentioned in his last letter. That only a few lives had been lost diminished her fears.

However, within days, the same newspapers were telling a different story. Words such as *'our losses have been severe'* and that *'men were mown down like grass'* did little to boost her hopes. One paper reported that *'when the men went over the top, they met with a hail of gun shot and rifle fire that wiped them out in hundreds'*. Was Jude one of the hundreds? Was he now lying dead on foreign soil, his beautiful body broken and mouldering? The more she read, the more she was afraid to leave the house should a telegram boy make a fateful delivery in her absence.

Telegram boys came to Wentworth Street at increasingly regular intervals. Amy went from one house to another offering comfort to the recipients of the dreaded yellow scraps of paper and all the while wondering if, in the next day or so, she would receive a telegram telling of her own loss? There were days when she couldn't decide which was worse, to receive a telegram or live with the uncertainty of not knowing what had become of Jude. And as Amy scoured obituary columns and lists of dead, missing or wounded that now filled several pages in the newspapers, Maggie made a daily visit to Barnborough Town Hall to check the lists that were posted there. Each day, on her return, Maggie said, 'No news is good news.' Amy wanted to believe her.

Then a letter came. Not from Jude, but from Bert's commanding officer, telling them Bert had been injured and transferred to a hospital in London. He wished him a speedy recovery and told them that Bert would soon return to the bosom of his family.

The bosom of his family . . . Beattie went into a flat spin. Where before she had brooded by the fire, she now paced restlessly from parlour to kitchen, kitchen to yard like a mad woman, settling to nothing.

'Why are you acting like this, Beattie? You should be pleased. Bert's injuries can't be too bad if the officer says he'll soon be back home.'

Beattie couldn't think of a reply. All she could think of was that Amy must never know about her condition and that she had to do something, anything, to alter it.

The next day another letter arrived, this one from Bert.

'Look, Auntie Amy!' Maggie waved the single sheet of paper under Amy's nose as soon as she arrived at the house in Grattan Row. 'Me dad's coming home an' when he does, he's going to start his own business driving a lorry.'

Amy grabbed the letter and read it. 'That's marvellous,' she cried, although deep down a snake of envy wormed its way into her thoughts. Why couldn't it be Jude coming home? She hugged Maggie, and turning to Beattie she said, 'Think of it, Beattie, Bert home and starting up on his own, isn't that wonderful?' She chuckled. 'You'll be a businessman's wife, Beattie.'

Beattie leapt out of her chair, and making

263

a strange howling noise like that of a wounded animal, she grabbed her coat and handbag and dashed out of the house.

Dumbfounded, Amy and Maggie watched her go.

★ ★ ★

The woman in Carcroft wouldn't do it; she said Beattie was 'too far gone'. The foreign doctor that the woman had recommended wanted twenty pounds, no questions asked. Where was she likely to find twenty pounds, Beattie fumed, as she boarded the bus back to Barnborough? On the bus, she pondered on what to do. She had to get rid of it. Bert might be lackadaisical but he'd not rear another man's child — not Bert the business-man. Tears stung her eyes. She pictured a yard full of lorries bearing Bert's name and a nice house and a wardrobe full of glamorous dresses; maybe they'd even have had weekends in Scarborough. She'd have liked being a businessman's wife, show all them toffee-nosed buggers like Amy Leas a thing or two.

Alighting from the bus in Barnborough, Beattie went to the tobacconists and the pub. Trudging back to Grattan Row, she walked straight past her own house and up to Connie Spratt's, a bottle of gin and ten Park Drive in her bag. Connie would know how to help her — hadn't she aborted her own daughter's unwanted pregnancy last year?

'Ooh, ta very much,' said Connie, accepting the bait and immediately lighting up a Park Drive and unscrewing the cap on the gin bottle. An hour later Beattie hurried back home, the instructions rattling inside her brain and the knitting needles and a long-handled spoon rattling inside her bag.

★ ★ ★

Amy had stayed with Maggie for almost two hours after Beattie's hasty departure. Then, tiring of waiting for her return and thinking she was drowning her sorrows in the pub, she had gone back home to soak dried peas to go with the small piece of boiling bacon for tomorrow's dinner. As she was opening the packet of peas the knocker on the front door rattled. Amy's heart missed a beat; what if it was the telegram boy? She squeezed the bag tightly; peas shot out, pit-pattering across the flagged stone floor.

Kezia laughed out loud, and as she chased the peas Amy ran into the parlour. On the mat was a letter. She snatched it up, the sight of the familiar handwriting sending her breath whooshing from her lungs. Only then did she realise she had been holding her breath from the moment she had heard the knock. Feeling somewhat lightheaded, she went back into the kitchen, scattering peas even further as she danced Kezia across the floor. 'Your daddy's sent us some news,' she cried, 'now leave those peas alone and let's sit down and read it.'

Out loud she read: '*My Dearest Amy and Kezia, it is the middle of the night and for the moment all is quiet where we are. It's a warm night, the moon is shining and the stars are big and bright. It's times like this when I miss you most of all. I feel very far away from you and Kezia and the distance lets me know what a lucky man I am to have you thinking about me and waiting for me at home.'*

Amy paused to scan the next few lines, then smiling at Kezia she said, 'There, isn't that nice? Daddy's safe and well and thinking about us.' Kezia's warm brown eyes were shining as she nodded her agreement. Amy's heart swelled with love. 'Now you pick up the peas for me like a good girl, whilst I read what else Daddy has to say.'

Kezia rattled peas into a pan as Amy silently read, *'The fighting here is still intense and every day I find myself seeing or doing things I never thought I'd see or do. I was with young John Cooper, Mary's boy, when he lost his life and although I did not see Freddie, the Howards' lad, die, I helped carry his body to where we buried him. Tell Fred and Clara we marked his grave with a cross bearing his name and number on it and prayed for his soul. Give them and Mary my condolences.'*

Again, Amy stopped reading, her heart heavy. Earlier in the week, she had commiserated with both neighbouring families, and as she forced herself to read on, she prayed that the letter contained no more sad news. Her prayer was answered.

'I've not seen or heard anything of Bert. I hope he is safe and well and that I will stay the same in the coming days. So far, I've escaped trench foot and dodged the bullets, and I'm still lending out books to the lads whenever we have rest periods. It seems like I've taken over your old job.' Amy gave a watery smile. Trust Jude to say something to amuse her; poor, brave Jude.

At the end of the letter he had written, *'I'm not*

266

sorry I joined up because I know I did the right thing, but I am sorry that it took me away from you. Take care of yourselves. You are very precious to me and I love you both very much.'

Choking back tears, for she never let Kezia see her crying, Amy made tea and later that evening she called with the Coopers and the Howards. Perhaps Mary would take some comfort from knowing that Jude had been with John at the end, that her son had died with a friend close by. At the Howards she showed them what Jude had written, the devastated couple's sorrows somewhat eased to learn that Fred had been buried with honour and respect.

After Kezia had gone to bed, Amy went out into the yard for a breath of air and taking the letter from her apron pocket she read it again by the light of the moon. Gazing up at the stars she selected the brightest, hopeful that Jude was watching the same star and if he wasn't then that, at least, the same bright star was shining down on him. With a heart full of love and longing she went indoors and to bed.

★ ★ ★

In the house in Grattan Row, Beattie Stitt gazed at her reflection in the mottled, greasy mirror hanging above the fireplace. She didn't like what she saw; she was getting old. Her cheeks were sallow and deep wrinkles framed her lacklustre eyes. Sadly she recalled the days when her eyes had flashed mischievously back at her, eyes that had attracted men looking for a good time. She prodded the puffed bags beneath each eye with her index fingers then moved them back to her hairline, tightening the loose skin. There, that looked better but it didn't matter anymore what she looked like, did it? She let her hands fall to her side and in an instance the bags reappeared, uglier than before.

All the bitter disappointments that life had doled out reared up in front of her. She had never fit in. She was like the wrong thread in the wrong colour, woven into a pattern that had gone badly wrong. From the very start she'd been a misfit. Hadley Elliot had wanted a son, and failing that a plump, fair daughter. Instead he'd had to make do with a skinny creature with swarthy skin and hair so black he likened it to boot polish. Not that it mattered now; he wasn't her dad, she was Raffy's daughter. But why if her mother loved Raffy had she never loved her, Beattie?

She turned away from the hearth, and resting her hands on her belly she thought of the life inside her. Poor bugger, it would have no more luck in life than she had. Heaving a gusty sigh, Beattie lifted her bag from the table and plodded upstairs, the clink and rattle of the knitting needles against the long-handled spoon causing her to shudder so violently that she had difficulty maintaining her balance.

★   ★   ★

Bright, early morning sunshine filtered through the window above the sink, glinting on the pan in Amy's hands. She had been up since six, the

268

restless energy that had coursed her veins ever since she had read Jude's letter making it impossible to stay in bed. Oh, but it was a beautiful morning; Jude was alive and well, and Bert was coming home soon.

Pouring milk into the pan for the morning's porridge, she planned her day. She'd call with Maggie, try and talk some sense into Beattie and then go up to Dr Hargreaves' garden and harvest the broad beans and cabbages. She took great pride in the flourishing vegetable garden, pleased to know that as Mrs Hargreaves distributed the produce to the needy families in Barnborough, she herself was doing something to make their lot easier. And now there are more needy families than ever, she thought, the shattered faces of Mary Cooper and Clara Howard springing to mind. This horrible war has a lot to answer for, she silently told the bubbling porridge. She shared it out between two bowls, and leaving it on the table to cool, she went upstairs.

Kezia was bouncing on her bed, a favourite nursery rhyme book open at her feet. 'Humpty Dumpty sat on a wall, Humpty Dumpty had a . . . ' she chimed. One bounce too many, and Amy dived closer, Kezia toppling into her mother's arms and Amy gasping her relief.

'Silly Humpty, you could have hurt yourself,' said Amy, hugging the warm, little body tight and speaking sharply. 'Jumping up and down on the bed's dangerous, don't do it again.' She set Kezia down. 'Keep your nightie on and come and get your breakfast.'

They were at the top of the stairs when they

heard the kitchen door crash open. 'Auntie Amy, Auntie Amy!' Maggie sounded frantic. Amy ran downstairs and through to the kitchen, Kezia at her heels.

Maggie, dressed only in her shift and her hair on end grabbed Amy by the arm, dragging her to the open door and crying, 'I can't waken me Mam an' there's blood everywhere.'

At the word 'blood', Amy's own blood ran cold. What had Beattie done now? Had she arrived home drunk and fallen and cracked her head? Without waiting to ask, she threw a shawl round Kezia and then grabbed her own coat. Maggie streaked ahead as they ran to Grattan Row.

Mary and Henry huddled in a chair by the dead fire, their eyes wide with fear.

'She's upstairs,' yelled Maggie, charging up the narrow stairwell. Amy plonked Kezia in the other armchair and followed Maggie. As she climbed, she had a strong presentiment that what she was about to see was far worse than she had imagined.

At the open bedroom door, she paused to gather her courage. The room was almost in darkness, a guttering lamp casting Maggie's shadow and that of the dark hump on the bed grotesquely across the wall. Amy stepped inside.

Beattie was sprawled in a pool of dark blood and fetid matter, her legs at a peculiar angle. Scattered on the bed were a pair of knitting needles, a long-handled spoon and an empty bottle of gin. Amy swayed on her feet, her shadow cavorting wildly on the whitewashed wall. She reached for the bedpost to steady herself, and with her free hand she felt for the pulse in Beattie's neck, her fingers trembling so much they were useless. She stooped so that her cheek touched Beattie's mouth, hopeful she might feel a warm breath, but her sister's lips were cold. Coming upright and swallowing noisily she gently closed Beattie's eyelids, shutting in the crazed, demonic stare.

'Shall I get t'doctor, Auntie Amy?'

Amy nodded dumbly, although she knew it was hopeless. Maggie clattered down the stairs and out into Grattan Row.

Amy stayed, staring at Beattie and blaming herself for not doing more to prevent this tragic waste of life. She had been too harsh. Instead of criticizing Beattie's drunkenness and dark moods she should have been seeking medical help. She gazed at the needles and the spoon. She had heard enough gossip to know what Beattie had done even if poor Maggie didn't. What was more, she thought she knew why; Beattie hadn't wanted Bert to know.

After Dr Hargreaves had examined the body, he drew Amy out onto the landing away from Maggie who was kneeling by the bed stroking Beattie's hair. Lowering his voice, he confirmed that Beattie had attempted an abortion and bled to death. He would inform the police, so that foul play could be ruled out.

The next two days passed by in a blur, Amy comforting Maggie and her siblings and at the same time arranging a funeral and attempting to get word to Bert. Raffy and Samuel helped where they could but Amy ached for Jude's presence: calm, loving Jude who knew what to do in a crisis.

On the morning of the funeral, a policeman

came to the house again. Amy presumed it was to do with Beattie's death. She didn't invite him inside to where Maggie, Samuel, Raffy, Bessie and the children were waiting for the undertakers to arrive with the coffin in the hearse. The policeman, whom Amy knew well having gone to school with him, gazed at her sombrely and mumbled his apologies before taking his notebook from his pocket.

'It is my duty to inform you that a Mr Herbert Stitt, known to reside at number two, Grattan Row, Barnborough was declared dead at Southwood Hospital in London on the 13th of August,' he read woodenly. 'His remains can be collected by arrangement. The constabulary offers Mr Stitt's family our deepest sympathy.' The policeman took a deep breath and then said, 'Sorry to bring you more trouble, lass.'

Amy's mind reeled. Beattie had died needlessly. Bert would never have known about the baby. She flopped onto the window ledge. How could she go back inside and tell Maggie and her brothers and sister that they had also lost their father? Too shocked for tears, she looked up into a sky as clean as a freshly laundered blue sheet. *I kept my promise, Bert, and I'll go on keeping it*, she silently told it. Then forcing her feet to move, she walked to the door saying, 'Thank you. I'll let Bert's family know.'

But not just yet, she thought, *not until we've buried poor Beattie.*

★ ★ ★

272

Miserable though they were, the family set about making arrangements for the future. Albert and Fred would live at Intake Farm with Samuel, Bessie and Raffy, and Maggie, Mary and Henry with Amy. 'It's bad doing that Jude didn't make it home in time for the funeral,' Raffy said, as he dismantled the bed that was Mary and Henry's to take to Amy's house. 'Maybe he'll be here in time for Bert's.'

Sighing heavily, Amy dumped a pile of children's clothing into a bag. 'His letter didn't say when he'd arrive, but at least we know he's been granted compassionate leave,' she passed a hand over her eyes, 'and he's on his way home not knowing poor Bert's dead as well.' She did not disclose that he had written, '*I might not have loved Beattie as a brother should, but coming to it the way we did left it too late to form a bond. Too much had gone before and she was already damaged goods, God rest her soul.*' She saw no purpose in adding to the guilt that Raffy and Bessie still carried for having kept the truth from him and Beattie.

'It's a bad business all round,' said Bessie. 'That lad should be coming home for a bit of happiness with his family and a rest from all that fighting instead of having to deal with all this.'

'No matter, we'll still have him home,' said Amy, her voice rich with emotion. For whilst she had foreseen that Jude would not arrive in time for Beattie's burial she now lived in hope that he would arrive in time for Bert's, to comfort her and the children in the aftermath of so much grieving.

★ ★ ★

273

Jude arrived two days later, on the same day as Bert's remains were brought back to Barnborough. Amy was shocked to see how gaunt and weary Jude looked. When she told him of Bert's death, he visibly sagged. She flung her arms round him, crying with him as she helped him into a chair.

'I thought Bert wa' invincible,' said Jude, choking on his tears. He reared up, the chair toppling as he stamped to the open door and gazed into the distance at the slag heaps and pithead winding gear. 'He wa' so full of life. He dodged death every day in that bloody pit, only for the bloody Germans to finish him off like a lamb to the slaughter.'

Amy comforted him as best she could, and on the day they buried Bert and in the days that followed, Jude hid his grief for the sake of Bert's children. They had enough to bear.

★ ★ ★

When time is short, every moment is precious. For minutes or hours in those next seven days Amy, Jude and Kezia left the ordinary world to inhabit one of their own making; a walk in the woods, a morning tending the vegetable plot, a trip to the park and a visit to Intake Farm that brought tears to Raffy's eyes as he gazed at his son and told him how proud he was to be his father. Evenings were spent in the cosiness of the parlour, each shared moment more magical than the one before.

Whenever Maggie wasn't at school, she joined them, wanting Jude's company for he had been where her dad had been and knew what went on over there, in France. Although Jude was deeply saddened by Bert's death, he wasn't averse to talking about him. He told Maggie what a marvellous driver Bert had been, that he had risked his own life to save others, and that his commanding officers held him in high regard. She laughed at his droll stories about Bert's escapades, her grief easier to bear as, in her eyes, her dad became a hero.

As for little Kezia, her dad, Jude, was already her hero. She couldn't get enough of his cuddles, games and stories, and Jude rejoiced in getting to know his little daughter all over again. But seven days, filled at first with deep sadness and then with love and happiness, pass all too quickly, and on a wet and windy Tuesday, Amy, Kezia and Maggie and Raffy stood on Barnborough Station to say farewell to Jude. Dressed in his greatcoat, puttees and boots and his rifle strapped to his back, once again he was being taken from them by this terrible war.

26

Of all Bert and Beattie's children, Maggie was the one who missed them the most. When she wasn't at school or helping Amy with the chores, she spent long hours reading or gazing intently into space. Amy let her grieve, and whenever Maggie wanted to talk about her parents, she was happy to listen. However, she grieved in private for the sister she thought she had failed. In the dark hours, she railed against Bessie for having made Beattie the unhappy woman she had always been, but this still didn't prevent her from feeling she should have been the one to rectify the wrongs.

Amy's mind often dwelt on the secrets and lies that were the root of all this suffering. Yet, as time went by, her generous heart would not allow her to wholly blame Bessie and Raffy; her mother had been a desperate young girl when she fell pregnant with Beattie and duped Hadley into marrying her. Sadly, she had then spent years hiding her secret, afraid of all she had to lose if she were found out, and taking out her misery on her innocent daughter. As for Raffy, he hadn't even known of Beattie's existence until it was too late. Time and again Amy tried to console herself that the past could not be undone, but sometimes it had a habit of catching up on her.

★ ★ ★

Amy wasn't the only one haunted by the past. Bessie also, couldn't let it go.

Today, as she looked at Jack and Fred shovelling a hearty breakfast into their hungry mouths, she felt a sudden, deep urge to acknowledge the misery she had caused. She set down the teapot and looked over at the two bent heads, one dirty fair, the other a tawny brown. She couldn't tell the boys how she felt; they were too young to be burdened with her sins, and she wouldn't tell Raffy. He would only say she was reaping what she had sown.

Twisting her hands in her apron, Bessie recalled how often those same hands had slapped little Beattie for no reason other than to assuage her own guilt. The cruel words that she had spoken then now stung her tongue as though she had just delivered them. Was this to be the pattern of the rest of her days, she wondered, crying deep inside over wrongs that she had committed and now could never put right? She let her apron fall, brushing at the creases and wishing she could smooth her life as easily.

The boys pushed back their chairs, ready to go and join Raffy in the fields. Before they left the kitchen, Bessie caught each of them by the hand. She plopped a fond kiss on Jack's cheek and then on Fred's. 'Have a good day, lads,' she said, 'don't be late back for your lunch.'

'As if we would,' Jack said, laughing as he and Fred went out into the yard.

Listlessly, Bessie did her chores, her thoughts crawling round like cockroaches inside her head and making it ache with remorse. She felt faint with relief by the time Amy arrived to collect some eggs. Now, at least, a diversion might dispel the awful memories.

Bessie bustled about the kitchen, brewing a fresh pot of tea and laying out cups and saucers, but her movements were clumsy, her hands unsure. 'Are you feeling all right, Mam?' Amy asked, concerned by her mother's distracted manner.

All at once, the doors inside Bessie's heart and mind, the ones she had struggled to keep shut fast, burst open. 'No, I'm not,' she said, a hot sweat making her body feel clammy as she slopped tea into two cups. She sat down heavily in a chair at the table. Amy also sat, a worried frown creasing her brow.

'Are you ill?'

'Not in me body,' Bessie said, 'but I'm not right inside my head.'

Amy's frown deepened. 'Whatever do you mean?'

Bessie took a sip of her tea then grimaced as though it was too bitter. The cup clattered against the saucer. 'I can't get Beattie out of my mind,' she cried. 'I keep thinking of her when she was a little girl.' She placed her fleshy arms on the table in front of her, her chin almost touching the freckled skin. Then she took a deep breath.

'I ruined that child's life,' she said, her voice low and thick with emotion. She closed her eyes as if to blot out the memory, and when she opened them, she stared bleakly into space. 'I was cruel beyond words,' she continued brokenly, her voice barely above a whisper, 'but the very sight of her made me do things that I'll never forgive meself for to my dying day.'

Amy didn't deny it; she couldn't.

'And I did it for my own selfish greed.' Bessie spat out the words. Then, cloaked in shame, she fixed her eyes on something above Amy's head and said, 'Do you know what I used to do when I was in bed with your dad? I pretended he was Raffy.' She twisted her lips distastefully. 'What sort of a woman does that make me?' She lowered her gaze, her eyes begging for her daughter to understand. 'I never felt for your dad what I felt for Raffy but I was a good wife to him in deed, if not always in thought, and I foolishly told myself that if I didn't show any love for Raffy's daughter then I'd somehow be making it up to your dad for having duped him. I hid my guilt so deep that it no longer bothered me, but now when it's too late to put things right it's eating away at me and I can't take much more.' Bessie was sobbing now, great gulping sobs that tore at Amy's heart.

Amy had, at the start, flinched at the intimate details, but the more she listened the more she realised what inner courage it must have taken for her mother to make her confession. Now, filled with the utmost compassion, she reached across the table for Bessie's hands. She squeezed them comfortingly. She couldn't undo the past, but she could ease her mother's suffering. 'It's never too late to admit you're sorry,' she said, 'and I know you can't make your peace with Beattie on earth, but maybe she's looking down and seeing what a wonderful job you're doing with her boys. She'd thank you for that.'

Bessie raised her sodden cheeks and blinked. 'Do you think so?'

'I know so,' Amy said firmly. 'I like to believe the dead know everything. She'll rest peacefully now she knows how you feel.'

'So help me God, I'll make it up to her,' Bessie said on her breath. 'Them lads'll want for nothing.'

'I know they won't,' Amy said sincerely.

Bessie wiped her face with the palms of her hands. 'I feel like I've been given a second chance,' she said, sounding more like her old self, and managing a wan smile.

'Like they say, Mam. God works in mysterious ways.'

★ ★ ★

There was a knock on Amy's door and Maggie answered it. 'It's me Uncle Ben and Auntie Dora,' Maggie called out to Amy in the parlour. She sounded surprised. Amy was equally surprised, for although they had attended his funeral, they didn't make a habit of visiting Bert's sister-in-law. They'd fallen out with Beattie shortly after she had married Bert. Had they come because 1916 was drawing to a close? Were they bringing Christmas gifts for their bereft nieces and nephews?

Amy made them welcome, and over a cup of tea Ben divulged the reason for their visit. 'It's like this,' he said, sounding frightfully nervous. 'Me an' Dora have been talking. What with our bairns all teenagers, we thought we should rear little Mary and Henry.' He looked anxiously from Amy to Maggie, their shocked faces making him hastily add, 'We'd give 'em a good home, an' it's

280

what our Bert wanted.'

'You mean take 'em away from us?' Maggie turned her ashen face to Amy.

'We'd bring 'em to see you often enough, an' you could visit us,' Dora blurted out, 'an' Ben here wants to do summat right by Bert. Afore your dad went off to France he came to see us. He said if owt happened to him he'd like me an' Ben to take 'em because what with your mam being like she was . . . ' Dora clamped her hand to her mouth as Maggie visibly bristled.

Ben tried to rescue the situation. 'Your dad said it 'ud interfere wi' your schooling and . . . ' he paused, looking at Amy. 'He told us he knew you'd see to Maggie an' the lads but he thought t'young 'uns would be better off wi' us. Sharing the load, he said. He couldn't trust Beattie to . . . ' He pressed his lips together, afraid to say more.

Amy made a fresh pot of tea, and leaving Ben and Dora in the kitchen she took Maggie into the parlour. She had often heard Bert singing Dora's praises, particularly when he wanted to annoy Beattie. She also knew Ben and Dora had a comfortable home and that Ben was a Pit Deputy earning good money. Gently, she pointed out these attributes, at the same time feeling guilty at offloading Bert's children when she had promised him to take care of them. But a loving home with his brother offered far more advantages than she herself thought she could give.

Maggie listened thoughtfully, agreeing or protesting and eventually seeing reason. 'I suppose you're right, Auntie Amy, an' if it's what me dad wanted it's only right we should let 'em go . . . but

I'll miss 'em somethin' awful.' Her eyes filled with tears as she added, 'An' what wi' me mam not being here anymore it does make sense. Me Aunt Dora'll be a good mam to them.'

'She will, Maggie,' said Amy, struggling with the thought that she wasn't exactly breaking her promise to Bert. Besides, when Jude came home, she had promised him the chance to go to college, a promise that would be easier to keep if they had fewer mouths to feed.

Dora and Ben crowed with delight when Maggie told them of her decision, and hurrying into the parlour, they began telling Mary and Henry what a wonderful time they would have once they were living with them. At first, the children looked warily from Amy to Maggie, not understanding, but as Dora cuddled little Henry and Ben told Mary about the dogs and the pony waiting for them at their new home, their anxiety turned to excited anticipation. 'Can I come as well?' said Kezia.

After tearful goodbyes on Maggie's part, and a deep sense of having made a wise decision on Amy's, the little family in the house in Wentworth Street settled into a new pattern, one that saw them living contentedly throughout the rest of that awful year and into the next.

★ ★ ★

On a warm, sunny morning in June 1917, Amy was down on her knees washing the flags outside her front door. As she lifted the donkey stone to draw the obligatory patterns on the clean step, she felt a tap on her shoulder.

'Letter from your old man,' the postman said gently. Jack Spivey knew how much these missives meant to the women who waited daily to hear from their husbands and sons and he hoped this one contained good news. Amy dried her hands on her apron and tore open the envelope. Skimming the letter she cried, 'Jude's been granted leave.' Whistling cheerily, Jack went on his way.

'Jude's coming home!' Amy's excited cry rang through the house, Kezia and Maggie rushing headlong from the kitchen into the parlour.

'When?' Maggie urged, her copper curls bouncing.

'The first week in July . . . ' Amy paused, and tapping her fingertips lightly on her chin she calculated, 'That's a week and two days from now.' Half-laughing and half-crying, she took hold of the girls' hands and together they jigged about the room.

★ ★ ★

Amy rarely left the house that first week in July but today, Tuesday, she had taken Maggie and Kezia up to the vegetable plot after Maggie came home from school. 'I've neglected it these past few days and the marrows will spoil if we don't pick them now,' she said, handing Maggie a large trug and a sharp knife. You cut them off and Kezia can put them in the basket.'

'Ah, there you are, Amy.' Mrs Hargreaves swooped across the lawn, beaming. 'I was anxious you had forgotten about us,' she said.

Amy assured her she hadn't. 'It's just that my

husband's coming home on leave and I don't want to be out of the house when he arrives,' she explained, 'so is it all right if I leave the girls here for the time being to gather the marrows?'

Mrs Hargreaves beamed again. 'How splendid,' she gushed. 'Now you pop off back home and I'll take charge here. We'll have a lovely time, won't we girls?' She gave Amy's arm an affectionate squeeze. 'I do so love having children about the place, and you've done such a wonderful job here I can hardly refuse.'

★   ★   ★

Amy was upstairs putting freshly ironed clothes into drawers when she heard footsteps outside her back door. It could be anyone of her neighbours, she thought, but what if . . . Leaving a pile of clothes on Kezia's bed, she ran downstairs.

Jude lounged in the kitchen doorway, a slow, sweet smile lighting his face as his eyes roved the familiar little room. A strange choking sound escaped his throat, and on hearing it Amy hurried towards him her hands reaching out, drawing him into the room. Then, as though wakened from a trance Jude clasped her to his chest, his lips seeking hers.

Breathless, they broke apart to gaze once again at each other, as though they could not believe what they were seeing. Amy reached up, her fingers caressing the taut, greyish skin on his stubbly cheek. *How gaunt he is*, she thought, *but still the most wonderful sight in life.* Jude rested his head against her hair and breathed in deeply. She smelt like meadow flowers, and he closed his eyes, holding the scent in his nose. As Amy's senses recovered, she wrinkled hers as the rank smell of the battle-field filled her nostrils but she didn't care. Words tumbling from her mouth, she spoke of love and longing, and the thrill of having him by her side.

Jude, still somewhat dazed, stood before her wearing his greatcoat and peaked cap. His rifle, mess tin and water bottle were strapped to his back and his puttees and boots caked in mud. Amy giggled.

'I can't get my arms round you and give you a proper hug,' she chuckled, patting the conglomeration of equipment. This simple remark made Jude come alive and he laughed out loud. Still laughing, he stripped down to his shirt and trousers and then took her in his arms and kissed her again and again. Beneath his shirt she felt the steady beat of his heart and her own beating in tandem. Jude glanced about him. 'Where's Kezia?'

Amy told him. 'Let's go and get her,' he said, and slipped on his tunic.

★　★　★

On his first night at home, after tucking an over-excited, sleepy Kezia into bed, Jude followed Amy into their bedroom. He had been longing for this moment like a thirsty man in a desert craves for an oasis, but suddenly all thoughts of lovemaking fled his mind.

'Where did you get all these?' he asked, stooping to read the titles of the books on the shelves. Amy smiled fondly. Here they were, coming together with their love of books. It was like starting over again but better.

'It's good to tell where your true love lies,' said Amy mockingly. 'Here am I waiting to be made love to, and you've got your nose in a book.'

Chuckling, Jude dived into bed and together they proved their love in the best way they knew how. Later, Jude rolled onto his back and gazed up at the ceiling, his lean, hard body pressed against Amy's arm and thigh. 'It's a grand collection; I can't believe it's ours. I'll read 'em all when I get home for good,' he said dreamily, 'and in the meantime I'll keep doling out my books to the lads. Do you know, some of 'em had never read a book before and now they're queuing up to borrow 'em? They can't get enough of Kipling's *Plain Tales from the Hills*. Mind you, I don't blame them, he can't half tell a good tale. He makes you laugh and, God knows, we don't have a lot to laugh about over there.' He shuddered.

Amy thought she could almost feel his spirits sinking, and putting her hand on his cheek, she gently turned his face to hers. 'Don't think about it, love. Let it go.'

Jude shook his head and then, as though he had emptied it of horrible thoughts, he grinned and rolled over, covering Amy's body with his own. 'Aye, there's much better things to think about right now,' he said, as she warmed to his urgent caresses.

★ ★ ★

286

The next morning, as Jude lingered over his breakfast with a look of sheer contentment on his face, Amy broached the subject of letting Ben and Dora take Henry and Mary to live with them. 'Do you think I've let Bert down?' she asked, this thought having troubled her ever since the children's departure.

'You'd never let anyone down; you've a heart as big as China,' Jude replied, the words full of love and admiration. 'You did your best for Bert's children and for poor Beattie — God rest her — and look how you coped with all that trouble your Samuel caused, not to mention Bessie and Raffy and all that carry-on. You've nothing to feel guilty about — you're a wonderful woman. And anyway, it makes perfect sense to let Mary and Henry go to a couple who can give them so much more than we can because,' he shrugged his shoulders, 'I've no idea what I'll do when this war's over. I don't want to go back down the pit but I will do if it means I can give you everything you deserve. I'd give you the world if I could.' He looked earnestly into Amy's face.

'You'll go to college and get your qualifications, young man,' Amy said severely. Jude stood and pulled her into his arms. Pressed against him, Amy silently promised that when he came home for good, she would move mountains to make sure that, in one way or another, his future involved working with books.

Two weeks later, Jude returned to France.

★ ★ ★

In the months following his return to France Jude marched, or shuffled, and fought wherever and whenever he was ordered. Now, having travelled north in a cattle truck he arrived at Neuve Chapelle, a damp, smoky region between cotton mill towns in the Lys Valley to the south and the French coalfields to the north. Years of warfare had destroyed the region, the towns and villages reduced to rubble. Unlike the chalky soil of Picardy, the trenches here were in marshy ground and Jude spent his days caked in the ooze of his surroundings. He was used to eating with fingers slimed with mud and resting his weary body on rotting sandbags. This was the pattern of his life.

★   ★   ★

On a night in July 1918 Jude was on revetting duty, packing sandbags into the top of the trench. Stars speckled the violet sky, Jude tilting his head to gaze up at them. These same stars were shining down on Amy and Kezia, he thought, feeling a moment of violent loneliness: God, how he missed them. Would he ever see them or hold them again?

A line from Shakespeare came into his mind, and although he didn't always understand old William's strange use of language, he liked the bit where Juliet said, 'And when he shall die take him and cut him out in little stars'. Was that what Amy would do with him, he wondered?

'Nearly done,' said Billy Cooper, breaking Jude's reverie as he rammed a sandbag into place. 'Maybe we can get us heads down for an hour or two.'

288

He had no sooner spoken than the sky lit up, red and yellow flashes accompanied by a dreaded shrieking. Jude and Billy dived to the bottom of the trench as an eleven-inch shell hit the ground above their heads.

'Bloody hell, that were close,' Jude said, as a minenwerfer tore into the sandbags they had so recently replaced. Shells rained down, Jude remarking, 'We'll be buried alive if this keeps up.'

Worming their way back along the trench to the fire step and their comrades they were stopped in their tracks by an almighty explosion, the sound reverberating above their heads and Jude wondering if the stars were about to fall. Turning the corner to approach the main trench, he staggered back as his eyes took in what lay before him.

'Bloody hell,' he whispered, his voice rising to a scream as he shouted, 'God almighty, what have they done?'

The main trench and the fire step were one gaping hole, the dismembered bodies of lads he had worked with only an hour before lying like butchered meat. Jude stumbled forward into the body of a young lad, one eye begging for help in what was left of his face, the other side blown completely away. Jude fell to his knees and gripped the boy's hand. 'You'll be all right in a minute, lad,' he mumbled.

The eye fluttered and closed, the lad's head rolling to expose the massive injury. Jude shuddered. 'See,' he whispered, 'I told you you'd be all right in a minute, an' now you are.' With gentle fingers he removed the young soldier's identification tag.

Billy had gone ahead and Jude now followed

him, crawling amongst the debris to tend their wounded and dying friends. The few who had survived without injury joined them and the following day, after burying their dead comrades and waving farewell to those who were carted away to the field hospital, the battalion reformed.

But that horrific scene would not leave Jude's head.

★ ★ ★

On the last day of July 1918 on the frontline at Warnerton on the River Lys, Jude tramped along a trench in the footsteps of his compatriots, the rank, raw stink of human excrement commingling with the ever-present mud. Jude lifted his sodden boots, suction protesting with every step as he ploughed on. Was this the way it would end? A perpetual trench to heaven or hell, littered with the detritus of all that man had to offer for king and country.

The smell grew stronger and his stomach heaved. Memories of the pit bottom in Barnborough flittered through his mind, the stink reminding him of the piles of shit left behind by colliers on the previous shift. Maybe Amy had been right; he should have stayed working down the pit. At least he had known why he was there, which was more than he could say for this place.

The line halted, a sharp blast of a whistle the signal to 'go over the top.' Jude scrabbled to the top of the ridge, rolling over into open ground and then up onto his feet. As he moved forward a dim uneasiness flitted across his mind like something you see but don't see out of the corner of your eye. The ground beneath his feet trembled and then exploded as an almighty roaring was thrown back from the sky.

In the following days Jude struggled with the fact that he was still alive and his physical injuries minor. However, his guts had turned to water and the left side of his face had developed an irritating tic. His body trembled at the slightest sound and his hands shook so badly he couldn't hold his rifle. When he could no longer walk in a straight line the orders came to 'get that man on the next shipment back to Blighty.'

Jude's war was over; he was going home.

$\star$ $\star$ $\star$

Amy didn't usually have premonitions, but from the moment she lifted the small, brown envelope with its typewritten address she knew to expect bad news. Inside was a single sheet of paper explaining that Sgt. Jude Field was suffering from war neurosis and had been transferred from the frontline to a hospital in East Suffolk from where he would shortly be transferred to a hospital in Leeds, it being nearer to his home address.

Over the past four years, Amy's ears had grown attuned to the postman's arrival in Wentworth Street. From whichever part of the house she was in she listened for the squeak of his bicycle's wheels or the rattle of the letterbox and the plop of a letter on the mat behind the front door. Waiting to hear the familiar sounds had become part of her daily routine, her feelings fluctuating between intense hope and impending sorrow. So far, each one of Jude's letters had filled her with pleasant relief, but for the past seven days she had waited for another letter with a typewritten address on its envelope, a letter from a stranger. And although she dearly wanted to hear that Jude was closer to home, each day of waiting left her with a feeling of cold dread.

Now, with her ears pricked, Amy waited in the silence of her kitchen for the flat iron to heat on the stove. She glanced at the clock — not long to wait if Jack was keeping to his usual time. *Please God, let him bring it today.* Amy lifted the iron and spat, her spit sizzling on its plate as she crossed from the stove to the table. The letterbox rattled. She thumped the iron face down on the blanket padding.

The same kind of brown envelope with the same typeface lay tantalisingly on the mat. At last, she thought, breath whooshing from her lungs.

The letter said much the same as the one before. Jude was now resident in the military hospital at Beckett's Park and would remain there until he was considered well enough to return to duty. A list of visiting times and a map showing directions to the hospital was included.

Dazed, Amy wandered back into the kitchen, her senses instantly alerted as the acrid smell of burned wool nipped at her nose. She lifted the iron from the blanket padding and gazed forlornly at the scorched imprint. She didn't know whether to laugh or cry. She read the letter again, and five minutes later, she was on the road to Intake Farm.

27

Beckett's Park Hospital

November 1918

Amy's spirits were high, and even though the railway platform had been crowded with fellow passengers all wanting to exchange the glorious news, and the journey had seemed to take forever she hadn't minded one bit. It was the 12th of November and everywhere was celebrating. All the towns and villages she had passed through sported flags and bunting, fluttering in the stiff breeze, and on the busy city streets passers-by stopped to smile and say how wonderful it was that war was over.

'Give them brave boys in there a cheer from me, an' tell 'em we've done for the Kaiser and the Hun,' said the cabby, as she paid her fare outside the hospital's front door. Assuring him that she would do just that, Amy pulled her thick, woolly scarf closely round her head to ward off the biting wind and hurried to get inside.

She was now an old hand at visiting and knew several of the doctors and nurses by sight, greeting them cheerfully as she trotted confidently down the long corridor. It seemed a lifetime since she had first walked its length worrying about where to go or saying or doing the wrong thing. Amy pushed open the door, a smile on her face.

Jude was sitting at a table littered with hanks of black wool and boxes holding all manner of bits and pieces. Alongside him, other men and nurses were doing the same. Last week he had woven a small cane basket, Amy carrying it home to proudly show everybody before placing it on the kitchen table and filling it with dried flowers.

Now, Amy nodded and smiled greetings to the nurses and the two women and a man who were also visiting their loved ones. She had spoken several times with the man, a retired colonel visiting his officer son, and both the women, one visiting her husband and the other her son. Talking with them had been a comfort; they were all in the same boat, desperate to regain the men they loved from the clutches of a war that had so terribly changed them, wanting nothing more than to release them from their torment and back to the men they had once been.

Amy went and stood at the worktable so that she was facing Jude. He was concentrating on stitching an eye in place, his own eyes narrowed and the tip of his tongue pressed against his upper lip — just like Kezia did when she was concentrating. Amy suppressed a giggle. Nurse Brennan looked up and said, 'Hi there, Mrs Leas, isn't it just great that the war's over?' Her smile was wide and Amy responded with one equally wide, but she couldn't help thinking that for some of the men in Beckett's Park, the war would never be over.

However, Amy agreed with the pleasant Irish nurse who had a soft spot for Jude, and at the sound of her voice Jude gave a start. He glanced this way and that, his face wearing the puzzled expression it so often wore these days. Then he saw Amy and his features crumpled into a half-smile. Lips trembling, he clumsily pushed back his chair and then shambled towards her. Amy clasped his hand and led him to the chairs by the window, pleased to see that he was walking more steadily than he had on her previous visits.

Before he sat down, she hugged him and kissed him on the mouth. His lips didn't respond, but neither did he push her away as he had on other occasions. 'The war's over, Jude, isn't it wonderful?' she gushed, holding on to him. 'Think of it, love! A world at peace.'

He pulled away from her and sat down heavily in the nearest chair, his face a blank. 'Over,' he echoed, but Amy wasn't sure that he understood. For the remainder of the visit they talked about Kezia and other things, although Amy did most of the talking, and then she read him a chapter from *Piccadilly Jim* — Wodehouse always made him smile — and even though Jude was now reading for himself he liked listening to Amy. 'Over,' he repeated, as she closed the book, Amy unsure whether he was referring to the book or the war.

It was time for her to leave, and as Amy kissed Jude goodbye, she felt a faint, familiar stirring in his lips and before she knew it, he was kissing her as warmly and sweetly as he had in the past. It was their first proper kiss since the visits began, and the blood sang in Amy's ears; he was coming back to her. When Jude ended the kiss, he gazed at her as though he was seeing her for the first time and then he sat down, a contented smile lighting his face and eyes. He appeared to have forgotten Amy was still at his side and, reluctantly, she left him with his thoughts and slipped quietly from the room.

Amy was almost afraid to believe in the progress Jude was making week on week, yet Dr Mackay had told her several times that the signs were good. Only last week he had said that whilst Jude still engaged in violent tremors and bitter speech, these fits were short-lived and increasingly rare. Amy had been delighted, and although Dr Mackay had warned her that Jude might have to contend with them for years to come, she was undeterred. She felt in her heart that Jude was recapturing his strong, beautiful spirit.

Now, she walked buoyantly down the corridor just in time to meet Dr Mackay coming out of his office. Falling into step with her, he asked had her visit gone well. She told him all about it, even the kiss, and before he left her in the foyer he said, 'You may well have him home for Christmas, Mrs Leas.'

28

Intake Farm, Barnborough

Christmas, 1918

'Do you think he'll ever work again?' Bessie glanced covertly at Jude as she whispered in Amy's ear.

Amy felt a prickle of irritation and pulled away sharply. 'He's only been home four days,' she hissed, lifting the jug of mustard sauce that Bessie had made to go with the pork she had roasted for their Boxing Day dinner.

'I was only asking,' whined Bessie, placing a conciliatory hand on Amy's arm. Amy shrugged her off and marched to the table, setting the jug down with a thud. Perhaps it had been unwise to come to Intake today. It was too soon to bring Jude into a crowded house, particularly when everyone kept fussing and talking to him as though he were deaf or stupid; or attempting to jolly him along as Freda was now doing. 'Come on then, Jude, give us a kiss.' She dangled a sprig of mistletoe above his head.

Samuel and Raffy laughed out loud but Jude sat woodenly, staring at his boots.

Albert and Fred cheered Freda on, Maggie yelling, 'Hey, Auntie Amy, she's stealing your husband.'

Jude raised his head and looked round anxiously. When his eyes met Amy's, she could see he looked tired, diminished, his expression haunted. Her heart aching with love, Amy went to his rescue but before she reached him Jude shot up out of the chair and blundered past her, out into the yard.

For a moment everyone was stunned into silence until Kezia let out a loud wail. 'See to her, Maggie,' cried Amy, heading for the door.

Outside, Amy peered into the dusk. Jude was leaning against the house wall, the glow from the kitchen window lighting his face. His eyes were closed and his jaw tilted upwards as he dragged deeply on a cigarette, its glowing tip sparking in the twilight. He looked utterly at peace. Amy stepped quietly back inside the house.

Kezia ran to her, pushing her tearstained face into Amy's legs and begging to be cuddled. 'He's just nipped out for a breath of air,' said Amy, lifting her daughter and trying to sound casual. 'Daddy's having a cigarette and a bit of peace and quiet, love.'

Freda arched her eyebrows and glanced up at the ceiling. Bessie bustled from the stove to the table with a large platter of sliced pork in her hands. 'Come on,' she said, overly cheery, 'let's all sit down. He'll be back in a minute.'

★   ★   ★

Outside, Jude flicked the butt of his spent cigarette onto the cobbles then ground it under his boot. He had sorely wanted to join in the fun but his mind and body wouldn't let him. No matter how hard he tried, he saw something looming beyond

298

his reach, something dark and impenetrable that got in the way of every happy moment. Mixed emotions surged through him and he didn't know what to make of them. On the one hand he knew he loved Amy and Kezia and felt a kinship with Raffy, Samuel and Bessie, but some inner reserve over which he had no control kept him detached, hard to reach. Strangely, it also made him feel safer: safer, but not better. He prised his back from the wall, and forcing himself to walk tall and straight, he went back inside.

'Just nipped out for a fag and a breath of air,' he muttered, unaware that he was repeating Amy's excuse. He essayed a grin and sat down at the table. 'This looks good. Well done, Bessie,' he said, as heartily as he could manage, but deep inside he doubted he would enjoy any of it.

'I hope the weather stays dry for New Year's Eve,' said Freda. 'I don't want to get married in a downpour.'

'It'll not rain, it won't dare, not if it knows it'll have you to listen to,' Samuel said jocularly. He addressed Jude. 'Does our Amy hold you responsible for everything, even t'bloody weather, cos this one does.' He flicked a thumb at Freda.

Freda laughed and pulled a face, but Jude just looked confused. Rain! Just for a moment his brain returned to a trench in Lys: mud, blood and pouring rain. Paralysed, he couldn't breathe, the glimpse of that other time so painful he didn't know what to do next. His knife and fork slipped from his fingers, clattering onto his plate, and for the remainder of the meal he sat motionless, his eyes fixed on the clock on the mantelpiece.

The others pretended not to notice, Freda and Bessie chatting about the forthcoming wedding, and Amy doing her best to join in. Raffy also tried to lighten the mood with a few funny stories, although his saddened eyes rarely left his son's face. Maggie, Albert and Fred led Raffy on in a bid to make things seem normal; after all it was supposed to be a celebration.

Amy didn't know which was worse. Everyone fussing over Jude and asking if he was all right, or doing as they were now by completely ignoring him. As she sat with Kezia on her lap, Kezia laughing giddily as they played a silly little game that involved clapping hands and tapping cheeks, chins and noses, Amy thanked God for her daughter. It was she who sustained her and calmed her when despair threatened to overwhelm her.

★ ★ ★

Later that night, Amy was in bed in the little house in Wentworth Street with Jude next to her. She fought back tears although her head ached with the effort. Jude lay flat on his back, wooden and still, just as he had each night since his homecoming. Now that he was beside her, she missed his questing fingers and his lovemaking more than she ever had in the years they were apart. She knew he wasn't asleep, and that if she reached for him his body would arch and stiffen and then, as he had on the other nights, he'd get out of bed and go back downstairs. But she had to keep trying; she had to reach him.

The moment he felt her hand on his cheek, he

rolled to the edge of the bed and when she whispered, 'Jude, love, tell me what it is that's troubling you,' he swung his legs to the floor and clumped from the room. Amy stayed where she was, her thoughts crashing uncomfortably inside her head. Then, concerned that she had driven him away, preventing him from getting the sleep he so desperately needed, she followed him.

He was in the parlour, humped in a chair by the dead fire, the smoke from the cigarette clamped between his lips spiralling up into his glazed eyes. Afraid that it would burn his lips, Amy carefully removed it and threw it into the ashes. Jude lunged forward, the crash of mortars and the flare of lights playing in his head.

'Bastard, bastard, bloody bastard war. Shoot you bugger, shoot.'

'Jude, it's me, Amy! It's me, love!'

Jude sagged and stared blankly at her for a second or two before shaking his head in bemusement. 'S . . . s . . . sorry, lass, I . . . I thou . . . thought you . . . you were . . . Shit!'

'I'll make a cup of tea.' Amy made her voice sound as though nothing untoward had happened.

'Aye, I could do with a cup.' Jude sounded equally calm.

The tea brewed, they sat and talked like other couples do late at night, Jude praising Bessie's dinner and then Kezia for her cleverness at reading him a story before she went to bed. *Anybody would think we were a perfectly happy family*, thought Amy, but as they climbed the stairs yet again her mind still dwelt on that massive, impenetrable barrier she could not breach.

301

Days crawled by, Amy feeling as though she existed in a nightmare state where nothing seemed solid, not even the ground beneath her feet. She went about her daily business with as much spirit as she could muster, taking Kezia to school then collecting her in the afternoon, and in between she cleaned and cooked meals, all the while edging round her husband's uncertain moods.

On the day of Samuel and Freda's wedding only she and Kezia attended the ceremony. It was a pleasant occasion, but not the joyful one Amy had hoped for, Jude having flatly refused to accompany them. During the service she recalled those first few blissful weeks of married life and wondered when, if ever, they would recapture the magic that had once been theirs.

Jude spent long hours reading his way through the books Amy had collected. Only then did he seem at ease. However, with Kezia his temper was inconstant, Amy afraid to leave them alone in case he lost his reason and harmed their daughter.

Jude was aware of this, and it only added to his problems. What sort of a man had he become that his wife considered him capable of hurting his beloved child? Yet he saw the way Kezia shied away from him, and he was hurt but at a loss as to how he could build the child's confidence when his own was so fragile. He didn't understand his own dark moods or sudden tempers, so why should she?

★ ★ ★

After several weeks of what, to Amy, felt like walking on eggshells she now dreaded each new day. When she wakened, she didn't open her eyes, she just lay there steeling herself to get out of bed, shafts of panic lancing through her as though she was in some strange dark place where nowhere was safe. When she did open her eyes, she turned them on Jude.

Today he was sleeping peacefully, although he had cried out twice during the night, his rambling shouts and thrashing arms disturbing her sleep. She gazed at his finely sculpted, handsome features thinking how sad it was that he looked the same but was not the same, and her heart felt heavy as lead as she slipped out of bed.

It was not yet seven, the kitchen cold and bleak as she raked the embers in the stove and set the kettle to boil. Tomorrow was the first day of spring; a day that Amy had always welcomed for this was the time of year that the earth was reborn: coltsfoot and celandines in the hedgerows, birds making nests, and the sun's brightening rays banishing winter gloom. But, as the day stretched in front of her, she couldn't help wondering if her life would ever bloom again.

She dropped a blob of lard into the pan ready to fry slices of stale bread to go with the last two rashers of streaky bacon. Food was scarce, but money was scarcer. The small pension that Jude received did no more than cover the rent and groceries. Had it not been for Bessie's generosity things would have been much worse; eggs, potatoes and the occasional chicken made a world of difference. But as Amy watched the bacon sizzle

303

she knew that if they were to improve their living standards and provide Kezia with anything other than the most meagre childhood then one or the other of them must go to work.

'I'm going to the Saturday market,' Amy said, when Jude slouched into the kitchen, his hangdog expression making her want to put distance between them.

He didn't answer. Hooking a chair with the toe of his boot, he pulled it out from under the table and then sat down reaching for the book he had left there the night before. Amy set the plate of bacon in front of him. If he didn't want to talk then neither did she.

Upstairs, she went into Kezia and Maggie's bedroom. 'I'm off to the market. Mind Kezia for me until I get back, there's a good lass,' she said to her niece.

Maggie nodded her tousled head and then asked, 'What about me Uncle Jude?' She asked this warily because, like Kezia, she found his uncertain temperament disturbing.

'I wouldn't know,' Amy said wearily. 'Just keep out of his way. I won't be long.'

⋆ ⋆ ⋆

The market was busy, a stiff breeze flapping the canvas awnings on the stalls set out in rows on a large piece of waste ground behind Barnborough Town Hall. The Saturday market attracted a variety of vendors and customers on the lookout for bargains. Holding on to her hat and glad to be out of the house, Amy strolled past stalls selling clothes, footwear, household linens, crockery, ironmongery and a host of other things, stopping to make purchases at the dried goods and vegetable stall. She would have liked to buy towels or the blue vase on a bric-a-brac stall but she had barely enough money for essentials.

About to go home, she passed by an old woman whose stall was nothing more than an old bit of tarpaulin spread out on the ground. On it were a few odd cups and plates, mostly chipped, a worn pair of slippers, a battered teddy bear, a dented brass jug and a few books with faded covers and pages curled up at the corners. Amy wondered who on earth would buy such rubbish? If the stallholder were to sell every bit of it would it even cover the rental on the plot? But now she came to think of it, this old woman came week after week, so it must be worthwhile. Amy retraced her steps.

'How much for this?' She picked up a plate patterned with a country scene. Amy bought it and asked a few more questions about running a market stall. The old woman, more than willing to chat, gave her the ins and outs of it. 'Hail, rain or shine, I allus goes home wi' a profit,' she concluded.

Amy walked back to Wentworth Street deep in thought. If people bought the shabby books the old woman was selling, what would they pay for books in good condition? The shelves in the bedroom and parlour were crammed with clean, interesting volumes, most of which she and Jude had read, and wasn't it rather fanciful to have your own library when you could barely feed and clothe your family? Maggie needed new shoes and Kezia a coat, and whilst she might once have felt guilty at selling books that had been given to her, surely nobody would object now that Jude was unable to work. Furthermore, it would give him an interest, something positive to do in the same way as his lending library had during the years with his regiment; he enjoyed encouraging others to read.

Her step lighter, she entered the house only to find Kezia in the kitchen in tears and Maggie trying to pacify her.

Maggie jerked a thumb. 'He had one of his fits. He's hiding under t'stairs.'

Amy hurried into the parlour. Jude cowered under the overhang clutching his head in his hands. Her gentle persuasion making no impression on him, Amy went back into the kitchen and lifted Kezia into her lap. 'What happened, Maggie?'

'A big gust of wind blew t'dustbins down t'yard. They'd just been emptied an' they were clanging and clattering on t'flags. He let out a roar an' ran under t'stairs.'

'I'll see to him. He'll be right as rain in a minute.'

Amy set Kezia down and went back into the parlour. Squeezing into the tight space under the stairs she embraced Jude, whispering what she hoped were comforting, encouraging words. He gazed at her sorrowfully and she could see that he was embarrassed, and when she gently led him into the centre of the room he became surly and unreasonable.

'I'm a coward — that's what they call men like me. If they hadn't sent me home they'd have shot me. That's what they did to chaps who couldn't fight anymore.'

Amy knew this to be true and she shuddered; the Presbyterian minister's son had suffered that fate. 'You're not a coward, love, you fought and did your best.'

Jude flopped onto the settee, and in the next second he appeared to have forgotten she was there. But he hadn't forgotten. The crazy feelings just wouldn't go away. He had been glad to leave the hospital and come home, but now that he was there, he felt helpless and a nuisance. At least, in Beckett's Park he'd felt safe: no responsibilities, nothing much asked of him, and now here was, expected to provide for his family and build for the future. He wasn't sure he could do it.

Back in the kitchen, Amy lifted her snivelling daughter. 'Daddy didn't mean to frighten you, love. He's just not himself yet, and loud noises frighten him but — ' she chucked Kezia under the chin and then kissed the tip of her nose '—we'll make him better, see if we don't.'

Kezia blinked away her tears and nodded.

★ ★ ★

'Why?' Jude asked, when later that evening Amy told him of her idea to open a market stall selling books. He turned his dark eyes on her, his expression troubled.

'We barely manage on your pension,' she said, her voice gentle as she took his hands in her own. 'I have to choose whether to pay the rent or buy new shoes for the girls, and we never have any money to spare for luxuries.'

'And that's my fault, I suppose.'

'No, love; you're not to blame. It's just the way it is. Think about it, you'll be working at something you enjoy, telling people that reading good books can change their lives. We've far too many, most of which we've read and some we'll never read. You can keep your favourites and I'll keep mine, but the rest we'll sell and let others have the pleasure of owning them.'

'And when you've sold 'em all, what then? Will you sell me?'

'Now you're being ridiculous.' She chuckled and then pecked his cheek. 'I can't do this without you, just like I could never feel whole if you weren't by my side. I love you, Jude Leas, and I'm doing this for us and our family.'

'I disappoint you, don't I?' he said, turning his back and walking into the parlour.

'No, Jude, you don't disappoint me, you disappoint yourself,' she called after him, her patience worn thin.

29

'That's the last of 'em,' said Samuel, carrying a box filled with books out to the landing. 'I'll load these and then we'll be off.' He went downstairs leaving Amy and Jude in the bedroom. It was a Saturday morning, two weeks after Amy had first mooted her idea of renting a market stall. She had grown independent during Jude's absence; now she was putting it to use.

'Are you coming with us?' Amy looked at Jude who was sitting on the bed gazing dismally at the depleted bookshelves. During the past week, he had made no mention of selling the books but Amy had, each time meeting with a negative response. Now, when he didn't answer, she went out to the landing and into the small bedroom.

'Come on you two, we're ready for off.' Maggie and Kezia excited at the prospect of selling books at the market, rushed out onto the landing.

'Come on, Dad, get your coat! We're going,' chirped Kezia.

Jude stayed where he was.

Out on the street the girls jigged up and down on the pavement whilst Samuel rearranged the boxes in the back of his new truck. When Amy had told him about her new venture, he had offered to transport her and the books to and from the market. Bessie had sniffed at the idea of Amy running a stall on the market. 'I think it's demeaning,' she had said, 'and anyway, there's a book shop in

Barnborough.'

'There is, but not like mine,' Amy had replied tartly. 'I'll cater for ordinary folks, those who'd never darken the doors of Metcalfe's bookshop with its snooty assistants and overpriced books. I'll give everybody the opportunity to buy books cheaply so that they can read marvellous stories and travel in their minds to different times and places. They'll not be frightened to come to me because they'll know I sell books they can afford.'

Now, with her coat on and the sandwiches she had made earlier in her bag, Amy went into the parlour, and finding Jude there, she made one last attempt.

'Are you coming or not?'

'Why on earth would you need someone as useless as me to help you?'

'Because I always need you, Jude. Always have, always will.' Without waiting for a reply Amy marched out to the street, surprised to see Raffy there.

'I thought I'd come along for the ride, lend a hand so to speak,' said Raffy.

Amy gave him a warm smile, suppressing the urge to say: *it's more than your son is willing to do*.

'Can I get in?' Kezia squealed, jigging excitedly by the truck's door.

Samuel strutted proudly round the truck and handed Kezia into the passenger seat. Her nose wrinkled. 'It's a bit smelly,' she said.

'That's because I've been carting animal feed in it.' Unabashed, Samuel refused to let the fetid stink detract from the thrill of ownership. 'Now, ladies up front wi' me, and you hop in the back,

310

Raffy. They all piled aboard, and Samuel climbed into the driver's seat and started the engine.

He drove to the bottom of Wentworth Street and, it being a dead-end, he turned the truck and was just level with Amy's front door when Jude darted out carrying his coat over one arm and using the other to flag them down. He had watched Amy march out, her head high and her back straight, and guilt had cloaked him. She was so beautiful and brave she was, so why was he sitting here? He jumped up and ran to get his coat.

Samuel stopped the truck and Jude climbed in beside Raffy. Amy twisted in her seat so that Jude could see her face, her broad smile and sparkling eyes letting him know he'd done the right thing. He sat with his back against the truck's side, a warm feeling washing over him.

* * *

'This is your pitch.' The market manager pointed to a stall at the end of a row on the edge of the market. Trying to hide her disappointment, Amy paid her dues; she would have preferred a pitch in the heart of the market. Leaving the others standing forlornly round the bare stall she went to guide Samuel to the appointed spot so that they could unload the truck.

'I'll call back when I've done my errands and see how you're getting on,' Samuel said, when the last box had been offloaded. Amy gave him a shaky smile. A few hours in which to succeed or fail. She lifted a handful of books from one of the boxes.

'Set them out like this,' she said to Maggie and Kezia, placing the books flat and in a neat row with their front covers showing. Feeling awfully important, the girls applied themselves to the task and Raffy joined in. Jude lit a cigarette and stood, cold and aloof, gazing into the distance. It wasn't that he didn't want to participate, but the clamour of the traders as they setup their stalls was unnerving him.

Soon, shoppers thronged the walkways, examining, haggling and purchasing: meat, vegetables, clothes, household linens and utensils. The bookstall earned no more than cursory glances.

By midday Amy had sold four paperback thrillers, a bundle of comics and a battered copy of *Heart of Darkness* to a deranged-looking young man. Shortly after, she sold several women's magazines that Mrs Hargreaves had collected from the comfort group. Raffy was doing his hearty thing, smiling at passers-by and calling out for them to look at the books, and though they sometimes looked they didn't always buy. Jude had wandered off taking Maggie and Kezia with him, to where Amy didn't know.

Her feet and heart aching, Amy jealously eyed the shoppers clustered round the next pitch. Transfixed, and eyes wide with amazement they watched plates soar skyward, releasing pent breath with gusto when the juggling stallholder deliberately let some smash to the ground, his glib, raucous patter gulling housewives into buying not one, not two but six plates, cups or dishes.

'Maybe if I throw a few books up in the air we might sell some of 'em,' Amy said despairingly.

Raffy gave her a forced a smile. 'It be early days. Don't expect miracles.'

Jude and the girls returned, disappointed to see the stall still covered in books. A gloomy silence fell over the afternoon no one pretending to make an effort. When Samuel arrived with the truck, Amy almost cheered. They all began packing books into boxes.

The plate juggler tossed a pile of plates to his assistant and, crunching over broken crockery, he edged round the audience into the empty space in front of the bookstall. 'You're not packing up already, are you?' Smiling broadly he stuck out his hand. 'Jeb Moxon,' he said. Jude returned the greeting.

'We might as well. We've hardly sold anything.' Amy's crestfallen expression spoke a thousand words and asked as many questions.

Jeb smiled sympathetically. 'Nay, you haven't given it a chance. You might not sell much at first but then, all of a sudden it'll take off and you'll be rushed off your feet.' He settled his bulk on the edge of the stall and leaned forward in a confidential way.

'You see, customers are funny creatures. Today they weren't expectin' you, so when they set out this morning they'd no notion of buyin' books or magazines. They came for meat and veg, a few pots and maybe a pair of boots. Now they've seen you they'll go away and think about it and next week they'll buy summat. You have to give 'em time to get used to you, and you have to attract 'em. If you sell 'em a book give a free magazine, or a comic if they have kiddies with 'em. That way

313

you'll build up confidence and improve your takings.'

Amy listened avidly. Even Jude appeared to be listening, nodding his head now and then in recognition of the sound advice. Jeb smiled appreciatively.

'Another thing,' he said, sliding off the stall, preparing to return to his own and the swelling crowd, 'don't just stand there looking miserable. There's nowt they like better than a bit o' banter, so shout out to 'em, tell 'em what you've got and why they should be buying it. Convince 'em they need it.'

Clapping his hands, Jeb strutted back to his stall to demonstrate his philosophy: a steady stream of raucous patter, a breathtaking display of juggling wizardry and passive onlookers became eager customers. Over at the bookstall Amy, Jude and Raffy, awed by Jeb's prowess gave each other meaningful looks.

'I wouldn't know what to shout,' Jude said, glaring at the other two. 'I can't juggle books, and I can't read exciting bits out of 'em — nobody would listen.'

No, they wouldn't, thought Amy, *but at least you're showing an interest.* A frisson of excitement had her clasping Jude's hand and saying, 'I think we can make a go of this, love. It was lousy today but we've still covered the rent on the stall and made a few bob. Let's give it another go. We're not beaten yet.'

Jude gave a glimmer of a smile, and then, returning the pressure of her hand and looking deeply into her eyes he winked lazily, that same old slow

314

wink that had captured her heart when first they met. Amy's spirits soared. He hadn't done that since returning home from the war. She squeezed his hand all the tighter, her joy bubbling over as he said, 'Aye, maybe next time we'll sell 'em all.' But he said it without enthusiasm.

★ ★ ★

On their second outing, Jude instructed the girls to set the books out in categories, not just at random. 'Start by putting all the crime here,' he said pointing to the edge of the table, 'then the westerns, the romances, and so on. People often like one kind of book more than another, and they'll be able to see at a glance all the titles we've got in that category.'

'Now why didn't I think of that?' said Amy. 'After all, I was a librarian.' Jude gave her a warm smile. Under his and Amy's guidance the girls arranged the books, Amy glowing inside at Jude's perspicacity and thrilled to see him taking an interest. The strategy worked, and they sold twice as many books that day.

Over the next few weeks of setting up the stall on Tuesdays and Saturdays, trade did improve. Furthermore, to Amy's delight and relief so did Jude, market days working wonders on his temperament. If prospective customers were deliberating over making a purchase, he gave them the gist of the contents of several books, helping them to make a choice. The customers liked this and came back for more. He also talked with the other traders, some who like him had fought in the war, and at the end of each day he was always more like his former self: a man with a purpose who had done something worthwhile.

Therefore, Amy was bitterly disappointed when, on a Saturday morning, he refused to accompany her. 'Why?' she asked. 'Is it because we've only a few books left to sell?' It was true that their stock was depleted, all the popular titles sold and the few they had left unappealing to their regular clientele.

'I've something better to do,' he replied, playfully cagey.

Amy widened her eyes. 'What like?' Her tone was sharper than she intended.

'You'll find out soon enough,' he said, gazing intently into her face.

Amy wished she understood the enigmatic expression in his deeply mysterious eyes, but when she pressed him he became sullen, his mood turning so quickly that Amy, nervous of further upsetting him, let it go. Even so, she couldn't help thinking that his refusal to go to the market seemed like a retrograde step and she wondered if she was fooling herself into believing that his condition was improving.

Out in the street, Samuel tooted the truck's horn to let them know he'd arrived with the books, which he stored at the farm.

'Are you not coming, Dad?' wheedled Kezia, tugging his hand. Although she was somewhat afraid of his sudden tempers, she hated to see him sad.

'Not today, pet. Your dad has a bit of business to see to.' Jude stooped to peck her cheek.

Mystified, but anxious not to keep Samuel

waiting, Amy ushered the girls out. 'I'll go without you then,' she said, and although she was still irritated, she placed a hand on each of his cheeks and pulled his head down so that she could kiss his lips. 'I love you,' she said softly.

He returned the kiss warmly, and when she broke away and turned to the door, he gave her backside a playful slap. Amy blinked her amazement. 'My, my, Mr Leas, we are feeling perky,' she said over her shoulder. She said it lightly, but inside her chest her heart swelled and in her stomach a thousand butterflies fluttered. How long had it been since he had done such a thing she wondered, walking out to the street? Perhaps she wasn't fooling herself after all.

Jude watched her go. Then, feeling guilty, he went into the kitchen and at the mantelpiece he hastily emptied Amy's savings jar before he could change his mind. A short while later, wearing his good, black suit he left the house, walking purposefully to Intake Farm. Bessie gave him a cup of tea whilst he waited for Samuel to return from the market. After a brief transaction with his brother-in-law he set off walking again, this time a mile or so into the countryside to Spring Vale House.

It was a beautiful autumn morning, the rustle of burnished leaves under Jude's feet lending a whispering calm as he strode along the road. White clouds scudded across a blue sky, the immensity of the heavens him making him feel small and insignificant. And yet, he told himself, what he was about to do made him feel more alive than he had felt in a long time. If today's venture proved successful, it would also prove that he was returning to the man he used to be, the man who made Amy proud to be his wife. His suffering had caused her to suffer too much and yet, day after day, she gave him her unstinting love and still had faith in him. The doctors had done their best to put his mind right but now it was up to him; he was going to repay her love. He'd take his life into his own hands and use it to overcome the damage that the war had done. It had torn them apart in more ways than one but today he resolved to change all that.

★　★　★

Spring Vale House stood back from the road, and as he walked up the driveway he felt the tic in his right eye spring into action. Perspiration moistened his upper lip, and his hands felt clammy.

He almost turned and ran.

Then steeling his nerves and willing himself to go on he mounted the steps and gave three sharp raps with the brass knocker on the imposing front door. A young girl wearing a smart white apron and cap opened it.

'Who shall I say is callin'?' Her breathless delivery made Jude smile.

'Mr Jude Leas, calling with regard to the advertisement.'

With much nodding of her head the maid committed his words to memory, mouthing them silently before blurting out, 'What did you say your name is, mister?'

Jude chuckled. 'Jude Leas, I've come about the books.'

318

Bobbing a curtsey, she left him in the vestibule, her dizzy reception making him feel more at ease. Perhaps she was new to the job, he thought.

The maid returned minutes later accompanied by a fashionably dressed woman of middle years. Confidently the woman extended her hand. 'Good afternoon, Mr Leas. I'm Marion Marchant.' They shook hands. 'Take Mr Leas' hat, erm, cap, Doreen and show him into the library.'

Jude would have preferred to be handing the maid a smart black bowler rather than a cloth cap, but when Marion Marchant led him into the library, all thoughts of his wardrobe faded into insignificance.

There were books everywhere: in serried rows on the shelves lining the walls, and in neat piles on several small side tables and on a magnificent desk by a window. More haphazard piles filled the brass studded, highbacked leather chairs and a long, green velvet couch in front of the hearth. Marvelling, Jude turned full circle.

'Yes, Mr Leas, quite overwhelming, isn't it?' Marion Marchant gave him an amused smile. 'Now! Down to business,' she said briskly. 'The books on the shelves are going to my late father's old university, the rest are for sale. They all have to go before the new owner moves in. I've selected and removed those I'm taking with me but, sadly, my apartment in London wasn't built to house the entire collection.' She paused. 'Pops never could resist books,' she said reflectively, a soft chuckle indicating her fondness for him.

Jude hardly knew where to start. He coughed, nervously. 'I couldn't afford to buy them all,' he muttered, perusing the books in the nearest pile, his touch almost reverent. Even the thirty shillings Samuel had loaned him and the money from Amy's savings jar wouldn't buy many books of this quality.

Marion saw the longing in his eyes and noted the way he handled the volumes. 'I wouldn't worry too much about that. I'm sure we can come to some arrangement. You're the first enquiry I've had and I can't afford to be away from London much longer. I'll leave you to it,' she said brightly, and swept from the room.

Jude pored over the books, many whose titles and authors he had never heard of.

Two hours later, in which the maid brought him a cup of tea and a slice of fruit cake, Jude's selected piles sat to the right of the door; ten times as many remained on chairs and tables. He ached to take more but was too afraid. Could he even afford those he had chosen, he wondered? If not, he'd haggle.

'Well, how are we doing?' Marion breezed back into the room, wearing a warm smile. 'I hope you found plenty to interest you. I don't want to be left with them.'

Jude indicated the piles of books by the door. 'I'll take these if the price is right.'

Her smile faded. 'Is that all?' she exclaimed.

'It's all I think I'll be able to afford. You see . . . ' Before he could prevent himself Jude's hopes and dreams took flight. He talked about his love for books, the market stall and the library he had organised in his war years.

'So you served your country in more ways than

one,' said Marion impishly. 'On one hand the fighting soldier and on the other a purveyor of pleasure.'

Jude grinned. 'Something like that,' he replied, the grin slipping as his eyes darkened and his mouth twisted bitterly.

'Was it truly awful?' Marion sounded genuinely concerned.

'It was for me,' Jude said, his tone hollow. Then he surprised himself by admitting that he had suffered from shell shock and dreaded the thought of returning to the pit, his only option if he was to give Amy and Kezia the kind of lives they deserved.

Words running dry and embarrassment shrouding him like an iron suit, he ended up mumbling, 'So I can't take — '

'Nonsense! You obviously love books as much as my father did and he would have gladly helped you get your life back together.' Marion flourished her hand. 'Look, take these and those over there, take as many as you like. Just get on with it.'

'But what about the money?' Jude stuttered. She named a ridiculously low figure and he stared at her in amazement, prepared to argue. Marion was having none of it.

'Look, I've already made my decision. You need books. I don't. So let's call it a deal.'

They celebrated with another cup of tea. 'How will you transport them? Doreen says you arrived on foot.'

Chagrin dampening his pleasure, Jude said, 'I don't own a car, but if I go now I can get my brother-in-law to collect them in his truck this afternoon.'

'Splendid, this afternoon it is then.' Marion

stood and held out her hand. 'I'm pleased we met and I wish you the very best of luck in your new venture. I'm pleased to be part of it in some small way.'

Jude walked back to Intake Farm in a trance.

★ ★ ★

'By, bloody hell, I've never seen so many books in my life,' Samuel said, as they made a final trip down the steps of Spring Vale House, Marion and Doreen waving them goodbye. Jude laughed as he stashed the last pile into the truck, a rush of blood singing in his ears. He felt as though his whole body was waking from a deep sleep. It was as though a dam had burst and that from now on, he would only go forward.

★ ★ ★

Meanwhile, as Jude and Samuel filled the parlour in 2 Wentworth Street with books, in the market-place Amy wearily began to pack up the few books left on the stall.

'It appears that demand has outstripped supply, girls,' she said.

Kezia screwed up her face. 'What does that mean?'

'It means we won't be coming again. We don't have enough books to attract any more customers,' said Amy, smiling sympathetically when she saw Maggie and Kezia's crestfallen expressions. They loved coming to the Saturday market, helping out on the stall or wandering between the alleyways looking at what else was on offer.

'But that means we won't be here for Fred to give us apples and Jeb to buy us a bag of sweets,' protested Kezia. She had grown used to the kindly stallholders who, at the end of a day often gave the girls left over fruit or, like Jeb, bought them a treat.

Maggie sighed. 'I'll miss Gertie most.' The friendly young haberdasher had given her odd bits of ribbon and a glittery purse minus some of its sequins and Maggie, about to start work as a trainee receptionist in Dr Hargreaves' surgery, had become fashion conscious. Amy had bought her two new outfits from Clara who ran the clothes stall but there was never enough money for all the frippery bits and pieces a teenage girl desired.

Amy sighed. 'They're such a friendly lot, I'll miss them all,' she said, sadly watching the nearby stallholders packing up their wares and at the same time keeping an eye out for Samuel's truck. He was late.

'See you next Tuesday, Amy.' Jeb slammed the doors of his van.

'I doubt it. We've run out of books.'

Jeb glanced over at Amy, wearing a bemused smile. 'Then go to t'wholesalers an' buy some more. You've built up a steady little business here. You can't just let it go.' He walked to the front of the van and climbed into the driving seat.

Had he stayed to listen, Amy would have told him they had no idea how to go about dealing with a wholesaler, and neither did they have enough money to open an account with one. Whatever profit they had made in the past few months had gone towards the rent and new coats and dresses and shoes for the girls. She might also have told him that she thought Jude had lost interest in the bookstall.

Samuel arrived at last, his beaming face making Amy wonder what he had to be so happy about. Riding homeward, she felt crushed by the sheer weight of responsibility as though she would snap under the strain. Yet, her family needed her to stay strong if they were to remain solvent so that's what she must do she told herself sharply.

'Cheer up,' said Samuel. 'There's a cloud with a silver lining coming your way.'

Amy harrumphed. 'If there is, it's taking its bloody time,' she replied heatedly.

They arrived at Amy's door. An elusive smile curved the corners of Samuel's mouth as he said, 'I'll not come in. I'll take these two up to see the lads an' bring 'em back afore bedtime.' Kezia and Maggie cheered.

'Suit yourself,' said Amy, too despondent to be persuasive. 'Thanks for the lift.'

Puzzled as to why Sammy was behaving so mysteriously, she climbed out of the truck and walked into the house.

Jude was sitting in the only available chair in the parlour, its matching partner and the couch, and the little table and part of the floor piled high with books — hundreds of books, some with green, brown and maroon leather spines, others clothbound in blue, grey and red. Boxes on the hearthrug held flimsy gazettes and women's magazines.

Amy gaped.

'We were running low on books so I went out and got us some more,' Jude said.

Amy didn't know whether to laugh or cry.

Later, Jude made love to Amy for the first time since his return from the war. It was truly, deeply, fantastically wonderful; more wonderful than anything she had ever known before. Afterwards, as he lay sleeping, she lay awake cocooned in happiness and awash with intense, deep and perfect love.

30

'Thanks, Sammy,' Amy said warmly, as Jude unloaded the last of the boxes and carried it to the stall. 'We couldn't do this without you. You're more than good.'

'Think nothing of it.'

'But I do. We can't keep dragging you away from the farm just for us to make a living.' Amy's voice was full of concern.

'Course you can! We're family. Anyway, it gets me away from Freda for an hour. This morning sickness has her proper tetchy.' Samuel's proud smile at prospective fatherhood belied his complaint.

Amy grimaced. 'It's no joke, let me tell you, but it'll pass an' come next spring you'll be the father of a bouncing baby girl or boy.'

'I can't wait. I never thought owt that grand 'ud happen to me.'

'Why not? You've turned into a lovely man since our Thomas . . . ' Amy's hand flew to her lips, her expression contrite.

Samuel gave a sad smile. 'I know what you mean, an' you're right.' He gazed off into the distance and added, 'It's a bugger that summat as bad as that had to happen to make me see sense.'

Words escaping her, Amy hugged him tight and said, 'You get back to Freda, love, and thanks again for all you do for us.'

By now, Jude had unpacked several boxes,

carefully categorising the books as he laid them out on the stall: westerns, crime, romance, thrillers and classics. Professor Marchant's eclectic taste should appeal to a wide audience.

'Don't they look grand?' said Jude, standing back to admire his handiwork. 'We'll not have any bother selling these.'

He spoke with such enthusiasm that Amy was reluctant to dishearten him, although the titles in the box she was unpacking made her wonder who on earth would want to read such dry tomes. *Essays on the Principles of Population* by someone called Thomas Maltheus sounded particularly dreary. Maybe *History of the Conquest of Peru* by William Prescott might be more exciting.

'They're absolutely marvellous and so are you,' she said, shoving Maltheus, Prescott and their companions under the stall and then filling the rest of it with women's magazines and comics.

All around them traders were setting up their stalls, a lovely feeling of camaraderie in the air as they called out to one another. 'I see you took my advice an' got more stock,' Jeb called out. 'I told you you'd be daft to let it go.'

Amy gave Jeb a cheery wave and Jude saluted him, his grin the widest she had seen it in a long time. She glanced up at the clear blue sky and threw a silent prayer of thanks to some unseen deity. Even the late autumn day, more like one in summer, was in their favour. Good weather always brought customers flocking to the market and the alleyways were already teeming with people.

A tired-looking woman, three children at her heels, paused by the stall to adjust her loaded bags. Taking the initiative, Amy picked up a copy of *Women at Home* and proffered it to the woman. 'Have you read this one?' The woman set down her bags.

'It's full of wonderful ideas for homemaking and saving money,' Amy gushed, 'and there's a free comic for the children with every copy.' The woman accepted it, flicked the pages, smiled and reached for her purse.

This exchange attracted the attention of a gaggle of housewives on the fringes of the crowd gathering at Jeb's stall. They inched closer, Amy pouncing and handing out copies of *The Gentlewoman*, *Annie Swains Magazine* and *Weldons Quilting*.

The women made their purchases and were about to depart when Jude found his tongue. 'What about books for your husbands, ladies?' The women faltered and one, more curious than the others said, 'He doesn't read much but I've a lad whose head's never out of a book.'

'What does he read?' Jude asked.

'Oh, anything that's exciting and full of adventure.'

Jude handed her a copy of Saki's short stories. 'Then he'll enjoy this,' he said, giving her an abbreviated version of the content, 'an' if he's a reader tell him to call next time he's in town.'

For the rest of the day Jude approached anyone who lingered at the stall with a raft of questions: 'Do you like a good mystery?' 'What about tales of adventure at sea?' and so on, his brief resumes so intriguing, sale after sale was made.

Throughout the autumn and approaching Christ-mas trade was brisk. Almost all of the more popular titles had sold, and whilst they had been to a few house clearances they had yet to investi-gate a more reliable source of supply.

'We might as well put some of these out,' said Jude, lifting one of the boxes containing books of the sort Amy consigned to under the stall. He began emptying the box. 'They'll make the stall look full if nothing else.'

It was a bitterly cold day in December and Amy shivered and felt a sinking feeling as she looked over their depleted stock. 'I can't see us selling many of these,' she said, jabbing a finger at books on philosophy, politics and religion. 'I could have sold two copies of *Howard's End* had we had any and I've lost count of the times I've been asked for *Zuleika Dobson, Clayhanger* and *Peter Pan.*'

'We need fairy stories and Christmas books for people like me,' Kezia piped up. She regularly helped out on the stall and had developed her own strategy for making a sale. 'Have you read this?' she would ask whenever children approached the stall. 'It's ever so good. You should ask your mam to buy it for you.' She rarely met with a refusal.

'She right,' said Jude. 'It's close on Christmas, and seeing as we have enough money to go to a wholesaler, we'll go to that one in Wakefield on Monday.'

'And maybe buy Christmas cards and calen-dars,' Amy suggested. They smiled at one another, smiles that said '*see, we're winning, we've broken through the barriers that were driving us apart and put the past behind us.'*

Amy watched as Jude arranged books on the stall, thinking how handsome he was and thanking God for returning him. Out of the corner of his eye, Jude looked at Amy. Her hair had flared rebelliously out of its chignon and her eyes sparkled determinedly. He thought how beautiful and strong she was, and that it was she who had brought him back from the brink of hell.

Taking advantage of a lull in trade, Amy said, 'Seeing as how we're not busy me and Kezia will take a walk and buy Christmas presents.'

'Yippee!' Kezia cried, raring to go. She never tired of roaming the walkways, fascinated by the sounds and smells and the variety of commodities on the stalls, and then returning with scraps of information and gossip. Eager to spend her weekend penny wisely she took hold of Amy's hand. Amy gave a friendly nod to the elderly gentleman peering at the titles of the weighty tomes Jude had put on display. Jude hovered, hopeful.

'You have some very fine books here, young man. It's unusual to see such volumes on a secondhand market stall.'

Flattered by the compliment and pleased to engage in conversation with someone who recognised the books' worth, Jude gave him his full attention. After lengthy discussion the gentleman purchased six books and departed, Jude elated by the experience and the lucrative sale.

When Amy and Kezia returned, he gleefully waved three one-pound notes under Amy's nose. 'That old chap, the one with the wispy beard and the Homburg hat bought six of Prof Marchant's books,' he said, handing the money to Amy. 'They call him Noah Wiseman, and it suits him because he knew their true value. He dictated the price he wanted to pay and it was three times more than I would have charged.'

Amy tucked the money in the leather pouch at her waist, her heart thumping at the unexpected turn of fortune. 'Oh, Jude,' she gasped, too astounded to say more.

★   ★   ★

The Christmas books and cards were selling well, the market crowded with eager shoppers getting ready for Christmas. Having made their first wholesale purchases the Leas family felt as though they really were in business.

'They've started celebrating early,' Amy commented, as two rowdy young men swaggered past, beer bottles in hands.

Jude was just completing the sale of a box of cards and a calendar when Noah Wiseman arrived at the stall. He had called regularly since his first visit, Jude always making time to talk with him and discuss the books Noah showed an interest in. 'Happy Hanukkah,' Jude said by way of a greeting, Noah's smile letting him know that the acknowledgement of his religion pleased him. Jude lifted a box containing books on philosophy and history from under the stall. 'You might be interested in some of these,' he said, sure that none of his other customers would find them appealing. He went back to serving. Loud jeering over at Jeb's crockery stall caught Amy's attention. Two young men were mocking Jeb. She recognised them as the men who had passed by earlier. Then, customers waiting, she attended to their needs.

Noah delved into the box. He was inspecting a copy of John Stuart Mill's *On Liberty* when a violent shove sent him reeling and the book flying from his hands.

'Dirty old Jewboy,' his attacker shouted. He shoved Noah again, sending his Homburg spinning, and was about to deliver another blow when Jude, his face livid, leapt from behind the stall and grabbed him. He twisted the assailant's arm up behind his back with one hand, and with the other he delivered a punch to his gut.

'Hey, what are you defending a filthy old Jew for?' shouted the thug's companion, moving in to assist his winded pal. Jude's eyes glittered blackly as he gave him a threatening glare. The lad backed down. Amy rescued Noah's hat and hurried to comfort him. By now they had attracted a crowd of onlookers.

'Get out of my sight,' Jude growled, releasing his hold on the thug and then forcibly pushing him into his companion. 'The only thing filthy round here is you two cowards. Now bugger off and don't let me see you by my stall again.' Jeb, and most of the onlookers, added their condemnation. To a chorus of catcalling and boos the thugs slunk off.

Amy had sent Kezia to the tea stall for a cup of hot, sweet tea, and now, as Noah held the mug in his trembling hands, he offered profuse thanks to Jude. 'I suppose by now I should be used to it,' he said, 'but each time hurts just as painfully as the time before.' He shook his head despairingly. 'Thank you so much for rescuing me.'

'I shouldn't have to,' Jude said bitterly, 'but scum like them know nothing but their own ignorance.' He stooped to retrieve the copy of *On Liberty* that had flown from Noah's hands. Grinning wryly, he handed it to him. 'We should have punished the pair of them by forcing 'em to read this before we let 'em go,' he said.

* * *

Two days later, snow threatening a full day's trading and business slack, Noah returned to the stall. Again, he offered his thanks, and after making his purchases he surprised them by requesting that they visit his home the following evening; he had something to discuss with them.

Amy glanced at Jude and he at her, seeing her expression flit from surprise to wariness. Knowing that his own expression mirrored hers, he waited and when she slowly nodded her head, he accepted the invitation.

* * *

The following evening, leaving Kezia with Maggie, Jude and Amy walked across town to Noah Wiseman's house, neither of them engaging in conversation for they were both deep in thought: why had Noah suggested this meeting? Amy presumed he was lonely and, based on their shared interest in good literature, had proffered the invitation so he and Jude could talk books. Jude suspected the instigators of this invitation were Marion Marchant's books but why exactly, he wasn't sure.

As they approached Noah's home in Bankside Street, Amy was reminded of the walks she and Jude had taken when first they met because the house was in the row whose backs overlooked the river. She recalled the hours they had shared in this same place and wondered if their meeting with Noah would bring about something equally wonderful — although she couldn't imagine what.

The house was three storeys high, the lower storey below street level and accessed by a shallow flight of steps. Another flight led up from the street to the front door, black iron railings guarding both. Light shone from a window directly above the basement. Lifting the brass knocker on the smartly painted black door, Jude rapped twice and turned to face Amy on the step below, his expression letting her know he was impressed by his surroundings. Whilst they waited Amy indulged in imagining how it would be to live in such a spacious dwelling.

'Good evening, I'm glad you came.' Noah Wiseman pulled back the door into a well-furnished hallway, a large, seven-branched candleholder on a table catching Amy's eye. Silently, she admired its elegance.

'Let me take your coats before we go through.' Noah took Jude's old black overcoat that had once belonged to Hadley, and as Amy handed him her worn navy blue coat she was glad that she had chosen to wear her best pale blue linen two-piece under it. Noah hung the coats on a huge hallstand

and then led the way into a sitting room crowded with overstuffed chairs, a settee and a table below the window. Several large bookcases lined the walls. Scattered on and in the spaces between the furniture were piles of books.

'Ignore the clutter,' Noah said, negotiating a path to chairs at the fireside. 'Only the most basic necessities of housekeeping are important to a man who lives alone.'

When they were seated, he poured three glasses of sherry from a decanter on a side table next to his own chair, handing one to Amy and another to Jude. Ill at ease, Amy clutched her glass in both hands, but she left the drink untried. As for Jude, he held the diminutive glass in fingers that felt more like sausages and sipped the amber liquid warily. Sensing their discomfort, Noah wasted no time on pleasantries.

'As you see, I live by books,' he said, gesturing expansively about the room, 'and, in a manner of speaking, so do you' — his gaze rested first on Amy and then on Jude — 'but the difference between us is I know the true value of books, you don't.'

Affronted, Jude straightened and opened his mouth to rebut the accusation. Noah waved him into silence.

'I don't mean to be offensive. I speak only the truth, and if I were a less honest man, I could have robbed you several times over. I chose not to because I admire you, I like your determination to succeed even though it's coupled with sublime ignorance.'

Amy's sharp intake of breath caused Noah to

smile and Jude to glance anxiously at her. 'What exactly are you trying to say, Mr Wiseman?' he asked, his expression a mixture of irritation, confusion and curiosity.

Noah leaned back in his chair, hands folded across his chest. 'I know from our many conversations that you both have a genuine appreciation for the books you sell but your knowledge of the trade is abysmal. Several times I was tempted to purchase books from you and pay the piddling amount you asked of me but my conscience wouldn't let me. Maybe it was my God telling me that the Talmud does not teach us how to dupe an innocent man. No matter, I brought you here to proposition you, so bear with me whilst I explain.'

Dropping his defences, Jude settled back in the chair. Amy took a small sip of sherry and, finding it pleasant tried to relax, resigned to hearing the older man out. Noah leaned forward, his eyes on Jude. Relieved that Jude had calmed down, Amy looked from one man to the other. Whatever Noah Wiseman had to say involved her too so she coughed discreetly to remind him of her presence. He reached out, patting the back of her hand in acknowledgement.

'I deal in books — have done for many years. I search for old or rare volumes and when I find them I sell them to collectors, men and women who have a particular desire for a certain author or subject. They pay good money to get the books they want.' He rubbed the palms of his hands together, his eyes twinkling.

'When I saw the books you had on display after you'd sold out of the most popular titles I was

336

sorely tempted to buy the lot, pay you a pittance of their true value and keep the profit for myself.' He smiled ruefully at Amy. 'However, my heart wouldn't allow it as by that time I looked on you as friends.' His eyes twinkled as he gazed fondly from Amy to Jude. 'Then, when you so bravely rescued me from those thugs the other day, I knew you were true friends. That got me thinking. How best could I repay your kindness, I asked myself?'

'Nay, we don't need repaying,' Jude intervened, 'we only did what any decent folks would do.' Amy murmured her agreement.

Noah held up his hand. 'Please, hear me out,' he said. 'I want to make you an offer. Give up the market stall and open a bookshop in the basement of this house. It's a good location, and you won't have to contend with foul weather or carting the books to and from the stall. In return for the premises I will sell the rare books you still have in your possession and you can carry on your everyday business. In between times I'll teach you the craft of recognising rare and valuable books.' He sat back, smiling beatifically, waiting for an answer.

'I didn't know any of them were rare,' Jude muttered. 'In fact, I thought we'd never get rid of most of 'em.'

'Exactly,' Noah said. 'You have to know your stock, and when it comes to the popular stuff, you do, but I know where the real money lies — you've at least two first editions and several rare volumes in the books you consider unsellable — so what do you say? Have we a deal?'

Utterly bemused, Jude turned to Amy. She felt

equally bewildered, but not too discomposed to find her voice. 'It's an intriguing offer, Mr Wiseman, and one we would like to consider. As I understand it, the premises will be rent-free in exchange for certain books, but once those books are disposed of, what then?'

Noah chuckled. 'Hopefully we'll find more, and if not the offer still stands. The basement is unused, and I'm a lonely old man in need of like-minded company. I have nothing to lose. I'm not just doing this for the books. I could have taken them had I wanted. It's more a shared venture I'm interested in, something to give me a reason to get up each morning.'

'I don't think I need to consider it any further,' Jude said, glancing at Amy for support. 'It makes damn good sense to me.' He grinned. 'And if you're that honest that you haven't robbed us yet, I can't see you doing it in the future. If Amy agrees we'll accept your offer and be grateful. Without you I'd be selling those books for nowt; this way we'll all make summat out of it.'

Her eyes gleaming, Amy nodded her assent. Noah topped up their glasses, and they toasted the success of the bookshop. As they talked, Amy's mind conjured up enticing images of a neat, cosy shop full of customers. Eventually, Noah stood and they exchanged handshakes. 'We'll have a solicitor write a contract so that your tenancy will be assured,' he said, 'and now, let me show you the basement.'

Amy descended the steps on feet that felt as though she was floating and, as Jude trod behind, his whole body became lighter and less substantial, as though caked mud was crumbling away,

338

leaving him with a sense of total freedom.

To their delight, the basement seemed perfect. It required decorating and shelving, and a counter from which to serve, but other than that it filled Amy and Jude with such anticipation of how it could be transformed that they let their imaginations fly. After further discussion reassuring them that they had made a wise decision, Amy and Jude bade Noah goodnight and began walking back the way they had come, their homeward journey, unlike the outward one, lively with talk. Cresting the brow of the slope leading to their part of the town, Jude slowed to a halt. Amy turned questioning eyes on him. Was he having doubts? Had they been too hasty in accepting Noah's offer?

Her excitement fluttered and began to fade, only to be revived as Jude pulled her into his arms saying, 'Look up, Amy. Look up.' He pressed his cheek against hers. 'Do you see all the stars, Amy? They're shining for me and you.' Amy tilted her head, and Jude continued. 'When I was in France I'd look up at 'em, knowing that the same stars were shining down on you and Kezia, keeping us safe for one another. They've seen us through good times and bad, always been there, just like you have for me, putting up with my crazy tempers and my foul moods. You're as constant as the stars and so is my love for you.' A passionate kiss sealed his words. In the warmth of his embrace, just at that moment, Amy believed that every part of her life was wonderful.

Arms linked, they resumed walking, a sudden flurry of snowflakes dancing in the light of the gas lamps and whitening the pavements. Amy's eyes moistened and she couldn't decide whether it was snow melting on her lashes or grateful tears seeking release. 'This is going to be the best Christmas ever,' she said, squeezing Jude's arm as she glanced up at him. 'We've weathered the storms and, God willing, we're on our way to securing a bright future for Kezia and us.'

Suddenly, they were running hand in hand, slipping and sliding and cheering and laughing, chasing away the dark shadows and running freely into the light.

31

Christmas trade was all that Amy hoped it would be. On Christmas Eve afternoon Jude and Amy bade fond farewells to the market traders they had worked alongside, whilst Kezia and Maggie ran from stall to stall saying their goodbyes and buying last minute Christmas treats.

Amy smiled up into Jeb's kindly face. 'Thanks for everything,' she said, 'and if our customers come looking for us don't forget to tell them we'll be opening in Bankside Street early in the New Year.'

'Don't you worry, I'll chase 'em up there if I have to,' said Jeb, giving Amy a swift hug and then shaking Jude's hand.

Back home in Wentworth Street, Kezia and Maggie finished decorating the tree in the parlour with the baubles Gertie had given them, Kezia declaring that it was the best dressed tree in Barnborough. 'This is a special Christmas, isn't it?' she said, turning to Jude and Amy who were sitting at the hearth drinking tea.

Amy's eyes glowed. 'It is. It's special for all of us, and the New Year will be even more special. We'll be proper book sellers, and Maggie will be the prettiest receptionist that Dr Hargreaves has ever had.' She didn't tell them that it might be special for another reason; she just hugged the hope deep inside. After Christmas she'd make an appointment with Dr Hargreaves.

Maggie flushed and tossed her glorious mane of red hair before bestowing a smile on the couple who had given her a loving home and the confidence to apply for what she thought was a far superior post to that of shop work or going into service. Although she still missed Bert and Beattie she couldn't have wished for kinder substitutes; even Jumpy Jude as she secretly thought of him. Silently, she made a solemn promise not to let them down.

★ ★ ★

On Boxing Day, Amy and Jude and the girls trudged through the snow to Intake Farm, stopping every now and then to throw snowballs, or for Kezia to plunge into the drifts blown against the hedges. They had spent Christmas Day at home, the house redolent with the smell of roast goose and mince pies as they ate a grand dinner and played games, everyone in high spirits and Amy basking in the shared love and happiness that permeated every corner. What a difference from last Christmas, she thought, as they arrived at the farmhouse door.

Bessie welcomed them fulsomely, Amy noting for the umpteenth time that her mother was mellowing with age. Albert and Fred whooped their delight at seeing the girls and wasted no time in persuading them to go out into the yard for a snowball fight. Jude sat talking over Noah Wiseman's offer with Raffy and Samuel, and Amy talked babies with Freda. Now in her seventh month of pregnancy, Freda lounged like a beached whale

342

revelling in Samuel and Bessie's ministrations.

'I hope to goodness it's a boy, for Samuel's sake,' said Freda, patting her bump.

'So do I,' said Bessie, plumping the cushion at Freda's back before handing her a cup of tea. 'Sons are yours forever whereas daughters go off and marry and make their own families. I always wanted sons.' She passed Amy her cup and then sat down.

Amy sipped and thought of Beatrice. Would Bessie have been kinder had Beattie been a boy? She contemplated sharing her own suspicions that she might be pregnant and then decided against it; Jude must be the first to know, and furthermore, the children had just trooped in from outside. Instead, she told Bessie and Freda about Noah Wiseman's lovely house and the wonderful offer of the basement.

Bessie's lip curled and her blue eyes sparked contempt. 'I'm surprised at the pair of you, taking up with a Jew. They're nothing but conniving moneygrubbers.' She got to her feet to expound her opinions. 'He'll feather his own nest and rob you blind, mark my words.' She looked pityingly at Amy. 'I'd have thought you had more sense, even if your Jude doesn't.'

Amy thought of Beattie again. What was it she used to say? *Mother can rip the heart out of things quicker than you can bat your eyelids.* Well, this time she wasn't going to let her away with it. 'That's where you're wrong, Mother,' she cried. 'Noah could have done that already but he chose not to because he's a decent man. Just because he's Jewish doesn't make him bad.'

'A lot of 'em are Germans, an' all,' remarked Samuel, adding fuel to the flame.

Jude, who had heard Bessie's remarks, called out, 'I fought alongside Jews in the trenches, Bessie. They were good lads fighting for king and country just like the rest of us.'

'It's not their country though, is it?' Bessie retaliated. 'They don't belong here.'

'Of course they do, Mother! Jews have lived in England for hundreds of years — this is their home. And let's face it, there's good and bad in everyone. I can think of some people not too far from here who are dishonest and manipulative, and they're not Jews.' Amy was generalising, not thinking of any particular persons, but a punch of fear hit her stomach as she realised what she had said.

The blood had leached from Bessie's face. Her hand was clasped to her mouth, tears springing to her eyes as they met Amy's. Amy jumped up, and eager to make reparation she threw her arms around Bessie. 'Oh, Mam, I didn't mean anything by it. I was just making the point that Noah's a good man.'

Bessie shook her off, and although the rest of the afternoon passed quietly there was a tension in the air that quelled the pleasure Amy and Jude had taken from their new venture.

'What's a Jew?' Kezia asked, as they made their way home.

'Somebody from Jerusalem,' Maggie piped, and before Kezia could enquire further her cousin began singing, 'There were three Jews from Jerusalem, Jerry, Jerry, Jerry-rusalem.' Kezia joined in

344

and, hand in hand, the girls skated on the snowy road carolling at the tops of their voices.

Amy raised her eyebrows and shook her head in disbelief as she caught Jude's eye.

'Trust Mam to stir things up,' she said, and then shouted, 'That's enough, Maggie. I don't want Kezia learning songs like that.' Surprised at the sharpness in Amy's voice, Maggie fell silent. Kezia looked peeved.

Under her breath, Amy said to Jude, 'I think we need to do some serious talking to both girls before we meet Noah again.'

'Aye, we'll sit 'em down one at a time and explain it, just to make sure they don't cause offence.'

'Why can't we sing the song, Mam?' Kezia whined. 'Is it because Jews are bad?'

Amy let out an exasperated sigh. Jude chuckled. 'It's your fault, you know. You're the one who nurtured her enquiring mind.'

Amy gave him a sharp dig in the ribs and pertly replied, 'Aye, and you can be the one responsible for satisfying it.'

★ ★ ★

In the basement of Noah Wiseman's house, a large square room with a smaller one behind, Jude and Amy surveyed their new domain for the second time. Barely able to contain their excitement they briskly set about sizing up the possibilities for shelves, a counter, and a few comfortable chairs and reading tables. Kezia danced about the empty space contributing ideas by the dozen.

'We could have a shelf here for children's books,'

she said, crouching low to the ground near the window. 'It'll have to be low down so that the little kids can reach it, and I can help you choose the books you're going to buy because I know what little kids like.' Her parents exchanged amused glances, acknowledging that their clever daughter knew what she was talking about; Kezia's love for books almost equalled that of her mam and dad's.

Back at street level, measurements and requirements recorded in Amy's notebook, Jude paused to gaze in awe at a dream come true. Noah came out to join them.

Swinging on the iron railings, Kezia called out, 'What will we call the shop? Will it have a sign with our name on it?'

Jude glanced at Amy. 'We've not thought that far ahead,' she said, turning to her daughter. 'We could call it Leas' Bookshop or — ' she aimed a deferential glance at Noah '—maybe Wiseman and Leas.'

'You should call it the book cellar,' Kezia said, 'cos that's what it is, a cellar where you sell books.'

'That's a splendid suggestion,' Noah said. 'I love a play on words — book seller, book cellar — that's what you should call it.' Glowing with pride at their daughter's perspicacity, Amy and Jude agreed.

A week later a long, rectangular sign was fixed above the window of the basement, and a smaller, square one attached to the railings. Large gold lettering on a dark green background spelled out 'The Book Cellar' and beneath it, in smaller case, 'Prop: A & J. Leas & N. Wiseman'.

A carpenter was hired to build shelving, and as the basement took shape Noah presented Amy

346

and Jude with yet another surprise. They had been busily painting and cleaning all day and now, as Amy reluctantly prepared to make the journey back to Wentworth Street, Noah came down into the basement.

'I'd really like to stay on and finish this,' said Amy, pointing at the half-scrubbed floor, 'but it takes me twenty minutes to walk home and I must be there for Kezia coming from school.'

Noah smiled understandingly. 'If you'd be so kind I'd like to make a suggestion that would ease the situation.' Intrigued, Amy nodded and Noah continued, 'Only yesterday my friend Isaac Cohen left to go to Israel for a year and he's charged me with the responsibility of finding a good tenant for his house. You could be the answer to my problem.'

Amy's brow puckered. 'How might we help?'

'By becoming the tenants.'

'Where is it?' Amy asked, fearing it might be even further away from the shop than their present home.

'Further along this street,' said Noah, gesturing airily. 'We could go and take a look at it now if you have time.'

'Jude,' cried Amy, 'put that paintbrush in the turps. Noah has something to show us. Get a move on or I'll be late for Kezia.'

'What's to do?' asked Jude, hurrying in from the back room.

'We'll find out when we get there,' Amy replied, pulling on her coat and hurrying to the door. A house in this street overlooking the river, she marvelled, her enthusiasm waning slightly when she wondered if they could afford the rent.

With Noah leading the way, Jude and Amy walked to the top end of Bankside Street, Jude somewhat bemused and Amy breathless with excitement as she explained why they were going to see Noah's friend's house. When they reached the part where the street met a grassy slope leading down to the river, Noah stopped at the gate of a small, square house surrounded by overgrown gardens. Its red pan-tiled roof and windows one either side of the door and three above came as a surprise in a street where all the other houses were tall and terraced. Amy loved it immediately. 'Can we go inside?' she urged.

Waving the key, Noah led them to the front door. 'Don't be too disappointed by the interior. Like me, Isaac is no housekeeper but he's stored his personal belongings in one room upstairs so you can do whatever you want with the rest of the place. No doubt cleaning will be your first priority.'

Four rooms on the ground floor included a kitchen, two sitting rooms and a dining room. Up above three bedrooms and a box room, and to Amy's delight a bathroom with a flush lavatory. Clapping her hands like a delighted child she tugged the chain, the gush of water mingling with her excited laughter. Noah and Jude joined in, their mirth echoing through the house.

'And how much rent is your friend, Isaac, looking for?' Jude asked cautiously.

When Noah named a modest sum, Amy threw her arms round him and pecked his cheek, and then did the same to a beaming Jude.

'Am I to understand you've solved my problem?' Noah said, his smile wide.

'Yes, yes,' Amy and Jude chorused.

32

The Book Cellar opened for business, Amy and Jude awed and delighted by the serried ranks of new books, purchased with their share of the money raised from selling the rare books. Other shelves contained clean, secondhand copies, Amy insisting they keep stock for less well-off customers.

'We mustn't forget them that bought our books from the market stall. It's them we've to thank for getting us this far,' she said, down on her knees emptying a box of books they had purchased from a house clearance.

In the first few weeks of trading, Amy and Jude took pleasure in helping their customers make their selections, but whilst their clients were loyal they were few and trade not as brisk as they would have liked. 'It takes time to be established,' Noah said. 'Don't worry about it.' But Amy and Jude did.

On a morning when trade was particularly slack, Amy kept her long-delayed appointment with Dr Hargreaves, although by now she was certain she was pregnant.

Walking back to the bookshop in a rosy glow, she suddenly recalled Jude's shock and disappointment when first she told him about Kezia. The warm feeling evaporated. Surely he wouldn't think that this child was detrimental to his ambitions, she asked herself. He had his bookshop, and although it wasn't making much profit, they were still more affluent than they had been. Even so, he might think that another mouth to feed, and Amy's time tied-up with caring for a new baby was an impediment they could well do without.

He'll just have to like it or lump it, she told herself as she turned into Bankside Street. *I want this baby, and so will Jude when he gets his head round it. Look how he was when he first learned I was expecting Kezia, and then when she arrived he fell head over heels in love with her.* Feeling much more positive, she ran down the steps into the bookshop. Jude was serving one of four customers, and Amy decided to keep her news until later although she was bursting to share it with him.

★ ★ ★

At the end of the afternoon, they closed the shop and walked the short distance to their new home, Kezia skipping ahead. 'Isn't she just the most amazing girl?' Jude said, having lost his grumpiness at the lack of trade. They had been quite busy in the afternoon. Kezia was now swinging round a lamppost chanting her seven times table. 'She was top of the class again in spellings and sums today,' he added.

Hearing the love and pride in his voice, Amy saw her chance. 'What would you say to having another one just like her — or maybe a son?' she asked, her heart fluttering uncomfortably.

Jude took two or three more steps and then stopped dead as Amy's words registered. She stopped too. He stared at her, his face crumpling, and she felt a sudden chill in her bones. It was happening all over again. She closed her eyes to stem the welling tears, and when she opened them she saw that Jude was crying.

'Oh, Amy,' he groaned, 'I thought . . . I thought I'd never be able to father another child after me being . . . ' He let out a whoop. 'That's wonderful, wonderful.' He scooped her up his arms and swung her round before planting a kiss on her mouth, which as it happens, was open wide in amazement. They clung to each other, rocking and laughing as Amy's misgivings took wing like a flock of startled sparrows.

'Hey, Kezia,' Jude called out, 'what do you say to having a baby brother or sister?'

Kezia stopped mid-swing and almost lost her balance. Her eyes grew wide. 'What did you say?' She ran back to them, her excitement palpable.

'Your clever mam's having a baby. What do you think to that?'

Kezia screwed her face thoughtfully and then said, 'I think it's smashing. It'll make us a proper family.' Jude lifted her into his arms, carrying her to their front door with Amy hanging on his free arm, and all of them chattering about the new baby. When Maggie arrived home from work, the wonderful news was repeated again. Whooping her delight, she threw her arms first round Amy and then Jude. 'About bloody time,' she crowed, before taking Kezia by the hand and jigging her round the kitchen singing, 'A sister, big sister, a blister for a sister.'

'I'm not a blister,' Kezia protested.

'No, you're not,' said Maggie. 'It's the only

352

word I could think of that rhymes with sister. So, you think on. Be the best big sister in the world.'

'You mean like you've been to me, Maggie?' Kezia said solemnly.

'Better than that,' Maggie said, hugging Kezia and then swinging her off her feet.

Amy and Jude exchanged heartfelt glances.

★ ★ ★

Kezia adored her new home, and most of all she loved the Book Cellar. Each day after school and all day Saturday she helped out, arranging books on shelves or concocting interesting displays on tables. In between serving in the shop, Amy spent her time cleaning her new home and arranging her own furniture around the pieces Isaac had left in place. As the year progressed, the neglected house became a haven of comfort and happiness.

On a sunny morning in July, as Amy washed the breakfast dishes in the bright, airy kitchen — so much pleasanter than the dank little scullery in Wentworth Street — she contemplated on her good fortune. Now in the final days of what had been an easy pregnancy she thought how different this baby's birth would be compared to Kezia's. This time she had no need to buy and refurbish secondhand furniture to make a comfortable home for a new baby and furthermore, this baby was fulfilling hopes and dreams rather than denying them.

Through the window she could see Kezia carefully snipping roses from the bushes in the garden to put in a vase on the dining table. *Something else we didn't have in Wentworth Street,* she mused, and stretched up high to place a pan on the rack above the sink. The baby jiggled, and Amy was suffused in a rush of glorious contentment.

★ ★ ★

That same afternoon, Jude and Noah went to an auction in Wakefield in search of rare books leaving Amy in the shop with Kezia who, off school for the summer holidays, was a much-needed help. Trade was brisk, and by closing time Amy felt utterly drained. The thud of feet overhead, in Noah's sitting room, let her know that the men had returned and a few minutes later Jude ran into the shop.

'Come and see what we've bought,' he cried, his excitement indicating that the trip had been successful. Intrigued, Amy followed him up the steps to Noah's front door although the pain in her lower back screamed for her to sit down and put her feet up. Jude strode ahead, Kezia scampering behind and Amy gasping, 'Slow down, this baby doesn't like moving at high speed.'

Jude slowed his pace, stepping back to offer her his arm. 'Sorry, love. I wasn't thinking.' But Amy could tell by his expression he was being anything but thoughtless. His chiselled features were tight and his eyes glittering with pent-up zeal.

Pulling her arm through his Jude matched his step to hers and Amy, perspiring heavily plodded forward, reluctant to deny Jude his pleasure but inwardly crying to get this over with and go home.

Noah gave her a beaming welcome, and through

glazed eyes Amy half-looked and half-listened as he and Jude reported on their finds: a first edition of this, a rare copy of that, the titles barely penetrating the fog inside her head. 'A fine collection,' Noah said, 'and most of it due to your husband's sharp eyes and increasing knowledge.'

Jude flushed at the compliment, and then crowed, 'What with these and the trade we're doing in the shop, our money worries are over.' He ran his hand over a leather-bound tome on the table, his mood suddenly changing. With a faraway look in his eyes he softly added, 'When me an' Bert were in France we promised one another we'd do something to make sense of it all, if we lived long enough. Bert wanted to do summat wi' lorries but the poor bugger never got chance.' The hot sweat coating Amy's body turned clammy and she shivered involuntarily. Jude turned and gazed lovingly at her. 'That was his dream . . . this was mine, and because of you it's now a reality.'

By now the pain in her back had moved deep into her womb and a trickling wetness tickled her inner thighs. Sensing her distraction and seeing her distraught expression, Jude anxiously asked, 'What is it? What's the — ?'

'Take me straight home,' Amy gasped. 'Me waters have broken.'

★ ★ ★

Seven hours later Jude sat beside Amy on the bed, his eyes absorbing the sight of his son feeding lustily and his thighs warmed by his precious daughter's bony little bottom. Amy lay propped-up with the

355

baby at her breast, her lustrous yellow hair fanning the pillows and her cheeks glowing rosily. Jude gazed over the top of Kezia's head, her hair as dark as his own, at the woman who had made all this possible: a home, a family and a sense of worth. He felt as though his heart might burst with love and gratitude. Kezia wriggled in his lap, and breaking the hypnotic spell of slurp and suck that seemed to have seduced both her parents she asked, 'Was I as ugly as that when I was a baby?'

Maggie, perched at the foot of the bed, giggled. But Amy, quick to ensure that Kezia shouldn't feel excluded or displaced by her brother cried, 'No, love, you were the most beautiful baby I ever saw.'

'And if he's half as clever as you, he'll be just grand.' Jude flicked the end of her nose with his fingertip.

Appeased, Kezia leaned over and smiled at her brother. He gazed back with eyes as blue as his mother's. A soft covering of wispy, blond hair clung to his scalp.

'You're right,' Kezia said, 'he doesn't look one bit like me.'

'That's because he takes after your mam,' said Jude. 'You take after me. You're my special girl. I knew that the minute you were born. You were beautiful.'

'All our young'uns looked like skinned rabbits when they were born,' Maggie reflected, her expression sad as she remembered a time she'd rather forget. Amy gave her a sympathetic smile as she too recalled her niece's miserable childhood. Maggie acknowledged it with a brave grin and then cried, 'But look at 'em now. Our Albert and Fred strapping young farmers as happy as pigs in muck, an' our Henry and Mary proper little toffs.'

'And you've done all right for yourself, Maggie. Dr Hargreaves is always singing your praises,' Amy told her, proud of the beautiful, diligent young woman Maggie had become. She smiled from one member of her family to the other. 'Now, me and this little boy are ready to go to sleep, so off you all go to your beds.'

'We can't keep calling him little boy,' said Kezia, as she slid from Jude's knee.

Amy looked at Jude. 'What do you think?'

'John Hadley Raphael Leas.'

'Then that's who he is,' said Amy.

'That's an awful lot of names! I've only got one,' cried Kezia.

'So have I,' said Maggie, taking her young cousin by the hand and leading her from the room.

Amy and Jude fondly watched them go and then turned their attentions back to their son.

★　★　★

Maggie had now lived with the Leas family for five years and looked on Jude and Amy as second parents. She loved Kezia like a sister and had willingly helped Amy through difficult times when Jude was still suffering from shell shock, her own tough childhood lending her a maturity beyond her years. She had worked diligently at school and learned from Amy and Jude, and when she was appointed Dr Hargreaves' receptionist she knew it was their careful nurturing that had enabled her to win the enviable position. A bright bubbly girl with a penchant for saying exactly what was on her mind, Maggie was a delightful addition to the family.

In return, Amy and Jude loved her like a daughter and were grateful for the fun she brought to their lives, her outspokenness causing them no end of amusement. 'Are we posh now?' she had asked when they moved to the house in Bankside Street. 'Cos if we are I'd better stop swearing an' start talking proper.'

Amy had laughed. 'That 'ud be an improvement, but don't start giving yourself airs and graces. We're just decent people getting on with life.'

For the first ten years of her life, Maggie had shared a bed with her siblings, and later a bedroom with Kezia. Now, she was thrilled to have her own bedroom and like most teenage girls she filled it with pretty clutter bought with her wages from Dr Hargreaves. She regularly, but silently acknowledged that none of this would have been possible if her parents had lived, and in her own way she tried to repay Amy and Jude. Although she worked every weekday for Dr Hargreaves, she loved helping out in the Book Cellar on Saturdays or keeping Kezia and John entertained whilst Amy dealt with the customers. Even though her Uncle Jude appeared to have made a full recovery, Maggie had feared he might relapse into the strange, angry man he was on his release from hospital. But now, with proof that Amy and Jude were 'at it' — her words for making love — she felt that her fears were groundless. John's birth had instilled in her a new hope for the future.

'I think our Maggie has an admirer,' Amy whispered to Jude one Saturday afternoon in November. She nodded her head at her niece and a tall, fair young man, deep in conversation by the window. 'He's been here for the last four Saturdays and he's yet to buy a book. He seems more interested in Maggie.'

'I can't say I blame him,' said Jude, 'she's a looker, and pleasant with it.'

Amy smiled her agreement. With her mane of red curls, sparkling green eyes and a pert figure, Maggie Stitt was indeed lovely.

'I think I'll be nosy and find out who he is.' Amy stepped from behind the counter and strolled over to Maggie. Maggie greeted her fulsomely.

'This is my Auntie Amy,' she said to the young man, and then, 'Auntie Amy, this is Stephen Netherwood. He's a student at the Technical College. He can't afford to buy books but he comes here because he likes looking at them.'

The lad's homely face reddened. 'I hope you don't object,' he mumbled, 'but the reading I do here helps with my studies.'

'And what might they be?' Amy enquired.

'History and Politics.'

'Let's go and talk to the man behind the counter. I'm sure he'll find you a book or two that might be useful,' said Amy, leading the way.

Introductions and explanations made, Jude took Stephen into the storeroom. He emerged half an hour later with three books under his arm and a smile on his face, the few shillings he had in his pocket still intact. Throwing Jude and Amy grateful looks, Maggie accompanied her beau out of the shop.

'He put me in mind of myself,' Jude said, when they had gone, 'and nobody else was likely to buy the books he chose.'

'I knew you'd help him out. You're a big softy,' said Amy. She put on her coat. 'I'm off now. Don't be late for tea.'

★ ★ ★

Later that day, as they sat down to tea in their cosy house in Bankside Street, Amy said, 'I can't believe we've lived here for almost a year. I keep pinching myself to make sure it's not all a dream and I'll wake up back in Wentworth Street.'

Jude nodded. 'I know how you feel. It's like being inside a brightly lit bubble waiting for it to burst.' He looked troubled. In the past year, they had built up a small, regular clientele but there were still days when they hardly made a sale, and this worried him. 'The rare books me and Noah occasionally find make things look more promising,' he continued, trying to be more upbeat, 'but we can't always rely on them. I just wish the shop could do better.'

Seeing Amy's downcast expression he thumped the table with his fist, making the cups rattle in their saucers. 'But hey,' he cried, 'it's coming up to Christmas and books make good Christmas presents.'

For the next few days Amy thought of little else other than how to boost trade. Jude had his success with the rare books, now it was up to her to

360

make the shop a success. She finally put her plan into action after a visit to Hepworth's tobacconists and newsagents. The Book Cellar had to reach out to people, let them know what it had to offer, and with that in mind she went out the following morning with John, returning later with a loaded pram and a fervent gleam in her eyes.

'What all this?' Jude gaped when she arrived at the top of the basement's steps with six stout cardboard placards balanced on the hood of John's pram, and a bag full of fat tubes of red, green and gold paint hanging from the handle. Jude helped her carry them into the storeroom. 'What are you going to do with them? What are they for?' he asked, his curiosity tinged with annoyance.

'Advertisements,' Amy said. 'Let the people know where we are and what we have to sell. I got the idea whilst I was waiting to buy your cigarettes and newspaper. The walls of Hepworth's shop are plastered with adverts for cigarettes and newspapers, and outside he has a board with newspaper headlines on it. They entice people to go in and spend money.'

'I don't need enticing to buy cigarettes, I can't do without them,' Jude said lugubriously, 'and everybody buys papers. I can't see it working with books.'

'That's 'cos you don't have the vision that I've got in my head,' Amy replied confidently, unpacking her shopping bag. 'I've brought you a pie as well. It's still hot so get it down you whilst there's no customers.'

'There's not much fear of that,' he groused, before biting into the pie.

Jude ate his lunch and went back to the shop. After eating her own pie and feeding John, Amy cleared the table in the storeroom and began to paint.

Books! Books! Books!

The Perfect Christmas Gift

Free wrapping in festive paper

Come and see our fine selection at the
Book Cellar, 37, Bankside Street.

Unable to hide his curiosity, Jude popped his head round the storeroom door.

'What do you think?' Amy said, as she began to artfully encircle the red and gold lettering with holly and ivy leaves. Would it catch your eye?'

Jude stared, amazed. 'That's fantastic!' He rewarded her with a kiss.

Thanking God for a placid son who only demanded feeding and changing, Amy painted for the rest of the day. At closing time Amy and Jude and a loaded pram went down into the town, and using stout twine, they tied the placards to lampposts and fences in various locations. 'Now they'll know where we are and once they find us I'm sure they'll buy something,' said Amy, as they plodded homeward.

★ ★ ★

'We didn't know there was a bookshop here until we saw your hoarding,' said an elderly woman who

362

had just purchased four books. Amy was delighted. She'd lost count of how many customers had said the same thing, and there had been many more customers in the past three days. Thrilled by the success of her idea, she wondered what else she could do to boost sales.

'Christmas is a time for celebration, lights, holly, baubles and festive spirit,' she told Jude, during a lull at midday, and with this in mind she hurried into the town. Again, she returned with the pram laden with her purchases. Outside the Book Cellar she tied bunches of holly trimmed with scarlet bows to the railings round the basement steps. Through the shop window Jude saw the flitting figure and ran out of the shop to see what was going on.

'What are you doing now?' he asked, amazed.

'I'm making the shop look Christmassy. That way it'll give people the idea that books make good Christmas presents. Wait till you see what I've got for inside.' She tied the last bunch of holly in place. 'Bring the pram down for me,' she cried, skipping down the steps.

By closing time the Book Cellar glittered and gleamed. Gold baubles hung from the rafters, the tops of bookcases sported holly and the counter a pile of pretty papers and green and gold ribbon, waiting to be wrapped round books.

Caught up in the spirit of Christmas, Jude created a window display of children's books and another of cookery books. 'Folk think of children and food at Christmas,' he said, 'bairns and eating, that's what it's all about.'

'Thank you, madam,' Jude said, handing over the six books that Amy had wrapped in festive paper tied with green or gold bows.

'Thank you,' the well-dressed woman replied, 'I wouldn't have chosen so wisely had you not assisted me. My appreciation is all yours.' She picked up her parcels. 'I didn't know you were here until I spotted your sign at the end of the street. I'll call again in the New Year.'

'And we'll be more than happy to serve you. The best of season's greetings to you and your family, madam.' Giving a polite half-bow, Jude ushered her to the door.

Amy glowed with pleasure although her fingers ached from wrapping and her tummy rumbled with hunger. Today they had had no time for dinner, keeping the shop open whilst ever there were customers to be served.

Glancing over at John in his pram in the back corner, she thanked God for such a good-natured, healthy boy, and then went on to thank Him for Christmas, a husband sound in mind and body, a kindly benefactor, Noah, an inquisitive minx of a daughter and a lovely niece before she turned back to serve yet another customer.

That Christmas and the two following it, and the months in between sealed the success of the Book Cellar and the Leas family's happiness.

33

Jude waited impatiently for the lone customer to leave to leave the shop. It was already past closing time. Outside, the street was empty and the balmy evening air tempting; he'd take Amy and the children for a walk in the park after they had had tea. Pleased with the idea, he emptied the cash drawer. The scruffy young man with a straggly red beard and hair continued to flit from shelf to shelf pulling out books but not really looking at them before shoving them back in the wrong place. Jude's spirits drooped. The last person he wanted to deal with at this time of day was Hubert Crank.

'Sorry, we're closing,' said Jude.

Hubert pulled a book from a shelf, riffling the pages carelessly.

Jude stiffened. It wasn't Hubert's first visit to the shop, he'd been in twice before and his attitude irritated Jude. On his second visit, Stephen, Maggie's beau had been in the shop. He'd briefly acknowledged Hubert, and Jude had asked who he was. When Stephen told him, Jude had replied, 'Crank by name and crank by nature.'

Stephen had laughed and said, 'You're dead right there.'

Now, Hubert looked smugly at Jude. 'Which one are you, Leas or Wiseman?' he asked sneeringly.

'Leas. As I said, I'm closing.'

Hubert, unaffected by Jude's terse response

365

asked, 'Do you live above the premises?'

Jude gave a monosyllabic 'no' and went and stood by the door, keys in hand.

Hubert sauntered towards the door, and as he drew level with Jude, he said, 'You Jews are all the same.'

Jude looked bemused.

'Jew,' Hubert repeated, making the word sound dirty. Before Jude could respond, he bounded up the steps and into the street.

'So that's what's eating you — you're an anti-semite,' Jude said to himself as he slammed the door behind him, savagely twisting the key in the lock. He detested bigotry. He'd come across it in the army, chaps who hated anyone they perceived to be different from themselves, those with brown skin or Jewish origins tormented the most. As Jude walked home mulling over the peculiar exchange, he made a mental note to keep his eye on Hubert Crank.

★ ★ ★

'It's beautiful, Maggie,' said Amy, her palm supporting Maggie's outstretched left hand as she admired the engagement ring on her niece's finger. 'Congratulations to both of you. Be happy.' Stephen blushed and shuffled his feet.

'Let's have a look at it then.' Jude was seated at the table scanning a large, old, leather-bound volume, a recent find on a day out with Noah to the auctions in Leeds. Swinging round in his chair he beckoned to his eighteen-year-old niece to come close, his eyes twinkling wickedly.

Maggie crossed the room and proffered her hand. Jude lifted the magnifying glass he had been using, and placing it over the ring on Maggie's finger, he gasped. 'By God, Maggie! Diamonds as big as the crown jewels.'

'You cheeky bugger,' said Maggie, withdrawing her hand and laughing merrily as she squinted at the minute diamonds. 'They might be small but me an' Stephen don't believe in wasting money just so we can show off.'

'Very wise too.' Amy gave Jude a warning glare.

'It's lovely, Maggie,' he said contritely and then, by way of making amends he added, 'I didn't buy Amy one. I couldn't afford to.'

'I'd never have been able to afford one either if I hadn't got the job with the *Barnborough Chronicle*.' Always a peacemaker, Stephen was keen to show he took no offence at Jude's playfulness. *He really is the nicest young man*, thought Amy. Jude gave him a smile filled with admiration.

'It's a job I wouldn't have minded having when I was your age,' he said, 'and before you know it you'll be their political editor, travelling up to London to report on what's going on in the government. We're proud of you, lad.'

Yet again Stephen blushed, and muttered his thanks then shrugged before saying, 'Last week I reported on a tailor's shop that had been deliberately set on fire after whoever did it had slashed all the suits to shreds, and today I was reporting on a church that was vandalised last night, out Melborough way. Whoever did it made a right mess. There's some crazy people out there.'

Jude sniggered. 'Aye, well, it was the 1st of April

yesterday — all fool's day. By the way, talking of fools. What do you know about that fellow, Hubert Crank?' He told them about the altercation in the shop.

'He's barmy,' Stephen said sneeringly. He put his index finger to his temple and made a winding motion. Laughing out loud, Kezia copied his action. 'He styles himself as something of a radical. He stands outside college dishing out leaflets and making crazy speeches. He's recruiting for a looney society who hate Catholics, Jews, black people, you name it — they hate the lot of them.'

'He sounds thoroughly disgusting,' Amy said, and then sent Kezia upstairs on the pretext of checking on John before she heard any more. Her perspicacious daughter's habit of storing and then repeating conversations she had overheard sometimes caused embarrassment or downright unpleasantness. Only the other day she had unwittingly told Noah it was a wonder he didn't get buried in all the clutter in his sitting room, a remark Amy had made to Jude after she had gone there to take Noah some buns she had baked that morning.

'If he shows his face again I'll soon give him his marching orders,' said Jude, rubbing one fisted hand in the palm of the other and imagining it to be Hubert's face. 'It's not as though he's a customer — he's never bought a thing.'

★ ★ ★

The next day, it being a Saturday and with Stephen otherwise occupied, Maggie volunteered to look after John and Kezia, leaving Amy free to serve in the shop. In the late afternoon, it being gloriously warm for April, she put John in his pushchair and they walked down Bankside Street to the Book Cellar. Kezia was skipping alongside keeping up a lively stream of chatter, but Maggie wasn't listening. She was thinking about the conversation Jude and Stephen had had the day before and worrying for Stephen's safety. Today he was reporting on a lock-out at a local pit, the miners protesting for better wages and working conditions. As they neared the shop, she saw Hubert Crank lounging at the top of the steps, his pale, shifty eyes watching their approach. He made no attempt to move out of their way. Kezia gave him a dirty look and wiggled her finger round her temple as she shoved past. Maggie wrinkled her nose, repulsed by his smell as she squeezed by, bumping the pushchair down the steps into the basement.

'He's hanging about outside, an' he stinks,' Maggie announced, seeing there were no customers in the shop.

'Who?' Amy glanced up from the low bookshelf she was tidying.

'That smelly man with the scraggy red beard and shifty eyes,' piped Kezia. She had no sooner spoken than Hubert sidled into the shop.

Jude strode over to him.

'Can I help you, Mr Crank?' The jaded question had a threatening edge to it and Jude's glowering expression reminded Amy of the days in Beckett's Park when Jude had had one of his bitter episodes. She cringed, wringing her hands and wondering if she should intervene before Jude exploded.

'Just looking,' Hubert drawled, pulling a book

from the shelf and letting it drop.

'Not anymore, you aren't.' Jude steered him towards the door, his features tight with anger. 'I don't object to anyone just looking but I do expect them to treat the books with respect.'

'Respect! Why should anybody respect you? You rotten Jews are all the same. You think because you own the banks and the fancy jewellery shops and run big businesses that you have a right to tell us what to do. But not me, I hate Jews and everything about them.'

'Get out!' Jude thundered, hustling Hubert through the doorway and up the steps, not letting go until they reached street level. With one almighty shove he sent Hubert sprawling on the pavement, watching with satisfaction as the miscreant scrambled to his feet and ran.

Jude bounded back into the shop. 'That's got rid of him.'

'He's bloody crazy,' Maggie cried, her green eyes flashing angrily.

'He's certainly unstable,' said Amy, 'and thank goodness there were no customers to witness his outburst.' *Or yours Jude*, she silently added, the violent display making her feel sick. Did he still feel a pain so great that the slightest word or look could trigger his anger and revive the horrendous memories he had struggled to forget? But rather than seething with temper Jude seemed elated, laughing as he picked up the book Hubert had dropped and then saying, 'There's never a dull moment in the place.'

Amy breathed a sigh of relief.

Later that evening, Stephen called to see Maggie. She cried when she saw his bruised face. 'Who did that to you?' she shrieked, pulling him into her arms. 'Whoever it was'll have me to deal with if I ever catch the buggers.'

'It turned out rough then,' Jude said, giving Stephen a sympathetic wry smile.

Stephen gratefully accepted the cup of tea Amy had shoved into his hand and then grinned. 'Just a flying stone,' he said casually. 'I didn't move quickly enough when all hell broke loose.'

'Who threw it?' Maggie demanded.

Stephen laughed. 'God knows, it was mayhem once the pit owner's hired thugs arrived.'

'It's history repeating itself,' Jude reflected. 'T'miners have always had to fight for their rights. You make sure you write a bloody good story defending 'em,' Jude said.

'I will,' he said, rubbing the bruise on his cheek and chuckling. 'I never imagined writing for a newspaper could be dangerous.'

'An' I never thought selling books would be. I had a run-in with that chap Crank this afternoon. I threw him out of the shop.'

'Good for you,' said Stephen. 'His sort are nothing but trouble.'

'Me Uncle Jude saw him off all right,' Maggie said proudly. 'He'll not be back. And the next time you're out on an assignment, you keep out of trouble. I couldn't bear it if owt bad happened to you.'

34

'I've seen that man again.' Kezia dumped her satchel and topcoat on a chair. 'He was standing across the road at the end of Mrs Booth's alley and staring across at the Book Cellar like somebody not right in the head.'

Her attention focused on the envelope in her hand, Amy only half-listened to her daughter who always found plenty to comment on. At ten, she was still diminutive but her heart-shaped face and her dark eyes, bright with learning and natural curiosity, frequently drew admiring glances from customers in the Book Cellar. Not that Kezia noticed. She was too busy making her own observations.

'I saw him yesterday as well, not here in the street but behind the house on the riverbank,' Kezia continued, helping herself to milk and biscuits.

Reluctantly, Amy broke the seal on the envelope and withdrew the sheets of flimsy paper. 'Who?' she asked distractedly. 'Who are you talking about?'

Kezia sighed, exasperated. 'Scruffy Red Beard: him who hates Jews and Catholics. He always hurries off when he sees me and knows I've seen him.' She waited for what she reckoned would be an interested response. When none came she cried, 'You're not listening to me.'

'I'll listen in a minute,' her mother replied distantly as she unfolded the pages in her hand. The letter was from Isaac. She recognised the post-mark and the handwriting; now all she had to do was read the dreaded contents.

For three happy years they'd lived in Isaac's house, two years longer than expected and, presuming this letter would inform them of his return, Amy hated the thought of having to read words telling them they would have to move.

'I think he's spying on us,' Kezia persisted, helping herself to another biscuit and somewhat surprised that her mother wasn't telling her to put it back.

Amy heard her daughter's voice but the words didn't register, lost as she was in a euphoric haze, her heart dancing and tears blurring her vision.

'Isaac isn't coming back. He wants us to buy the house! We don't have to move after all.' She flung the letter on the table, laughing and crying as she hugged Kezia. Then she lifted John in her arms and together they ran to the Book Cellar to tell Jude and Noah the news. In her excitement at not having to leave the house in Bankside Street, Kezia forgot all about Hubert Crank.

When Maggie dropped into the Book Cellar on her way home from the surgery she was delighted to hear the news although she would soon be looking for a home of her own. She and Stephen were getting married in August. 'I'm glad for you, Auntie Amy,' she said, giving her a hug and then rounding up her young cousins. 'I'll take these two with me and have a celebratory tea waiting for you when you come home.'

Left alone, Amy and Jude rejoiced at their good

fortune and just before they closed the Book Cellar they stood, arms linked, gazing wondrously at all they had achieved. Kipling, Forster, D.H. Lawrence, Arnold Bennett, H.G. Wells and many more lined the shelves, along with a ready supply of cheap secondhand books, magazines and comics, for they remained loyal to their initial motives and their customers from the market. Now, standing back to admire the latest delivery from the Union Jack Library they blessed Sexton Blake and his thrilling intrigues and then locked the shop, walking home to a house that they soon would own.

★   ★   ★

His long vigil over, the shrouded figure furtively waited in the passageway opposite the Book Cellar. Nervously, he fingered his scruffy red beard and then plunged his hands into the pockets of his overcoat, feeling for his means of revenge. He had watched Jude and Amy lock up some hours before and sneered at their departing backs. They hadn't seen him; not this time or any of the occasions he'd lingered in Bankside Street over the past fortnight. Only that brat of a daughter appeared to be aware of his existence. Whenever their paths crossed she pulled a face and stuck out her tongue, the ignorant Jewish peasant.

Burning with revulsion, Hubert pictured them seated round the table in the house further along the street, warm and well fed, sure of their position in life, afraid of nothing, not even the dark,

374

for hadn't he once peered through their undrawn curtains, watching and hating. Hating them like he hated the Jewish landlord who had turned him and his mother out on the street because they couldn't pay the rent, or like the Jew who ran the sweatshop where his mother had worked until she died, her lungs choked with fibres from the cloth she sewed into coats. They had infiltrated his country, making it their own, just like the Irish priest who had turned him out of the church one cold, winter night when he had nowhere else to sleep. He hated them all.

Hubert fingered the box of matches in one pocket and the paraffin-soaked rags in the other and then picked up the iron bar at his feet, his evil thoughts lighting his face with a demonic smile. 'Well, you who have everything in life will soon find out what it's like to have nothing. I lost my home and my mother. Now it's your turn.'

★　★　★

Muffled shouts and thuds became part of Jude's nightmare as he struggled to dig his way out of an endless trench, German soldiers at his back. He wakened lathered in sweat, the black hole and the Germans gone but the hammering and yelling persisting.

'Fire! Fire!'

Leaping out of bed he dived into his trousers, and shaking Amy by the arm he dashed out of the bedroom. No smoke, no smell of burning. Where was the fire?

Amy, eyes fearful, hair awry, joined him on the

landing crying, 'What is it?'

'Get the bairns and Maggie,' Jude urged, plunging downstairs, along the hallway to the reverberating front door.

'T'bookshop's afire,' gabbled a pyjama-clad neighbour.

Jude's grief-stricken roar rocketed up to Amy at the head of the stairs. With John in her arms and Kezia and Maggie at her heels she descended frantically, and from the open doorway she watched her demented husband haring up the street, bawling like a bull to the slaughter. 'Stay with the children,' she ordered Maggie, and flinging a coat over her nightdress she followed him.

Doors in Bankside Street opened, bands of light lancing the pavement as she ran. Outside the Book Cellar a small gathering of neighbours, coats over their nightclothes, gazed in dismay at the smoke and flames belching up the basement steps. 'Waken Noah and get him out,' Jude bawled to a man in the crowd. Then, barging past them Jude hurtled down the steps and, heedless of his own safety, he unlocked the door and rushed inside. The window display was ablaze.

Oblivious to the swirling smoke, he dashed into the storeroom. One mighty shove sent the table crashing into the rear wall, freeing the rug from under its legs. Back in the shop he tossed the rug over the burning books to smother the flames, stamping on it with both feet.

Whoosh! A trail of hungry flames crept insidiously along a shelf to his left. Out of his eye corner, Jude saw Amy wielding a furled umbrella left behind by a customer. 'Go back,' he yelled, but Amy paid him no heed. She continued raking books from the shelves nearest to the window with the umbrella's curved handle, creating a break that left the hungry flames with nothing to burn.

The window display now a blackened mass of charred books and the scorched rug, Jude left off stamping. 'Are you all right, love?' he cried, clutching Amy's shoulders and pulling her into the safety of his arms. Thick, black smoke swirled round their feet, rising steadily towards the low ceiling.

'Grand,' she panted, her eyes streaming and her throat raw from the fumes. She leaned her weight against his firm body and felt the thud of his heart against her own. Her panic subsided only to rise again as, over his shoulder she spotted a trail of flames flickering in the fug, licking their way along the varnished floorboards.

'Behind you,' she cried, leaping away from him. Jude swung round, and like a manic rumba dancer began stamping again. By now, the shop was filled with smoke so dense that they could barely see one another. Feeling her way to the storeroom, Amy found a bucket, filled it, and stumbled blindly back into the shop towards Jude. Using both hands to tilt the bucket she sloshed the water from it, Jude letting out a yell as it cascaded down his back.

'Are you trying to drown me?' he said, feeling for her and both of them laughing foolishly as the clanging of a bell signalled the arrival of the fire brigade. 'Better late than never,' said Amy, too exhausted to summon any more emotion.

'Don't start pumping water all over the place,

t'fires out,' Jude cried, as the firemen clattered into the shop, one dragging a hose and another a hand pump. 'Wait for the smoke to settle before you start doing owt an' causing more damage.' The firemen glanced at one another, nonplussed.

Gradually, the smoke cleared enough for them to properly assess the situation.

'Just douse this lot here and check there,' said Jude, pointing to the charred mess in the window and the smoking shelves. 'It didn't reach any further, and we might be able to salvage all the other books — but not if you wet 'em.'

Cautiously, one of the firemen lifted the corner of the singed rug with the toe of his boot. Smoke swirled upwards, but no flames. The acrid smell of paraffin stung their noses. 'This were started deliberately,' he said.

Amy and Jude exchanged alarmed glances.

The fireman sifted through the debris, his gloved fingers prodding the piles of burned paper. 'Ah ah!' he cried triumphantly, holding up the remains of a length of charred rag and waving it about. The smell of paraffin grew stronger. 'This is your culprit,' he said, 'and whoever put it here did so by shoving it through that hole in the window.'

'It wasn't broken when I locked-up this evening,' said Jude, noticing the smashed pane for the first time.

The dousing administered and the building declared safe, Jude and Amy climbed the steps to the street to be met by Noah, his hair on end and a coat over his pyjamas. 'Thank the Lord you're safe,' he gasped. 'Is the damage bad?'

'It could have been worse,' Jude said, thinking

how easily it could have spread to Noah's living quarters, 'but nobody was harmed, thank God, just the books.' The horror of what could have been, and the loss of his beloved books suddenly hit him and he staggered visibly.

Amy caught him. Devastated though she was by the damage to the shop she was more concerned for Jude's peace of mind. Shell shock had impaired him, his temperament fragile. Although his outbursts were rare, he was still beset by bouts of bitter depression and occasional nightmares. Was this setback about to revive the dark days of the war?

The crowd of onlookers, held back by two burly policemen, cheered when Amy and Jude appeared at the top of the basement steps. They mingled with their neighbours, all of whom were anxious to hear every detail. Lurking at the edge of the crowd, his hooded coat hiding his face, Hubert looked on. He enjoyed watching the results of his destruction. In St Patrick's Catholic Church in Melborough he'd sat for an hour admiring the defiled altar and broken stained-glass windows, and he had laughed uproariously as he slashed the suits in the Jewish tailor's shop in Wenbury before setting the premises alight — and getting away with it. However, tonight he felt somewhat deflated; he had expected a roaring inferno that destroyed both the bookshop and the house above, where the evil, old Jew lived. But he hadn't reckoned on that arrogant, hard-faced bookseller's interference. Now, as he watched Amy approach, he gave a satisfied smirk; he'd caused enough damage to let them know he meant business.

Amy was coming to enquire if old Mrs Booth who lived opposite the shop had seen or heard anything — she was an inveterate nosy parker, awake at all hours — when she caught a distinct, strong whiff of paraffin. Mrs Booth forgotten, she dashed to find Jude.

'Over there,' she hissed, 'the one with the hood. He reeks of it.' As she ran to alert the policemen, Jude lunged through the crowd. Coming up behind the man Amy had pointed out, his nose told him that she had not been mistaken. He swung the man round to face him and pulled off the hood.

'You bastard! You miserable, bigoted bastard.' Jude's roar had his neighbours turning as one as he grappled with Hubert.

Amy and Noah and the policemen closed in. 'Leave this to us, sir,' said a beefy constable wresting Hubert Crank from Jude's clutches and then holding onto him whilst his colleague frisked Hubert down. A paraffin-soaked rag and a box of matches and an iron bar in his pockets were proof enough.

'How could you?' Amy's expression was one of utter revulsion.

Hubert, his eyes alight with a demonic zeal, sneered. 'It's my duty to destroy Jews and all the other filth that thinks it rules this world.'

The policemen dragged him away.

★ ★ ★

Later that morning they all gathered in Noah's sitting room. 'Now I know what it means to see dreams turn to ashes,' Amy said.

'I never for one moment thought that my religion would harm you or your business,' said Noah apologetically. He looked positively shaken.

'You can buy more books, Dad,' said Kezia.

Jude smiled ruefully. 'We might be able to sell off some of the smoke-damaged stuff but it'll cost a fortune to replace what we had. I think we're done for.' He buried his head in his hands to hide his tears.

Noah chuckled wryly. 'Don't despair, Jude. Kezia is right, as usual. We have the money — insurance money.'

Jude looked at Amy, his eyes hopeless. 'We weren't insured,' she said softly. 'You see, Noah, for all your teaching we're still rotten businessmen.'

Noah's eyes twinkled. 'But I'm not. We Jews have great faith in insurance. Everything will be replaced at no cost to you, other than the sweat of your brow when you come to refurbish the place.'

★ ★ ★

The garden at the rear of the house in Bankside Street was bathed in glorious sunshine and the people in it flitted like butterflies or soporific honeybees as they celebrated the day. Flashes of pink zigzagged across the lawn as, like a pair of pretty flamingos, Kezia and Mary chased after Henry and John and Hadley Jr. 'Those bridesmaid dresses are going to be ruined,' Bessie remarked dryly to Freda.

Freda bounced Thomas Jr on her knee and agreed, but Raffy said, 'It's a wedding, Bessie, they be having fun.' He drained his glass and turned to

Samuel. 'It'll be no time afore this boy'll be racing round like his brother and cousins. Time flies, so you be there to make the most of it.' He didn't say, 'not like me' although he thought it.

Bessie gave him a knowing glance and Samuel, his eyes brimming with love and pride said, 'Give him here, Freda,' and taking his younger son into his arms he wandered over to introduce him to Stephen's parents, holding him aloft and calling out to Maggie and Stephen, 'It'll be your turn next.'

Maggie laughed raucously, a laugh that seemed at odds with the beautiful vision she presented. Wearing white silk, and her magnificent red tresses accentuating her creamy complexion she was the picture of loveliness. By her side, Stephen looked like the proudest man on earth. 'She's a beautiful bride,' said Mrs Netherwood dreamily, gazing from Maggie and Stephen to Thomas Jr and imagining being a grandmother before adding, 'It might not be long till we have one as handsome as this little chap. He's a credit to you.' Samuel beamed.

Albert and Fred, serious in their first proper suits, talked with Stephen's brothers and Noah, the conversation flitting from farming to mining and selling books. Dr and Mrs Hargreaves kept company with Stephen's grandparents and Maggie's Uncle Ben and Aunt Dora. Maggie had insisted that she couldn't possibly get married if Mary wasn't a bridesmaid along with Kezia, and Henry, John and Hadley Jr pageboys.

At the doorway leading down into the garden, Amy and Jude paused. They were on their way into the house to replenish plates and glasses for their guests but, as one, they were drawn to observe the assembled company. Amy's gaze and thoughts lingered on the beautiful bride and her siblings. Looking up into the clear, blue sheet of sky she silently said, *I kept my promise, Bert; I hope you can see them now.*

Jude lovingly watched Kezia running hand in hand with John and then rested his gaze on Amy. She was still the same beautiful girl he'd fallen in love with at a dance in the village hall, the girl whose constant love had brought him back from the brink of hell and helped him to achieve his dream.

Yesterday had seen the opening of the newly refurbished bookshop, a grand affair attended by local dignitaries, family members and faithful customers, and some who came for nothing more than free tea and buns. Without this girl at his side none of it would have been possible, thought Jude. He placed his arm around her waist and pulled her close.

Amy gazed up into his dark eyes, her own alight with love, a love so deep she could barely breathe. Here was her man, strong in arm and sound in mind; in the garden, happy and healthy, were the fruits of their enduring love. And further down the street was the Book Cellar. She had kept her promise.

Acknowledgements

First and foremost I thank my agent, Judith Murdoch. She works tirelessly on my behalf and her sound advice and encouragement keeps me going. I am also extremely grateful to the wonderful team at HoZ/Aria for their friendly guidance, particularly the fantastic Rhea Kurlen and Dushi Horti; as usual, their sharp eyes and broad vocabularies improve any story. Thanks also to Vicky Joss and Holly Domney for the beautiful cover and the work they do in promoting my novels.

As always, my sincere thanks to my son, Charles, and his wife, Martina, and Paul and Annemarie Downey and Andrew and Sharon Downey. Their daily love and support make my life worthwhile. To Helen Oldroyd for her friendship and the interest she takes in my writing, and to Marie Duffy another loyal reader always willing to talk about my stories and encourage me. Thanks also to Tom Duffy for promoting my books locally.

I am indebted to David S Halstead of Cudworth, a guide at the Yorkshire Mining Museum, Caphouse Colliery, for his wealth of knowledge about the working lives of coal miners and the dangers that they face in the hewing of every bucket of coal I throw on my fire. I hope I got the facts right, David. Thanks also to the Tolson Museum, Dalton, Huddersfield for its wealth of WW1 information.

Writing is one of my greatest pleasures and it's a privilege to have my stories published so I send a huge thank you to all those who have read my novels *The Girl from the Mill* and *The Child from the Ash Pits* and given such encouraging feedback; your support is invaluable. I look forward to hearing what you think of *The Collier's Wife*.

Finally, thanks to my grandson Harry Walsh and the Downey boys, Jack, Matthew, Lewis and Alex for making me a proud and happy grandmother.

We do hope that you have enjoyed reading this large print book.

Did you know that all of our titles are available for purchase?

We publish a wide range of high quality large print books including:
Romances, Mysteries, Classics
General Fiction
Non Fiction and Westerns

Special interest titles available in large print are:
The Little Oxford Dictionary
Music Book, Song Book
Hymn Book, Service Book

Also available from us courtesy of Oxford University Press:
Young Readers' Dictionary
(large print edition)
Young Readers' Thesaurus
(large print edition)

For further information or a free brochure, please contact us at:
Ulverscroft Large Print Books Ltd.,
The Green, Bradgate Road, Anstey,
Leicester, LE7 7FU, England.
Tel: (00 44) 0116 236 4325
Fax: (00 44) 0116 234 0205

THE CHILD FROM THE ASH PITS

Chrissie Walsh

In the aftermath of the General Strike, times are tough for coal miners and their families. When Cally loses her beloved mum, she hopes her father will comfort her. But instead she soon acquires a cruel stepmother, and Cally begins to fear that she is on her own. Through uncomfortable years in service, to a terrifying brush with the streets, through hard work and determination, Cally finally finds a place for herself. She even trusts enough in the future to create her own family, despite being abandoned by her own. Cally has all she ever hoped for but, with World War II looming, how long can she hold on to the people she loves?